D0644191
NCIS
NOVEL THREE
BLOOD
Saravan
Souvannakhili
Bolovens
Plateau
Attapu
Muang Kao
Dak To
Kon Tum
Play Ku
Phiafai
Khong
Siem Pang
Virachei
Lomphat
Stung Treng
Chhep
Kohnieh
KAMPUCHEA
Ban

TYNDALE HOUSE PUBLISHERS, INC. >> CAROL STREAM,
LINES
Savannakhét
Taphan
Saravan
Khemmarat
Khôngxédôn
Souvannakhili
Phibun
Mangsaban
Bolovens
Plateau
Ubon
Ratchathani
Pakxé
Attapu
Sisaket
Champasak
Phiafai
Mounlapamôk
Không
Range
Cheom Ksan
Kompong Sralao
Chhep
Samrong
Chong Kal
Melouprey
Sèn
Thalabarivat
Koulen
Rovieng
Chikreng
Angkor
Siem Reap

ILLINOIS
MEL ODOM
Binh Son
Que Son
Son Ha
2598
Muang Kao
Dac To
Tam Qu
Hoai A
Kon Tum
Binh Kh
An Khe
Play Ku
Virachei
Phum Kompadou
Cheo Reo
Kohnieh
Ban Don
Buon Me Thuot
2405
Kien Duc
Gia Nghia
Senmonorom
Kratie
Chhlong
Snuol
Khtum
Bo Duc
Da Lat
Di Linh

Visit Tyndale's exciting Web site at www.tyndale.com

TYNDALE and Tyndale's quill logo are registered trademarks of Tyndale House Publishers, Inc.

Blood Lines

Designed by Dean H. Renninger

Published in association with the agency of Ethan Ellenberg Literary Agency, 548 Broadway, #5-E, New York, NY 10012.

Library of Congress Cataloging-in-Publication

Odom, Mel.
Blood lines / Mel Odom.
p. cm. — (Military NCIS ; #3)
ISBN 978-1-4143-1635-2 (pbk.)
1. Coburn, Will (Fictitious character)—Fiction. 2. Murder—Investigation—Fiction. 3. United States. Naval Criminal Investigative Service—Fiction. 4. Vietnam—Fiction. I. Title.
PS3565.D53B68 2008
813′.54—dc22 2008037937

Printed in the United States of America

14 13 12 11 10 09 08
7 6 5 4 3 2 1

God,

I ask for you to watch over me as I go through my life with my children and my wife. There are times that they don't understand me, and there are even times I don't understand myself. But you have kept my love for them strong even in times of crisis and loss. I know that is one of the best blessings you've ever given me.

I would be a less compassionate husband, a less understanding father, and a much weaker man without knowing you. Thank you for everything you've done in my life. Please continue to bless my family, especially the two new babies added to the mix in June 2008. I only hope that you guide my children to love their children as much as I've learned to love the ones you gave me.

And thank you for being a father to me, for counseling and caring for me during times I didn't want to listen and thought I was smarter than you were. That's just the relationship fathers and sons have.

Mel

ACKNOWLEDGMENTS

Without Jan Stob and Karen Watson, the acquisitions team at Tyndale, and Jeremy Taylor, who edited me into a much cleaner form, though I had to coach him on a few Southernisms, this book—one of the most important I've written to date—wouldn't be in your hands. People, thank you very much.

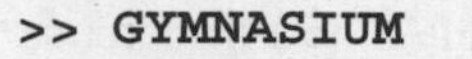

>> GYMNASIUM
>> CAMP LEJEUNE, NORTH CAROLINA
>> 1203 HOURS

"Did you come here to play basketball or wage war?"

Shelton McHenry, gunnery sergeant in the United States Marine Corps, shook the sweat out of his eyes and ignored the question. After long minutes of hard exertion, his breath echoed inside his head and chest. His throat burned. Despite the air-conditioning, the gym felt hot. He put his hands on his head and sucked in a deep breath of air. It didn't help. He still felt mean.

There was no other word for it. He wanted the workout provided by the game, but he wanted it for the physical confrontation rather than the exercise. He had hoped it would burn through the restless anger that rattled within him.

Normally when he got like this, he tried to stay away from other people. He would gather up Max, the black Labrador retriever that was his military canine partner, and go for a run along a secluded beach until he exhausted the emotion. Sometimes it took hours.

That anger had been part of him since he was a kid. He had never truly understood it, but he'd learned to master it—for the most part—a long time ago. But now and again, there were bad days when it got away from him. Usually those bad days were holidays.

Today was Father's Day. It was the worst of all of them. Even Christmas, a time when families got together, wasn't as bad as Father's Day. During the heady rush of Christmas—muted by the sheer effort and logistics of getting from one place to another after another, of making sure presents for his brother's kids were intact and wrapped and not forgotten, of preparing and consuming the endless supply of food—he could concentrate on something other than his father.

But not today. Never on Father's Day.

The anger was bad enough, but the thing that totally wrecked him and kicked his butt was the guilt. Even though he didn't know what to do, there was no escaping the fact that he should be doing something. He was supposed to be back home.

Usually he was stationed somewhere and could escape the guilt by making a quick phone call, offering up an apology, and losing himself back in the field. But after taking the MOS change to Naval Criminal Investigative Service, he was free on weekends unless the team was working a hot case.

At present, there were no hot cases on the horizon. There wasn't even follow-up to anything else they'd been working on. He'd had no excuse for not going. Don, his brother, had called a few days ago to find out if Shel was coming. Shel had told him no but had offered no reason. Don had been kind enough not to ask why. So Shel was stuck with the anger, guilt, and frustration.

"You hearing me, gunney?"

Shel restrained the anger a step before it got loose. Over on the sidelines of the gym, Max gave a tentative bark. The Labrador paced uneasily, and Shel knew the dog sensed his mood.

Dial it down, he told himself. *Just finish up here. Be glad you're able to work through it.*

He just wished it helped more.

"Yeah," Shel said. "I hear you."

"Good. 'Cause for a second there I thought you'd checked out on me." Remy Gautreau mopped his face with his shirt.

He was young and black, hard-bodied but lean, where Shel looked like he'd been put together with four-by-fours. Gang tattoos in blue ink showed on Remy's chest and abdomen when he'd lifted his shirt. Shel had noticed the tattoos before, but he hadn't asked about them. Even after working together for more than a year, it wasn't something soldiers talked about.

Before he'd entered the Navy and trained as a Navy SEAL, Remy Gautreau had been someone else. Most enlisted had. Then whatever branch of military service they signed on for changed them into someone else. The past was shed as easily as a snake lost its skin. Men and women were given a different present for that time and usually ended up with a different future than they would have had.

But they don't take away the past, do they? Shel asked himself. *They just pretend it never happened.*

"Where you been?" Remy asked.

"Right here." Shel broke eye contact with the other man. He could lie out in the field when it was necessary, but he had trouble lying to friends. "Playing center."

Remy was part of the NCIS team that Shel was currently assigned to. His rank was chief petty officer. He wore bright orange knee-length basketball shorts and a white Tar Heels basketball jersey. Shel wore Marine-issue black shorts and a gray sweatshirt with the sleeves hacked off. Both men bore bullet and knife scars from previous battles.

The other huddle of players stood at their end of the basketball court. Other groups of men were waiting their turn.

Shel and Remy were playing iron man pickup basketball. The winning team got to stay on the court, but they had to keep winning. While they were getting more tired, each successive team rested up. Evading fatigue, learning to play four hard and let the fifth man rest on his feet, was a big part of staying on top. It was a lot like playing chess.

"You've been here," Remy agreed in a soft voice. "But this ain't where your head's been. You just been visiting this game."

"Guy's good, Remy. I'm doing my best."

The other team's center was Del Greene, a giant at six feet eight inches tall—four inches taller than Shel. But he was more slender than Shel, turned better in the tight corners, and could get up higher on the boards. Rebounding the ball after each shot was an immense struggle, but once in position Shel was hard to move. He'd come down with his fair share of rebounds.

Basketball wasn't Shel's game. He'd played it all through high school, but football was his chosen gladiator's field in the world of sports. He had played linebacker and had been offered a full-ride scholarship to a dozen different colleges. He had opted for the Marines instead. Anything to shake the dust of his father's cattle ranch from his boots. None of the colleges had been far enough away for what he had wanted at the time. After all those years of misunderstandings on the ranch, Shel had just wanted to be gone.

"You're doing great against that guy," Remy said. "Better than I thought you would. He's a better basketball player, but you're a better thinker. You're shutting him down. Which is part of the problem. You're taking his game away from him and it's making him mad. Problem is, you got no finesse. He's wearing you like a cheap shirt. If we had a referee for this game, you'd already have been tossed for personal fouls."

"Yeah, well, he doesn't play like a homecoming queen himself." Shel wiped his mouth on his shirt. The material came away bloody. He had caught an elbow in the face last time that had split the inside of his cheek. "He's not afraid of dishing it out."

"Don't get me wrong. I didn't say that fool didn't have it coming, but I am saying that this isn't the time or the place for a grudge match." Remy wiped his face with his shirt again. "The last thing we need is for Will to have to come down and get us out of the hoosegow over a basketball game. He's already stressed over Father's Day because he's having to share his time with his kids' new stepfather."

Shel knew United States Navy Commander Will Coburn to be a fine man and officer. He had followed Will into several firefights during their years together on the NCIS team.

The marriage of Will's ex-wife was only months old. Everyone on the team knew that Will had taken the marriage in stride as best as he could, but the change was still a lot to deal with. Having his kids involved only made things worse. Before, Father's Day and Mother's Day had been mutually exclusive. This year the kids' mother had insisted that the day be shared between households.

One of the other players stepped forward. "Are we going to play ball? Or are you two just going to stand over there and hold hands?"

Shel felt that old smile—the one that didn't belong and didn't reflect anything that was going on inside him—curve his lips. That smile had gotten him into a lot of trouble with his daddy and had been a definite warning to his brother, Don.

The other team didn't have a clue.

"The way you guys are playing," Shel said as he stepped toward the other team, "I think we've got time to do both."

Behind him, Shel heard Remy curse.

✪ ✪ ✪

>> 1229 HOURS

At the offensive goal, Shel worked hard to break free of the other player's defense. But every move he made, every step he took, Greene was on top of him. Shel knew basketball, but the other guy knew it better.

A small Hispanic guy named Melendez played point guard for Shel and Remy's team. He flipped the ball around the perimeter with quick, short passes back and forth to the wings. Unable to get a shot off, Remy and the other wing kept passing the ball back.

Shel knew they wanted to get the ball inside to him if they could. They needed the basket to tie up the game. They were too tired to go back down the court and end up two buckets behind.

Melendez snuck a quick pass by the guard and got the ball to Shel. With a fast spin, Shel turned and tried to put the ball up. But as soon as it left his fingers, Greene slapped the shot away. Thankfully Melendez managed to recover the loose ball.

"Don't you try to bring that trash in here," Greene taunted. "This is my house. Nobody comes into *my* house." Sweat dappled his dark features and his mocking smile showed white and clean. "You may be big, gunney, but you ain't big enough. You hear what I'm saying?"

Shel tried to ignore the mocking voice and the fact that Greene was now bumping up against him even harder than before. The man wasn't just taunting anymore. He was going for an all-out assault.

Melendez caught a screen from Remy and rolled out with the basketball before the other defensive player could pick him up. One of the key elements to their whole game was the fact that most of them had played ball before. Greene was a good player—maybe even a great player—but one man didn't make a team. Special forces training taught a man that.

Free and open, Melendez put up a twenty-foot jump shot. Shel rolled around Greene to get the inside position for the rebound. Greene had gone up in an effort to deflect the basketball. He was out of position when he came back down.

Shel timed his jump as the basketball ran around the ring and fell off. He went up and intercepted the ball cleanly. He was trying to bring the ball in close when Greene stepped around him and punched the basketball with a closed fist.

The blow knocked the ball back into Shel's face. It slammed against his nose and teeth hard enough to snap his head back. He tasted blood immediately and his eyes watered. The sudden onslaught of pain chipped away at the control that Shel had maintained. He turned instantly, and Greene stood ready and waiting. Two of the guys on his team fell in behind him.

"You don't want none of this," Greene crowed. "I promise you don't want none of this." He had his hands raised in front of him and stood in what Shel recognized as a martial arts stance.

Shel wasn't big on martial arts. Most of his hand-to-hand combat ability had been picked up in the field and from men he had sparred with to increase his knowledge.

"You're a big man," Greene snarled, "but I'm badder."

Despite the tension that had suddenly filled the gymnasium and the odds against him, Shel grinned. This was more along the lines of what he needed. He took a step forward.

Remy darted between them and put his hands up. "That's it. Game's over. We're done here."

"Then who wins the game?" another man asked.

"We win the game," one of the men on Shel's team said.

"Your big man fouled intentionally," Melendez said. "That's a forfeit in my book."

"Good thing you ain't keepin' the book," Greene said. He never broke eye contact with Shel. "Is that how you gonna call it, dawg? Gonna curl up like a little girl and cry? Or are you gonna man up and play ball?"

Remy turned to face the heckler. "Back off, clown. You don't even know the trouble you're trying to buy into."

Greene was faster than Shel expected even after playing against the man. Before Remy could raise his hands to defend himself, Greene hit him in the face.

Driven by the blow, Remy staggered backward.

E SCENE ✪ NCIS ✪ CRIME SCENE

NAVAL CRIMINAL INVESTIGATIVE SERVICE

>> GYMNASIUM
>> CAMP LEJEUNE, NORTH CAROLINA
>> 1238 HOURS

Shel exploded into action, throwing himself forward and lifting his hands to protect his face and head. Greene tried to take advantage of his longer reach and hit Shel, but the big Marine slapped the blows aside like they were nothing.

Greene pulled his arms in to better defend himself and even managed to get off another punch, but Shel ducked his head and took the blow on his forehead. Something in Greene's hand snapped. He roared and cursed in pain as he tried to backpedal.

Mercilessly, Shel drove forward and caught his opponent around the throat with his left hand. He clamped down hard enough to shut Greene's air off.

Panic widened Greene's eyes. He flailed at Shel. Instead of releasing his hold, Shel tucked his head between his arms and squeezed harder. Blood veins swelled in Greene's eyes. He struggled to speak, but it came out only as a cough.

One of Greene's men came up on Shel's right and threw a punch at his head. Shel leaned forward, pressed his face into Greene's, and let the blow slide by across his shoulders. Then he swept his fist back over his attacker's arm and caught the man on the side of the face.

The man dropped like a poleaxed steer.

Another man kicked at Shel from the left side, but Shel lifted his arm to block the effort, felt the impact shiver along his forearm and elbow, and drop-kicked the man in the crotch.

The man sank to his knees and retched. Before he could get up, Max ran to join in. Trained in combat, the Labrador seized the man's arm and yanked him to one side into a sprawl. The man tried to get up. Max growled threateningly. The man got the message and lay still.

For a moment, Shel was lost in the anger that he normally kept locked away. He stood in the center of a gray fog and nothing seemed real. Then Remy was there. At first, Shel couldn't even hear what the other man was saying. He saw Remy's lips moving, but nothing reached his ears.

Then, in a rush, the world came back into focus.

"Shel!" Remy cursed and grabbed Shel's arm. "Let him go! Shel! You're going to kill him!"

Shel suddenly realized that Greene was deadweight hanging at the end of his arm. Remy had hold of Shel's thumb and was peeling it back.

With effort, Shel bottled the anger and put it away. He made himself breathe out. Then he opened his hand and let Greene sag to the floor. He knew he wouldn't have killed Greene. He still possessed enough control to stop short of that. But he wanted the man humbled.

By that time several Marines and sailors were closing in. Most of them hung back, uncertain about what to do.

"Calm down," Remy ordered the crowd. "We got everything under control here." He fished his ID card out of his pocket. "Special Agent Gautreau. NCIS. Anybody who wants to go home from this will stay out of it."

⊛ ⊛ ⊛

>> LOCKER ROOM
>> CAMP LEJEUNE, NORTH CAROLINA
>> 1307 HOURS

"You want to tell me what that was about?"

Shel tucked his shirttail into his jeans, buttoned the fly, and cinched his belt. He had pulled his boots on right after his pants the way he always did. The shirt always went on last.

Remy, still dressed in basketball clothes, leaned against the lockers in the dressing room. Everyone else in the room gave them plenty of space.

MPs had arrived within minutes and started sorting everything out. Remy had interfaced with them and cut Shel loose, which had suited Shel just fine.

"What?" Shel asked. "The part where Greene was ticked about potentially losing the game because he got tired of me hanging with him? Or the part where you stepped into that haymaker and nearly ended up lights out? Because, honestly, neither one of those things makes sense to me."

Remy looked flustered. "I didn't see him because I was busy watching you."

"*I* wasn't going to hit you." Shel calmly put his gear into a gym bag and zipped it.

"At the time, looking at you, I thought you might hit anybody."

Shel flashed Remy a crooked-toothed grin. He didn't feel humorous, but he'd learned that a show of gentler emotion sometimes defused a situation even if he didn't feel it.

"I wouldn't have hit you," Shel said. "I wouldn't even have hit him if he hadn't hit you." And maybe that was the truth.

"It was just a game."

"Yeah. I had a good time. Glad you invited me."

Remy looked at Shel as if he thought he were insane. "We could have gotten waxed out there."

"Me and you?" Shel shook his head. "We could have taken a dozen guys like Greene. Maybe two dozen. He crawfished out of the situation quick enough once things started to go south."

"This isn't funny."

"That's because you didn't see that look on your face when he pasted you."

Remy frowned and touched his jaw tenderly. "We could have gotten in a lot of trouble."

"Not from Greene and his buddies." Shel reached back and ruffled Max's ears.

"From the MPs. We could have spent Father's Day in lockdown."

"We aren't. C'mon. I'll buy you a beer at the canteen."

Remy didn't readily agree.

That bothered Shel. He believed in working closely with his team. Remy's reluctance, though understandable, hurt.

A cell phone rang shrilly and cut through the hiss of water coming from the showers. Remy reached into his pocket, pulled out his phone, flipped it open, and spoke his name.

Shel leaned up against the lockers and waited like he was totally relaxed. Instead, his insides twisted even tighter. His anger was an old acquaintance. He knew from experience that it wasn't going to be easily dismissed. He needed another diversion.

And the canteen's probably the last place you need to be, he told himself honestly. Thinking about it, he figured beer and a pizza would be a better choice. He felt the need to apologize to Remy. That was normal too.

Remy listened to the phone conversation for a few minutes, then said, "Sure" and closed the phone. He looked at Shel in idle speculation. "That was Maggie."

Shel waited. Special Agent Maggie Foley was the team's only civilian agent. She specialized in interrogation and profiling. Before landing the post at NCIS, she had been a Boston police officer.

"I thought maybe she was calling because she'd heard about what went down here," Remy said.

Shel had figured the same thing.

"But she's calling about something else," Remy went on. "How do you feel about doing a job on Father's Day?"

"What kind of job?"

"Fugitive recovery op. Got a guy on the local Most Wanted board that just turned up in Charlotte."

"Sure." Shel grabbed his gym bag. "You got a change of clothes?"

"Yeah."

"You coming?"

"Planned on it. I don't know that you're safe out there alone."

Shel gave Remy another crooked-toothed grin and slid his mirrored sunglasses into place. "Grab a shower and change while I go get my truck. If you're not out front in ten minutes, you'll have to catch up."

Remy cursed at him but started working on the combination to his locker.

Shel stepped out of the room. He was aware that most of the men were staring at him. He didn't like the attention, but he blew it off and concentrated on the job in front of him. Being in motion helped soothe him.

This was what he needed.

⊛ ⊛ ⊛

>> GYMNASIUM PARKING AREA
>> CAMP LEJEUNE, NORTH CAROLINA
>> 1326 HOURS

Shel sat behind the steering wheel of his black Jeep Rubicon and ignored the fact that two MP Hummers now occupied the parking area in front of the gym. He knew they were there because of what had happened earlier.

Violence was part of every soldier's world. If it wasn't present out on the battlefield or in whatever country he was policing, then it lurked in the camps, posts, and bases where those warriors gathered. Violence was a necessary product of the trade they practiced, and it didn't always stay under control.

Max sat patient and quiet in the backseat. The dog had learned to adjust to Shel's dark moods when they stole up on him.

After checking his watch, Shel popped the glove compartment open and took out a dog treat. He called the dog's name, then flipped the treat over his shoulder. Max caught it easily and devoured it with a couple of noisy chomps.

"You're not the most polite company I could have," Shel told the dog's reflection in the rearview mirror.

Max barked at him.

"When we get back from this, if there's time, I'll take you down to the beach," Shel promised.

Max barked again.

One of the first things Shel had learned after being paired with a K-9 unit was how smart the dogs were. He knew that Max didn't understand his words, but he also knew the dog understood his intent. There were more good things in store for him than just the dog treat.

Lynyrd Skynyrd played on the stereo. Shel could listen to—and appreciate—a lot of different music, but it was Southern rock that took him back to his roots outside Fort Davis, Texas.

His daddy hadn't cared for the rock and roll too much, but Shel knew Tyrel McHenry was acquainted with it. The Rolling Stones and the Beatles had been big during the Vietnam War when Tyrel had served.

But back home, Tyrel only listened to country and western music. Hank Williams Sr., Bob Wills, and a handful of others made up the core of his musical library. He had cut off anything new about the time Conway Twitty and Loretta Lynn were singing together. But he had made allowances for George Strait and Randy Travis.

His daddy, Shel reflected, was some piece of work. He was a hard man to understand and a harder man to get to know. But he'd been fair when Shel and his brother were growing up.

Just never warm. Especially not after Shel and Don's mama had died. That was how Tyrel had always referred to her. "The boys' mama." Never his wife.

And just like that, Shel was thinking about his daddy and his daddy's ways all over again.

⊛ ⊛ ⊛

>> 1328 HOURS

Remy jogged to a fire-engine red Camaro Z-28 that he had restored and continually worked on. He opened the trunk and dropped his gym bag inside, then hauled out the duffel containing his gear. All of the team carried spare weapons and tactical armor everywhere they went. It was the nature of the job.

Shel pulled up behind Remy and waited as the other man threw his duffel in the back. Remy kept out a 9 mm Beretta M9 pistol in a paddle holster. He wore a loose basketball jersey outside of his khaki pants that would cover the weapon.

Weapon already in place, Remy slid into the passenger seat. Golden yellow wraparound sunglasses masked his eyes.

"You ready to do this?" Remy asked.

"Yeah."

"'Cause after that scene on the basketball court, I'm not so sure."

Shel throttled the angry response and concentrated on breathing out. Pleasant or not, Remy's concerns were warranted.

"I'm fine." Shel slipped the Jeep into gear and headed out of the parking lot.

"You're fine?"

"Yeah."

"Just like that, you're fine?" Remy clearly had a hard time believing that.

Shel glanced at him. "Yeah."

"Then you tell me what that business back at the basketball game was."

"An aberration."

"Cool," Remy said sarcastically. "I feel all relieved now. You're using big words and everything."

"You're really going to make this hard, aren't you?"

"We're lucky we're still outside a cell, still walking around. So, yeah, I'm gonna make this hard."

"I got a thing," Shel replied.

"What kind of thing? About winning basketball?"

Shel made himself tell the truth. "About Father's Day."

Remy stared at him in silence for a moment. "Oh. Okay." Then he relaxed back into his seat like he was hesitant about saying anything else.

3

E SCENE ✪ NCIS ✪ CRIME SCENE
NAVAL CRIMINAL INVESTIGATIVE SERVICE

>> INTERSTATE 40
>> WEST OF JACKSONVILLE, NORTH CAROLINA
>> 1403 HOURS

Charlotte was just under five hours from Camp Lejeune. After they were out of Jacksonville, the town surrounding the Marine camp, Shel headed west on Interstate 40, chasing the sun.

"If the traffic stays good," Shel said, "we'll be in Charlotte around seven."

Remy nodded. He leaned back in the seat and played a PSP game. Earbuds filled his head with the sounds of battle on the brightly lit screen. He had pulled out the game system before they'd cleared the main gates at the camp.

"Is our fugitive still going to be there?" Shel asked.

"Yep."

"You're sure?"

"Yep." Remy twisted and turned slightly in his seat as he followed the game's shifting environment.

"And if he's not?"

"Then maybe I saved Camp Lejeune from Shelzilla. Bad thing is nobody knows, and I don't get a medal or a commendation."

Shel took in a deep breath and let it out.

"That ain't gonna work," Remy said.

"What?" Shel asked irritably.

"Trying to suck in all the oxygen in the Jeep and hoping I pass out from asphyxiation."

The growing irritation inside Shel almost broke free. "You planning a comedy routine?"

Remy grinned a brilliant white smile. "Nope. This is what you call natural humor. But if you want, I can use hand puppets. Might make it easier for the slow kids to comprehend."

Shel ignored him. And he continued to do so for the next 137 miles.

⊛ ⊛ ⊛

>> INTERSTATE 40

>> OUTSIDE GREENSBORO, NORTH CAROLINA

>> 1619 HOURS

Shel pumped gas at the small convenience store while Remy went to grab some burgers from the fast food franchise located inside. Max ran around the dog-walking area.

By the time Shel paid for the gas, cleaned up after Max, hit the head, and returned to the Jeep, Remy stood waiting with two paper sacks of burgers and fries and a tray containing a half-dozen bottles of water. They divvied the food, and Remy emptied one of the water bottles into a dish beside the Jeep for Max.

"Who's the fugitive?" Shel unwrapped one of the burgers and took a bite.

"A lowlife named Bobby Lee Gant." Remy bit into his burger, then winced a little; Shel saw him try to cover the reaction. Remy's jaw was still swollen from the punch he'd taken.

Shel chewed, thought for a moment, then swallowed. "The biker guy who did the carjacking in Jacksonville back in April?"

Remy nodded. "That's the one."

The carjacking, which had involved a young Marine and his wife, had been particularly heinous. The couple had been shopping in Jacksonville. The Marine had just returned from Iraq. While they'd been stopped at a light, Bobby Lee Gant and three of his buddies had driven up beside them on their motorcycles. Gant and one of his buddies had ridden doubled up.

At the light, Gant slid off the motorcycle he had been a passenger on, crossed to the young Marine's car, and smashed the window with a tire iron. Then he'd taken a pistol from his belt and shoved it into the Marine's face.

Just back from Iraq and the horrors he had seen there, the Marine hadn't reacted well to the open violence. He'd grabbed for Gant's pistol automatically and ended up getting shot in the face. He had survived but had been forced to undergo cutting-edge reconstructive surgeries to repair the damage. His right eye had been lost, and his military career had ended at the same time.

One of the other men had yanked the wife out onto the street. Then Gant had driven off in the car while his friends followed on the bikes, leaving the couple behind. Luckily the Marine's wife had her cell phone and was able to call for medical assistance immediately.

NCIS had been trying to get a lead on the biker for the last two months. It was the kind of assignment Shel enjoyed: danger with a hint of vengeance.

"How'd we find him?" Shel asked.

"Charlotte PD nabbed Gant's girlfriend on a holding charge. She's pregnant. A fall like that, she'd be inside county lockup and the kid would end up on its own. She tried to pull hardship, claimed that her family had disowned her and nobody would take care of her kid. Charlotte DA froze her out."

"Hard."

"Yeah."

Despite the years of military life, wars, and what he had seen while with NCIS, Shel hadn't hardened to the struggles of others. He empathized with the young mother. A lot of people who trafficked in crime weren't evil. Not like Bobby Lee Gant. They were just people looking for an easy or quick way out of a bad situation.

"The girlfriend rolled on Gant?" Shel asked.

"Like a log." Remy pushed the last of his first burger into his mouth, chewed, and swallowed. Afternoon sunlight glinted on his yellow gold lenses.

"Did Charlotte PD check her story out?"

"Maggie says no. They don't have any paper outstanding on Gant and we're not going to let them play on our court. They forwarded it to us."

Shel unwrapped his second burger, then tossed one of the meat patties Remy had purchased for Max to the dog. The Labrador snapped the patty out of the air like a Frisbee and gulped it down.

"Don't see how he does that," Remy commented.

"I trained him to eat like a Marine," Shel said.

"I kind of got that from the way he chews with his mouth open."

Shel ignored the gibe. He wasn't ready to play yet. "You think Charlotte PD took an honest pass on this and left Gant undisturbed?"

"Nope."

"Me neither."

"Gant will probably know something's up."

"Yeah." Shel dropped the wrapper into the bag. "So if Gant knows the police have located him, why's he still there?"

"Maybe he doesn't know. Maybe Charlotte PD has a stealth mode like none we've ever seen."

Shel folded his arms across his broad chest. "Let's say they don't."

Remy grinned. With the swelling in his face, the effort was lopsided. "Gant's daddy is in Charlotte. Maggie says he's a bad dude. Runs the local chapter of the Purple Royals."

"Motorcycle gang."

"That's the one."

Shel sipped his iced tea. NCIS had encountered the Purple Royals before. They were a dangerous motorcycle gang fueled by meth and arms running. Most of the inner circle was made up of "one percenters," men who were confirmed criminals.

"Me and you against a biker gang?" Shel asked.

"Well," Remy said, "we don't have to bring them all in. Just Gant."

"True." Shel warmed to the coming encounter. He tilted his head back to look at the sun. "It's getting late."

"Let's roll."

⊛ ⊛ ⊛

>> INTERSTATE 85
>> NEAR SALISBURY, NORTH CAROLINA
>> 1703 HOURS

"Are you going to play that thing the whole way?" Shel asked.

Remy paused the PSP and pulled the earbuds out of his ears. "You want to talk?"

"Thought maybe you wanted to tell me about Gant's daddy."

"We're not planning on hooking him up."

"In case we happen to cross paths. I noticed you were looking through a file Maggie sent you."

Remy put the PSP away and reached into the backseat for his back-pack, then pulled out the small notebook computer all the team members carried as part of their equipment. He settled the computer across his knees and brought it to life.

"Victor Gant's in his late sixties," Remy said. "He was a ground pounder in Vietnam. Pulled three tours."

"Three?"

"Yeah. Put in his twenty altogether. Pulled the pin at thirty-nine."

"Then turned to a life of crime as a biker?"

"Back then there weren't as many openings for military-issue as there are now. Especially not for somebody who liked to stay in the bush. Today he probably would have segued directly into the private security sector. He mustered out as sergeant first class after the first Gulf War."

"Came back to spend time with Bobby Lee and his mom?"

Remy snorted. "Not likely. Bobby Lee's mother had already divorced Victor back in the seventies."

"Any special reason?"

"Maggie didn't dig deep into this. She stayed with Victor Gant's crime side. It was intense enough. Besides that, he's not the focus of our little trip. Not long after Victor Gant mustered out, he got into a bar fight and killed a man."

"Why?"

"It was part of a turf war. Maggie's notes indicate that the police investigating the homicide thought Gant should have taken a fall for murder one. The DA couldn't make premeditation stick, so he didn't try. Gant was convicted of manslaughter and spent seven years inside. He did his whole bit, so there's not even a parole office in his life."

"Not much father-son time there," Shel observed.

"No. But Bobby Lee started hanging around anyway."

"Is Bobby Lee a Purple Royal?"

"No. They don't have an interest in him."

"Except that Victor Gant's his daddy."

"That's about the size of it." Remy looked at Shel. "So what is it you hate about Father's Day?"

CRIME SCENE
NCIS
NAVAL CRIMINAL INVESTIGATIVE SERVICE

4

E SCENE ✪ NCIS ✪ CRIME SCENE

NAVAL CRIMINAL INVESTIGATIVE SERVICE

>> TAWNY KITTY'S BAR AND GRILL
>> SOUTH END
>> CHARLOTTE, NORTH CAROLINA
>> 1705 HOURS

"You ask me, Victor, this is just wrong."

Victor Gant glanced at Fat Mike Wiley and said, "Ain't asking you, am I, Fat Mike?"

Fat Mike shrugged and sighed. His broad, beefy face turned down into sadness only a basset hound could show. "No, I guess you ain't. But if you woulda asked, I'd have told you I didn't like this none."

"Don't expect you to like it. Just keep my back covered while we're having this little set-to."

"Ain't got no problems with that. I been there for you over thirty years."

Victor knew that was true. He'd met Fat Mike in Vietnam. They'd hunted Charlie in the bush, blew him up when they found him, and partied hard in the DMZ next to Charlie. Those had been some crazy times. Some days—in a weird way he didn't quite understand—he missed them.

In those days Fat Mike hadn't been fat. Lately the man was starting to earn his name. He stood an inch or two over six feet and tipped the scales at nearly three hundred pounds. Back in the day, Fat Mike had been called Fat Mike because he rolled his marijuana joints thick as sausages when he blazed.

Now his biker leathers didn't fit him quite so well. But he wore his hair long and sported a Fu Manchu mustache like he'd done when they'd been in the bush, even though the first lieutenant they'd had at the time had tried to keep his troops disciplined and clean-shaven.

One night, while the lieutenant was sleeping and probably dreaming up new ways for his men to risk their lives out in the jungle, Fat Mike and one of his buddies had rolled a grenade into the lieutenant's tent. Three seconds later, they'd needed a new lieutenant. The one they'd gotten had been a little smarter than the last one and knew to stay out of their way.

Victor was gaunt and hard-bodied. No spare flesh hung on his six-foot-two-inch frame. He was sixty-seven years old and was still whipcord tough. He wore a full, short beard that had turned to pewter over the last few years, but he'd kept his hair, and it hung down to his shoulders in greasy locks.

He wore his colors, and his jacket covered the two Glock .45s he carried in shoulder holsters. His jeans were clean but held old mud, blood, and oil stains. Under the jacket he wore a sleeveless black concert T-shirt featuring Steppenwolf. Square-toed biker's boots encased his feet.

Fat Mike sat astride his Harley next to Victor. There were a lot of other sleds in the gravel parking lot. Tawny Kitty was a biker bar and not a tourist attraction.

There were a few cars there too. Victor swept them with his gaze. Some of the vehicles belonged to college kids still in town for summer classes who thought slumming would be cool. Or they belonged to young women looking for bad boys.

The bar was a rough-cut square of stone and wood. Neon lights promising "Beer" and "Live Entertainment" hung in the windows. Another sign advertised Open. The sign advertising Tawny Kitty showed a young blonde in revealing clothing with a saucy glint in her eyes. The years had faded the colors of the sign, but it still drew salacious attention.

Victor stretched and reached into his jeans pocket. After a moment of digging, he brought out a crumpled cigarette pack. He unfolded it and stuck a cigarette in his mouth, then lit it with a skull-embossed Zippo lighter.

Without another word, he swung his leg over the motorcycle and stepped toward the bar. As always, Fat Mike was right behind him.

✪ ✪ ✪

>> 1707 HOURS

The interior of the bar was a little better than the exterior but not by much. Tawny Kitty was twenty years out of date. Two dance stages equipped with brass poles and backed by mirrors divided the large room into distinct areas. The long bar serviced both areas.

The stench of beer, cigarettes, reefer, sweat, nachos, and cheap perfume hung in the turgid air. Victor barely noticed it. He'd spent more time inside places like this than he had outside of them.

Young women—their bodies hollowed out by drugs and years of having their pride stripped out of them to leave only hard-edged anger or dulled acceptance—gyrated on the stages to an old 38 Special song. Nearly two dozen men and a handful of women sat around the stages. None of them appeared especially entertained.

Victor swept the bar with his gaze and didn't see the man he was looking for. He wasn't surprised. He and Fat Mike had arrived a little early. Victor did that when he was meeting with people he didn't particularly trust. Staking out the terrain first was important. That had been one of the first lessons he'd learned in Vietnam.

A petite hostess approached them. She wore immodestly cut jean shorts and a chambray shirt with the sleeves hacked off and tied well above her waist. Her dishwater blonde hair held a green tint under the weak light. Tattoos covered her arms and legs and ringed her navel.

"Can I get you boys something?" the waitress asked.

"Beers," Victor said.

"Domestic or imported?" the waitress asked.

"American," Victor said. "I fought for this country. I'll drink the beer that's made here too."

"You want me to take you to a table?" the young woman asked. "Or do you want to pick one out for yourselves? It's early yet. Got plenty of room."

Victor waved her off. "When you get those beers, we'll look just like this." He walked through the tables and took one against the back wall that gave him a good view of the room. Then he dropped into a chair.

Fat Mike sat at another table nearby and to one side. They always left each other clear fields of fire in case they needed it. If the waitress thought the seating arrangement was odd when she returned with the drinks, she didn't mention it.

⊛ ⊛ ⊛

>> 1717 HOURS

Minutes passed as rock and roll pounded the bar's walls.

Victor drank his beer and gazed around the bar. Other bikers lounged nearby, but none of them were Purple Royals. The Tawny Kitty was a neutral zone, a lot like the DMZ back in Nam.

"You seen your boy today?" Fat Mike asked from his table.

"A little."

"A little?" Fat Mike shook his head sadly. "Don't he know it's Father's Day? He should be hanging with you. A boy should be with his daddy on Father's Day."

"This ain't exactly something I want Bobby Lee hanging around for." Victor took another sip of beer. "Boy's got enough problems."

"That beef with them jarheads down in Camp Lejeune?" Fat Mike waved the possibility away. "If they was gonna do something, they'd have done it by now."

"They been looking for Bobby Lee."

"Well, they ain't found him."

"We met a lot of jarheads while we were doing our bit," Victor said. "You know the problem with jarheads."

"Ain't smart enough to know when to give up on something. I know. Bobby Lee shouldn't have left any witnesses behind when he jacked that car. Me and you wouldn't have done that."

"Me and you wouldn't have jacked no car."

Fat Mike shrugged. "Me and you was always too smart for that. We learned what we needed to know back in the Army." He grinned like a sly old hound. "But you got to cut Bobby Lee some slack. You wasn't always there. He's learning the best way he knows how."

That rankled Victor. He hadn't even known Amelia was pregnant with the boy until he'd gotten served with the papers. He'd married her while on a weekend bender, then come to his senses when he was sobered up back in South Korea. He hadn't come home again.

He'd told himself that Bobby Lee wasn't his, that Amelia was just sticking it to him for the child support the Army made him pay. But then he'd come back home after the Gulf War and seen the boy. There had been no denying it then. The boy had been the spitting image of him.

Victor could remember how weird that had felt. With everything he'd done, everything he'd seen, he'd never once thought about being a daddy. He didn't run with guys who had kids—in the Army or out. He remembered his old man, but there weren't any fond memories there. His daddy was the reason Victor had joined the Army at eighteen and quit high school midterm to go to Vietnam. Fighting the Vietnamese made more sense than trying to fight his daddy.

At first Victor and Bobby Lee had only grudgingly admitted the other existed. Victor hadn't held that against the boy. He didn't hold it against him now.

He could remember when the child support had been pushed through and the Army had given a big chunk of his pay to Amelia every month. Victor hadn't had much love for Bobby Lee then. But things were different now. Victor liked the idea that the boy was a lot like him and that there was some part of him that would continue existing after he was gone.

He just wished Bobby Lee wasn't so reckless. That carjacking in Jacksonville had been boneheaded. But Victor figured the apple hadn't fallen far from the tree there either. If Uncle Sam hadn't covered Victor's mistakes, then found a use for them, he might have ended up the same way.

"Bobby Lee and me are gonna hook up later," Victor said. "Gonna be down at Spider's. I'm buying Bobby Lee a new tattoo."

"Boy's got a fetish about them, don't he? I'm surprised Spider can find a place to put a tattoo on him."

"Been saving a place right over his heart. For when he was in love."

"Bobby Lee's in love?"

"Thinks he is. He's got a girl pregnant who says she loves him. She ran off from her folks and they're thinking about getting married."

"Is the kid his?"

"He thinks it is." Victor could barely remember having the conversation with his son. They'd both been blitzed at a recent cookout when the chapter had gotten together to celebrate the prison release of one of the members. Victor couldn't even remember the girl's name.

"Be good if it is."

Victor nodded and sipped beer.

"Hey," Fat Mike said, "I just realized he's about to make you a granddaddy."

"Yeah." That concept was still new to Victor. It sat among his thoughts like a poised rattlesnake and made him feel uneasy. He was just now starting to get comfortable with the idea of Bobby Lee. Adding to the confusion wasn't a good idea.

And there was no telling what Amelia might try to do. Back when Victor had mustered out and come home, after Bobby Lee had started coming around when he was twelve or thirteen, Amelia had tried to stop it. She'd even taken out a restraining order to keep Victor from the boy. The problem with that was that Bobby Lee was coming to see Victor, not Victor to see Bobby Lee.

Then Victor had gotten busted on the manslaughter charge. There hadn't been any way around it, and he'd been lucky they hadn't gotten him stuck with murder one. Time inside the pen hadn't been easy, but he'd done it standing up.

When he'd gotten out three years ago, Bobby Lee had ridden up with the other Purple Royals like he belonged. Fat Mike had even given him the keys to Victor's ride, and Bobby Lee had ridden home behind his daddy for the first time ever.

Of course, that hadn't fixed everything between them. There was too much history that had been bad, too much time that had been lost. Bobby Lee's own arrogant rebelliousness—honed to a razor's edge fighting his mama and stepdaddy—had kept him from getting too close to Victor.

The fact that Victor didn't want the boy in the Purple Royals was another stumbling block. It wasn't to keep Bobby Lee from a life of crime. Bobby Lee'd had a long history with juvie even before he met Victor for the first time. There was no keeping the boy out of trouble.

The attack on the Marine in Jacksonville was going to be a problem sooner or later, though. The best thing Bobby Lee could have done was leave North Carolina. Go out West to California.

The reason Victor didn't want Bobby Lee in the Purple Royals was because he didn't have enough of what it took to be a member of the gang. Bobby Lee was too independent and boneheaded. Victor had seen a lot of young men like him. He'd seen them blown up and shot down in the bush.

Maybe in time Bobby Lee would change.

"You a granddaddy." The thought seemed stuck in Fat Mike's mind. Thoughts often got that way for him. He was rattlesnake smart and junkyard-dog clever, but his mind tended to run in the same track when left to itself. "Means only one thing. Me and you are getting old."

"Speak for yourself. I intend to stay young until they scrape me off the highway." Victor upended his beer and drained the last of the bottle's contents.

Then the door opened and the man Victor was waiting for entered the bar.

He was young, and his appearance was rough. His road leathers were scarred and dusty. His black hair hung wild and tousled to his shoulders. When he lit a cigarette, his jacket separated long enough to reveal the semiauto pistol tucked into his waistband.

Most people, Victor reflected as he looked at the guy, would have been surprised to learn that the man was an undercover FBI agent.

His true name was unknown to Victor, but on the street he went by Thumper. He even had a tattoo of the bunny from the Disney film on one shoulder. Except that the image wore biker's leathers and breathed fire. One guy had made fun of the tat in a bar, called him Bambi, and Thumper had put him in the hospital.

Whoever the federal agent truly was, Victor knew the man had been around the track.

Thumper nodded at Victor, then crossed the room and dropped into a chair on the other side of the table.

"How's it hanging, bro?" Thumper asked.

"I'm not your bro," Victor said. He moved his hand on his thigh slightly. The butt of one of the Glocks was only inches from his fingertips. "I'm here to do business. Not make friends."

Thumper smiled slightly. "I can live with that. So tell me what's on your mind."

CRIME SCENE
NCIS
NAVAL CRIMINAL INVESTIGATIVE SERVICE

E SCENE ✪ NCIS ✪ CRIME SCENE

NAVAL CRIMINAL INVESTIGATIVE SERVICE

>> INTERSTATE 85
>> NEAR SALISBURY, NORTH CAROLINA
>> 1718 HOURS

For a long moment, Shel thought about just ignoring Remy's question. He knew if he decided not to answer, Remy wouldn't push it. Finally he said, "We've never talked about family."

"No."

Since Remy had been pulled into the team to replace Frank Billings, who had been killed in South Korea, he'd gradually warmed up to everyone else. But—like Shel, Nita, and Maggie—he hadn't talked much about family.

Only Will and Estrella did that. Will's current situation was screwed up, what with figuring out the pecking order with his ex-wife's new husband in the picture. And Estrella had never gotten over her husband's death. Both of them had pictures on their desks and computers, and they had stories to tell about what was going on in that part of their lives.

"Did you get along with your daddy?" Shel asked.

Remy looked ahead at the interstate. His face was as expressionless as his tinted sunglasses. "I never knew the man. My grandmère raised me and my brother." The French Creole influence from New Orleans sometimes crept into Remy's words.

"Didn't know you had a brother."

"I don't. Not anymore."

Shel knew there was a story there. He could feel the jagged pieces of it in Remy's words. But he let it go.

"My daddy's a hard man to get to know," Shel said. "All my life he's been distant. Not really a part of my life. Like he was just somebody curious and looking in through a window at me."

Remy didn't say anything.

"When Mama was still alive," Shel went on, "it wasn't so bad. She buffered everybody. Kept us all on an even keel. But Daddy was distant with her, too."

"You ain't the most talkative man I've ever met," Remy commented.

Shel had to grin at that. It was true. "Neither are you, kemosabe. And that's why you and me having this conversation is . . . odd."

"We don't have to have it."

"Unless we play another basketball game."

"Never again on Father's Day."

Shel knew Remy was giving him an out and gently letting him know he didn't have to continue talking. Or maybe the topic was a little uncomfortable for him too. Shel wasn't sure.

But Shel discovered that once he'd opened the can, the worms insisted on crawling out. Most of the reason for that, he was sure, was because he was confident Remy would never tell another soul. And because Remy wouldn't waste time trying to correct Shel's thinking or tell him how he should feel.

⍟ ⍟ ⍟

>> 1723 HOURS

"Mama always said Daddy got messed up in the war," Shel said. "She knew him before he went to Vietnam. His daddy raised him to be a rancher, but when he got old enough, he signed on with the Army."

"Not the Marines?"

"I was never one to follow in my daddy's footsteps." Shel admitted that honestly. "It started long before the choice of service in the military."

"Your father was in Vietnam?"

Shel nodded. That was a source of pride for him despite the confusion that generally roiled up when he thought of his father. "Pulled four two-year tours. Got released in '72 when his mama took sick. He had to go back and help work the ranch—the Rafter M. Mama said that taking care of Grandma was the only thing that brought him home."

"But somewhere in there he met your mother."

"Somewhere." Shel reached back and patted Max on the head. Having the dog with him 24-7 was a blessing. "Mama said they knew each other in grade school, all the way through high school. She said they talked like they were going to get married, but Daddy wouldn't do it because he thought he might get killed."

"A lot of boys did. Today isn't much better."

Shel nodded. "She said Daddy was surprised when he came home and found out she hadn't married."

"Eight years was a long time to wait."

"That's what Daddy said. But Mama said that eight years wasn't any time at all when you were waiting for the right man."

Remy grinned, and the ease that the expression created on his face had Shel grinning before he knew it too.

"So they had a love story going on," Remy said.

"The way Mama told it."

"How'd your father tell it?"

"He didn't. Never said one word about it. And my brother and I never asked him. Not even after Mama passed. Daddy came back to the ranch, and he worked it hard. He still does."

"Sounds like Kurt Russell should be a ranch hand there."

Shel grinned at that despite the bad mood the day had left him in. "It's a working cattle ranch. The living's hard and the profits are lean, but Daddy's a simple man and keeps at it. Mama's buried there with Grandpa and Grandma McHenry. Two of Daddy's brothers are buried there too."

"Sounds like a big commitment."

"He'll never leave that piece of ground. I reckon when the time comes, we'll plant him there too. My brother, Don, isn't happy about that, but that's how it goes. Daddy's leaving me control of the land. According to the will, I have to buy Don out if he wants me to."

"I didn't know you had a brother."

"One. Don."

"Is he military too?"

"Nope. He found a way to irritate Daddy even worse than I did. Of course, Don doesn't see it that way. He became a Bible-thumper." As he talked, Shel heard his accent thickening. His words—his thoughts even—turned more toward how he'd been raised when he was talking about his daddy.

"A preacher?" Remy asked.

Shel nodded.

"I still don't see why Father's Day bothers you so much. A lot of people have father issues."

Shel took a moment to think about that. It was hard, he was discovering, to get everything he felt into words that someone else would understand.

"I joined the Marines because I wanted my life simple," Shel said.

"That was your first mistake."

Shel ignored the comment. "I liked the idea of organization and structure, of knowing how I was supposed to treat other people."

"You don't think you got that at home?"

"From Mama, sure. And from Daddy, too, I guess. He taught me how I was supposed to treat other people, but—" Shel stopped, suddenly embarrassed. He had already revealed far more than he'd intended to.

"But not how to act around him," Remy said.

Shel wanted to tell Remy to just forget they were having the conversation, but he couldn't. It was on his mind. And today was Father's Day. Tomorrow it wouldn't be, and he might not feel inclined to talk about any of this. Then it would lie waiting to ambush him, as patient as a circling buzzard, for another year.

"I knew how to act around him," Shel said. "I just didn't know how we were supposed to act together."

"You were into sports. You don't have any father-son moments in there?"

"Daddy came to some of the games. Don and Mama shamed him into it on occasion."

"He didn't like coming?"

"Daddy doesn't like being around other people. He didn't make friends. He was what we always called *standoffish*."

"Why?"

"I don't know."

"Do other people make him uncomfortable?" Remy asked.

Shel shook his head. "I've seen Daddy walk into a bar filled with people, most of them wanting to form a lynch mob, and take command of the whole situation. We had a vaquero in from Mexico one summer. His name was Miguel. He was eighteen. I was twelve at the time. The way he could stick on a green mount and break him was amazing. I wanted to be just like him."

The road noise filled the pauses between Shel's words.

"Anyway, Miguel got into a fight with one of the local guys," Shel went on. "Words were said. Pride was hurt. And it was all over a girl."

"Now there's a bad mix," Remy said.

"Yeah. Miguel was outnumbered, and those boys pulled out baseball bats. Miguel pulled a knife. Jimmy Dean Harris got cut pretty bad and ended up in the hospital. It was his daddy that gathered up the lynch mob that night."

"Exciting little town you grew up in."

"I've heard New Orleans isn't exactly filled with saints," Shel countered.

Remy displayed a flat, mirthless grin. "My grandmère would agree with you. She wanted to move out of that place, but she never could. Even after Katrina, she's back where she grew up."

"A lot of people get stuck in their ways."

"I know that's true. But anyway, your father walked into this bar."

⊛ ⊛ ⊛

>> 1729 HOURS

"He did walk into that bar that night," Shel continued. "I followed him, but he didn't know it. Daddy got a call from one of the men inside the bar, and I followed him into town on my dirt bike."

"Where were the police?"

"We didn't have police. We had a sheriff's deputy. And he didn't want any part of what was going on."

"Brave soul."

"This was Texas. Old Texas. And it was twenty years ago."

"Not exactly prehistoric."

"Not if you're going by a calendar." Shel looked at the interstate stretched out before them. "But things hadn't changed much since the frontier days. At least, most folks living around there didn't think they should have. Daddy got out of his truck with an old Colt .45 on his hip and a pump-action shotgun in his hands. He didn't hesitate about walking straight up to that bar."

"I would have at least thought about it. Why didn't he call for help?"

"Because Miguel was a Mexican, and nobody else would have risked their neck for him. And because that's just the way Daddy is. He skins his own cats."

"I thought you said it was a cattle ranch."

Shel started to explain. The country accent came back to him so naturally when he started talking about things back home. Then he saw Remy grinning.

"I know you didn't mean that he really skinned cats," Remy said. "That's just one of those country terms."

"City boy," Shel snarled good-naturedly.

"So what happened at the bar?"

"I peeked in through a window. I didn't know what to do. I was scared to death for Daddy, but I don't think I'd ever been more proud of him."

"But it wasn't his fight."

"The way Daddy saw it, it was. He'd brought Miguel there to break horses and help out with the stock for the summer. What happened to Miguel—according to Daddy's way of thinking—was his responsibility. Daddy faced all those men in that bar and told them he'd kill the first man who hurt Miguel."

"Would he have?"

"They thought so."

"What did you think?"

Shel looked at Remy and nodded. "He'd have killed any man who laid a hand on Miguel that night. That's gospel truth."

"Not exactly Joe Average."

"Daddy never has been." Shel took a deep breath and let it out. "Anyway, Daddy left with Miguel. He saw my bike and knew I was there. I thought he was going to kill me. He'd told me to stay home. Instead, he had Miguel and me load my bike into the back of his pickup, which wasn't easy, and we went back to the ranch."

"And that's where it ended?"

"The sheriff came out the next day and told Daddy he didn't want him going into town waving guns around and threatening folks. Daddy told him he wouldn't have had to do it if the deputy would do his job, and he was lucky he didn't bill him for keeping the peace and preventing a murder that night. Mama came out and gentled things down before the sheriff made a bad mistake. She was the only one who could do that where Daddy was concerned. Don talks to Daddy, and sometimes Daddy listens. But I think it's more out of respect for him being a preacher."

"What kind of relationship does your brother have with your father?"

"After Mama died of cancer while I was in high school, Don got relegated to the role of family peacemaker. I think that's part of the reason he became a preacher. He figured out how to keep the peace in his life, and he mostly kept it between Daddy and me. But we never made it easy for him."

"Does Father's Day affect your brother in the same way it does you?"

Shel grinned at the thought of what was probably going on back home right now. "No. Don's got a whole new set of problems. He has a hard time giving up on an idea, and he wears like leather. So he goes to see Daddy on Father's Day whether Daddy likes it or not."

6

E SCENE ✪ NCIS ✪ CRIME SCENE
NAVAL CRIMINAL INVESTIGATIVE SERVICE

>> FOUR-MILE TAVERN
>> OUTSIDE FORT DAVIS, TEXAS
>> 1629 HOURS (CENTRAL TIME ZONE)

Don McHenry was aware of the sudden quietness in the bar as he stepped into the long, deep cool of the building. Outside, the Texas countryside was parched and sun blasted. The heat called up twisting mirages over the baked countryside. Scars were already starting to show from the heat, and summer wouldn't even officially begin for a few more days.

Don gazed around the bar but knew that most people there wouldn't meet his eyes. Fort Davis was a small community. Most people knew he was a preacher either from attending church or from seeing the televised Sunday morning meetings or just from the presence he had in the community. He served on the development boards and umpired games at the Little League ballpark.

So some of the drinkers were anxious about him being there.

Although Texas wasn't a dry state, it was still close enough to the Bible Belt of the country that some shame was attributed to drinking. A few of the churches still spoke against it. Don didn't feel that way and sometimes enjoyed a quiet beer when he took his sons to a Texas Rangers baseball game in Arlington.

Four-Mile Tavern was named for its geographic location. Built along the highway leading into Fort Davis, the bar was four miles outside the city limits. At one point it had been a small house. The story went that the owners had built a small room onto the front of the house to sell moonshine to locals. Over the years its reputation had grown, and people from outside the city had started to drive in to drink there and hang out in front of the building.

So new construction had begun. Within a few short years, the house had more than quadrupled in size. Unable to keep up with the demands and fearful of law enforcement frowning on their homegrown business, the owners had gotten a liquor license and gone legit. They'd also purchased some secondhand restaurant equipment and started serving lunches and dinners to truckers, tourists, and those in the city who preferred to do their drinking outside of it.

As Don stood there in the door, he saw a handful of men and women slide out the back way. A few of the others gave him a hard-eyed stare.

"Hey, preacher," an older woman with frosted hair said as she walked up to him. "If you're here on business, we don't want any. You got your shop, and I got mine. And looks like you done chased off some of my customers."

"Well, Katie," Don said with a smile, "chasing your customers off wasn't my intention."

The woman's severe face relaxed a little. She tossed her bar towel over one shoulder and put her hands on her hips. She even offered a smile.

"It ain't your fault, Pastor McHenry," Katie said. "I get too many Protestants in here and not enough Catholics. At least Catholics ain't afraid to drink in front of the priest. Why, I've even seen nights Father Bill bought a round for the house when he became an uncle or he'd shot a good game of golf." She winked at him. "Of course, Father Bill always waited till there weren't very many people in here at the time."

"You know I don't preach that consuming alcohol is a sin when it's used in moderation."

"You just scared out the backsliders, is all. And maybe a few of them who was here with people they oughtn't have been here with. But I guess you know that."

"I wasn't taking names."

"You never do." Katie looked at him a little more tenderly. "I suppose you're here to see your daddy."

Don nodded. "I am if he's here."

"He is. He's in the back. In the TV room." Katie looked a little sympathetic as she jerked a thumb over her shoulder. "You know the way."

"I do. Thanks." Don headed for the back of the tavern. His steps rang against the hardwood floor. It sometimes amazed him how solid and big that tavern sounded and how much his footsteps sounded like they did when he was alone in church before service started. The sound seemed right, though, since the tavern and the church were both places people took their troubles when they got too big for them.

"Can I bring you anything?" Katie asked.

"A vanilla Diet Coke, please." The tavern kept a range of flavorings to add to soft drinks. Don had drunk his first vanilla Coke in the tavern as a boy and still liked one on the rare occasions he was there.

"I'll bring it on back," Katie promised.

⊛ ⊛ ⊛

>> 1632 HOURS (CENTRAL TIME ZONE)

When Don was growing up, everyone in the neighborhood who owned a TV called their living room the TV room.

Television reception hadn't been very good in rural Texas for a long time—still wasn't in some areas. There wasn't much air-conditioning back then either; installing units was too expensive, and the wiring was problematic. Relaxation had come on shaded porches at the end of the day when the work was done. Most people enjoyed the radio, and Don remembered neighbors sitting around on porches on cool evenings listening to baseball games together. Church had often been held under tents too.

Those were the things Don remembered most about his childhood, and they were the things he kept with him when he'd grown up. He liked to keep things simple. Unfortunately, in the hurry-up world that was forced onto young minds—and maybe not-so-young minds as well—through television and the Internet, simplicity was all but lost these days.

When personal satellite dishes had come along, families had started investing in televisions. The TV became a status symbol of sorts, and so they started calling living rooms the TV room the way that empty nesters started calling their children's rooms the hobby room.

The Four-Mile Tavern had been one of the first to put TVs in for public viewing in the 1960s. Boxing, NASCAR racing, baseball, and horse races had all been big. And the patrons of the Four-Mile often placed wagers on those events. Gambling was illegal in Texas, but back then the laws had been hazy, and the sheriff and his men had turned a blind eye to anything that didn't involve cards, dice, and roulette. As long as nobody reached for a weapon.

Coupled with beer, air-conditioning, and TV, the tavern had become a booming local enterprise. Some of that success was mired in blood, though. Fights broke out over bets, over women, and over perceived slights. In rural Texas, fights were settled with fists, tire irons, and—occasionally—guns. It had helped that the local sheriff's deputies usually did their drinking there too.

When Don led church retreats in large metropolitan areas, other pastors he met had trouble understanding everything he faced while shepherding his flock. But to be fair, he didn't quite understand the problems those city preachers dealt with either. Of course, there was more about gang violence in the news than there was about rural feuds and murders.

Don chose to believe that God gave each of his teachers their own burdens to carry. He also believed that God gave them each the strength and tools to deal with those burdens.

All things considered, Don loved living in Fort Davis, keeping church there, and raising his sons and daughter on the baseball and softball fields. He'd been to the big cities and hadn't seen anything there that he couldn't live without.

Shel, on the other hand, seemed bound and determined to see the whole world.

Not see the world, Don amended. *Just get off the ranch and stay away.*

During his service as a youth minister, as choir leader, and finally as preacher of The Blessed Word Church in Fort Davis, Don had handled everything God had ever put before him to do. By all counts, he'd been successful doing God's work, and he gave thanks every day that he could make a difference.

But there was one man whose heart Don felt he'd never touched the way God would want it touched. Don had failed time and again, but through God's grace he had never given up.

And maybe, Don sometimes thought, hoping that he wasn't being irreverent, *I haven't given up because of that stubbornness I got from Daddy. Maybe his own bloodline will be the end of his reluctance about accepting God.*

Tyrel McHenry, his daddy, was the most stubborn man Don had ever met. And Don was there tonight to make another stab at getting through to the man.

7

SCENE ✪ NCIS ✪ CRIME SCENE
NAVAL CRIMINAL INVESTIGATIVE SERVICE

>> TAWNY KITTY'S BAR AND GRILL
>> SOUTH END
>> CHARLOTTE, NORTH CAROLINA
>> 1737 HOURS

"Don't know why you feel you gotta come on all hard and everything, Victor. We're all friends here."

Gazing across the table at Thumper, Victor knew that the man had been in tight places before. He knew how to handle himself. Not just with guns and fists, but with words and emotions as well. He didn't panic at the first sign of trouble.

That was good and it was bad. The fact that he'd weathered the initial blast meant he had backbone. Now it remained to be seen if he had any brains.

"You don't like it, maybe you should leave." Victor kept his voice flat and neutral.

Wraparound shades kept Thumper's eyes hidden, but Victor knew the man was assessing and reassessing the situation in seconds. The first thing Thumper had to be worried about was how much danger he was in.

Guys that went deep undercover knew from the moment that choice was made that they didn't have a friend left to them in the world. If they were found out by the gang or organization they were infiltrating, they were dead. If they turned dirty while they were under, unless they had really good evidence to the contrary, they were incarcerated with the same people they had started out trying to lock down. If they forgot for a moment where their loyalty—and ultimately their safety—lay, their lives were worth less than nothing.

Thinking about the situation an undercover agent would find himself in, Victor reflected that it wasn't far removed from looking for Charlie in the bush. It took nerves of steel to play the game.

Or drugs to mute the fear.

If Thumper had been legit, he should have gotten up from the table and walked out. No biker worth his salt took an insult straight up like that. He'd have been into the wind or he would have busted Victor in the chops.

Unless you figure you're sitting right next to what you want and you won't pick up your cards from the table because you think you're going to win, Victor thought. He was about to disabuse Thumper of that notion.

The biker's face hardened a little, but it was all for show. Thumper just didn't know that yet.

"I don't know what you're trippin' on, dude," Thumper said, "but I don't appreciate it."

"I'm gonna lay somethin' down for you, man, and you can decide if you want to pick it up or if the weight's too much for you." Victor's eyes never left those of the other man.

Thumper glanced away. He didn't bother to meet Fat Mike's gaze either.

Victor wondered if Thumper's cop buddies were listening to the conversation. He didn't think Thumper was stupid enough to wear a wire, but there had been plenty of time to wire the tavern before the meeting took place. Frankly he didn't care.

"I know you're a cop," Victor stated. For a moment, the accusation hung in the air.

❂ ❂ ❂

>> 1741 HOURS

Thumper turned back to Victor and proved just how good he was at playing the role. He laughed. And he sounded like Victor had just told him a really good joke.

"Dude, I seriously don't know what you been smoking, but if you got any of it left, I want some."

"You went to school, right?"

After a brief hesitation, Thumper smoothly nodded and tossed in a devil-may-care shrug. "Sure. Before I got old enough for juvie. After that, it was splitsville for me and the public school system. I was just a product of the state."

"Is that so?" With his free hand, Victor reached into his jacket pocket and took out a few photographs. He noted that Thumper reached a little more deeply under his own jacket.

From the way Fat Mike moved in his seat, Victor knew that he had his sawed-off shotgun out under the table and leveled at Thumper's midsection. If the man made a wrong move, Fat Mike was going to blow him in two.

"You ever hear of an East Coast motorcycle chapter called the Iron Goblins?"

Thumper's face seemed frozen. No emotion showed. "Lots of chapters out there now," Thumper countered.

"You see, I went to school," Victor said. "I learned to add, and I learned when things don't add up. And you? You don't add up."

"Maybe I should just call it an afternoon," Thumper suggested. "I got things to do and places to go." He slid his chair back.

"If you leave before I'm through talking to you," Victor stated, "you aren't going to live to see morning."

Thumper tried to cover his nervousness by reaching into his jacket for a cigarette.

Fat Mike eased the hammers back on his shotgun. The clicks sounded ominous and loud enough to be heard over the music.

"Chill, bro." Thumper's voice sounded strained and brittle. "I'm just going for a packet of cigarettes."

"Leave your hands on the table where we can see them." Victor leaned back in his seat and fished out his own cigarettes. He slid the pack across to Thumper, then added his Zippo lighter. "Smoke one of mine. Keep it friendly."

Thumper took the pack, shook a cigarette out, and lit up. He almost looked calm. Except for the fact that his hands were shaking as much as a man going through the DTs. He breathed out a thick plume of smoke.

"You guys are *waaaayyyy* too intense, bro," Thumper said.

Victor smiled, but the effort was cold and calculated. There were people who'd seen that smile who never walked the earth again. He thought he could stop short of that with Thumper. In fact, Thumper—if he could be reasoned with—could make other things much simpler.

If Victor had not been able to figure out a way to use Thumper and his cop connections, he and Fat Mike would have buried the guy tonight. In fact, Fat Mike had been happier with that idea than with what Victor had in mind.

Thumper made a show of smoking calmly. "I'm starting to feel offended. I have to tell you that. That business we've been talking about doing? That's pretty much over at this point."

"Guess what, genius," Victor said. "Once I figured out you were a Fed, whatever business you and I might have had was taken off the table."

Thumper's eyes hardened. "We were talking about a supply of meth."

"I got to be honest with you about that," Victor said almost pleasantly. "That was just me and Fat Mike setting you up. We were just yanking your chain."

Thumper glowered at him. "Setting me up for what? To rip me off?"

Listening to the desperation in Thumper's voice, Victor knew that someone was monitoring the encounter. Maybe Thumper hadn't worn the wire to the meeting, but that didn't mean he'd arrived without any backup.

"We got hookups," Victor said. "You want something, we know a guy who can get it for you. We just take our cut out of the middle."

Thumper looked at Victor, then at Fat Mike, then back again. "You guys have got cooks working for you." He was referring to meth cooks.

Victor fanned the photographs in his big, callused hands. "Don't know what you're talking about."

Thumper snarled a curse that was loud enough to draw the brief attention of two bikers at a table only a short distance away. Victor looked at the men for a long, hard minute and they looked away.

"You know what I'm talking about," Thumper stated angrily. "You garroted Hobo Simpson. Garroted him and dropped him into a hole somewhere out in the woods."

Victor smiled coldly. "I don't know what you're talking about."

"Yeah, you do."

"If you got proof of that, then arrest me." Victor shoved his hands out in front of him. He hadn't planned the move and it caught Fat Mike by surprise too. Fat Mike shifted uneasily and for a moment Victor thought he was going to bring the shotgun into play.

"I ain't no cop." Thumper sounded sullen.

"Yeah, you are." Victor spread the photographs across the desktop in a move so smooth it would have done a riverboat gambler proud. "Got you a six-pack here, Thumper. Isn't that what the cops call mug shots?"

"Don't know."

"If you've been arrested and held for questioning, you'd know that." Victor delighted in turning the knife a little, letting Thumper know he wasn't thinking straight enough to keep himself out of trouble.

"Okay. Maybe I heard it called that." Thumper's eyes never went to the photographs.

"Take a look," Victor said in a soft voice. "See what I see."

"I ain't here to play games," Thumper said. "I got people who are gonna be all up in my grill if I don't hook them up with the meth I promised them."

"The meth won't be a problem," Victor stated. "Like I said, I know a guy who knows a guy." Passing on information about someone selling drugs wasn't illegal. Not as long as he didn't ask for money. "Look at the pictures."

After a moment, Thumper did. As soon as he recognized the people in the pictures, he froze. Then he called Victor a vile name.

Victor knew that the undercover cop had recognized the people immediately. They were his ex-wife, son, and sister.

"Where did you get those?" Thumper demanded in a hoarse voice.

"Chill, dude. They're just pictures." Victor turned the photographs over, then spread them again.

"They're of my family," Thumper said.

Victor knew the name Thumper had called him was a tell. He'd known it as soon as Thumper had said it, and he knew they weren't going to finish their conversation alone.

Victor left the photographs lying facedown on the table. He passed a magazine he'd brought with him to Fat Mike, who got up and walked away without a word. From here everything was a gamble, a desperate roll of the dice. The kicker was that the club had an excellent attorney on retainer, and Thumper had recognized his family.

Quietly Victor sipped his beer and waited. Less than a minute later, FBI agents in black riot gear burst through the doors with guns drawn. They started shouting at once. There was a brief flurry of activity as some of the bikers tried to escape. The agents put them down with stun batons, then screwed the muzzles of their weapons into the base of those men's skulls.

Victor finished his last sip of beer and put his hands in the air. He didn't resist when one of the men grabbed him out of the chair by his hair and made him drop to his knees.

"He had pictures of my family," Thumper said to a grizzled guy wearing glasses. "I wouldn't have blown cover if he hadn't."

Victor just grinned.

Without a word, the grizzled agent reached for the photographs on the table and flipped them over one by one. Victor laughed as he saw the surprised look on Thumper's face. The pictures—each and every one of them—showed Thumper drunk and drugged out with other members of the Purple Royals. None of the pictures, though, were of Victor or Fat Mike.

He'd made sure they weren't compromised.

Thumper picked up the photographs. "I don't understand. I saw them! I swear I did!"

The grizzled agent swung his attention to Victor. "Like to think you're cute, don't you?" the agent asked.

"Cute enough," Victor responded. "And about to get cuter. Me and you, we gotta talk. Now that I got your attention."

8

E SCENE ✪ NCIS ✪ CRIME SCENE

NAVAL CRIMINAL INVESTIGATIVE SERVICE

```
>> FOUR-MILE TAVERN
>> OUTSIDE FORT DAVIS, TEXAS
>> 1648 HOURS (CENTRAL TIME ZONE)
```

Seated at one of the small round tables that dotted the floor in the tavern's TV room, Tyrel McHenry looked like he'd been carved from stone. He was sixty-three years old. Age and a lifetime of hard work had eroded the excess flesh from his lean body.

He was not quite as tall and broad-shouldered as Shel was, but looking at the two of them together, a person would know where Shel had gotten his build.

Don had always thought—though he would never mention it to either one of the other men in his family—that his daddy and Shel were more alike than they were different. If anyone didn't fit into that family, Don felt certain it was him.

Tyrel's hair had finished going iron gray a few years back. Long exposure to a blistering sun and harsh winters had bronzed his skin. Permanent wrinkles wreathed his cold blue eyes and pleated his leathery cheeks, which he kept smooth and shiny with a straight razor he used every morning and every evening if he was going to go out.

He wore straight-legged jeans tucked into cowboy boots. Tyrel had always maintained that the difference between a working ranch hand and a drugstore cowboy had been whether the jeans were worn on the outside of his boots or tucked in. A ranch hand tucked them in so they didn't catch in the stirrups or get caught on anything while he was working.

The black Western shirt was carefully pressed and had white pearl snaps. Tyrel's high-crowned black cowboy hat sported a silver hatband etched with Native American symbols. Don's mama, part Lipan Apache, had made the hatband for her husband and marked it with signs that she'd claimed would bring him peace.

Though his mama had been a devout Christian woman who went to church every Wednesday and Sunday, she'd also held on to some of the old ways because she hadn't wanted the culture to disappear. And if her husband was dead set against believing in the works of the Good Lord, maybe he'd have been a little more open to something else. Anything that would have brought him peace.

Tyrel smoked an unfiltered Camel cigarette and kept his gaze focused on the baseball game on the big-screen TV on the wall. A handful of other men sat quietly and watched the game as well.

Don approached his daddy and stood nearby. Even as a grown man, he'd never walked up to his daddy without being acknowledged first.

"What do you want, boy?" Tyrel asked in his coarse voice. He never turned his gaze from the TV.

"I came to see you, Daddy," Don said.

"I thought you just did come to see me."

"Yes, sir. But that was back in May." Don's mother had succumbed to her illness on May 12, and Don always visited on that anniversary so his daddy wouldn't have to be alone.

"You came out to put flowers on your mama's grave."

"Yes, sir."

Tyrel nodded in quiet satisfaction. "She'd have liked that. You looking after her like that."

"Yes, sir." When he'd arrived at the grave, Don had discovered a woven flower blanket that covered his mama's final resting spot. His daddy made them himself. At least, Don hadn't ever found out if anyone else did them. And the braiding was similar to the rope mending his daddy had taught him to do.

"Well, you planning on standing there all night?" Tyrel asked. "I thought you had a church to run."

"You don't exactly *run* a church, Daddy," Don said. "It's not a business."

"Seems to me you get paid by people who go there. That's a business."

Don knew his daddy was deliberately baiting him and avoided the old argument. "People go there to be with God. They leave money so they have a house to do that together in. And to help out people in the congregation that aren't able to fend for themselves."

Tyrel flicked ash from his cigarette in annoyance. He took another draw on the Camel and breathed out a cloud of smoke.

"You say toe-may-toe; I say toe-may-tah."

Don had long since given up trying to caution his father about smoking. Tyrel McHenry wasn't a man much given to listening to advice he didn't want to hear.

"Don't you gotta get back to that church soon?" Tyrel asked. "Must be an evening prayer or something you gotta give."

"We're not having service tonight till seven," Don said. "I wanted families to have time to spend the day together." He paused. "Do you mind if I sit with you, Daddy?"

Tyrel hesitated for a moment, and Don thought he almost looked over. "Suit yourself. You're a grown man."

"Yes, sir. Thank you, Daddy." Don took a chair beside his father. As he looked at Tyrel, he realized that the years were marking him harder. Don couldn't help wondering how much longer his daddy would be with them.

Then Don felt miserable because his daddy had never truly been with any of them.

That's not true, he reminded himself. *Daddy was always there for Mama.*

All throughout the time he was growing up, though, Don couldn't remember much softness between his parents. Tyrel had worked from sunup to sundown, and he'd been early to bed after he'd washed the supper dishes for his wife.

Don could recall nights he'd sat by the fireplace and listened to Rachel McHenry read from the Bible. They were always stories from the Old Testament, filled with wars and fearful things, because those were the ones Tyrel tolerated best.

The stories of David from the books of 1 and 2 Samuel were Tyrel's favorites. Don could remember his mama asking his daddy one night why he liked those stories so much.

Tyrel had thought long and hard about his answer before he gave it. That was usually his way. Tyrel had always taken longer to answer deeper questions. Responses to general questions about right and wrong, about the code Tyrel McHenry lived by, came lightning quick, but things beyond mending fences and how a man should react in everyday situations took him longer.

"I like that book," Tyrel had said, "because even though David did a powerful lot of wrongful things, God still loved him. It just seems uplifting. Can't see how it would be true, but I like those stories."

Don had read the books several times to try to figure out what drew his daddy to them. He'd finally given up in frustration. Whatever secrets lay in those pages had eluded him.

⊛ ⊛ ⊛

>> 1654 HOURS (CENTRAL TIME ZONE)

"You want something to drink?" Tyrel asked.

"No, thank you, Daddy. Katie's bringing me a soda."

At that moment, Katie appeared, placing a cocktail napkin and the soft drink glass in front of Don.

Tyrel smiled in disbelief and shook his head. "Come to a bar to drink a soda pop. Don't that beat all."

"I got to deliver a sermon tonight, Daddy. I'd rather not do it with beer on my breath." Don took a sip of his drink.

On the screen, the Rangers turned a double play against the Yankees. Their success spurred a spate of happy curses from a couple of the men.

"And I didn't come here to drink a soda pop." Don looked at his daddy, who had yet to turn his full gaze on him. "I came here to be with you."

"I came here to be alone," Tyrel said.

"If you'd wanted to be alone, you'd have stayed at home."

"But you already been by there, ain't you?"

Reluctantly Don nodded. He'd gone by the Rafter M Ranch first and found only Gonzalez snoozing on the porch. Gonzalez was nearly Tyrel's age, but Tyrel took care of the other man and gave him lodging and payment for his help around the ranch.

"I wanted to ask you to come to church tonight, Daddy," Don said.

"I'm not interested in church," Tyrel replied. "What happens between me and God stays between me and God. Don't need to go airing it out in public."

As always, that bit of insight into his daddy's spiritual affairs made Don relax a little. His daddy was a believer or was at least paying belief lip service. That was a start.

"It's Father's Day," Don went on. "I thought maybe you'd like to spend part of it with me."

"You're here, ain't you?"

"And my family," Don went on patiently.

"Son, we've had this conversation a hundred times if we've had it once." Tyrel stubbed his cigarette out in the ashtray. "Comes a time in a man's life when he cuts loose from his family to make one of his own.

A man can't ride two broncs. You gotta choose one or the other. I think you'll find that in the book of Ecclesiastes." He paused. "Personally, I think you made a fine choice in leaving. You married a pretty little gal, and you got two fine boys and a daughter. You got your family."

"They'd like to see more of their granddaddy."

"You and yours are welcome to come on out to the ranch any time. You know that. I've told you enough. And you're coming out there enough that them boys are learning to ride good enough. Might even be as good as Shel someday."

"We'd like to have you to supper after the service." During Don's eleven years of marriage, his daddy had never once stepped inside his house other than to help repair or install something. Even that was done after protest, after Tyrel became convinced his son really couldn't manage it on his own.

Occasionally, if he moved fast enough, Don managed to lay out steaks or burgers on the grill and get a meal together before Tyrel could leave. But despite Don's best efforts at being cordial, he'd known his daddy wasn't comfortable being there.

He just didn't know why that was so. Tyrel liked small children, and they liked him. Don's sons and daughter adored their grandpa, and he doted on them when they were around. He just kept his distance.

"I'm planning on stopping by the truck stop on my way home. They got that coconut pie I like."

"You can always stop by there on your way home. After you have supper with us."

"I already got my plans in order."

"Change them. It's Father's Day."

Tyrel turned and looked at his son. In that unflinching gaze, Don felt somehow diminished, like he was looking at something that would always and forever be larger than he was. He was ashamed that he felt this way in front of his daddy. He didn't like feeling weak and helpless, and he truly believed that God had put this work before him.

"I'm not changing my plans," Tyrel said. "They're good plans. They fit me. I don't plan my life around you, and you ought not plan yours around me."

"It's just supper, Daddy."

"I thought it was church, then supper."

"Church won't last too long tonight. I want to get everybody home early."

Tyrel sipped his beer. After a minute, he shook his head. "No thanks.

I already got my mind made up. Don't mean to not be social, but I got a lot to think about."

"What?"

"Where to move them cows. Gonna be hot and dry come August. Pasture might not survive. Hay's expensive if you have to feed it during the summer. I don't want to do that."

"You get through every year."

"It gets harder. Ain't like that job you do. Just memorize a few lines of Scripture and quote 'em at people now and again."

Don knew that if he'd been Shel and had just heard his work tossed off so casually, an argument would have broken out then and there. Shel had always been defensive around their daddy.

"Yes, sir," Don said instead. He'd always found it easier to keep the peace than to fight with his brother or his daddy.

"There's a science to ranching," his daddy said. "A man that don't pay attention and learn what he needs to survive ends up sacking groceries somewhere. I'm too old to do that."

"Yes, sir." Don sipped his drink. "Have you heard from Shel today?"

Tyrel fished his pack of smokes out of his pocket and lit up a new cigarette with a Zippo lighter. He squinted and waved the smoke out of his face with a hand. "No."

"I haven't been able to get ahold of him either." Don had called several times just in case Shel had forgotten it was Father's Day. The calls had gone unanswered and unreturned.

"I haven't tried to get hold of him," Tyrel said simply. "Likely he's busy. No reason he should be calling anyway."

"It's Father's Day. He should call." Don felt irritated and a little sad. Over the last few years, Shel had seemed to be drifting farther and farther away from their daddy. It hurt Don to see that and recognize it. It hurt even more when he realized there was nothing he could do to prevent it. Both men needed each other, but neither of them seemed willing to admit it.

"I didn't raise either of you two boys to be soft." Tyrel knocked ash from his cigarette.

"Calling your daddy on Father's Day isn't being soft. It's about respect and love."

Tyrel turned and looked at Don. "You ain't your brother. You don't feel what he feels. Shel's got his ways, and you got yours. What works for you ain't necessarily gonna work for him. He don't say what's on his mind as easy as you do, that's all."

Shel and Don had been different almost since day one. Don got that they were different, and that they would probably always be different.

But on Father's Day, Don didn't want to have that conversation with his daddy. He knew it would probably lead to an argument. And if there was any arguing to be done, Don fully intended to set his sights on Shel.

"Ball game's almost over," Tyrel said. "Reckon you need to be getting back to the church before long."

"That's all right, Daddy. I got a few more minutes. If you don't mind, I'll just sit here and watch the game with you for a little bit."

"Do what you want, but there's men in here who come to watch the game. Not to listen to you and me talk."

"Yes, sir." Knowing his daddy wouldn't take part in any more conversation, Don quietly sat and watched baseball. It wasn't the ideal Father's Day, but he knew it was the best his daddy would allow him to have.

There in the darkness of the tavern, he quietly loved his daddy and asked God to help him understand how Tyrel McHenry had come to be the cold, hard man he was. And he hoped that Shel had a good reason for not coming home and not calling.

Otherwise Don was going to have that argument after all.

CRIME SCENE
NCIS
NAVAL CRIMINAL INVESTIGATIVE SERVICE

E SCENE ✪ NCIS ✪ CRIME SCENE
NAVAL CRIMINAL INVESTIGATIVE SERVICE

>> NCIS OFFICES
>> CAMP LEJEUNE, NORTH CAROLINA
>> 1909 HOURS

"Are you trying to hypnotize that computer screen?"

United States Navy Commander Will Coburn's voice broke the spell of Maggie Foley's cycling thoughts. She glanced away from the computer and looked at her commanding officer.

"Because if you're trying to hypnotize it," Will continued, "I don't think it's going to work."

"I was trying to catch up on some of the files." Maggie leaned back in the ergonomic chair and tried to find some of the relief the design promised. "We've all got court appearances to do in the next few weeks, so I wanted to start prepping everyone."

Court appearances were a major part of an NCIS special agent's life. Coming in weeks or months after the fact—oftentimes nearly a year because they dealt with civilian courts as well as military ones—preparation was important. Cases came and went, but an agent had to be ready to make the jury or the judge believe he or she remembered everything as if the events had happened only yesterday. That kind of confidence wasn't gained just overnight.

Will paused at the coffeepot and poured a cup.

The NCIS offices weren't completely deserted, but only a skeleton crew of agents was in place. Crime never truly came to a halt. Most of the cubicles were silent, but Maggie knew it would be business as usual in the morning.

"You could have let that go for tonight."

Maggie knew she could have, but she hadn't wanted to stay in her apartment or go out. Over the last few years, the NCIS offices had gotten comfortable for her. It was Father's Day, and she didn't want to sit at home and feel guilty about not calling her father. Not that Harrison Talbot Foley III would have truly cared other than to tweak whatever guilt she might have felt.

"I didn't feel like going out, and I didn't feel like staying in," Maggie said. "I needed to work on something that was mindless. Organizing files does that for me."

Will blew on his coffee and sipped. Then he grimaced and put the coffee down. "I take it you haven't been drinking the coffee."

Maggie held up an extra-large Starbucks cup that was still almost half-full. "Nope."

Will busied himself brewing a new pot. "Well, at least it's peaceful tonight."

"It *was* quiet tonight. At least, it was until someone gave us a lead on Bobby Lee Gant."

Quiet contemplation passed over Will's face for just a second; then he nodded. They all remembered who Bobby Lee Gant was.

"Anything solid?" Will asked.

"We hope so."

"'We'?"

"Shel and Remy are en route."

"Where?"

"Charlotte."

"How did you find out Bobby Lee was supposed to be there?"

Maggie told him about the woman who'd been flipped by the Charlotte PD investigators.

"Whom does Bobby Lee know up there?" Will asked when she'd finished.

Maggie brought up Bobby Lee Gant's file. "His father. Victor."

The man's grim visage filled the screen. Maggie had worked in law enforcement long enough to know that pure evil existed in the world. Looking at Victor Gant, she couldn't help but get the feeling the man was intimate with all aspects of that dark force.

Will nodded and ran a hand through his short-cropped black hair. "The biker guy."

"Right." As she studied Will, Maggie knew he was tired and struggling. Even without her degrees in psychology and years of profiling suspects and victims, she would have known that.

"You could have called me," Will said. He was a little over six feet tall and rugged looking. He was bigger than Remy Gautreau but nowhere near as developed as Shel McHenry. His green eyes looked bloodshot. He was tan from the sun and the sea, and he wore the Navy like it was a part of him. During the last few months he'd been out sailing with his kids on the weekends every chance they'd gotten.

"You were with Steven and Wren, and it's Father's Day," Maggie said. "I wasn't going to interrupt you. It's just a quick look-see. If it doesn't feel right, Shel and Remy will shadow Bobby Lee and wait till we can get someone there. They know the drill."

Will watched the coffee drip into the glass pot. "Bobby Lee's elevator doesn't go quite to the top."

Maggie smiled. "That sounds like something Shel would say."

"That's because it is something Shel said. And he said it because Bobby Lee is dangerous."

"Shel and Remy can handle themselves. There's no sense in sending three men on a two-man job. Shel could probably collar Bobby Lee himself." *Besides,* Maggie thought, *you needed the time with your kids.* But she knew better than to tell Will that. He already felt torn in different directions enough by the job and his family. Getting that balance right had always been a struggle for him.

"How far out are they?"

Maggie brought up her GPS program and entered the ID designation for Shel's Jeep. It took only a second to locate the vehicle and mark its position. "They're in Charlotte now. It shouldn't be long."

Will took a fresh cup of coffee. "When you know something . . ."

"You'll be my first call."

⊛ ⊛ ⊛

>> 1915 HOURS

Will stood in his office and peered out the window. The camp was still light enough that he could easily see the surrounding grounds. Everything was green and full. He knew if he opened the window he'd be able to smell the ocean.

Maybe I should have gone fishing, he thought. But he knew that wouldn't have helped his mood. If anything, it would have made the situation worse.

"Trying to hypnotize that window?"

Refocusing on the glass, Will saw Maggie's reflection as she leaned in the doorway behind him. She was petite, a handful of inches over five feet, with an athletic body kept taut and fit through rigorous exercise. Her dark brown hair dusted her shoulders, and she regarded him with deep hazel eyes. She wore a black skirt and a white blouse, looking like all she had to do was throw on a jacket to have dinner at one of the best restaurants in Jacksonville, the city just outside Camp Lejeune. She was intelligent and insightful and incredibly competent in the field.

"Maybe," Will replied. "I think I've almost got it."

Maggie smiled. "So how did today with Steven and Wren go?"

Will hesitated long enough to make sure he spoke in a conversational tone. "I didn't come here to get counseling."

"Of course you didn't. You came here because you didn't want to go home and sit there alone."

Will sipped his coffee. She was right; he had been avoiding the emptiness of his living quarters.

"I have a counselor I talk to these days," he said. Maggie had helped him get in touch with one of the people on base.

"Is it helping?"

It was the first time she'd asked. Will was a private person about a lot of things, and he was especially private about the painful things. What he was still going through—even after the divorce—hurt more than he wanted it to. And he didn't like talking about it.

"I think so," Will replied.

"Good." Maggie waited, then prompted him again. "So how's it going tonight?"

"I'm planning on talking to Doug about it next session."

"Doug's not here right now. A lot has changed the last month. Your ex-wife has a new husband. Steven and Wren have a new stepfather. Those are big things. And Father's Day is a red-letter day." Maggie shrugged. "I thought maybe you might want to talk about it."

Will did. And he didn't. It was a brief struggle before the balance tipped. He took a deep breath and let the air out, and some of the tension inside his chest broke.

"It's kind of confusing actually," he admitted.

"Because now Barbara is married again and you're not."

Will thought about that. "Because Barbara is married again," he agreed. "Not because I'm not. The last thing the kids or I need right now is another stepparent involved in the mix."

Maggie smiled. "You're probably right. I suspect Barbara wouldn't handle you getting married with the same grace you've handled her marriage."

"The way I've handled it hasn't felt very graceful." In fact, Will sometimes felt certain that he wouldn't have made it through the transition at all without God's help. That closeness he felt—though at times it was still strained because of all the horrors he saw in his line of work—had gotten stronger in him. He'd learned to acknowledge God's presence as his quiet strength.

"I think you have been," Maggie said.

"I appreciate the vote of confidence."

"I also suspect that her new husband—"

"Jesse," Will said.

"—doesn't care for the situation either."

"Probably not."

"He's not a kid person," Maggie said, "so having them around is . . ." She paused, searching for the right, technically inoffensive term.

"Inconvenient," Will said.

"Having to share them with you is more than inconvenient to him," Maggie said. "I've seen his type. He likes to be top dog. He wants it to all be about him."

Will looked at Maggie then. "You haven't mentioned this before," he said.

"It's because I mind my own business."

Will cocked an eyebrow. "But here you are in my office."

Maggie smiled guilelessly. "Yes."

Will gestured to a seat across from his desk. Maggie slid into it and sat attentively.

"So now you don't have any more questions?" Will asked.

"You know what you want to talk about more than I do," Maggie replied. "A good counselor only leads a conversation when that isn't the case."

Will hesitated for a moment and wondered if talking at all was a mistake. But he felt the need to. Today had been harder than he'd expected. Taking Steven and Wren back to be with their new "dad" for part of Father's Day hadn't been easy.

"You're right about Jesse," he said. "He does want it to be all about him." Will shook his head. "I honestly don't know what Barbara sees in him."

"He's always home. He's always around. It's all about him, and he wants to be there so it *can* be all about him." Maggie shrugged. "It's not rocket science. Barbara wanted a man who was home."

"And I wasn't."

"Not enough for her, no. But the work you were doing with the Navy was important, Will. Never forget that. Military careers are hard on everybody. You went through the same things that she did, and you got to see your children a lot less."

That had been one of the things Will had sought to redress after taking the NCIS posting.

"Not everybody can do what you and those other men do on a daily basis."

"She blamed me."

"She blamed your job. You just got caught up in the fallout. Jesse wants home to be all about him. So he's there. By default, even though it's not exactly for the right reasons, his desire meets Barbara's needs."

"He didn't like it that Steven and Wren were with me most of today. And he didn't like it when they called and asked him if they could stay the night and come back tomorrow."

"That would have been a big concession."

Will nodded.

"But he wasn't big enough to make it," Maggie said.

"No."

"Why do you think he felt that way?"

Will folded his hands together and leaned across the desk toward her. "I'm not the professional here."

Maggie shook her head. "That's not how we do the work. I don't just give you the answers. You have to look for them yourself. Besides, you know the answer to this one."

Will did because the answer was simple. "Jesse didn't want them to be with me because it was a distinct reminder that it's not all about him. Not where they're concerned."

A pleased look flashed in Maggie's hazel eyes. "Bingo. But it cuts deeper than that."

Will's momentary triumph faded. "I don't understand."

"You were one of the youngest lieutenants ever promoted to commander," Maggie said. "You can figure this one out." She sipped her coffee.

Will was silent for a full minute as he tried to wrap his brain around what Maggie was saying.

"Do you think Jesse would have usurped Father's Day from you if he could have?" Maggie asked finally.

"Yes." Will answered without hesitation.

"But he didn't."

"No."

"Why do you think he didn't?"

"Because it's Father's Day."

"Is the visitation written out in the divorce papers?"

Will gave that consideration and shook his head. "No. But it only seems fair. Barbara gets them on Mother's Day."

"Because you allow it."

"Yes." Then Will understood. "And *she* allowed me to have them today."

"In spite of the fact that Steven and Wren have a new father figure in the house. This was Jesse's first Father's Day with them as their stepdad. It was probably kind of a big thing to him."

"Because it's all about him. Only today wasn't, because Barbara didn't let that happen."

Maggie nodded.

"Maybe I shouldn't feel as angry at Barbara as I have been for not having Steven and Wren all day."

"You're going to feel the way you feel, Will," Maggie said. "I just want you to understand that you had something good today—several hours of almost stress-free time with your kids—that could have been much harder."

"Barbara wanted me to be with Steven and Wren today."

"I think so. But that can't have set well with her new husband."

"Because it's not all about him."

"Exactly. But even if they'd been there, he wouldn't have appreciated them as much as you did. The emotional ties and investments aren't there."

Thinking back over the way Steven and Wren had reluctantly left him when he'd dropped them off, Will realized that what Maggie was saying was true. It helped a little.

"Father's Day has gotten complicated," he said.

"But not impossible."

"No." *And please, God, never let it be impossible.* Will relaxed a little more and glanced at the clock on the wall. "Have you eaten?"

"Not yet."

"Neither have I. I could order Chinese in."

"Sure."

Even as Will reached for the phone on his desk, though, it rang. He lifted the handset and identified himself.

"Commander," a no-nonsense voice on the other end of the connection said, "I'm Special Agent-in-Charge Scott Urlacher of the Federal Bureau of Investigation. If I may, I need a moment of your time."

CRIME SCENE NCIS
NAVAL CRIMINAL INVESTIGATIVE SERVICE

10

SCENE ✪ NCIS ✪ CRIME SCENE
NAVAL CRIMINAL INVESTIGATIVE SERVICE

>> NCIS OFFICES
>> CAMP LEJEUNE, NORTH CAROLINA
>> 1923 HOURS

Will covered the mouthpiece and looked at Maggie. "FBI. SAC Urlacher?"

Maggie shook her head, letting him know the name meant nothing to her.

"What can I do for you, Agent Urlacher?" Will hit the speakerphone button, motioning for Maggie to stay quiet.

"Do you know a man named Victor Gant?" Urlacher responded.

Will didn't hesitate about answering, but he was instantly wary. "I do."

"You've got paper out on his son, Bobby Lee."

Will agreed to that as well, wondering why the FBI agent had called him.

"I've got a situation I was hoping you could help me with," Urlacher said.

"If I can," Will replied. He wasn't in the habit of making blind promises.

"Victor Gant is in a bad bit of business out here in Charlotte," Special Agent-in-Charge Urlacher said. "He runs with a local biker gang."

"The Purple Royals," Will replied as he gazed at the file Maggie had opened up on his computer in front of him. "He doesn't just run with them. He leads it."

"Yes, sir. Our intel suggests that the Purple Royals deal meth and weapons."

The notes in the folder agreed with that assessment. Will didn't say anything.

"We've had an undercover officer on-site in Charlotte for months," Urlacher said. "He made contact with Victor Gant and was trying to negotiate a sizeable drug buy. Gant has a resource for opium that beats most anything we've seen down here."

"Down here" let Will know immediately that Urlacher wasn't from the South.

"How can I help you?" Will asked.

Urlacher hesitated. "I need some leverage to use against Gant."

"I don't have anything. We've been working the case against Bobby Lee."

"I understand that. What I was wondering was if you'd gotten any closer to bringing Bobby Lee Gant in."

Will swapped looks with Maggie, and he knew what the FBI man was about to ask.

"Not yet," Will said.

"With everything Gant's done, I can hold him for a few days before we have to charge him," Urlacher said. "To hold him any longer, I'm going to have to charge him with something. I can make a case for threatening a federal officer, especially in light of how he confronted our undercover, but that's not going to be enough." The FBI agent sighed. "We might not even be able make that stick. Gant maneuvered the situation so it's his word against my undercover's."

Will didn't say anything.

"I'm wondering if you could heat up your search for Bobby Lee Gant," Urlacher said.

"Trust me," Will said evenly, "nobody wants him more than we do." He'd interviewed the young Marine in the hospital and seen firsthand the damage that Bobby Lee Gant had wrought. Even after everything he'd seen while at NCIS, the atrocity had sickened Will.

The young Marine had looked small, helpless, and defeated in that hospital bed. His wife hadn't looked much better. But she'd asked Will to find the man who had done that to them.

Will had promised he would.

"I need to put pressure on Gant to turn his opium source," Urlacher said. "But to do that, I need something to offer him in return."

"You want to offer him Bobby Lee?" Will couldn't believe it. Anger stirred in him. "There's no way Bobby Lee is going to walk after what he did."

"He's a young man," Urlacher said in a matter-of-fact voice. "Still has a lot of years ahead of him. Hasn't been in a whole lot of trouble, judging from the jacket I'm going by. A jury could be persuaded that young man could be rehabilitated."

Will didn't think so. Neither did Maggie, judging from her sour expression. Her profile of the man had shown him to be a career criminal. Salvation wasn't in the cards for Bobby Lee Gant. Not once the jury saw the damage the young Marine and his wife had suffered at Bobby Lee's hands.

"I'm willing to take my chances in court," Will replied. In fact, he wanted a jury to handle the case because he felt certain they would punish Bobby Lee Gant more than a deal between the DA's office and a defense attorney would.

NCIS had processed the evidence, and the case was airtight. The only trick would be in making the civilian DA stick to his promise to prosecute to the fullest extent of his office.

"Maybe you misunderstand what I'm getting at," Urlacher said.

"I think I understand perfectly," Will said. "For whatever reason, your undercover operation against Victor Gant was blown. You still want to salvage something. Since you don't have your guy in the wringer, you want to offer to free the guy I've got in the wringer. That pretty much sum it up?"

Urlacher was silent for a moment. "I don't think you understand the gravity of the situation we're dealing with here. Victor Gant and his motorcycle gang are responsible for an increase in opium feeding into this county. I want to shut that pipeline down."

"I don't blame you."

"Ultimately a lot of those drugs are going to find their way onto military bases. They always do."

"And when they do," Will said, "we'll take them off the board. Bobby Lee Gant is another matter entirely. He's going to take the fall for what he did."

"I understand why you feel the way that you do. I heard about what he did to that young soldier—"

"He was a Marine," Will corrected automatically. "One of the Marines that I'm supposed to help. I couldn't be there to stop Bobby Lee Gant, but I am going to help see that Bobby Lee goes away for what he did." He let out a breath. "If you're a betting man, Agent Urlacher, I advise you to bet on that."

"I think the DA in Jacksonville can be persuaded to do business with us," Urlacher said. "All cases involving civilian personnel go through him."

That was true. Only cases that involved strictly military personnel went through military courts.

"We have a good working relationship with the Jacksonville DA," Will said.

"He might like to have a new one with the FBI."

"I don't see how working with the FBI would be in his best interests."

"The FBI is a good friend to have."

"The FBI," Will said, "can't fill the DA's court with civilians violating ordinances in Camp Lejeune. The DA can't hold military personnel in jail if this camp decides those men are better off working at their jobs. Trust me when I say that we make his life a whole lot better than you ever could."

"I don't think you can muscle up that much resistance."

"It's not just me," Will said. "With the military, it's never just an individual. Civilians make the mistake of seeing an individual, but we're never alone. And these are the Marines. They'll want justice done."

"I think the federal government can pony up more respect than that."

"I've worked with the DA over the years," Will said. "He's not a guy who likes getting strong-armed. You take that approach with him, I might not have to do a thing."

Urlacher cursed.

"Now, if there's nothing else," Will said, "I've got work to attend to."

"I'll be talking to you, Commander." Urlacher broke the connection before Will could respond.

"Sounds like he has issues," Maggie said.

"Maybe a few." Will took out his Pocket PC and scribbled Urlacher's name onto a Post-it note. He'd write up a file about the conversation later on the off chance that they might bump heads again. "Let's get hold of Shel and Remy. If Urlacher has Victor Gant, he's probably holding him in Charlotte."

"Are you thinking they might cross paths?"

Will nodded. "We got the tip about Bobby Lee Gant from the Charlotte PD. If Urlacher finds that out, he might want to pursue Bobby Lee himself."

⊛ ⊛ ⊛

>> INTERVIEW ROOM
>> FEDERAL BUREAU OF INVESTIGATION FIELD OFFICE
>> CHARLOTTE, NORTH CAROLINA
>> 1941 HOURS

Calm and at ease, Victor Gant sat in the uncomfortable straight-backed chair like he didn't have a care in the world. He actually sat too far from the table, but he couldn't move the chair because it was bolted to the floor.

He didn't know if anyone stood behind the one-way mirror to his left, but it didn't matter. He wasn't going to go to jail long—if he went at all. He wasn't worried about that. What concerned him more was whether or not he'd be able to sell the other part of the plan.

That was questionable, and it was important.

The FBI agents had left Victor his cigarettes even though the building was supposed to be smoke-free. He knew that was an attempt at buying him off, but he didn't care. If the cigarettes hadn't been there, he wouldn't have smoked them. Time would have passed just as slowly, but he would have been more aware of it.

He inhaled carefully, drawing the smoke deep into his lungs to absorb the nicotine. When he let the smoke out in a steady stream, he saw the past coiled in the gray mass. He was never far from the past. Maybe it was thirty years and more on a calendar, but it remained only a single thought away.

One thought and he was right back in those green jungles with Charlie all around him.

The interview room door opened.

Victor barely glanced up.

The hard-nosed FBI agent who had arrested him at the Tawny Kitty stepped into the room. He carried a slim folder in one hand.

Victor knew at once that the folder wasn't his. He'd seen his folder. It was thick with past brushes with the law and the evil that he'd done. There was a dark part of him that took pride in that work.

Urlacher dropped the file on the scarred conference table.

Victor grinned at the man. "Catching up on your reading, Hoss?"

"Do you know what genealogy is?" Urlacher countered.

A cold chill spilled through Victor's stomach. "Family history. I ain't dumb."

"I never thought you were." Urlacher put a big hand on the file. "But I find family histories mighty interesting. Not always good reading, but interesting nevertheless."

Victor lit a fresh cigarette from the butt of the old, then crushed out the old one and fanned the smoke. His handcuff chains rattled and pulled at the connection to the belt around his waist.

"Take you, for instance," Urlacher said. "You've got an interesting family tree. Father and grandfather were both hard-core military guys. Noncoms, both of them. Your father served in Korea and World War II. Your grandfather fought in World War I. Both of them were decorated heroes."

Victor leaned his head back and blew a perfect smoke ring that floated toward the ceiling.

"You," Urlacher said, "weren't quite so decorated."

"Vietnam was a different kind of war," Victor said.

"I know. I was there."

Interested in spite of himself, Victor leaned forward. "Where?"

"I was a PJ."

Now that was interesting. PJs were pararescue jumpers, men who'd parachuted into hostile territory under enemy fire and pulled out survivors. Everyone respected the PJs.

"I knew some PJs," Victor said. "They had a saying."

"'That others may live,'" Urlacher responded.

"They always said you guys went to Superman school."

"We did."

Victor smiled at Urlacher. "I know you ain't here to rescue me."

"I'm not. If I had my way, I'd drop-kick you into the deepest, dankest cell I can find."

"Love the way you sugarcoat things. Must make you a real heartthrob with all the guys you bust."

Urlacher's face hardened. "Let's get something straight, melonhead. I'm not your friend. I'm not going to be your friend. If push comes to shove, I'm going to rip your ears off and feed them to you. Are you hearing me all right?"

"So far. I've still got my ears." Victor took another drag on his cigarette.

"You've also got a son." Urlacher opened the file.

11

E SCENE ✪ NCIS ✪ CRIME SCENE
NAVAL CRIMINAL INVESTIGATIVE SERVICE

>> INTERVIEW ROOM
>> FEDERAL BUREAU OF INVESTIGATION FIELD OFFICE
>> CHARLOTTE, NORTH CAROLINA
>> 1941 HOURS

Before he could stop himself, Victor glanced at the file Urlacher had brought into the room. Bobby Lee's picture was on top. Bobby Lee looked bruised and cocky.

"You don't want to go down that road," Victor said quietly.

"Sure I do," Urlacher stated. "It's the same road you took getting to my guy."

Victor didn't say anything.

"You build a road," Urlacher said, "it goes both ways. My guy says you threatened his family. Now I'm telling you that I can hit you right back."

"I never threatened his family. You saw the photos."

"I saw the ones you wanted me to see. But my guy also says your friend hightailed it with a magazine just before we showed up. So you show some pictures, do a little sleight of hand, then send them away with your buddy. That might fly in a kiddie show, but this is serious business."

"The FBI's got no interest in Bobby Lee."

"No. But more than that, I can make the interest the Marines have in Bobby Lee go away."

Victor leaned back in his chair. "If I cooperate? Tell you what you want to know?"

Urlacher nodded and smiled. "See? I told you I didn't think you were stupid."

Victor didn't say anything. His thoughts felt scrambled. He hadn't seen this curve coming.

"Bobby Lee's pregnant girlfriend ratted him out," Urlacher said. "She told the Charlotte PD where to find Bobby Lee. The Charlotte PD called Camp Lejeune and talked to the NCIS agents there. You know who they are?"

Victor nodded. "I know who they are."

"The word I get is that they want Bobby Lee pretty bad after what he did to that Marine." Urlacher grinned mirthlessly. "You and I both know soldiers. Probably every bit as old school as one-percenter bikers when it comes to taking a pound of flesh back from someone who's wronged them."

Silently Victor agreed. "Do they know where Bobby Lee is?"

"Yeah." Urlacher closed the file. "But so do I. And I've got a team headed there now."

Victor thought about that. "The boy's green to trouble. He's not going to know how to handle himself. If your people confront him, surrendering is gonna be the last thing on his mind."

"Then I guess that'll just be bad all the way around."

A million thoughts rattled through Victor's head all at once. He felt them surge like a tide of writhing snakes, and none of them were friendly or comforting. He kept seeing Bobby Lee shot up and dead. Both of them were caught like rats in traps.

Only Bobby Lee didn't know that yet.

Let it go, Victor told himself. *They'll bring Bobby Lee in. They're the FBI. They're trained for situations like this.*

But Victor also knew his son. Bobby Lee envisioned himself as some Old West gunfighter. He was determined to die with his boots on.

And the idea of going to prison for what he'd done to that Marine would have been impossible for the young man at his age.

The emotion that rushed through Victor surprised him. He wouldn't have believed how much he didn't want to see his son get hurt. They hadn't known each other long, but it had been long enough for Victor to see himself in the young man and know that he had a bid for immortality. Especially with a grandson already on the way.

Victor stubbed his cigarette out in the overflowing ashtray. "Let me talk to Bobby Lee."

Urlacher didn't say anything.

A curse ripped through Victor's lips. "Let me talk to Bobby Lee, get him to give himself up. If you do that, I'll give you my connection."

And then, Victor knew, the war would be on. He and Tran went back over thirty years. But he didn't doubt for a second that Tran would have him killed for rolling over on him.

Slowly Urlacher nodded. "I can do that. But if you're lying to me, I'll carve the rock they'll set over Bobby Lee's grave and stomp it into place myself."

⊛ ⊛ ⊛

>> SPIDER'S TATTOO SHOP
>> DOGGETT STREET
>> CHARLOTTE, NORTH CAROLINA
>> 2026 HOURS

Shel stood across the street from the tattoo shop and gazed at the neon blue spider holding tattooing needles in all its legs. As the animation kicked in, the neon spider's legs blurred into motion, and a cloud of black webbing spurted up.

"Nifty," Shel said as he adjusted his sunglasses. The sun was still up and would be for another fifteen or twenty minutes. But shadows had already started to steep themselves between the buildings. Pools of darkness spread across the sidewalks.

Remy looked at him. "People still say *nifty*?"

"Some do," Shel said. "The really cool people do."

"I never heard anybody say *nifty*."

"I would say that's because you don't hang with cool people, but you're here with me now."

"I've never heard you say it before."

"That's because you haven't been listening."

"I listen just fine." Remy turned his attention back to the tattoo parlor. "How do you want to do this?"

Shel studied the area. The tattoo parlor was flanked by a deli and a Chinese restaurant. Both businesses still had customers. So did the tattoo parlor.

"Straight ahead," Shel answered. "Go in. Introduce myself to Bobby Lee. Then take him down."

"Oh yeah, I really like how inconspicuous that's going to be. Especially after Will called to give us the heads-up about the FBI."

"The fact that the FBI is involved at all is putting pressure on our timetable." Shel glanced down the street and searched for any unmarked cars that might have been filled with FBI agents. For the moment, he didn't see any. "If we had time, we'd go with my other great plan."

Remy shot him a look. "I'm afraid to ask."

"We'd build a giant wooden horse and climb inside. Pretend to be a gift to Bobby Lee. On second thought, maybe we could disguise ourselves in a giant wooden Harley."

"Wow. I can see you've been giving this a lot of thought."

"I stopped thinking about how we're going to do it after Will called. We're all out of time." Shel glanced at the tattoo-artist spider again. "I'm not going back without Bobby Lee."

"He could have friends."

"I don't think his friends would be all that friendly. Bobby Lee doesn't strike me as the dedicated friend sort."

"This part of your Father's Day mad-on?"

Shel shook his head. "Just me doing my job. I'm going to go check out tattoos."

"Why you?"

"Do you see any black customers in that tattoo shop?"

Remy looked, then shook his head. "That place has probably got a rear exit."

"Probably."

"Maybe I should slip around back and set up there. In case Bobby Lee somehow gets wise to your stealth ninja moves."

"Sure."

"Give me five minutes."

Shel nodded and reached down to pat Max on the head. The Labrador sat quietly and contentedly beside him as Remy walked down the block and crossed the street.

Despite the tension that coiled in his stomach—more from the possibility of FBI interference than from the idea of facing Bobby Lee—Shel remained calm and cool. This was business as usual, no matter if it was Father's Day.

He scratched Max behind the ear, listened to the dog pant in the heat, and felt the sweat trickle down his back under the slim-line Kevlar vest he wore. A sleeveless flannel shirt softened the edges of the vest, and the tails of the shirt left outside his pants covered the matte black Mark 23 Mod 0 SOCOM .45-caliber semiautomatic pistol in the pancake holster at the base of his spine. Extra magazines rode in his jeans pockets, but he doubted he'd be able to work a reload inside the shop if things went awry.

Excitement flooded Shel's veins with adrenaline. He lived for this.

⊛ ⊛ ⊛

>> 2027 HOURS

Bobby Lee Gant lay in the chair with his eyes closed, riding on a pleasant wave of alcohol and pills. He felt the sharp bite of the tattooing gun as it chewed through the flesh over his heart. The raucous buzzing echoed inside his head over the thundering bass of the heavy metal music blasting through the tattoo parlor.

Someone slapped his forehead.

"Hey!" Bobby Lee opened his eyes and tried to push up from the chair. "Don't you be slapping me, you big piece of—"

"Stop moving!" Spider spoke gruffly around a fat cigar shoved into his wide mouth. He was a big man in his fifties, with a flat, rugged face and beard and hair that roped down to his broad shoulders. He held the tattoo gun off to one side and dabbed at Bobby Lee's chest with a wipe with the other hand. "You keep moving around like that, this tat's gonna look like a three-year-old done it. And if you walk out of here with a bad-lookin' tat and you tell everybody I done it, I'm gonna charge you double."

Juiced by the drugs and whiskey, Bobby Lee grinned. "Okay, okay." He started to raise his hands in surrender.

Spider cursed. "Keep your hands down!"

Bobby Lee put his arms at rest beside him. It was hard to be still. With the drugs and the music working, he wanted to be up and dancing. More than that, he wanted to be with Lorna, his girl. He closed his eyes and thought about that.

The tattoo gun started buzzing again. Pain seeped back into his skin.

"You spell Lorna with two *o*'s, don't you?" Spider asked.

"What?" Bobby opened his eyes again and tried to peer down at his chest.

Spider barked laughter that echoed even over the heavy metal. He put a big hand on Bobby Lee's forehead and pushed him back into the chair.

"Man, relax," Spider guffawed. "I'm just screwing with you."

Bobby Lee lay back.

"I know it's spelled with a *u*," Spider said.

Irritated, Bobby Lee reached for the pistol tucked into his waistband.

Spider's demeanor changed in a flash. He dropped a hand to Bobby Lee's arm and trapped it against his body. "Hold on there, boy."

"Let go!" Bobby Lee shouted. "I ain't in here for you to make fun of." He held on to the pistol, but Spider's strong hand prevented him from pulling it.

"Chill, bro," Spider said. "I was just havin' a little fun."

"It ain't fun for me. That's the name of my woman. I don't want it spelled wrong."

"It ain't gonna be spelled wrong." Spider held up a forearm. There in ink he'd written *Lorna*. "Got her name right here. As long as you spelled it right, I spell it right."

Bobby Lee stared at the man a little longer, then relaxed in the chair.

"We cool?" Spider asked.

Bobby Lee nodded. "Cool."

"Then you just get mellow, bro, 'cause we're in the home stretch."

But before Spider could start in with the ink gun again, Bobby Lee's cell phone rang. It was just a track phone, a cheap, disposable handset he'd had Lorna purchase for him. He waved Spider off, pulled the phone out of his pocket, and flipped it open.

"Got some bad news, man," a voice said after Bobby Lee answered. "Lorna told the cops where you are. They're on their way there now."

Panic flooded Bobby Lee as he scrambled up from the chair despite Spider's protests. He wasn't going to jail. No way.

12

E SCENE ✪ NCIS ✪ CRIME SCENE
NAVAL CRIMINAL INVESTIGATIVE SERVICE

>> SPIDER'S TATTOO SHOP
>> DOGGETT STREET
>> CHARLOTTE, NORTH CAROLINA
>> 2033 HOURS

"Something I can help you with, man?"

Shel looked at the slim young woman behind the counter to the right of the door inside the shop. She was dressed in black jeans and a black Anthrax concert T-shirt. She was pale enough to pass as a vampire. Metal studs gleamed in her eyebrows and at the bottom of her lower lip. Her long blonde hair was the color of old bone.

"I wanted to see about getting a tattoo," Shel said. He let the Texas drawl slide naturally into his words. In the military he'd learned what he called "TV talk," that flat Midwestern accent used by news anchors and sports announcers.

The woman looked at him and smiled. "You don't seem the type."

Shel smiled back and stepped toward the counter. His gaze took in the closed-circuit monitor hanging from the wall.

"And what type do I seem like to you?" Shel asked.

The woman folded her arms and leaned a hip against the counter. "Mama's boy. Joe Average. Joe Military."

Shel knew he couldn't help looking military. Even when he was in disguise—even better ones than his current effort—he still looked like a Marine poster boy.

"Actually," the young woman went on, "you look like you could be some superhero's secret identity."

Terrific, Shel thought. But he kept his smile in place. "Actually, it's worse than that."

She cocked an eyebrow and waited.

"I'm afraid of needles," Shel said conspiratorially.

The woman looked at him askance. "A big guy like you?"

"I know. Shameful, isn't it?"

"Well . . ."

Shel nodded and shrugged. "If I hadn't met this girl, and if she wasn't into tattoos, I wouldn't be here tonight." He paused. "And I have to be honest—unless I see something I really want, I'm not even getting one."

"A girl, huh?"

"Yeah."

"Pretty?"

"Yeah." Shel shrugged again. "I guess that makes me sound pretty dumb, huh?"

"As long as you don't do anything really stupid, you should be okay."

"What's really stupid?" Shel asked.

"Getting her name tattooed on you. Then you have to explain to all your other girlfriends why you got that one's name . . . wherever you put it."

"Maybe I won't show it to them."

The young woman grinned. "Oh, they'll look for it. I would."

"I could just date only girls with that name," Shel suggested.

"Right." The woman took a book down from a shelf over the counter. "Got some designs here you might like. Small. Distinctive." She looked at his biceps. "Big as your arms are, I'd check out some tribal tats. That would look cool."

Shel grinned again. He'd learned a long time ago that women of all ages liked his grin.

Noise erupted from the back. The door opened, and Bobby Lee Gant stepped into the room with a 9 mm pistol tightly gripped in his fist. He was young and thin, at least twenty pounds too light for his five-foot, nine-inch frame. He wore holey jeans, square-toed boots, a Confederate flag bandanna that held back his greasy hair, and a motorcycle jacket without a shirt. Drops of blood glinted in the center of a tattoo of a skull with a rose clenched in its teeth. *Lorna* was inscribed beneath the skull.

"Hey, Bobby Lee," a gruff voice said. "Get back in here, bro."

Judging from the young man's jerky reactions and his unfocused gaze, Shel figured Bobby Lee was higher than a kite. Shel didn't move. Beside him, Max set himself, hunkering low and getting prepared to separate and go for the pistol.

Shel signed to Max, and the dog sat with a quiet but forlorn whimper. Max wasn't used to quietly sitting out while guns were in evidence.

Bobby Lee whipped his pistol toward Shel. "Get your hands up!"

❂ ❂ ❂

>> 2033 HOURS

When Remy saw three unmarked sedans suddenly whip by the end of the alley, he knew something had gone badly wrong. Or was about to. He slid his Beretta out from under his shirt and held it ready as he catfooted through the alley toward the tattoo parlor's rear exit.

His cell phone buzzed against his hip. He braced against the wall in the deepening dark of the approaching evening and slid the phone out so he could read the caller ID as it buzzed again.

A loud voice sounded inside the shop. Someone screamed.

Caller ID showed that the call was coming from NCIS headquarters in Camp Lejeune.

Remy pulled the earpiece connector from his shirt pocket, slipped it into his ear canal, and tapped it to open the line. "Gautreau."

"Remy." It was Will's voice, calm and intense at the same time.

"Yeah."

"We just got word from Charlotte PD that the FBI is on-site at your twenty."

The sound of running feet echoed down the alley.

"Oh yeah," Remy agreed. "They're here."

"Where's Shel? He's not answering."

"Shel's inside." Remy tried the back door. It was locked.

"What's going on there?"

Remy watched helplessly as four men entered the alley from either end. They carried flashlights and military-style assault rifles.

"Put the pistol on the ground!" one of the arriving men yelled. He wore an FBI jacket over his bulletproof vest. "Do it now!"

"You might want to get hold of the FBI," Remy stated calmly. He let his pistol drop to hang from his finger. "Let them know that you've got two men out here working this."

"They know," Will said. "Maggie's already sent them copies of your photo IDs."

"Good to know," Remy said. But it didn't make him feel any better.

The four FBI agents locked into position along the alley.

"Drop the gun!" the man bellowed again.

Ruby lights glowed to sudden life against Remy's chest. He knew he was only a heartbeat from death. Carefully he bent over and placed the pistol on the pavement and awaited further orders even though he was pretty sure he knew what they would be.

"Get on the ground!" the man ordered. "On the ground now! Facedown! Hands on top of your head!"

Remy followed orders and took care that his hands were always outstretched from his body so they wouldn't think he was reaching for a weapon. His heart felt like it was going to explode.

Memories of other times he'd been arrested back in New Orleans flashed through his mind. It was hard to believe that he was going to survive such an encounter when there had been so many close calls back then.

The rough pavement chewed at his cheek. He had to force himself to lie there when footsteps pounded in his direction. In the next instant someone blinded him with a flashlight beam while someone else jumped in the middle of his back and raked his arms behind him.

Hard metal bit into his wrists and secured his hands behind his back.

"I'm with NCIS," Remy said. "My ID—"

Someone punched him in the back of the head and snarled, "Shut up."

"Hang in there, Remy," Will said over the earpiece. "We'll get you out of there as soon as we can." Then one of the FBI agents stripped the earpiece.

Blood from a split lip tasted warm and salty inside Remy's mouth. He shut up and stayed where he was as he was roughly frisked. But he hoped Shel was still safe.

⊛ ⊛ ⊛

>> 2035 HOURS

Slowly, not offering any sudden movement that might panic Bobby Lee Gant, Shel raised his arms. "Hey, bro," Shel said. "I don't know what you're smoking, but I just came in to check out tattoos."

"Who is he?" Bobby Lee demanded.

The young woman behind the counter shook her head. "He just came in. He was asking about tattoos."

"Bobby Lee!" the big man from the back room roared.

Shel recognized the man from the file Remy had downloaded. His name was Ralph "Spider" Gemmell, a known associate of biker clubs.

Bobby Lee swiveled and pointed his pistol at Spider. "Back off, man!"

Spider came to an abrupt halt. "You don't want to do this, bro. It's gonna end bad if you do."

"I ain't going to jail!" Bobby Lee screamed. His eyes rolled in panic like an animal's. "They ain't gonna take me to jail!"

"Dude," Spider said, "it's just jail. Ain't like they're gonna lock you up forever."

"They ain't locking me up at all!"

Shel thought about reaching for the pistol at his back. But he knew if he did, he was going to have to use it.

Let it ride, he told himself. *Let this develop. He's smart enough to realize he isn't going to get out of this without getting hurt.*

At least, Shel hoped that was true. Whether Bobby Lee was sober enough to do the right thing was another question.

Outside, through the large windows that overlooked the parking lot and Doggett Avenue beyond, two unmarked sedans with flashing lights shrilled to halts. Car doors jacked open, and men in Kevlar armor and FBI jackets took up ready positions behind cover.

"FBI?" Bobby Lee said in surprise.

Well, Shel thought, *he isn't so high or panicked that he can't read.*

"It ain't supposed to be the FBI," Bobby Lee moaned. "It's the Marines. The Marines are supposed to be after me."

"Maybe they're not after you," the woman behind the counter suggested. "Maybe they're here after somebody else."

"Who?" Bobby Lee demanded.

The young woman flinched back. "I don't know. I was just saying."

In the next minute, though, a man on a loudhailer stripped away that illusion. "Bobby Lee Gant! This is the FBI! Put down your weapon and come out with your hands up!"

Bobby Lee whirled around just in time to get lit up by ruby spotter lights. He glanced down at his chest and cursed.

"Give it up, bro," Spider advised. "They got you cold. You can still get out of this in one piece."

A lithe movement put Bobby Lee next to the young woman at the counter before anyone could move. He roped an arm around her neck and pulled her body back against his.

"I'm getting out of here!" Bobby Lee declared. "Or I'm going to kill her stone dead! I swear I am!"

NCIS
NAVAL CRIMINAL INVESTIGATIVE SERVICE

13

SCENE ✪ NCIS ✪ CRIME SCENE

NAVAL CRIMINAL INVESTIGATIVE SERVICE

>> SPIDER'S TATTOO SHOP
>> DOGGETT STREET
>> CHARLOTTE, NORTH CAROLINA
>> 2037 HOURS

The young woman screamed and tried to break free from her captor. Bobby Lee popped his forearm up and hit her in the mouth. She stopped screaming and remained still.

"Try that again," Bobby Lee yelled, "and I'll hurt you bad! Do you understand me?"

The young woman nodded and shivered in fear.

"Don't do that, bro," Spider said. His voice was more calm than Shel expected. "If you just stay calm, Bobby Lee, you'll come out of this all right. I promise. But if you go off half-cocked, you're gonna get a lot of people hurt."

Shel forced himself to remain still. Any move on his part would turn the tattoo shop into a bloodbath. He didn't know why one of the FBI snipers outside didn't drop Bobby Lee Gant in his tracks. Shel also wondered where Remy was.

Spider stepped forward slowly. "Give her to me. She don't deserve none of your trouble."

"Well she's in it now," Bobby Lee snarled. "All of you are. Whatever happens to me is the same what happens to you."

Moving slowly, Spider took another step toward Bobby Lee.

Shel's breath locked down in his lungs. *Don't,* he thought. Bobby Lee wasn't holding together well. He wasn't going to handle the situation.

"Give her to me, bro," Spider said.

Bobby Lee shook his head. "I can't. I can't. ICANTICANT-ICANTICANT."

"Yeah, you can." Spider took another step. "That there's my blood, Bobby Lee. My sister's girl. I promised my sister I wouldn't let any harm come to her." He gestured with one hand. "You got to give her to me an' let me get her outta this. C'mon now, bro."

"No." Bobby Lee shook his head like a scared child. Unshed tears gleamed in his eyes. "I heard stories about what prison's like, man. I ain't gonna go. They ain't gonna do something like that to me. I ain't gonna be no . . ."

Spider wouldn't stop moving.

Shel knew that was a mistake, and it was like watching a train wreck happen in slow motion. He wanted to tell Spider to stay back, that the FBI snipers would put Bobby Lee down without hurting the young woman if it came to that, but he couldn't. If he spoke, he would further split Bobby Lee's attention and ratchet up the tension.

It was at a time like this, Shel knew, that his brother Don would have told him to pray. But Shel had never been a big believer in the power of prayer. He had prayed on occasion, but he'd never been able to put his heart into it or really believe.

Instead, he remained still and hoped that he was wrong about how events were about to unfold.

"Bobby Lee, listen to me." Spider took another step. He was close enough now that he could have reached out and touched the pistol in Bobby Lee's hand.

Bobby Lee pointed the pistol and squeezed the trigger without warning. The detonation filled the tattoo shop with rolling thunder.

Spider recoiled only slightly. His head jerked to one side. Shel saw the ugly wound in the side of his face and the huge exit wound in the back of Spider's head. Death had to have been instant, but he remained on his feet for just a moment. Then his legs went out from under him and he sank to the floor.

"I told him!" Bobby Lee shouted. "I told him to stay back! It wasn't my fault he didn't listen!"

Even though he'd seen it happen before, Shel couldn't believe the suddenness with which the violence had erupted. He watched Spider fall in the periphery of his vision, but he kept his eyes on Bobby Lee. Beside

Shel, Max bunched, ready to leap into action. Shel stilled the Labrador with a hand signal and Max subsided.

One of the sniper's ruby dots flicked to the exposed side of Bobby Lee's head and tracked across his face. Even though he couldn't see the light, Bobby Lee instinctively pulled back more tightly behind the young woman. She shuddered as she cried. Tears tracked her face and blood ran down her chin.

Shel continued to hold his hands up and offered no threat. He debated saying anything until the young woman started fighting against Bobby Lee.

"Don't fight him," Shel instructed. "Just—"

"Shut up!" Bobby Lee roared. "Shut up! Shut up!" He brought the pistol around and pointed it at Shel. Shel saw the young man's finger tighten on the trigger and knew he was going to shoot.

Before Shel could move, two sledgehammer blows chopped into his chest and one caught him in the right shoulder. The impacts vibrated through him and drove him back as pain washed away his thoughts. The sharp bite of intense agony told him the vest hadn't stopped all of the bullets. As he fell, he managed to grab Max's left foreleg.

Hold on, Shel told himself. *Hold on.* He tried because he knew that Max might attack. Without him there to back Max up, Bobby Lee would gun him down. Shel tried to maintain his grip, but the white-hot pain sucked him into a whirling pool of blackness.

⊛ ⊛ ⊛

>> 2040 HOURS

Helplessly Victor Gant sat handcuffed in the back of the FBI sedan and watched his son write his death warrant. Victor spoke through the wire mesh that locked him in the rear seat.

Urlacher was crouched behind the driver's side door with the loud-hailer clutched in one hand and a pistol in the other.

"If you kill my boy," Victor threatened hoarsely, "the deal's off. I won't tell you nothing. You hear me?"

"Hold your fire," Urlacher said over the radio. He didn't turn around or even acknowledge that Victor had spoken. "Nobody shoots until I give the word."

Adrenaline flooded Victor's senses. In frustration, he pulled at the handcuffs that kept his arms behind his back. He watched the violence unfolding in the tattoo shop and tried not to be sick.

For the first time in years, Victor was afraid. Fear hadn't touched him like that in a long time. And he couldn't remember the last occasion he'd been concerned over anybody outside of his own skin. Not even for Fat Mike, who'd been with him for over thirty years.

But he was afraid now for his son, whom he'd barely gotten to know. A man was supposed to be afraid for his son. Victor didn't want to be, but he saw so much of himself inside Bobby Lee that he didn't want anything bad to happen to him.

And he was scared to death that something terrible was about to happen. All he could do was sit and watch.

"Bobby Lee," Urlacher said over the loudhailer.

Inside the tattoo parlor, Bobby Lee spun toward the line of cars out in the parking lot. He brought the pistol up to the side of the young woman's face. The barrel was superheated from the recent firing. She jerked her head away as the barrel seared her flesh.

Don't shoot, Bobby Lee. Victor willed his son to hear him. *She's just scared and hurt. You still got her.* But for a moment he thought Bobby Lee was going to shoot anyway.

Instead, Bobby Lee pulled the pistol back and clubbed the woman's ear. She stumbled and nearly fell, but she stayed on her feet in front of him. A handful of ruby laser dots danced across Bobby Lee's face.

Victor stopped breathing and waited for one of the snipers to empty Bobby Lee's brainpan.

"Hold your fire," Urlacher ordered.

Bobby Lee yanked the woman in front of him again. He propelled her to the door and opened it a little. "I want a car!" he yelled. "And I want an airplane standing by at the airport."

"Kid's seen too many movies," the FBI driver said quietly.

Victor cursed at him and kicked the back of the seat.

Urlacher and the FBI driver ignored him.

"Bobby Lee," Urlacher said, "I've got your father in the car with me. He doesn't want you to get hurt. He wants you to surrender."

"You lie!" Bobby Lee yelled. "My old man wouldn't give in to nobody like you!"

Urlacher turned to Victor and spoke through the mesh. "It's your play. You want to talk to him or sit on the sidelines?"

Victor hesitated only for a moment. "I'll talk."

Urlacher nodded at the driver. "Get him out of the back."

Gingerly the driver eased back and opened the rear door.

Looking back, Urlacher locked eyes with Victor. "You try to run, I'm gonna shoot your legs out from under you. That'll probably spook Bobby

Lee; then these men out here will blow him out of his socks. You be sure and think about what you're doing."

"I am," Victor gritted. He didn't try to get out of the car. "Can you make this go away too? If I give you what you want?" If Tran didn't kill him first.

Urlacher hesitated. Victor wouldn't have believed the man if he'd just said yes like it was nothing.

"It'll take some doing," Urlacher said, "but I can convince the right people that what you're going to tell us will be worth it."

"Even after Bobby Lee killed them men?"

"It'll be a tough sell," Urlacher admitted. "But I've sold worse."

Victor nodded. "Okay. Let's do this." He slid off the seat and stood beside the car. He raised his voice. "Bobby Lee, can you see me?"

Bobby Lee jerked his head around. His Confederate flag bandanna hung askew and allowed his hair to trickle down into his face. He looked worried and scared and lost.

Just like a kid, Victor realized.

"I can see you," Bobby Lee said. "What are you doing with them?"

"They got me under arrest." Victor smiled like it was all one big joke and he was just getting to the punch line. He turned slightly so that the handcuffs showed.

"Why?" Bobby Lee demanded. He looked more lost than ever. He kept turning his head from side to side, trying to take it all in.

"Bobby Lee," Victor said, afraid he was going to lose him, "look at me."

Bobby Lee settled a little.

"You're gonna have to turn yourself in," Victor said.

"No way." Bobby Lee shook his head vigorously. "I ain't going to prison. I got me a hostage. They're gonna give me a car and a plane, or I'm gonna kill this girl."

The ruby lights hung on to Bobby Lee's head, face, and exposed shoulder like a clutch of predatory insects.

"That's stupid talking," Victor said. "I cut you a deal. They're gonna let you go free."

Thirty years and more of dealing with Tran, and Victor was going to burn that bridge in a heartbeat for a son he barely knew. It almost didn't make sense, but blood was blood, and Bobby Lee was his boy.

"Don't need you to cut me no deal," Bobby Lee shouted back. "I'm gonna cut my own deal."

"They ain't gonna let you out of here, Son," Victor said in the calmest voice he could manage. "They can't. Goes against FBI rules." He didn't want to tell Bobby Lee they could kill him in an eye blink because that might unnerve him even more.

"You scared?" Bobby Lee asked.

The question startled Victor. "No. Why?"

"Because you ain't never called me *son* before."

Victor hadn't, and he only then realized he'd called Bobby Lee that. But it had seemed so natural calling him that when he was trying to calm him down.

"Just give up the girl," Victor said. "Put your weapon down. We'll get through this just fine."

Bobby Lee hesitated; then he shook his head again. "I can't. I don't want to go to prison."

"You ain't gonna go to no—"

"Shut up!" Bobby Lee roared. "I don't know how they got you here to lie to me, but I ain't gonna believe you! You ain't never cared about me!" He pointed the pistol at Victor.

Not knowing what to do, Victor stood silent and helpless. His stomach turned sour, and bile burned the back of his throat.

"Get me a car!" Bobby Lee ordered. "Get me a car and a plane or I'm gonna kill her and kill as many of you as I can before you get me!" He fired three shots at the unmarked sedan where Victor stood.

The bullets smashed through the windshield and caromed off the top of the car. The federal agents ducked to cover. Victor never flinched, but he grew cold and still inside as he waited for the FBI to return fire.

"Hold your positions!" Urlacher ordered. "No one shoots!"

You're a greedy man, Victor thought. *Still wanting what I can give you.* He watched the FBI agent from the corner of his eye, but his attention was focused on Bobby Lee.

"Get me that car!" Bobby Lee shouted.

Pride thrummed through Victor, but it was short-lived as he watched the big man with the dog slowly push himself to his feet behind Bobby Lee. Victor had clearly heard all three gunshots when Bobby Lee had shot the man at almost point-blank range. There was only one way the man was getting to his feet.

He'd been wearing a bulletproof vest.

And if he'd been wearing a bulletproof vest inside the tattoo shop, that meant he was some kind of cop.

"Bobby Lee!" Victor yelled. "Look out! Behind you!"

If Bobby Lee had turned instantly, if he'd trusted the warning, Victor knew he would have caught the big cop stone-cold. But he didn't. He hesitated for just an instant, and by then it was too late.

14

E SCENE ✪ NCIS ✪ CRIME SCENE
NAVAL CRIMINAL INVESTIGATIVE SERVICE

>> SPIDER'S TATTOO SHOP
>> DOGGETT STREET
>> CHARLOTTE, NORTH CAROLINA
>> 2043 HOURS

Shel struggled to focus through his swirling senses as he stood unsteadily on his feet. Bobby Lee was in front of him, his back to Shel, hugged in tight to his hostage.

Chest straining as his empty lungs tried to kick into action again, Shel ignored the burning pain in his right shoulder and reached for the SOCOM .45 holstered at the small of his back. His fingers found the grip, but the pistol felt alien to him and his hand felt too big and numb.

It's just shock, he told himself. *You've been here before. Just work through it.* He was dimly aware of the action out in the parking lot, the shouting voices, and the traffic beyond.

Bobby Lee started turning. His pistol dropped away from his hostage, and he shoved it forward to track toward Shel.

Shel tried to bring his right arm up, but it wouldn't work properly. Pain arced through his shoulder and chest. He gave up and managed the SOCOM in one big hand. Ruby laser sights danced over his body and lit up his left eye, but he ignored them and hoped the FBI sharpshooters held their fire.

Either way, Shel had decided Bobby Lee was leaving the picture. The young man was too unstable to deal with and more people were going to get hurt—beginning with the woman he was holding.

Bobby Lee's mouth moved. Shel couldn't hear the words. His ears still rang from the previous gunfire, and the pain had detached his brain to a degree, leaving only the part of him that focused solely on survival. But that part was Marine-trained, the best military training in the world.

Despite the danger, despite the fact that he'd already been shot, despite the fact that he might get shot again by Bobby Lee or the FBI, Shel held his fire until he had his target cleanly in his sights.

Bobby Lee's pistol had almost gotten all the way around toward Shel. The barrel belched a muzzle flash that stood out bright and hard in the tattoo shop, but the bullet went wide. Shel centered his sights at the bottom of Bobby Lee's chin just over the woman's shoulder and squeezed the trigger. The pistol bucked against his palm and he rode the recoil slightly up. He fired again and he knew the second shot was a few inches higher than the first.

Without a sound, Bobby Lee fell backward. He dragged the woman down with him, or her legs gave way out of fright. Shel wasn't sure which. He was just as surprised when the FBI didn't open fire on him.

⊛ ⊛ ⊛

>> 2044 HOURS

Grimly Shel marshaled his reserves and went forward. His balance wasn't too good, and he knew he wasn't very strong. But he had to secure the weapon.

Max got there first. The Labrador bunched and sprang into action. Before Shel could take another step, Max seized the pistol in his teeth and tore it away. He flung it to one side and stood guard over Bobby Lee.

One look at the young man's face told Shel there was no need to guard, but the dog had been Marine-trained too, and Shel wasn't going to break that. In fact, Shel wasn't certain he was going to stand up much longer. But he did.

"You okay?" Shel asked the young woman.

Her face was covered with Bobby Lee's blood, and she was seriously freaked. She couldn't answer.

"It's going to be all right, ma'am," Shel said. "You're going to be all right now."

"Special Agent McHenry," the loudhailer announced, "this is Special Agent Urlacher of the FBI. Put down your weapon. We're coming in."

Shel turned and put the pistol on the counter. He reached for the woman's hand, took it in his, and gently pulled her to her feet.

"Come on now," he said. "Let's get you away from that."

She started to look back at the body.

Shel caught her chin in his hand and gazed into her eyes. "That's not something you want to do," he told her gently. "Just let this part of everything go."

The woman nodded; then she wrapped her arms around him and wept uncontrollably. "I thought he was going to kill me."

"Yes, ma'am. But that didn't happen, did it? You came through this just fine." Shel stroked her hair and patted her back like he would for one of Don's kids. Bad situations could make children fearful of everyone, and it took a gentle hand to bring back courage and confidence.

She looked up at him. Tears had tracked through the blood, but she'd smeared a lot of it on Shel's shirt. "He was going to kill me, wasn't he?"

Shel thought about lying to spare her from those thoughts, but he knew she'd see the truth in him. He'd never learned to lie very well except while he was undercover.

"Yes, ma'am. I believe he was," Shel said.

FBI agents rushed the door.

"Thank you," she whispered.

"You're welcome." Shel held her for just a moment longer; then the FBI agents invaded the room.

Two of the agents advanced on Shel. Max barked at them furiously and bared his gleaming white teeth.

One of the agents pointed his pistol at Max.

"Mister," Shel said in a cold voice, "if you hurt that dog, I'm going to put you in the hospital."

"Call the mutt off," an older agent ordered. "I talked to your commander. Coburn. We'll get this sorted out in a little while, but until then I'm taking you into custody."

"That's fine," Shel said. "But the dog goes with me. He's not going to allow us to get separated."

The agent nodded.

Shel stood still and endured the pain as one of the FBI agents secured his hands behind his back with disposable cuffs.

"Get him to a medical unit before he bleeds out," the older agent said. He glanced back at Bobby Lee Gant lying on the floor and cursed fluently enough to impress Shel, who'd been around Navy men most of his life. "This is a total mess." Then he cursed some more.

❂ ❂ ❂

>> 2056 HOURS

Light-headed and hurting, Shel sat on the bumper of the ambulance while the emergency medical technicians worked on him. They cut the disposable cuffs, freeing his hands, then cut off his shirt and unfastened the Velcro straps of the Kevlar vest. One of the two bullets embedded in the vest dropped to the parking lot pavement.

The EMTs kept working on him and ignored it.

"Hey," Shel said. He had to struggle for the words, and he didn't understand that. He'd been shot before.

"I got no exit wound," the lanky black EMT said as he searched Shel's massive shoulder. "Bullet's still inside."

"Don't worry about that," the blonde EMT said as she examined the massive bruises already forming across Shel's chest. "The OR can take care of that. Let's just get him stable."

"Can't get him to stop bleeding." The first EMT threw another bloody compress into a bucket at his feet. He tore open a package to get a fresh one. "I think we've got a bleeder inside him somewhere." He glanced at Shel. "How are you feeling?"

"Like I just got shot," Shel said. "I need that bullet that fell off the vest." He tried to lean forward, then discovered he was so woozy he almost fell over.

The EMTs braced him and shoved him back against the ambulance. But that only got Max excited and he started growling.

"I've got to have that bullet," Shel insisted. "It's evidence." The habits he'd learned while serving with NCIS were ingrained, and he'd always been one for training.

"Lie still," the blonde ordered. "Tony, get that bleeding stopped."

"I'm trying. I told you that."

Max barked more loudly and bumped up against Shel's legs.

"He's bleeding too much."

"I know that. That's what I've been trying to tell you."

Shel tried to speak, to remind them about the bullet; then he thought maybe he should tell them that he really wasn't feeling very good. Before he could say anything, though, he blacked out.

❂ ❂ ❂

>> 2057 HOURS

Hands cuffed behind him, Remy sat in the back of the unmarked sedan and watched as the FBI agents secured the tattoo parlor. They were good at what they did. He had to admit that.

Still, knowing that didn't make him feel any better about being on the wrong side of the wire mesh in the vehicle. Too many old memories sat there with him. He kept remembering his brother, and remembering how Marcel had died in his arms.

"I forgive you, Remy. So does God. Find peace in your life. Just ask God to help you."

The door opened and tore Remy from those dark thoughts. One of the FBI agents stood in the doorway and reached for Remy.

"Come with us," the agent said. "We got a problem."

Remy allowed himself to be pulled from the back of the car. "What problem?"

"Your partner." The agent shoved Remy toward the ambulance where other agents had taken Shel. "He went down and now the dog won't let anyone near him. The EMTs say if they don't get to him quick, your buddy's gonna die."

Max's warning growl hung in the air. Remy heard it then. The car had muffled the noise. He quickened his steps.

CRIME SCENE

CRI

15

E SCENE ✪ NCIS ✪ CRIME SCENE
NAVAL CRIMINAL INVESTIGATIVE SERVICE

>> SPIDER'S TATTOO SHOP
>> DOGGETT STREET
>> CHARLOTTE, NORTH CAROLINA
>> 2058 HOURS

Shel lay sprawled on the parking lot. His color was bad. His normally tan complexion had turned the color of whey. Blood pooled across the pavement from his injured shoulder.

Max stood braced over him. His fangs were bared as he growled at everyone around him.

"If you can't get that dog to calm down so the EMT can work on your buddy," the FBI agent told Remy, "we're gonna have to shoot him."

"No." Remy looked at Max and tried to focus on the fact that he could still see Shel's chest rising and falling. But the motion was too slow and too shallow. "You can't shoot the dog."

"We can't let that man die either."

"Free my hands," Remy said. He turned his back toward the agent.

"You're in custody."

Remy cursed. "Have you got concrete between your ears? Free my hands. If I'm not free, that dog isn't going to listen to me. Do it *now*."

"Do it, McKinley," a gruff voice ordered. The salt-and-pepper–haired FBI agent came up beside the ambulance. Max growled at him.

McKinley unfastened the cuffs.

Remy massaged his wrists and went forward. "No guns," he told the

FBI agents. "Anyone pulls a gun right now, the dog may go for you. And he won't let anybody close to Shel."

They stood around him. The revolving red and blue lights striped the scene.

"Max," Remy called. "Hey. Take it easy now."

The Labrador kept his fangs bared. He straddled the big Marine's midsection protectively. Only a dog that big could have done that job.

"Max. It's me. Remy. We're friends."

Max gave him a sideways look.

Remy held his hands up to show he meant no harm and carried no weapon. He squatted down almost within reach of Shel but no closer. Max wouldn't have allowed anyone to get any closer without going for a throat.

"Tango, Max," Remy said. "Tango." It was their secret word, the one that Shel had taught the Labrador that would tell him to obey Remy. Each member of the NCIS team had a secret word. If something happened to Shel, the dog wouldn't leave his side unless someone else with a code word commanded him to.

For a moment Remy didn't think Max was going to obey. He'd never used the word for real, never when Shel hadn't been right there to enforce it.

Then Max lowered his head and tail. The liquid uncertainty in the dog's brown eyes was almost heartbreaking.

Carefully Remy reached for Max, aware that the control word might not hold under the circumstances. "Shel's hurt, boy," Remy said in a soothing voice. "Shel's hurt and we gotta let these people take care of him." He curled his fingers in Max's fur and gently pulled him off Shel.

The dog came reluctantly and sat beside Remy. Quivering and fearful, Max licked Remy's face. Though he wasn't a fan of dog saliva, Remy dealt with it. He patted the Labrador's head and stroked his fur.

"Can we get him now?" the blonde EMT asked.

"Yeah," Remy said. "And plug that shoulder wound. You've got a nicked artery in there." He tried to say it calmly, but the idea of an artery hosing Shel's blood out with every heartbeat was scary.

The blonde started to pick Shel up from the ground. "I hardly think—"

Remy stood without a word and kept hold of Max's fur. The dog stood with him at once. "Back off," Remy snarled. Anger settled into him.

The blonde EMT stepped back. "What makes you think you can just—?"

"Urlacher." Remy focused on the medical supplies in the kit beside Shel. "Back them off."

"What do you think you're doing?" Urlacher asked.

Remy hunkered down and popped open the first aid kit. He pulled on a pair of surgical gloves. "I'm a combat medic. This is a combat wound. I know what I'm doing. I'm saving my friend's life. That's what the Navy trained me to do."

"He can't—," the blonde started to protest.

"He can," Urlacher said. "He is. You step back out of his way and prepare to transport."

Remy worked feverishly to pack the wound and staunch the bleeding. Once he had that done, the rest of it was in a surgeon's hands. He blinked sweat out of his eyes as the black EMT knelt beside him to assist. When the man didn't get in his way, Remy allowed it.

❂ ❂ ❂

>> NORTH CAROLINA AIRSPACE
>> 2134 HOURS

Tension knotted Will's stomach as he flew through the night. He tended to the airplane's needs out of habit and training rather than thinking, and he didn't like that he was doing that. Flight was less risky than driving a vehicle on the ground—and, thankfully in this case, faster—but a pilot still had to pay attention.

Maggie sat beside him in the copilot's seat. She wasn't trained to fly, but she coordinated the communications loop so he wouldn't have to. She turned toward him. "Director Larkin is online now."

Before becoming the director of the NCIS, Michael Larkin had been a homicide cop and then division leader in New York City. His record and his no-nonsense handling of cases and personnel had won him his current position. Although they sometimes butted heads over procedure—especially in regard to the military way of handling things—Will liked and trusted the man.

"Will," Larkin said quietly.

"Sir," Will responded as he made an altitude adjustment. "Sorry to interrupt your trip."

"It's all right. I'm just glad we've got phone service out here." Larkin had gone on a family fishing trip, and they were currently staying at a cabin in Cape Hatteras along the Atlantic shoreline. "How's Shel?"

"I can't tell you anything more than Maggie did, sir. Remy said the OR took Shel back about twenty minutes ago. We haven't gotten any word yet."

"Remy said it looked bad."

"Shel's been through worse." Will had kept telling himself that from the moment after he'd received the news.

"I guess what I really want to know is how you're doing."

"I'm fine."

"One of your men is in the OR," Larkin said. "I know you're not fine."

Will silently admitted that. Shel's getting shot, the severity of it, created painful echoes of the loss of Frank Billings. Frank had served with Will aboard the aircraft carrier where he had made commander, then followed him into the NCIS billet. When the business in South Korea had started up, Frank had been the first casualty Will's team had ever suffered.

The only casualty, Will amended. *God willing.*

"I'm fine as I can be, sir." Will stared through the plane's Plexiglas windows and listened to the even throb of the dual engines. "There's going to be some confusion in Charlotte."

"I understand that. Apparently my answering service has already received several phone calls from Special Agent-in-Charge Urlacher. I take it he's the point man on the confusion."

"Yes, sir."

"How did he get involved?"

Swiftly, with cool efficiency despite the tension inside him, Will relayed the story.

"Urlacher is trying to flip Victor Gant on his opium supplier," Larkin said when Will finished.

"That's the way I understood it."

"Well," Larkin said, "I suppose there's not much chance of that now, is there?"

"No."

"The rest of it, whatever Urlacher's business is with Victor Gant, doesn't concern us."

"No, sir," Will agreed. "I'm just going to Charlotte to bring Shel home."

"Do that, Will," Larkin said. "I'll keep Urlacher off your back. Let me know if you need anything else."

"Yes, sir. Thank you."

Larkin broke the connection.

"Will."

Will glanced at Maggie.

"I've got Shel's brother, Don, on the line. I still haven't gotten an answer at Shel's father's house."

"I'll talk to him," Will said.

16

E SCENE ✪ NCIS ✪ CRIME SCENE

NAVAL CRIMINAL INVESTIGATIVE SERVICE

>> RAFTER M RANCH
>> OUTSIDE FORT DAVIS, TEXAS
>> 2057 HOURS (CENTRAL TIME ZONE)

The whole time Don drove his Toyota Camry down the long dirt road that led to the house where he'd spent all his childhood years and become a man, he felt his father's gaze on him. The ranch house sat far enough back off the highway that no one could approach without Tyrel McHenry noticing.

It was still early enough, Don knew, that his daddy would be up. Probably watching a baseball game and soaking homemade corn bread in a glass of fresh buttermilk. That was one of the treats his daddy loved, though he wasn't much for pies and cakes outside of the occasional piece of coconut pie.

Don still wore the suit he'd delivered his message in at church only an hour ago. He and his family had barely gotten home before he'd received the call about Shel from the NCIS.

He parked beside his daddy's Ford F-150. After a minute, because he knew his daddy didn't like any sudden movement out in the yard, Don got out of the car and walked toward the home.

The ranch house was a small three-bedroom that Tyrel McHenry had built with his own hands before he'd asked for his wife's hand in marriage. He'd wanted to give her a good home, and he had. He still managed the roofing and upkeep on his own, though Don and Shel had both spent considerable time helping out while they were growing up.

Don was just stepping up onto the wooden veranda that ran around two sides of the house when he heard his daddy's voice from the side.

"Kind of late for you to come calling, ain't it?" Tyrel asked.

Don froze where he was and—for just a second—felt as guilty as he had when he'd tried to come sneaking home back in high school after staying out too late with Shel. That hadn't happened often. Shel had stayed out a lot, but Don hadn't.

"Yes, sir," Don said. "I wouldn't have come if it hadn't been important."

Tyrel sat in the dark of the porch in one of the two rocking chairs that had been on the veranda as long as Don could remember. They'd taken some mending over the years too, but they'd stood up under the weather and the time. Tyrel had built them as well.

"Your brother was shot," Tyrel said flatly.

"Yes, sir."

"I already know that. Them people he works with called."

In the dark, Don couldn't see his daddy's face. He had no idea how his daddy was taking the news, but he sounded as calm as ever.

"They said they couldn't get hold of you," Don said.

"They left a message."

Confusion spun through Don. "They called more than once."

"They did." Tyrel rocked gently in the chair.

"You didn't answer the phone."

"Didn't need to. I heard their message. If anything changes, I expect they'll leave a different message."

Feeling overcome, Don sat down on the edge of the porch like he'd often done when talking to his daddy. They hadn't ever talked for long. God knew Don had tried, but Tyrel McHenry had just never been one for long-winded conversations. It came to Don then that he'd probably talked to his daddy more that day than he had in years.

"They say Shel's hurt pretty bad," Don said.

"He'll be all right." Tyrel's voice was firm and unyielding. "He's been hurt before."

Don sat there for a moment and tried to figure out what he was going to say next. Then he realized that there was no other way than to just say it.

"I'm going up there, Daddy," Don said. "Commander Coburn said Shel needs to take some time off to heal up. Now I know Shel; he's not going to want to do that. So I figured I'd go up there and bring him on back here so he could be with family."

"That sounds good. But I'm betting you won't get him to come."

"I've decided I'm not coming home without him. For one, he needs to rest. And for another he hasn't been around his family—" *his daddy*, Don wanted to say—"in a long time."

"Good luck with that. You know how stubborn Shel can be."

And I know who he gets that from, Don thought, but he didn't dare say it.

"Maybe," Don said cautiously, hoping he was sounding like he'd just come up with the idea on the spot, "he'd listen if *you* told him that."

Tyrel stopped rocking. "Ain't my business to be telling a man full growed what he ought to be doing."

"You're his daddy."

"Both of y'all are an age you don't need a daddy telling you what to do."

"Then come with me and *ask* him to come home." Don tried to stare through the darkness to see his daddy. But he couldn't quite see the older man's hard face. "I can get another plane ticket."

For a long moment, Tyrel didn't say anything. During that time Don thought his daddy was actually considering the possibility.

"You go ahead on and do that if you've a mind to," Tyrel said. "But it ain't for me to do."

"Why not?"

"Because I just told you it wasn't."

Anger got past Don's defenses. He didn't understand his father. He never had. Not when it came to being involved in family.

"That's your son up there lying in that hospital bed," Don said hoarsely.

"He's gonna be fine."

"You don't know that. They don't know that. That's why they called."

For a moment Tyrel didn't speak. "Don't go getting yourself all worked up into a lather, boy. Come morning, everything is gonna be fine, and you'll find out you just got yourself upset for no reason at all."

Shaking, Don stood. "Daddy, I'm going to tell you something I haven't ever told you. Maybe I should have. I just don't know."

"Maybe you should just hold on to that," his daddy cautioned, "before you say something you can't take back."

"I've held on to it too long already." Don took a deep breath and asked God to stand beside him while he spoke. "When Joanie was pregnant with Joshua, I was so afraid of becoming a father because I didn't know how to be one. I was afraid I wasn't going to be able to love him enough. I was afraid we weren't going to have anything in common."

"You didn't have no cause to think that way."

"Didn't I?" Don couldn't believe it when he stepped up onto the porch. "You raised Shel and me, but you haven't been the best father you could have. Half the time—especially after Mama died—I don't think you even cared."

"Yet here you are," Tyrel said. "Standing on your own two feet and telling me man-to-man what's on your mind."

"You weren't there, Daddy. You weren't there when my children were born. You weren't there when I was scared to death I didn't know how to take care of them. You weren't there when Shel shipped off to the Marines. You weren't there when most of his unit had gotten killed in the Gulf War and the Marines thought he was dead too." Tears stung Don's eyes and he let them flow.

"I think maybe it's time you went on home," Tyrel said quietly. "You're getting too worked up. You're worried about your brother, and that's understandable."

"You know when I realized how little of a father you'd been?" Don asked. His voice was so tight with emotion he almost couldn't speak.

"Don—"

"When I held Joshua in my arms the first time," Don said. "That's when. I held my son and realized how good it made me feel. That's when I realized how much Shel and I had missed growing up."

"I never cut and run on you boys," Tyrel grated. His voice was tight with some emotion too, but Don didn't know exactly what it was. "I was there every day. Putting in time on this ranch. Making sure you had a roof over your heads, plenty of food on the table, and clothes on your back."

"There's more to being a father than that, Daddy."

Tyrel pushed up out of the rocking chair. Don felt afraid for just a moment. He'd seen the deep anger that resided in his daddy. Tyrel had never turned those hard hands on his sons, but Don had always thought it was possible. Although since Tyrel had never flattened Shel while he was growing up, maybe it wasn't. Because Shel had sorely tried his patience.

"You know the biggest thing I was afraid of when Joanie was pregnant?" Don asked in a quieter voice. "I was afraid I was going to be *you*. I didn't want any child of mine to grow up with a daddy like I had."

"It's time for you to go," his daddy said. "You need to get some sleep if you're gonna catch a plane outta here in the morning."

Don tried to think of something else to say and couldn't. Helplessly, he watched his daddy walk to the front door, enter, and lock the door behind him. The house was completely dark inside.

Although he thought about going to the door and demanding to be let in, Don knew that wouldn't do any good. Tyrel was through talking, and when that happened, there was nothing else to be done.

In the quiet darkness on the porch, Don took a deep breath and wondered if he'd destroyed what little remained of the fragile connection he had with his daddy. He tried to tell himself that he'd be better off.

Shel had walked away from their daddy for the most part. He only stopped in often enough to remember why he'd left home.

"Daddy," Don said loud enough to be heard through the closed door, "I'm sorry if I hurt your feelings. But I'm not sorry I said what I said."

There was no answer from the darkened house.

After a few more moments, when he was sure his daddy wouldn't be answering, Don turned and walked back to his car. He stood beside it for just a moment and bowed his head in prayer.

God, you want me to honor my mother and my father. You have to know how difficult this is. Please show me how, because I can't find a way on my own.

Lifting his head, Don got into his car and drove back toward home. There was a lot to be done by morning.

⊛ ⊛ ⊛

>> INTERVIEW ROOM
>> FEDERAL BUREAU OF INVESTIGATION FIELD OFFICE
>> CHARLOTTE, NORTH CAROLINA
>> 0017 HOURS

Victor sat motionless and stared at the one-way mirror. Occasionally he took note of his reflection, but there was nothing there he wanted to see.

He kept seeing Bobby Lee.

As he sat there, Victor tried to assess how he felt. He hadn't tried to do anything like that in years. Normally he didn't bother. Normally there was enough whiskey, drugs, and women at hand that he didn't need to feel much of anything. He'd always operated on instinct.

Instinct is the survival of the species, Victor told himself. *Having kids is part of it.*

Only someone had gunned down his kid.

When he'd seen the EMTs walk the big man out of the tattoo shop and seen all the blood gushing out of him, Victor had known the man was in trouble. Only an artery pumped like that.

Personally, Victor hoped the man died. But in case he didn't, Victor had memorized his face. If the man lived, retribution was going to be swift and final. It didn't matter who he was. Some other father was going to lose his son too.

The door opened, and Urlacher entered.

Victor didn't even glance at the FBI agent. He kept track of him in the mirror.

"Don't know what you're doing here, supercop," Victor said. "The deal's off. It died with my boy."

"That's not how I see it," Urlacher said.

Victor grinned slow and easy. "Then you need to get your eyes checked."

Urlacher sat at the table. "You're still in a world of hurt. You aren't free of me yet."

"If you could make anything stick, we wouldn't be in here talking, would we?"

With a tired sigh, Urlacher leaned back in his chair.

"Do you really think all your fed bosses are going to let you just hang around here trying to trip me up?" Victor asked.

Urlacher didn't answer.

"I don't think so. Especially not as deep as you like to run personnel on a job."

"Are you just talking to hear yourself?"

Victor grinned again, even though he didn't truly feel like it. "I was going to offer your undercover buddy a deal tonight. Before you decided to be a hard case about it. Maybe you're ready to listen to that now."

"I'm here about the opium that's showing up in North Carolina."

"There's a Salvadoran gang running opium through North Carolina." Victor shook out a cigarette, the first one he'd had since he'd been returned to the interview room. He lit up and dragged a deep lungful. "Maybe taking them down would be enough to satisfy the people you're banging heads for."

Urlacher seemed to contemplate that for a moment. "What Salvadoran gang?"

"Mara Salvatrucha," Victor said. "They named themselves after some kind of army ant. Whatever they are, they're mucho trouble. You interested in them, supercop?"

"You don't get your opium from them."

Victor grinned. "I don't deal in opium. Don't know where you get that idea."

"It's more than an idea."

"Then prove it. Arrest me. Let me call my lawyer. Then I'll be out of here as soon as he posts bail for me. And whatever you get some DA to charge me with, my attorney's going to beat. Then we'll turn around and sue you for false arrest. It'll make a nice retirement package."

Urlacher frowned. "I've heard of the Mara Salvatrucha. They also call themselves MS-13."

"One of the most notorious gangs operating out there right now," Victor agreed. "Those guys are big-time hard-core. They'll bury you soon as look at you." He knew that from personal experience; they'd already crossed paths a couple times, and blood had spilled like water. "They've even got themselves a History Channel special."

"What do you have?"

"I got names. Places. Players. Routes they use to bring cargo in from Houston right up Interstate 35, then out Interstate 40 to here. If I give you what I got here, then you can follow the play back there and bring down some major players."

"Are they getting work from the same place you are?"

Victor smiled and spread his hands. "I don't sell drugs. I already told you that."

Urlacher cursed.

"These guys deal opium," Victor said. "Get it from a Yakuza connection down in Mexico. The Japanese mafia is treading on the toes of the Colombian cocaine cartels. Gonna be a real shooting war down there when this all breaks loose. Might help domestically if you could start working on getting a handle on it now."

Urlacher only stared at him.

"So what's it gonna be, supercop?" Victor asked in a flat voice. "That's the deal on the table. You want to ante up and play with the big boys? Or are you gonna roll the dice with Mr. DA?"

S
SERVICE
CRIME SCENE
NCIS
NAVAL CRIMINAL INVESTIGATIVE SERVICE
CRI

17

E SCENE ✪ **NCIS** ✪ CRIME SCEN

NAVAL CRIMINAL INVESTIGATIVE SERVICE

>> INTENSIVE CARE UNIT
>> PRESBYTERIAN HOSPITAL
>> CHARLOTTE, NORTH CAROLINA
>> 0814 HOURS

When he tried to open his eyelids and found that they weighed about a hundred pounds each, Shel knew he was on serious pain medication. The too-bright illumination from the overhead track lighting was another clue. The fact that his nose itched told him that at least one of the prescribed meds was Demerol. His nose always itched when he was on Demerol.

"Hey."

Woozy, Shel rolled his head to the side. The room seemed to spin. He closed his eyes involuntarily.

"Easy," a soft feminine voice suggested. "Go slow."

Shel checked his teeth with his tongue. It was a habit after all the fights he'd been in. At least this time it didn't seem like any dental work was involved. Everything was where it was supposed to be.

"You still with me?" the woman's voice asked.

When he recognized her voice then, Shel said her name. "Maggie."

"Got it in one, Marine."

Shel didn't want to try to smile. He always looked goofy when he was on Demerol and smiled. Some of the guys he'd toured with had pictures to prove it. But he smiled anyway because Maggie was there and he thought it was great she was there. In fact, everything seemed kind of great.

He blinked his eyes open again. "Good to see you, Maggie."

"I bet." Maggie stood at the foot of the hospital bed. "How are you feeling?"

"Better than I've felt in a long time."

Maggie laughed.

"Didn't know you were twins." Shel tried to focus and bring the two images back into one. He almost had it, but it took nearly everything he had to accomplish that.

"I think I'll suggest to the nurse that they cut back on the meds," Maggie said.

"Sure."

"If you start hurting, you'll want to let them know."

Shel nodded, and the effort seemed like it took forever. The room spun again too.

"Can I get something to drink?" he asked.

"You can have ice."

Shel sighed.

"Sorry, big guy. Nurse's orders. With all the painkillers you're on, if you drink water, it might come back up."

"Ice," Shel agreed.

Maggie fed him a few ice chips with a plastic spoon.

Shel savored them, holding them in his mouth till they slowly melted and relieved some of the parched sensation in his throat. That was from the tube the emergency room people had shoved down his esophagus to keep the airway open. The next couple of days weren't going to be pleasant swallowing.

"How bad is my arm?" he asked.

"Nothing permanent," Maggie replied. She spooned more ice chips into his mouth. "The bullet tore into your upper thoracic cavity and struck the underside of the glenohumeral joint. There was some—"

"English," Shel protested.

"The bullet hit you in the chest and caught the underside of the ball and socket joint in your shoulder."

"Now that I can understand," Shel said, "but only because I've had a few shoulder separations."

"The surgeon did mention there had been previous operations."

Shel nodded. "Football."

"Then you know the rehab you're going to have to do to get everything back in shape."

"No permanent damage?" Shel asked again because he wanted to hear it once more. One of his biggest fears was that he'd get disabled somewhere along the way, then shelved at a desk job or released on a medical discharge. All he had was the Marines. If something like that happened, he didn't know what he'd do with himself. He didn't have a family like Don, and he was pretty sure he didn't want one.

"No permanent damage," Maggie agreed. "The bullet deflected downward and went into your right arm. It nicked the brachiocephalic artery just enough to cause problems." She paused. "Remy probably saved your life. Twice. When you went down, the EMTs couldn't get to you."

"Max," Shel said, understanding at once.

"You passed out from blood loss. Max went into total protective mode. Unfortunately that wasn't what you needed at the time."

"Max is okay?" Shel knew there were times when a dog had to be put down so medical teams could save an unconscious and wounded K-9–equipped soldier.

"Max is fine," Maggie said. "He's downstairs with Remy. They've become best buds."

Shel grinned. "You won't believe how sad a day it is when a man's dog deserts him."

"Hardly. Max knows you're here. Somewhere. How he knows is anyone's guess, but—"

"He's a trained Marine. Never underestimate Marine training."

Maggie gave him a wry look. "—but he's refusing to leave the hospital now that he's here. He walks the corridors a lot looking for you."

"Remy?" Shel deadpanned. "I knew he was starting to warm up to me, but—"

"Oh, if you can do humor, maybe you can get your own ice chips."

Shel smiled and thought again how he shouldn't be doing that. "I give."

Maggie gave him another helping of ice chips. "Anyway, the EMTs should have started you on an IV immediately. And packed the shoulder wound. Remy did that and kept you alive until you reached the ER."

"Naahhh," Shel said. "I'm too tough to kill." Fatigue washed over him then, or it might have been the Demerol. He closed his eyes and quietly went away.

Somewhere in there, though, he heard Maggie whisper, "I hope so."

❀ ❀ ❀

>> FEDERAL BUREAU OF INVESTIGATION FIELD OFFICE
>> 400 SOUTH TRYON STREET
>> SUITE 900
>> CHARLOTTE, NORTH CAROLINA
>> 1126 HOURS

Dressed in a suit, including jacket and tie, Will Coburn sat in the waiting area outside the FBI offices. He referenced his notes on his Pocket PC and ignored the attention he was getting from the young FBI agent seated on the other side of the office. The agent had been put there to bird-dog him. Will didn't mind. As long as the agent was there, it was a sure indication that whoever had assigned the detail to him was in the building as well.

Will had been kept waiting for over two hours. But he didn't think of sitting there as waiting. He was guarding the door. Special Agent-in-Charge Urlacher was in the building. Will intended to see to it that the man didn't leave without talking to him.

Ten more minutes passed; then Urlacher emerged from the back offices with Victor Gant and three other agents. Gant, Will noticed, wasn't in handcuffs. That, he decided, was interesting.

Will stood and put his Pocket PC back on his hip. He straightened his jacket over the holstered Springfield XD-40 snugged under his left arm and followed Urlacher and his entourage out into the hallway.

"Special Agent Urlacher," Will called.

Urlacher looked over his shoulder but didn't break stride on his way to the elevators. He nodded at one of the younger FBI agents. The agent peeled off from the group and headed back toward Will.

"I'm sorry," the agent said. "Agent Urlacher can't be bothered right now."

Without saying a word, Will stepped around the man, moving too fast to be stopped because he'd never slowed his pace.

The agent grabbed Will's right wrist and pulled. "I said—," he started.

Will smoothly slid his hand over the agent's wrist, rotating his own wrist toward the man's thumb to pop it free. He grabbed the man's jacketed shoulder before he could react, then twisted him around and shoved him face-first into the wall hard enough to jar the picture hanging there. He jacked the wrist he'd captured up toward the man's shoulder blades.

The man grunted in pain and stood in place.

"Touching me without provocation is assault," Will said in his commander's tone. "I'm a federal officer, so that's a federal violation."

The other two agents reached under their jackets for their weapons. Will held his captive and stared straight into Urlacher's eyes. Victor Gant seemed amused by the situation.

Urlacher raised his hands and the two agents pulled their hands back. "Commander Coburn."

"That's right," Will said. "I thought maybe we could have a word." He forced a smile. "A polite word."

"It's hard to be polite when you're wallpapering the hallway with one of my men."

"It's hard not to wallpaper the hallway with your men while one of my team is lying in the hospital because you had to try to high-hat us," Will said. His captive struggled, so he lifted the man's arm higher till he was tiptoeing to keep the pain at a tolerable level.

"Pretty harsh talk from a single man," Urlacher said.

"Trust me," Will said, "I'm all that's standing between you and a base full of Marines that happen to think a lot of my gunnery sergeant."

"What do you want?"

Will stepped back from his captive and released him. He watched the man. The agent nursed his arm and walked over to join Urlacher and the others.

"There's going to be a review by the Charlotte police department crime teams of what went down last night," Will said.

"You mean the shooting."

"I *do* mean the shooting," Will said. "I expect my gunney to be cleared in the matter. I thought I'd come talk to you and get this worked out ahead of time. In case you or your men had problems remembering exactly how everything happened last night."

"You're with the NCIS?" Victor Gant asked. A crooked smile twisted his thin lips.

Urlacher put a hand on Victor's chest and held him back. "Stay out of this," he said.

"Do you know who I am?" Victor demanded.

"I do," Will said. "I don't have an issue with you at the moment, Mr. Gant. I'd like to keep it that way."

"Maybe I have an issue with you," Victor said. "Your man killed my son. Shot him down like he was a dog." His voice was hoarse with anger.

Will met the man's angry glare and didn't look away. He couldn't. Both of them knew it hadn't happened the way Victor Gant said it did, but any weakness on his part would have confirmed the other man's story in his mind.

Urlacher grabbed Victor by the arm and shoved him back. "Get moving."

Victor continued to stare at Will.

"Take it outside," Urlacher said, eyeing the man vehemently. "Or I will arrest you."

Victor went, accompanied by two of Urlacher's agents, but he glared at Will until the elevator doors closed.

18

SCENE ✪ NCIS ✪ CRIME SCENE

NAVAL CRIMINAL INVESTIGATIVE SERVICE

>> FEDERAL BUREAU OF INVESTIGATION FIELD OFFICE
>> 400 SOUTH TRYON STREET
>> SUITE 900
>> CHARLOTTE, NORTH CAROLINA
>> 1132 HOURS

Urlacher wheeled on Will. "Your timing stinks, Commander."

"I'd have preferred to meet in your office," Will said. "You're the one who forced this."

Urlacher stepped to within inches of Will. "I didn't force anything."

"You did." Will didn't budge an inch. He locked eyes with the older man. "If you hadn't gone there last night, my guys could have taken Bobby Lee Gant without anyone getting hurt."

"You don't know that."

"I do. They've worked a lot of pickups. And did it without anyone getting hurt." Of course, there were some that didn't turn out so well, but Will wasn't going to mention those.

"What do you want?" Urlacher asked.

"Like I said," Will replied, "I want that shooting report squared away. No problems for my gunney. He's a good man and a fine Marine. His record's going to stand clean and without blemish."

"And if I don't see it that way?"

"Then you're going to be in a world of hurt."

Urlacher laughed, but the effort didn't sound convincing. "There's nothing you can do to me."

"You seem to be getting awfully chummy with Victor Gant," Will said. "My guess is that you're going to try to get him to snitch on some people for you."

"I can't hold him on what I've got."

"He wasn't wearing cuffs when he went through here."

Urlacher didn't say anything.

"My gunney took three bullets and nearly died," Will said, "so he could take down the problem *you* lit a fire under without getting that woman hurt. If your report doesn't corroborate that, I'm going to look into Victor Gant's business with a microscope." He smiled slightly. "I'm betting that'll throw a kink in whatever tea party you've got planned with Victor Gant."

"You can't do that."

"I can." Will kept his eyes locked on the other man's. "When Bobby Lee Gant hurt that Marine in Jacksonville, he had three men with him. I'm still looking for those three men. For all I know, they're part of Victor Gant's little motorcycle club."

Urlacher growled a curse. "You're making trouble for yourself."

"Not if I don't have to. I'll take a clean report on that shooting and I'll pack up and leave."

A frown tightened Urlacher's lips and he gave a grudging nod. "It'll be like you said."

"Not like I *said*," Will told him. "Like it *was* last night. You owe my gunney that. He might have saved the lives of your men."

"You'll get your report."

"By end of day," Will said. "Or we start turning over rocks in Victor Gant's neighborhood." He reached into his jacket pocket and took out one of his business cards.

"I'll have it there." Urlacher scowled as he took the business card. Without another word, he turned and walked away.

Silently Will watched the FBI agent go, but he couldn't help wondering what it was that Urlacher was working on. For the agent to have capitulated so quickly, it had to be something big.

Let it go, Will told himself. *You've got enough on your plate.* He let out a deep breath, then turned and walked away.

But he couldn't get Victor Gant's eyes or voice out of his mind. The man had radiated pure evil and hate. Will decided he was going to be happy when he could get Shel out of the hospital and back home.

⊛ ⊛ ⊛

>> 1137 HOURS

Surrounded by FBI agents, Victor stared at the elevator indicator lights as the cage dropped to the bottom floor. One of the agents had stopped the cage and waited for Urlacher to get on again. Victor had only heard a muffled version of Urlacher's conversation with the NCIS agent. The cage swayed and the two men next to him bumped against him.

"Don't go getting any ideas," Urlacher said.

"Wouldn't think of it," Victor replied.

"You tangle with the NCIS, make this personal, I don't have enough juice to pull them off you."

"Understood." Victor nodded. It was already personal. How could somebody killing his son not be personal?

"What happened to your boy—"

"Bobby Lee," Victor interrupted.

Urlacher looked at him.

"My boy," Victor said. "His name was Bobby Lee. Don't you go remembering him as just another dead kid."

Urlacher didn't back off. "Stay away from those NCIS people."

Despite the No Smoking sign posted in the elevator, Victor took out his pack of cigarettes and lit up. Overhead, the smoke alarm shrilled.

"I heard on the news that Marine who shot Bobby Lee lived," Victor said.

"If you go around him, I'll toss the deal and put you in jail."

"For what?"

"For whatever," Urlacher said. "Jaywalking. Spitting on the sidewalk."

Victor smiled. "You act like I should be afraid of them."

"They run a pretty tight crew."

The elevator dinged and came to a gentle stop. The doors opened. Victor got out with the cigarette in his fist.

Two matronly women gave him discourteous looks. One of them pointed at the No Smoking sign posted inside the elevator cage.

Victor said something offensive and both women stepped toward the next elevator cage.

"I've got half a mind to take you and stash you in protective custody," Urlacher said.

"Quickest way to guarantee that I won't tell you a thing." Victor walked through the downstairs hallway. His eyes roved the people and stared through the glass doors at the front of the building. "You leave me be, I'll get you what you want." He stopped and looked at Urlacher. "And this is where we go our separate ways, gentlemen."

Hesitation soured Urlacher's features. In the end, though, Victor knew that the FBI agent didn't have a choice. Not if he wanted to nab all the opium he had his eye on.

"All right," Urlacher said.

"Then I guess I'll be seeing you." Victor took his sunglasses from his shirt pocket and slipped them on. He took his cell phone—returned to him with all his other possessions that morning after he'd agreed to the FBI's deal—from his pocket as he walked away. He punched in Fat Mike's number.

"Yeah," Fat Mike answered.

"Me," Victor said. "I need a ride."

"Where are you?"

"Walking out of FBI offices."

"Cool, bro. I'm just dipping my beak at the strip club over on Tyvola Road."

"That place seems a little upscale for you."

Fat Mike laughed. "Maybe it was, but after I walked through the door, its standing dropped through the basement."

"I'll be out front." Victor stepped through the glass doors and out into the heat of the day. "Got a question."

"Okay."

"Do you know where they took that cop? The one that killed Bobby Lee?"

Fat Mike sucked in a breath. "Yeah."

"I want to go there."

"Now?"

"Yeah." Victor closed his cell phone and pushed it into his pants pocket. He lit another cigarette while he waited and thought about what he wanted to do to the big Marine who had killed Bobby Lee.

⊛ ⊛ ⊛

>> PARKING LOT
>> PRESBYTERIAN HOSPITAL
>> CHARLOTTE, NORTH CAROLINA
>> 1208 HOURS

Will pulled the dark gray Taurus he'd gotten from the rental company into the parking lot and started to get out. When he opened the door, a blast of superheated air slapped him in the face. It was hard to believe that it was going to be hotter still in a couple more weeks.

Before he could get out, he tracked movement in the side mirror, and a big hand fell onto his door. He'd already abandoned his jacket when he'd gotten into the car, so it took only a second to reach up under his arm and free the Springfield pistol.

In the next instant, Victor Gant stepped to the window and smiled at him. "Hey, cap'n," the biker said. "I come in peace."

Will kept the XD-40 in hand as he checked his mirrors. There were no other bikers in sight, but that didn't mean they weren't there.

"Just me," Victor said good-naturedly.

Will didn't say anything. He knew the man would say what was on his mind when he was ready. After all, he'd come all this way and somehow even beaten Will to the hospital to say it.

"Ain't you got nothing to say?" Victor asked.

"It's your show," Will said calmly. "Why don't you run it and I'll see if I find any conversation starters."

"A man of few words," Victor said. "I like that." He kept his hands in plain sight. "I liked how you stood up to Special Agent Urlacher and told him off. That was choice. And all he could do was stand there and eat crow."

"I'm pretty sure you didn't come here to congratulate me for that."

"No, I guess you're right. I didn't. I was wondering if you'd do a favor for me."

Will waited, sensing what was coming.

"Do you know if the big Marine that shot my boy believes in God?" Victor asked.

"You want to be careful what you say next," Will said.

"No foul, cap'n," Victor said. "Just asking for a little information, that's all. Sometimes I stand around on street corners and hand out them pamphlets what's got God's Word on 'em. I was just asking about that sergeant."

Will said nothing, but he felt the naked, cold threat that blew in off the man.

"Tell him for me that if he don't believe in God now, he should start real soon. Things come at you in life and everything changes so fast that sometimes you don't get the time to do the things you should. Tell him I said he should get to know God because him and God could be on a first-name basis before you know it."

As he gazed into the dark hate in Victor's eyes, Will's stomach lurched a little. It wasn't because he was afraid, though it was normal to be fearful at a time like this. It was because he knew that Victor couldn't be scared off his chosen course.

"You just give him that message," Victor said as he turned and walked away. He threw a hand in the air and a big motorcycle engine rumbled to excited life. Without turning his back to Will, the biker stepped out to the edge of the parking lane. "And you have yourself a nice day, cap'n."

A motorcycle and sidecar sped into view and stopped behind Will's rental car. Victor threw a leg over the sidecar and dropped into it. He tossed Will a final salute and rode out of sight.

Will remained where he was and listened intently. He was certain Victor Gant hadn't put in an appearance by himself. Sure enough, less than a minute later, a handful of other motorcycle engines roared to life all around Will.

Hard-faced men wearing their colors rode slowly up behind the car; then they too roared out onto the street and were gone.

Carefully Will took his suit jacket and used it to cover his forearm and the pistol in his fist. He wasn't going to take any chances. Moving slowly, he slid out of the rental car and turned his steps toward the hospital. The sooner they could move Shel—even if it was only to get him back to the base hospital—the happier Will was going to be.

19

E SCENE NCIS CRIME SCENE

NAVAL CRIMINAL INVESTIGATIVE SERVICE

\>> INTENSIVE CARE UNIT
\>> PRESBYTERIAN HOSPITAL
\>> CHARLOTTE, NORTH CAROLINA
\>> 1233 HOURS

Maggie stood at the observation window overlooking the private intensive care room Will had arranged. She had her arms crossed and looked worried.

The two Marine guards stationed out in the hallway carried assault rifles and holstered pistols. Their orders were to inspect the sleeve IDs that had the pictures of all personnel allowed to enter the area. As Will approached, they immediately formed a human wall.

Their BDUs were crisp and clean, and they were alert.

When they recognized Will, they stepped back to allow him passage. They stood at attention.

"Afternoon, Commander," one of them said.

Both saluted.

"At ease," Will said.

The Marines sat back down in folding chairs that creaked under their weight. Neither of them was a small man. They kept their assault rifles across their knees.

Maggie glanced up at Will and smiled. Some of the fatigue dropped away and she looked a little more hopeful.

"How did it go?" she asked.

"Urlacher's on board," Will said.

"Did he have a problem with that?"

"I didn't give him a lot of choice."

"No. I suppose you didn't."

Will stood beside Maggie and gazed through the window. On the other side of the glass, Shel looked like death warmed over. It hurt Will to see the big Marine looking like that. Shel had always seemed like a force of nature, as unstoppable as the morning sun.

"How's he doing?" Will asked.

"In and out," Maggie said. "He lost a lot of blood, and it's going to take him a while to build his strength back up. But the real danger is past."

"That's good." Will glanced down the hall. "Did you get a chance to talk to the doctor?"

Maggie nodded. "She's a good woman. She knows her stuff. According to her, the surgery couldn't have been any better."

"Good to hear. Did she say anything about when we could move him back to Lejeune?"

Maggie studied his face. "What happened?"

"I ran into Victor Gant out in the parking lot."

Worry creased Maggie's face. "I thought the FBI was going to lock him down."

"They didn't. Evidently Victor is cutting some kind of deal with them."

"Must be a pretty big deal."

Will shrugged. "Not our concern."

Maggie blew out an angry breath. "No, but Victor Gant is."

"I know." Will glanced back into the hospital room. "I'm going to work on that a little."

"What?"

"I'll tell you about it if I turn out to be as bright as I think I am. In the meantime, why don't you give the director a call and ask him to request a few more Marine volunteers to cover security here at the hospital."

"All right. I could go with you."

Will shook his head. "Stay with Shel. When he wakes up, when he needs something, I want him to know we're here."

"Remy's here too."

"I'm going to need Remy with me. I've got a few places to go."

"Where angels fear to tread?"

Will smiled at her. "Those places too."

❁ ❁ ❁

>> MECKLENBURG COUNTY MEDICAL EXAMINER
>> 618 NORTH COLLEGE STREET
>> CHARLOTTE, NORTH CAROLINA
>> 1352 HOURS

Will parked his Taurus behind the redbrick building that housed the county medical examiner's office and got out in the heat. The severe lines of the building were only partially blunted by the trees and landscaping.

Remy got out the other side and flared his Tar Heels basketball jersey so it covered the pistol at his hip. Gold chains shone around his neck.

"You want to go over what it is we're doing here?" Remy asked.

"When Bobby Lee was brought in, he was carrying drugs," Will said as they headed toward the glass door. "Heroin. I thought maybe we'd pick it up and have a look at it."

"Okay."

Will opened the door and allowed Remy to enter. "Then we see if we can't get some leverage."

"Where are you going to get the leverage?"

Will held up two fingers. "Bobby Lee had two things we can work with regarding our investigation."

"And what investigation is that exactly?"

"When Bobby Lee attacked our Marine in Jacksonville, he had two buddies."

"I read the reports."

Will led the way down the cool hallways and followed the posted signage to the medical examiner's office. "We're investigating the identities of the two men who were with Bobby Lee."

Remy smiled. "You're hoping that at least one of those men belongs to the Purple Royals."

"I wouldn't say *hoping*."

"But you wouldn't be surprised."

"No," Will said. "I wouldn't."

"If they are, Victor Gant isn't going to like you putting pressure on him."

"At the hospital today, he came on our turf and fired a warning shot," Will said. "We're going to return the favor."

"The drugs—" Remy stopped himself. "The heroin Bobby Lee was carrying is part of your leverage."

"Yes."

"How?"

"We're going to have it couriered to the labs at Camp Lejeune and analyzed under a spectroscope. The tests should be able to identify the trace elements of metals in the heroin. Those are based on geographically related patterns."

"Gant isn't growing his heroin empire here."

"No, he isn't. But it's being grown somewhere."

"If someone could trace the heroin back to its native soil, you'd think it would've been done before now."

"It would've been. That's not what we're going to do. The mixture of those trace elements—from one crime scene to the next—is as distinguishable as a fingerprint."

"A lot of guys could have been caught holding a stash Gant or the Purple Royals sold them."

"I know." Will turned to Remy and smiled. "All I need to do is find one biker who knows the guys Bobby Lee hung with in his father's gang."

Remy smiled and nodded. "I like it. Not exactly gonna make us popular with the FBI."

"I'm not in a popularity contest. I'm trying to make sure my Marine is safe while he recovers."

The young woman at the desk looked up from her computer monitor. "Hi."

"We're here to see Dr. Greer." Will held his NCIS ID open for her.

Remy did the same.

The woman lifted the phone and called the doctor.

⊛ ⊛ ⊛

>> 1406 HOURS

The morgue was cold, but Will was too intent to really notice.

Remy seemed a little uncomfortable. The Tar Heels jersey was too lightweight to blunt much of the cold. He stood with his arms folded.

"Which of you is Commander Coburn?" Dr. Allen Greer asked.

"I am," Will said. "This is Special Agent Gautreau."

"Okay." Greer gazed at Will for a moment, then shifted his attention back to the corpse on the table. The medical examiner didn't seem overly disposed to a friendly personality. He was heavyset and wore thick sideburns that had gone gray with age. He leaned over the open chest cavity of a middle-aged man. "What can I do for you?"

"You're holding the body of Bobby Lee Gant for us," Will said.

"You're here to take custody of the body?"

"No."

Greer looked at him again. "I was assured that body would be gone before morning."

"It will be."

"Then why are you here interrupting my work?"

"I came for Bobby Lee's personal effects that were on the body."

"I see." Greer pulled off his bloody gloves and threw them into a biohazardous materials container. "I heard about the shooting yesterday. It happened in front of several witnesses."

"Yes."

"I was told there'd be no problems clearing the man responsible."

"There won't be."

Greer walked over to a wall of small vaults and checked a notebook. Then he searched the vaults till he found the one he wanted. He reached inside and brought out a large plastic Baggie containing the last things Bobby Lee had had with him that day.

"That's good," Greer said. "If you ask me, more force should be shown to those motorcycle outlaws. But they're making good money in the area, which means they can hire the lawyers necessary to keep them in business and out of jail."

"Maybe we can change that a little," Will said.

"Just sign the chain of custody book and the contents of that bag are yours."

⊛ ⊛ ⊛

>> OFFICE OF THE CHIEF OF POLICE
>> CHARLOTTE-MECKLENBURG POLICE DEPARTMENT
>> 601 EAST TRADE STREET
>> CHARLOTTE, NORTH CAROLINA
>> 1437 HOURS

Charlotte-Mecklenburg Police Chief Ben Tarlton was a young, energetic, and simple man. In his late thirties, he was one of the youngest police chiefs the city had ever seen.

He was a no-nonsense man with an open and honest face that he kept meticulously shaved. His brown hair was cropped short, and his hazel eyes were sincere. His uniform was neatly pressed with creases that looked sharp enough to slice cheese.

His office was compact, filled with law enforcement manuals as well as pictures of his family. Most of the photographs revolved around Little League sports.

One of the plaques on the wall was a toastmaster award, and others were for coaching and Bible study. There were also pictures of Tarlton in a Marine uniform.

"Commander Coburn, sir," Tarlton greeted as he stood up behind his desk and offered his hand.

"Chief Tarlton," Will responded. He introduced Remy, and they shook hands as well. "I appreciate you seeing us on such short notice."

"Not at all. It's my pleasure. How is your agent?"

"He's fine," Will said. "Thank you."

"He's a lucky man."

"He's a good man," Will said. "God seems to take care of those." Even as he said it, though, Will felt a pang as he thought of Frank Billings.

"More times than not, I'd agree with that assessment." Tarlton gestured to the chairs in front of the modest metal desk. "Please. Have a seat."

Will and Remy did.

"So what brings you here?" Tarlton asked.

"We thought we'd share information," Will said.

Tarlton leaned back in his chair and smiled. "You'll forgive me my cynicism, but it's been my experience that federal agencies aren't in the habit of sharing information with local law enforcement agencies unless they want someone to blame or just to throw their weight around."

"That's not why I'm here," Will replied.

Tarlton waited, but he rolled his wrist over and glanced at his watch.

"We ran the pistol that Bobby Lee Gant used on those people last night," Will said. "We didn't pull any federal hits. No wants, no warrants."

"You get a clean gun every now and again," Tarlton said.

"I know. But generally only weapons that have been used in the commission of a murder or a drug deal get logged through channels."

"Not every weapon hits the Bureau of Alcohol, Tobacco, Firearms, and Explosives' regional crime gun center," Tarlton agreed.

"But," Will said, "one of the things I've learned while working at the NCIS is that local PDs often have records of their own."

Tarlton maintained a level gaze. "Some do."

"I know you by reputation," Will said. "You do an honest job here."

"Flattery?" Tarlton smiled a little then.

"I didn't figure you were susceptible to something like that."

"I'm not."

"I'd like to know if the serial number of the pistol Bobby Lee Gant used last night is in your database."

For a short time, Tarlton just stared at Will. The hesitation, Will knew, wasn't anything meant personally. But the chief had some departmental pride to salvage.

"You and the FBI," Tarlton said, "came into my city without so much as a by-your-leave—"

"That's incorrect, sir," Remy interrupted. "Shel and I checked in the minute we were inside city limits. The commander insists on that. We let your office know about the pick-up order we had on Bobby Lee Gant. We played by the rules and kept the house respect."

"The FBI then," Tarlton said.

"Yes," Will agreed.

"And between the two of you, one of my citizens was killed."

"We didn't have control of that situation," Will said.

"I'm fully aware of that."

Will felt a little exasperated. He knew Tarlton was distancing himself from the situation on purpose. Straining relationships with the FBI wasn't a good thing to do. Maybe Tarlton didn't depend on them, but they obviously helped him out every now and again.

"You were a Marine," Remy said, nodding to the picture of Tarlton on the wall behind him.

"Yes, I was. I made my way up to captain; then I pulled the pin and took the position here. I grew up here. It was a good fit, and it came at a good time."

"Shel," Remy said, "my *friend* Shel, is a Marine too."

Tarlton sat silent.

"Most of the NCIS agents you hear about," Remy said, "are drafted out of civilian law enforcement agencies. Commander Coburn's team isn't. All of us are Navy except Shel. And we take a lot of pride in our Marine."

Tarlton looked at Remy and grinned. "Leave it to a sailor to lay it on so thick."

Remy smiled back. "I'm not a sailor. I'm a Navy SEAL."

"Oh, a poor man's Marine."

"But trained to take over when a Marine fails out."

Both of them laughed at that. Will was still trying to sort out all the posturing that had just gone on.

Tarlton turned to Will. "You said you had a serial number on that weapon. Let's have a look at it."

CRIME SCENE
NCIS
NAVAL CRIMINAL INVESTIGATIVE SERVICE

20

E SCENE ✪ NCIS ✪ CRIME SCENE

NAVAL CRIMINAL INVESTIGATIVE SERVICE

>> OTIS'S SALVAGE YARD
>> 5000 WILKINSON BOULEVARD
>> CHARLOTTE, NORTH CAROLINA
>> 1507 HOURS

"You've got to watch yourself while you're dealing with Gerald," Tarlton said as he put the police car's transmission in park. "He's what you might call a few sandwiches short of a picnic."

"I'll follow your lead," Will said.

"That'll probably make us all a lot happier." Tarlton got out, then reached back in for his baseball cap and pulled it on.

Will and Remy got out on the passenger side.

The salvage yard was large and gave the sense of a long history. A ten-foot-tall white fence with peeling paint and graffiti lined the yard. A hand-lettered sign made from a four-by-eight-foot slab of plywood hung on the fence and advertised "Otis's Salvege Yard."

"Hasn't anyone ever told him he misspelled *salvage*?" Remy asked.

"Sure." Tarlton stepped around to the rear of the police car and took out a pump shotgun. "I've told him myself. He says he misspelled it on purpose because people remember something that's wrong a lot longer than they remember something that's right." He closed the trunk. "For what it's worth, I think he's right. But I don't think that's why the sign's misspelled. Gerald's just not that bright."

Will nodded at the shotgun. "Is there anything we should know?"

"Don't stand in front of me when this thing goes off." Tarlton grinned. "This is probably a little overkill, but Gerald's got a couple uncles who ran their wife through a wood chipper almost forty years ago. They got out of prison year before last."

"'Their' wife?" Remy echoed.

"Yep. She married one of them. Then divorced him and married the other. She cheated on both of them. So one night they got drunk and decided they'd had enough. None of the Otises have got enough brightness between them to power a lightbulb, but they know how to scrap cars just fine."

Will reached under his jacket and released the safety catch on his shoulder holster.

"The shotgun's not really for Otis or his uncles," Tarlton said. "It's for the guard pigs."

"He has guard pigs?" Remy asked.

"Yeah. Arkansas razorbacks. When the uncles ran the salvage yard, they went hunting in Arkansas and brought back a half-dozen young pigs. Started raising them up to be guard pigs."

"Meaner than a junkyard pig?" Remy asked.

Tarlton smiled. "Sounds catchy, doesn't it?"

"It sounds insane is what it sounds. But I knew a guy down in New Orleans who kept a guard alligator in his gris-gris shop. It actually caught a burglar one night."

"Interesting. But if the Otis junkyard pigs ever caught anybody, there wouldn't be anything left of him come morning."

⊛ ⊛ ⊛

>> 1511 HOURS

Sobered by Tarlton's nonchalant explanation of one of the strangest things he'd ever heard of, Will trailed the police chief to the salvage yard's main building.

The building had evidently started life as a small home, probably a two- or three-bedroom. Then a few extra rooms had been added on. Somewhere in there, the salvage yard had been tacked onto it, and the fence ran in two directions. The house was covered with the same peeling white paint and graffiti as the fence.

Tall oak trees butted up against the house and the junkyard wall. Although houses were on either side of the salvage yard and a large street ran in front of it, the business looked like it should be located out in the middle of a rural wasteland.

Tarlton had gotten a hit on the gun's serial number almost immediately. He'd turned to his computer and worked from a short list of known gun dealers in the area. Keeping track of weapons was a problem in smaller towns, he'd pointed out, because people had a tendency to swap them out, sell them, and borrow them for years.

Gerald Otis had once owned the pistol Bobby Lee Gant had used yesterday on Shel. Tarlton had been forced to take it from the man during an altercation at the junkyard. A group of young drivers barely old enough to drive had been liberating parts to build a race car. Upon discovering them one night, Gerald had held them at gunpoint till Tarlton arrived. No other police officer would do.

During the heated moments that had transpired, Tarlton had taken the gun from Gerald. He'd later returned it, along with a polite explanation of why he'd taken it.

In the meantime, though, Tarlton had logged the weapon into his own private records system. He'd been doing that with the merchandise of every pawn shop and private dealer that he could. The list was nowhere near complete.

Tarlton walked to the front door and knocked loudly. Then he stood there and waited.

A frazzled woman in her fifties answered the knock. She peered at them owlishly from the other side of the screen door. Her hair was so white it shone like pale fire.

"Afternoon, Chief Tarlton," the woman said in a cigarette-roughened voice.

"Afternoon, Maisie. I came out here to see Gerald. It's official business."

"Who's your company?"

"Investigators from the Marine base at Camp Lejeune."

"Military men?"

"Yes, ma'am."

"Now you know Gerald don't like nothing to do with the government."

"I know. But they need his help."

Maisie frowned at that, as if trying to figure out why Tarlton would sell her such a big bill of goods.

Will waited patiently even though time was getting away from him.

"All right, you can go on back." Maisie slipped the lock open on the door and pulled it wide.

"Thank you, Maisie." Tarlton carried the shotgun across his chest with both hands as he entered.

Inside, the house smelled like motor oil and rust. An engine occupied a table in the center of the living room. A block-and-tackle assembly had been mounted on the roof.

The television in one corner of the room broadcasted a soap opera.

"Gerald's out back in the garage with Woody and Taylor," Maisie said. "You can see yourself out."

Tarlton tipped his hat and went through the room to the door that let out to the back.

As he looked around the smoke-stained room, Will remembered other people like these who'd been frozen in time and pretty much forgotten about.

"You just mind them guard pigs while you're out there," Maisie said. "Gerald's not feeding 'em like he should. They might get a little out of hand."

"Thank you," Tarlton said as he stepped out the rear door and onto shaky wooden steps.

Will and Remy followed.

❂ ❂ ❂

>> 1514 HOURS

Outside the house, the ground was barren in all directions. The earth was stained black where automotive oil and all kinds of other fluids had been dumped for years.

The salvage yard was primarily filled with automobiles. But there were also boats, motorcycles, and farm equipment. Two 1950s airplanes interested Will immediately.

Snuffling from under the house startled Will. He turned just as three lean shapes burst into view. The hogs stood almost up to Will's hips. Yellow tusks curled up from their lower jaws. They were an indiscriminate brown color, covered by sparse curling hair. Rings festooned the wiggling pink noses.

One of the hogs tried to put its snout against Tarlton's pocket. The police chief popped the animal in the nose with the butt of the shotgun.

Surprised and hurt, the hog let out a bleat of pain and ran away. The other two hogs backed off and snorted and grunted indignantly. Their ears flattened against their low-browed skulls.

"Chief Tarlton," a deep voice called. "That you?"

Looking forward, Will spotted a tall, rawboned man in an olive uniform shirt and blue uniform pants standing next to a ramshackle building. He was bald on top, but the hair around his head trailed down to his shoulders. He looked like he was in his forties.

"Gerald," Tarlton called back. "Need a few words with you if I can."

"Sure. Come on ahead."

⊛ ⊛ ⊛

>> 1517 HOURS

Gerald Otis stood at least six feet seven and was built broad enough that he made Shel look small. But his weight was from overeating and had gone to fat. He smelled like oil, gasoline, and bacon grease.

The shed was a study of contrasts. Barely standing, it housed a pristine 1969 Pontiac GTO that had been lovingly restored and seemed incongruous to its surroundings. The bright red paint seemed to glow with an inner fire.

"Man," Remy said as he examined the car, "that is some sweet ride."

"It is." Gerald Otis smiled broadly. "I've been taking my time putting it together." He shifted his attention to Tarlton. "What brings you out this way, Chief?"

"I'd like you to talk to someone if you would," Tarlton said. "This is Commander Will Coburn of the NCIS."

Otis's brow furrowed in confusion. "Don't know what that is."

"I'm a military cop," Will said. "I specialize in Navy and Marine crimes."

"I never been in no service. Don't see how I could help you."

"The chief tells me you sometimes deal in guns," Will said.

Gerald hesitated. He ran a big hand across the back of his neck. A guilty flush flamed his face. "I ain't supposed to do that, I know. Chief Tarlton done explained that to me."

"I'm not here to give you any trouble over that," Will explained. "I just need to know if you can identify a gun for me."

Gerald's face cleared as worry lifted from him. "Sure."

Will took a picture of the pistol Bobby Lee had used from his shirt pocket and showed it to the big man. "Have you seen this gun before?"

"Sure. I sold it."

"If someone asked you to identify it, how would you do that?"

"Serial number. Each one of 'em's different."

"Did you write down the serial number of this pistol?"

"Nope." Gerald frowned again. "That's one of the problems I got into with the chief. I didn't write enough stuff down."

Will looked at Tarlton. The police chief had a twinkle of merriment in his eyes.

"Ask him to identify the pistol for you," Tarlton suggested.

Will did.

And Gerald rattled off a string of numbers and letters.

"That's the serial number," Gerald said when he'd finished.

From the picture, Will couldn't tell. He took out his iPAQ and brought up his notes on the pistol. Then he asked the man to recite the numbers back again. The numbers and letters matched perfectly.

"Gerald has a gift for numbers," Tarlton explained. "Once he sees them, they're his. Always."

Will was quietly amazed.

"The few times the DA has had to put him on the stage to hammer someone else for trying to sell Gerald something, he's run numbers forward, backward, and sideways," Tarlton said. "You could come back a year from now, and he'd still know the serial number without ever seeing it in the meantime."

Will knew Tarlton was letting him know that acquiring unimpeachable testimony was entirely possible. He concentrated on smoothing out the testimony he'd need.

"Did you sell this pistol to Bobby Lee Gant?" Will asked.

"No. I sold it to another biker. That big guy that always hangs around with Victor Gant. Victor is Bobby Lee's father."

"You sold the pistol to that man?"

"Yeah. Fat Mike. That's what he goes by."

"If I needed you to testify to that in court, would you be able to do it?"

Gerald looked troubled. "Would it be like the other times the chief has had me do it?"

Will looked to Tarlton for guidance.

Tarlton nodded.

"Yes," Will replied.

"Then I can do it."

21

E SCENE ✪ NCIS ✪ CRIME SCENE
NAVAL CRIMINAL INVESTIGATIVE SERVICE

>> THE BLOODY SKULL
>> CHARLOTTE, NORTH CAROLINA
>> 2156 HOURS

The bar was more a clubhouse for the Purple Royals than a business enterprise. The bikers came there when they were in town, and they circled the wagons there when they were under attack from the outside world.

Victor Gant sat in the back office and gazed at the security monitors mounted on the wall in front of him. Although no sheet of paper showed it, he owned the bar. The business and the employees were wholly subsidized by the Purple Royals.

The people he'd hired to run the place didn't exactly have it made. But they could at least live well enough. All they had to do was be available for the nights the gang was in town.

And the gang was definitely in town. Word had gotten out—over the phone, by word of mouth, and through the TV—that Victor's son was dead, shot by a federal agent. Now the place was packed.

Heavy metal crashed through the surround sound system. The dancers worked the crowd, more enthusiastic than they'd been in months because the money was flowing like water. Victor thought the bikers were acting like children; certainly they were creating a mess in the bar.

He tried not to let the men's pursuit of a good time bother him. But it did. He couldn't isolate himself that well. He felt Bobby Lee's absence in a way he never would have thought possible before.

He reached for the longneck bottle on the desk and took a sip. The beer was warm and flat. He didn't know how long it had been sitting there. Too long.

His eyes roved the security monitors, searching for anything to distract him. Some of the women were attractive, not the used-up specimens the bar usually held. A lot of those women were on their last legs, coked up and decaying from the inside.

Today, not even the new ones held his attention.

You're bordering on dinky-dao, brother, he told himself. *Totally whack. You need to pull yourself together.*

But it was hard. He kept seeing Bobby Lee in his mind. The young man had been all the immediate family Victor knew he was ever going to have. And that family had been wiped out in a heartbeat.

Reluctantly Victor dropped his feet off the scarred wooden desk and threw the flat beer into the nearly filled trash can. The glass bottle shattered and tinkled down among the others.

His leathers creaked as he walked out of the room and onto the main floor. Bikers stepped aside in front of him like the Red Sea parting for Moses.

He paused at the bar and called Creeper's name. Creeper wasn't the man's real name, of course, but so many people knew him by Creeper that likely only the law enforcement agencies would know what his given name was now.

Creeper was young and hard. He hadn't pulled Nam with Victor and Fat Mike and the others, but he'd made his bones in the first Gulf War. The vets got together and argued over who'd had the worst war, those who'd slogged through the jungles or those who'd slogged the desert.

They even each had their own conspiracy theories. The Nam vets pointed to Agent Orange as being responsible for so many cancer-related deaths. The first Gulf War vets had the mysterious "malaise" that had descended on them and might have been part of a biological weapon Saddam Hussein had been bankrolling.

Creeper turned and looked at Victor.

"Hey, boss man," Creeper said. "What'll you have?"

"Beer."

"Coming up." Creeper squatted and reached into the cooler beneath the counter. He brought up a fresh longneck, peeled the lid with the church key, and slid the bottle down to Victor's waiting hand.

Victor took a long draw. "You seen Fat Mike?"

"Not yet."

"Soon as he gets here, send him in to me."

Creeper shot him a thumbs-up.

Victor made his way back to the office, a pit of roiling rage in his chest. He sat at the desk once more and used the remote control to flick through the television stations.

The need to do something vibrated through him. His hand actually shook as he brought the longneck to his lips. That hadn't happened even when they were back in the bush taking heavy fire.

News footage of the standoff at the tattoo parlor started to roll on-screen. Victor muted the anchor's commentary and just stayed with the images.

There behind the glass, he saw Bobby Lee standing with his hostage. He knew how scared his son had been. He looked so young; this was the first time he'd gotten into a situation that was so far over his head.

In another minute, Bobby Lee would be dead—again.

Victor sipped his beer, but he couldn't turn away from the impending violence.

His cell phone rang.

Victor thought about not answering the call. But he was looking for a distraction of any kind.

He flipped the phone open and said, "Yeah?"

⊛ ⊛ ⊛

>> 2203 HOURS

"Ah, my friend, it is good to hear your voice."

"It's good to hear yours." *But you're a little late calling in condolences.* Victor drank some more beer. Tran was his partner in the heroin business. No one knew that. They'd been very careful to set the business up that way. Rather, Tran had been careful to set things up like that.

They'd met in Vietnam. Tran had been a Kit Carson scout, one of the regulars who'd defected from the North Vietnamese army to lead recon missions for the American troops.

That had been back when both sides had figured the Americans were going to win the war.

A Kit Carson's life expectancy hadn't been high. If he was caught by his old army buddies, they tortured him as long as they could before they killed him. And his new army buddies weren't the most trusting. A number of Kit Carsons had gone down under "friendly" fire that was anything but. The Department of Defense had a name for such things too. *Misadventure* sounded equally innocuous.

Tran, though, had seemed to flourish as a traitor to his people. When the tide of the war had changed, Tran had changed with it by going back to the NVA and claiming to have been a prisoner.

However, the friendship he'd had with Victor Gant had included a lucrative black market trade that involved drugs and women. During the thirty-plus years between, they'd found a way to do business. The latest thing with the heroin was by far the most lucrative.

"I just found out the bad news and wanted to call and see how you were doing," Tran said.

"I'm fine."

"You sound a little rocky."

"I said I'm fine. Drop it."

Tran didn't acknowledge that one way or the other.

Victor sipped beer. Both of them were careful not to mention the other's name.

Tran was based in Vietnam, where he oversaw the poppy growing and the production of raw opium. Back when he'd first gotten everything together, he had contacted Victor and explained how he'd gone into the drug business in a big way. It had taken them almost two years to work out the ocean transport through a shipper based in Singapore.

"I was told there'd been a problem," Tran said.

Victor knew the man meant he'd heard about the arrest. "It's taken care of. I negotiated my way out of it."

"How?"

Victor grinned a little. After all these years, Tran didn't completely trust him when the pressure started to mount. But that was okay. He didn't completely trust Tran either.

But it made Victor wonder who among his group was selling him out to Tran.

"I'm going to give them something," Victor said, answering Tran's question. "Our southern competition."

"Do you think that's wise?"

"Are you questioning my decision?"

Tran didn't respond right away. "What happened?"

"A business negotiation with one of their men went south. His people were taking more of an interest than I thought, and they chose to make everything personal."

"Couldn't you have negated that?"

"The guy I had to deal with wasn't local. He was based in Virginia. The domestic arm." Meaning the FBI in Quantico, Virginia, and not the CIA at Langley, Virginia.

"I'm sure you did what was best."

"I did. In fact, I streamlined the pitch I was giving the associate of the Virginia team."

"And they went for it?"

"I didn't give them a choice."

"I see."

Victor drained the beer bottle and dropped it into the wastepaper basket. It shattered with a brittle pop.

"I didn't have a choice, either," Victor went on, his voice tightening till it was edged steel. "The business I'm taking care of at this end isn't easy. Sometimes deals have to be cut to preserve what we've got going on."

"I realize that. But you have them off of you?"

"Till next time. Unfortunately the reality is that this business of ours is established. People are going to talk. Customers as well as rivals. When that happens, we'll have to stand prepared to take care of it."

"What about this man? The one who cost you so much?"

"I'm going to cost him."

Tran was silent for a moment. "I could take care of him for you."

Victor took a moment to think about that. The offer came with subtext, but he wasn't sure exactly what it was. For Tran to offer to reach across the Pacific Ocean to whack the Marine meant that he'd come into more muscle than he'd had before.

The offer also served to put Victor on notice that he wasn't as insulated as he had been.

"No need," Victor said. "I'm going to take care of this. I'm going to take the time I need to do it right."

"I know you see this as a personal challenge," Tran said. "But you can't allow any harm to come to what we've got going on. We've worked too long and too hard to get what we have."

"You just worry about your end. I'm going to take care of things here. You'll see."

"It would be better for you—and for what we're doing—if you put this behind you."

Victor couldn't believe the suggestion had been made. "Put the murder of my son behind me?" His voice was cold and hard.

Tran hesitated for only a moment, then—showing that their relationship *had* changed over the years—said, "It wasn't murder. I saw the news footage. He killed a man and tried to kill that Marine. I'm sorry for your loss, my friend, but he'd been given every chance to come out of that encounter alive."

"He was my flesh and blood," Victor snarled. "My family."

"I know."

"Do you?" Victor tried to control the anger that threatened to break loose inside him. "Do you remember what happened when your family was killed?"

Tran's voice was soft, but a hard edge rang in his words. "I do."

"Me and you," Victor said, "we found out who the soldiers were that killed your family. And they were American soldiers."

It had been one of those incidents that didn't come out of Vietnam until years later. The military and the media had worked together for a time to shut down all the atrocities that young American soldiers committed while they were overseas.

Everybody back home was so interested in the John Wayne image of the American soldiers, they didn't think of what it had really been like to be there. There wasn't a day most of those young men hadn't been afraid. Never a day passed that sudden, harsh death hadn't dogged their footsteps through that hellish jungle.

As a result of that fear, the quickness that death could reach out, and the merciless nature of the enemy they'd faced, a lot of soldiers had gone feral and become pitiless killers who saw only enemies in everyone outside their own group.

Chaplains and officers had tried to keep those young soldiers from becoming barbarians. Their efforts had broken down and failed on several occasions. Sometimes those chaplains and green second lieutenants got fragged by the very men they were trying to save.

"We buried your family, me and you," Victor said. "We dug those graves with our hands and laid your family to rest. Then we found out who those men were . . . and we killed every last one of them."

That had been a bloody business. They'd hunted the men down and ambushed them in the jungle. Some of them had gotten loose. It had taken four days to find the last one. Under Tran's cruel skills, it had taken the man two days to die.

For just a moment, the smell of burned flesh filled Victor's nostrils at the memory. He didn't remember any good times from his tours in Nam. But he just hadn't been able to escape the jungle till Uncle Sam had finally called him home. Even then, the jungle still lived inside him today. It was only a heartbeat away.

"I remember," Tran said.

"You'd better remember."

"But in the end, killing those men didn't bring my family back."

"I know that. But the idea of the man who killed Bobby Lee walking around breathing the same air that I do offends me."

"Vengeance is for the young," Tran said quietly. "We are older now.

We know the things that matter. This business we're doing matters. You've got a good life. You shouldn't be thinking about throwing it away. I'm asking you, as your friend, to let this be."

Irritation filled Victor. In the beginning, Tran had been the low man on the totem pole regarding the operation. He hadn't had any contacts. Victor had provided everything.

Now that he had control over the product and thought he could easily pick up another distributor in the United States, Tran wasn't quite as closemouthed about how the operation was conducted as he had been.

The thing was, Tran also knew what Victor was about. If Tran tried to freeze Victor out, Victor would go over to Vietnam and finish a final piece of the war.

"I can't," Victor said.

Tran sighed. "I was afraid that would be your answer."

"Was there anything else?" Victor asked.

"No."

"Then I've got a few things to do around here."

"Of course. I just wanted to express my condolences and to check on you."

"You just take care of your end of things."

"If you need anything, you'll call?"

"Of course," Victor replied.

"Get some rest. You sound exhausted."

Victor broke the connection and tossed the phone onto the desk. Then his eyes roved over the security monitors showing the street outside.

He zoomed in on the undercover police car parked in the alley across the street. Every time the Purple Royals gathered, Police Chief Tarlton put people there. It would have been comical if Victor had been thinking about the cops and not about getting revenge.

CRIME SCENE

22

SCENE ✪ NCIS ✪ CRIME SCENE

NAVAL CRIMINAL INVESTIGATIVE SERVICE

>> INTENSIVE CARE UNIT
>> PRESBYTERIAN HOSPITAL
>> CHARLOTTE, NORTH CAROLINA
>> 2308 HOURS

Even with the pain medication coursing through his system, Shel knew someone was in the room with him. Fear bumped against his mind as he struggled to lift his eyes.

"Hey, Shel."

Shel recognized the voice before he was able to focus. "Don."

"I'm here." Don's hand settled on his uninjured shoulder and squeezed. "Are you all right?"

"Yeah." Shel tried to nod, but the effort seemed to loosen his head, and he was afraid it would float away. "What are you doing here?"

"I came to see you."

"Waste of time," Shel said. "I'm going to be fine."

"That's what Commander Coburn told me. But I've been saving up for a vacation. Thought I'd get out of town for a bit. See how the other half lives."

Shel grinned. "I appreciate it. You doing okay?"

"A little tired. We got word late last night. I caught the first flight out this morning. I've been in airport terminals or on planes all day. Nobody flies straight through anymore, it seems."

Shel rolled his head around and tried not to be obvious about it. Although he couldn't imagine his daddy leaving the ranch, there was that possibility.

Don grimaced. "Daddy's not here."

"I didn't think he was," Shel lied. It was funny how much it bothered him that his father hadn't come. He was a man, full-grown, blooded in a couple of wars. *How old do you have to be before you stop looking for your daddy when you get hurt?* He didn't know. "I was looking for Max."

"Max is fine. He's sacked out in the waiting room with some woman named Maggie."

"You got to meet Maggie?"

"I did."

"Maggie's good people, Don. You'd like her." Shel hated the fact that pain meds also sometimes gave him a bad case of motormouth.

"She seems like she is."

"She should be in a hotel, not here. When you go back out there, tell her to go on and that I'll be fine."

"I told her I was going to stay the night with you. She pointed out that there was no one Max could stay with."

"She could take him with her. He'll go."

"They tried taking him earlier. He'll go outside for a little while to answer the call of nature, but he won't get in any vehicles. He just sits at the hospital door waiting to get in."

"That dog's a Marine's Marine," Shel said.

Don grinned. "I'd say there is a resemblance."

"Have you met Will?"

"Just over the phone. I'd hoped to meet him. It seems he and another agent—"

"Remy."

"That's the one. They're out working on something."

Shel tried to think about that, but it was hard getting his thoughts to stay connected long enough to make sense of them. "Bobby Lee Gant was the only business we had here."

"I don't know."

"Maggie would know what's going on."

"You can ask her in the morning. Both of you need to get some sleep."

"I can't sleep. How's the family doing?"

Shel tried to listen as Don told him about soccer games and birthdays. It made him sad to think he'd missed all those things, but he knew it was the pain meds. They tended to depress him too.

Somewhere in there, though, he hung on to Don's voice and felt more at home than he had in a long time. And he slept.

❂ ❂ ❂

>> THE BLOODY SKULL
>> CHARLOTTE, NORTH CAROLINA
>> 0119 HOURS

Fat Mike knocked at the office door.

When Victor looked up, he saw his second standing there with a sheaf of papers rolled up in one big fist.

"Where have you been?" Victor demanded.

Fat Mike entered the room and dropped into a chair in front of the desk. The chair squeaked in protest. He took a pull on his longneck.

"I been out doing what I always do," Fat Mike said. "Keeping your six clear."

"You didn't tell me you were going to leave."

"You were on the verge of pulling a mean drunk. You still are. Nobody wants to be around you when you do that. Me included."

Fat Mike, Victor reflected, was probably the only person in the world who could talk to him like that. The only reason Victor allowed it was because Fat Mike was being truthful, not disrespectful. There was a difference.

"I'm not drunk," Victor said.

"No, and I'm surprised. If I was you, I think I would be. Or maybe seriously messed up about now."

Victor nodded at the sheaf of papers. "When did you take up reading?"

"A long time ago. I'd do it more often but my lips go numb after a while." Fat Mike leaned forward and spread the pages on the desk.

Victor was in a mean mood and knew it. He glanced at the pages and saw that there were photos in the midst of the blocks of type. "At least it has pictures."

"Yeah," Fat Mike said, taking no offense. "Did you get a good look at them pictures?"

Intrigued, Victor slid the pages over to his side of the desk and studied them. He recognized Shelton McHenry's photo at once. The man was in Marine dress at some military function.

There were a lot of other pictures. Evidently the Marine's career had been extensive. His work at the NCIS had gotten him mentioned on several occasions.

"So this is our jarhead," Victor said.

"Yeah." Fat Mike took a pull on his beer. "He's still military-issue. Assigned to an NCIS team in Camp Lejeune. I've got more information coming on the rest of the team."

"Where'd you get the info?"

"From Beetle. Computers are his thing."

Beetle was a computer whiz. He was also a hanger-on of the Purple Royals. He was a paraplegic, the victim of a motorcycle-van collision when he'd stolen a sled at fifteen. He still rode on a specially converted three-wheeler, but these days he did most of his cruising on the cyber highways.

"Beetle was glad to do this research," Fat Mike said. "But I think it would mean a lot to him if you'd give him a kind word."

"I will." There was more information on Shelton McHenry in the printout pages than had been on the television all day. "Did you pay him?"

Fat Mike grinned. "Yeah. Gave him enough cash and drugs to keep him smothered in the vice of his choice for months."

Victor nodded. "When he gets information on McHenry's friends, pay him again."

"Happy to. Beetle'll probably be happy too."

"Somebody thinks this jarhead is some kind of hero," Victor grated.

"Guy's been around," Fat Mike said. "Pulled Iraq. A lot of special-ops assignments. He's looked death in the face."

Victor studied the Marine's classic handsome face. "Pretty boy."

"That he is."

The dark, violent anger writhed inside Victor. He felt it moving, and he embraced it. When he had that, he could do anything.

Victor read through the bio on the man again. "McHenry. Where do I know that name?"

Fat Mike grinned. "Now that was the part I was waiting for you to remember."

Victor put the papers down and looked back through all those years. "That skinny farm boy we ran into in Qui Nhon was named McHenry."

"Yeah, he was." Fat Mike rifled through the pages till he found the one he was looking for. He pushed it across to Victor. "Turns out maybe we should have killed him that night too."

"We needed him to get us through the checkpoints." Victor remembered that night like it had been yesterday. They'd sweltered in the truck as the kid, McHenry, drove along Highway 19 out of the coastal city. "If he hadn't been along, we wouldn't have gotten out of the city."

"I know. And without him, we wouldn't have gotten one of those guys that killed Tran's family." Fat Mike took in a breath and let it out. "Once we dumped that body off, I wanted to kill him. But you didn't."

"We needed him to get back into Qui Nhon."

"We coulda walked back in," Fat Mike said. "We did it plenty of times before." He tapped the paper. "You read that report, you'll see Shelton McHenry's father is Tyrel McHenry."

Victor couldn't believe it. "That guy was the same grunt we jobbed in Qui Nhon?"

"Yeah. Ain't that a kick in the head? Just proves how small this world is. If we'd killed Tyrel McHenry back then, he wouldn't have had a boy that grew up to kill Bobby Lee."

CRIME SCENE
NCIS
NAVAL CRIMINAL INVESTIGATIVE SERVICE

23

E SCENE ✪ NCIS ✪ CRIME SCENE
NAVAL CRIMINAL INVESTIGATIVE SERVICE

>> RAFTER M RANCH
>> OUTSIDE FORT DAVIS, TEXAS
>> 2441 HOURS (CENTRAL TIME ZONE)

The mare delivered her foal without any trouble, but Tyrel McHenry stood watch all night just in case. Since he'd laid the foundations of the ranch house, there hadn't been a horse born on his ranch whose birth he hadn't attended.

The same could be said, more or less, of the cows. When the calving season began in the winter and extended into the spring, it made for long days and long nights. Tyrel stayed horseback for days on end, making cold camps and watching over his flock. From time to time, he had to help out with the birthing. Sleeping on the ground when it was still holding on to winter temperatures had gotten harder over the years, but when the day came that he couldn't do it anymore, he figured they could just cover him on over.

Sitting there on a bale of hay and watching the mare nudge her new baby to its feet, Tyrel reflected that maybe he wouldn't have too many more years to watch miracles like the birth of a new animal. He was getting older. He could see it in the wrinkles on his face and the slackness and weathered cracks of his skin.

Growing old bothered him. He disliked the idea of infirmity. He'd seen people—some of them younger than him—who just couldn't seem to take care of themselves anymore. If he ever reached that time in his life, he figured it would be better to just cash in his chips and get up from the table.

But it doesn't really happen like that, does it? he told himself. *You just keep right on drawing cards, even if you got a losing hand, because you just can't stop yourself.*

Death itself didn't bother him. A good part of him had died in Qui Nhon all those years ago.

Grimly Tyrel turned his thoughts from that time. He'd promised himself that night while looking down on the dead man's face that he wouldn't think of what had happened ever again.

He had been unsuccessful. Even when he didn't think of that terrible event, the weight of it rode him around like a determined bull rider. No matter what he did to shake that weight—drinking and fighting and just pure cussedness—it would never go away.

The only person who had ever been able to remove the old fear and gentle him down had been his wife. He missed her. Every minute of every day. There wasn't a thing about the ranch that didn't remind him of her. And he was trapped by everything that had happened in his life.

It would have been better for her if they'd never met. Or if he hadn't fallen in love with her despite the fact that he knew better. But he hadn't been able to help himself, no matter how much he felt that he hadn't deserved her love.

If she hadn't loved him back, he could have walked away from everything. Vanishing into the back roads would have been better than trying to pretend he was a normal person.

Because he hadn't been normal since that night in Qui Nhon.

His wife had paid the price; he couldn't talk to her about anything that had happened in the war. His sons had paid the price as well.

And now you got grandbabies paying that same price, you inconsiderate old fool.

Although he'd never admit it, Don's words on Father's Day had hurt him in ways he didn't know he could still be hurt. When he'd put his wife into the cold, hard ground, he'd thought it would be the end of those feelings.

Life was like that, though. He'd never truly been able to figure out what it was he was supposed to do.

Or why.

Mostly it was the *why* of things that got to him and made everything difficult.

He reached for the insulated cup of coffee he'd brought out with him and took a sip. The coffee was cool now because he'd been out in the barn so long, but it was still strong. He liked his coffee strong. He made it the way his daddy had. Strong enough to put hair on a rock.

His daddy had been a tanker in World War II. That had been the last of the simple wars, where everything was black-and-white, and a man could fight for what he believed in and know that he was right for doing it. The same couldn't have been said about Vietnam.

Tyrel sat there and thought thoughts he'd promised himself he'd never think again, and he didn't know why he was thinking them. Nothing good could come of this.

Maybe, he mused, he was putting himself through his own particular hell again because he'd stayed at the ranch instead of going with Don to check on Shelton.

What kind of daddy wouldn't go to the hospital to see his nearly shot-to-death son?

Your kind, that hard voice said in the back of his mind. *The kind that's scared of what's lying out there for him.*

But that wasn't all of it, he knew. He didn't go because he didn't want Don or Shel—or the grandbabies—to think on him too hard. He couldn't be there for them. He couldn't ever be there for anybody.

He'd known that since Qui Nhon.

⊛ ⊛ ⊛

>> 0112 HOURS

Satisfied that the mare and her new colt were going to be fine, Tyrel got up from the hay bale. His knees cracked in protest.

When he was standing, he walked over to where Ramon Sanchez lay. Ramon was fourteen years old, the oldest grandson of Miguel. He was a handsome boy and looked a lot like his granddaddy.

"Hey," Tyrel said gruffly. He kicked Ramon's boots hard enough to wake the boy.

Ramon came awake instantly and looked apologetic. "Sorry," he said in Spanish. He rubbed his eyes. "I must have fallen asleep."

"You were snoring so loud I thought you were gonna spook the horses," Tyrel said. He spoke in Spanish, but his was awkward even after all these years. Shel was the one who had taken to the language like a native.

Embarrassment flushed Ramon's face. "My grandfather is going to be upset with me. He told me to watch over you—I mean, the horses."

"Well then," Tyrel said, "I guess we ain't gonna tell your granddaddy. Get up and let's get you to bed. We got an early morning coming if we're gonna get everything done." He reached down and pulled the boy to his feet.

"The mare? How is she?" Ramon glanced at the pen.

"She's fine. Baby's fine too. It was an easy birth."

"Good." Ramon sounded relieved. Then he focused on Tyrel. "You can deduct tonight from my pay."

"Ain't gonna do that," Tyrel said. "The agreement was that you'd be here if I needed you, not that you'd stay awake the whole time. The way I look at it, you held up your end of things."

"Thank you."

"Now let's get you on to bed."

⊛ ⊛ ⊛

>> 0127 HOURS

Despite his fatigue and the long day he'd put in, Tyrel couldn't sleep. That wasn't unusual. He hadn't slept all that much when he was a young man, and he'd always been told that old people needed even less sleep.

In front of the television, Tyrel reached for the remote control and switched on ESPN.

For the most part, the ranch operated the way it had when he'd grown up. He still worked the cattle on a horse, and both his sons had learned to ride.

Shel had been the one to bring a motorcycle home one summer, and he'd used it for a while. Until it had broken down on him and left him with a five-mile walk home. Tyrel had taken great satisfaction—maybe a little too great, looking back on it now—pointing out that a horse didn't break down.

For a time, Shel had nurtured his love for motorcycles anyway. The boy was stubborn, but Tyrel had to admit that Shel hadn't gotten that from his mama. He'd been cursed with that by his daddy.

The only concession Tyrel had really made to the twenty-first century was the satellite television receiver. He'd done that mostly for Don's kids, but Tyrel had learned to love the fact that ESPN had sports programming on around the clock.

He checked a few box scores, but none of them really interested him. He hadn't had a vested interest in a baseball team since Hank Aaron had stepped out of the box and Nolan Ryan had come off the hill.

Those were men in Tyrel's book. They weren't necessarily supermen or even men who always did the right thing or always succeeded. They were just quiet men who stepped in and got the job done.

That was the kind of man he'd always wanted to be.

That was the kind of man, he realized, that both his sons had become.

The old sadness filled Tyrel then. It had a bittersweet ache that plumbed the very depths of his soul. He closed his eyes and was back there in Qui Nhon staring at the dead soldier's eyes.

Tyrel hadn't meant to kill him.

It had just happened.

CRIME SCENE
NCIS
NAVAL CRIMINAL INVESTIGATIVE SERVICE

24

E SCENE ✪ NCIS ✪ CRIME SCENE

NAVAL CRIMINAL INVESTIGATIVE SERVICE

>> NCIS OFFICES
>> CAMP LEJEUNE, NORTH CAROLINA
>> 0258 HOURS

"Estrella?"

The voice, quiet and unexpected, startled United States Navy Petty Officer Third Class Estrella Montoya. She turned from her computer and looked at the forensics tech Will had called in to handle the couriered drug sample he'd sent from Charlotte.

"Yes?" Estrella said, then cleared her throat. She hadn't spoken in hours. The last time she'd had conversation with anyone, it was to tell her son, Nicky, a bedtime story. He was currently staying with Nita, Joe, and Celia for the night since Estrella had to run files.

Actually, she didn't have to. Will had cleared her for the evening. But Estrella had worked with Will long enough to know that he wasn't going to stop trying to figure out a way to get Victor Gant away from Shel.

After she'd heard the story of how the motorcycle gang leader had walked out of FBI custody and accosted Will in the hospital parking lot, Estrella had known she wasn't going to rest until she found Will the leverage he was looking for.

She thought she had that now. If forensics had come up with the physical tie they needed to the unsolved case she'd found, they were golden.

The forensics guy was a human scarecrow. Philip Carmichael was tall and lean, with a lantern jaw and razor-cut blond hair that sprouted from his head like a weed. His ill-fitting white lab coat hung on him. Despite the soft drinks and candy he habitually ate, nothing seemed to find a home on his too-thin frame.

"I got the spectroscopy results from that sample Will sent." Philip pushed them in her direction.

Estrella leaned back in her ergonomic chair as she took the pages. Her Latino heritage marked her with bronze hair and an olive complexion. She had brown eyes and a full figure that belied the strength and endurance she had.

A quick scan of the printouts confirmed what she'd hoped for.

"The two samples are a match," she said.

"Definitely." Philip leaned back against the desk behind him. He fished an energy drink from the pocket of his lab coat.

"Have you got electronic copies of these printouts?"

"I've already e-mailed them to you. I wanted to stretch my legs, so I thought I would bring you the paper copy."

"I appreciate the extra effort. I know Will does too."

"Hey," Philip said, "I love being here. This job is so much cooler than the video store I worked at till I got my science degree. I just appreciate Commander Coburn taking a chance on me."

"Will's a good judge of character. You brought your good luck on yourself."

Philip smiled.

Estrella logged on to her e-mail, brought up the messages Philip had sent her, added the files she'd been working on, and started sending.

If this didn't give Will the leverage he needed, Estrella didn't know what would.

✪ ✪ ✪

>> DENNY'S RESTAURANT
>> 4541 SUNSET ROAD
>> CHARLOTTE, NORTH CAROLINA
>> 0311 HOURS

"Having Gerald willing to testify that he sold that pistol to Victor Gant isn't going to give us anything," Tarlton said.

Will nodded. They all knew that, but someone had to say it. They sat at one of the restaurant's back booths. None of them was operating at prime. Tarlton looked burned, and Will knew he and Remy were operating on even less sleep than the police chief.

"There's nothing in any of these files we can hope to use against Victor Gant." Tarlton waved at the copious piles of paper he'd dug out of the police department records. They sat in cardboard boxes in the booth beside him.

"If there'd been anything there," Will said, "you'd have taken him down before now. We were just hoping to find something that you hadn't."

"Last best shot," Tarlton agreed. "The only thing I could possibly get Gant for is carrying concealed. With his prison record, I could get an arrest warrant for that."

"But you weren't there when the FBI took him into custody," Will said.

"No. I could get some witnesses from the bar who saw them take weapons off Gant, but then I'm sure I could get other witnesses who say that only Fat Mike Wiley had a weapon."

"Gant's also got a deal in place with the FBI," Will said. "They're going to protect him as much as they can."

"Kind of makes you wonder whose team they're on."

"Theirs," Remy said. "First, last, and always. That's how they operate when they got their own fish to clean. Then when they're helping you clean yours, they just want to hang back and tell you how to get it done."

"Why, Special Agent Gautreau, I suspicion that's a cynical attitude you have." Tarlton smiled.

"This guy Urlacher is a political climber," Remy said. "You find his type everywhere. Gant's moving enough heroin through the area that finding his source is going to be a big deal."

"You can't blame a guy for having ambition," Tarlton grinned. "I say that with all the false sincerity I can muster."

"We can still shadow Gant for a few days," Remy said. "Keep him in a full-court press till Shel gets out of here and we can take him home." He cut his gaze to Will. "Unless Director Larkin says different."

"He won't," Will said. "At least not yet." Larkin knew how badly Frank Billings's death had affected all of them. "But the time will come." Will looked at the notes he'd scribbled on his iPAQ and didn't see anything there that looked the least bit promising. "My problem is that I don't feel good leaving this for Chief Tarlton now that we stirred up the hornet's nest."

"I appreciate the sentiment," Tarlton said, "but I've been making my way around here for a long time before you guys showed up. I expect I'll be doing the same after you leave."

"I know." Will sighed. "I just like cleaning up any messes I've made before I pull up stakes."

"You didn't make this one. Victor Gant has been here for a while."

The waitress came by and took away the last remnants of their dinner. When she left the check, Will reached for it.

"Nope." Tarlton picked up the check. "Your money's no good here. My town, my treat."

"It seems like the least we could do after keeping you up half the night," Will said.

"You offered me a shot at taking Victor Gant off the streets, and you had enough clout to make the FBI dry up and blow away if it came to that," Tarlton said as he dropped a credit card over the check. "And who knows? Maybe I'll need some help farther down the line."

Will's iPAQ vibrated for attention. He glanced at the screen and saw Estrella's icon float to the top. He tapped the icon and held the iPAQ to his ear.

"Estrella? You should have been home hours ago."

"Nita and Joe are keeping Nicky tonight," Estrella said. "Nicky told me that was okay and that he didn't miss me."

Even though she tried to disguise it, Will heard the slight pain in Estrella's voice. She took motherhood seriously.

"Take tomorrow off," Will suggested. "Catch a movie."

"I can't. Too much work has piled up here. Everything will be fine. One of the reasons Nicky's so excited about staying with Nita and Joe is because Joe has promised to take him and Celia sailing in the morning."

"I'd be excited too." Will sailed with his own kids every chance he got. Since he'd gotten divorced, it seemed there were more opportunities to take Wren and Steven out on the boat.

"I can make you more excited," Estrella offered.

"Okay."

"Philip finished the analysis of the heroin you couriered to us. We've got a match. If you want to bring your computer up, I'll walk you through it."

Will reached into the messenger bag he used to carry his computer. Remy and Tarlton leaned in closer.

"Something?" Tarlton asked.

Will nodded. He opened the computer and powered it on, then waited for it to connect to the mini satellite that provided the encrypted Internet connection to the NCIS transmissions.

The Web page Estrella had set up for her presentation appeared on the screen. Will put the phone on speaker. No one in the restaurant was close enough to overhear.

"Let me walk you through the time line as I've constructed it," Estrella said. "Thirty-one hours ago, Bobby Lee Gant used his pistol to murder one man and threaten Shel and a young woman."

Will rubbed his eyes tiredly. It was hard to believe so little time had passed. But the first forty-eight hours of any investigation were always the most important. If something didn't break during that time, things generally went badly.

"Nine months ago, Fat Mike Wiley bought the pistol from Gerald Otis," Estrella continued. "So somewhere in there, the pistol went from Fat Mike's hands to Bobby Lee's."

Will studied the time line and saw those two incidents marked.

"Four months ago, a man named Walter Simpson went missing," Estrella said.

"I worked that case with the sheriff," Tarlton said. "Simpson lived in Charlotte, but everybody knew he was a meth cook. The sheriff and I suspected he worked for Victor Gant."

"As a matter of fact," Estrella said, cycling the Web presentation forward so that another page opened up on the computer monitor, "I did some digging. Five men who've been tentatively identified as Purple Royals were busted in Mecklenburg County, Robeson County, and Guilford County. At the time of their arrests, all of them had meth on them that came from the same batch."

"You said *tentatively*," Tarlton said.

"I think a little digging could improve the standing on that point," Estrella acknowledged. "The important thing is that these men were carrying meth that could be tied to Simpson."

"How was it tied?" Remy asked. "Recipe or product?"

Will knew that meth cooks almost always created the drug the same way every time and that the individual products tended to be unique enough to identify. Further chemical breakdowns could verify that beyond doubt. Recipes were filed with law enforcement departments, and drug samples were kept in federal clearinghouses.

"Both," Estrella answered.

"That indicates there was a tie between Victor Gant and Simpson," Will said, "but how does that help us?"

"Because a month ago hunters found Simpson's body, and it had a bullet from Bobby Lee's gun in it."

And that, Will knew, was the beginning of something they could work with.

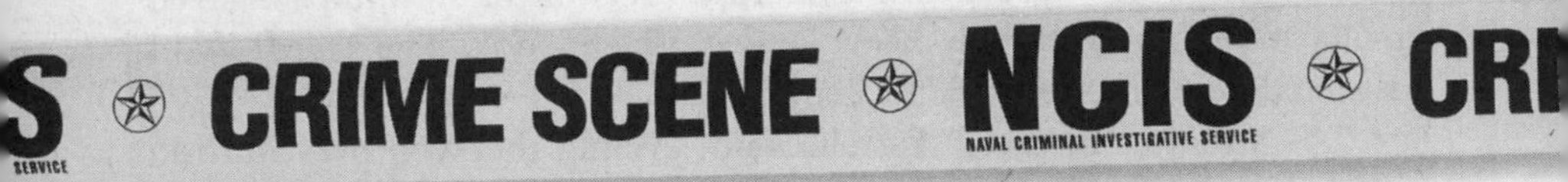
S
SERVICE
CRIME SCENE
NCIS
NAVAL CRIMINAL INVESTIGATIVE SERVICE
CRI

25

E SCENE ✪ NCIS ✪ CRIME SCENE

NAVAL CRIMINAL INVESTIGATIVE SERVICE

>> RAFTER M RANCH
>> OUTSIDE FORT DAVIS, TEXAS
>> 0231 HOURS (CENTRAL TIME ZONE)

Restless, Tyrel flicked through channels. He knew he had insomnia bad when he couldn't even focus on baseball. In fact, not even cold corn bread soaked in buttermilk had taken the edge off, and generally that would guarantee he'd sleep like a baby.

He flicked through the channels and ended up on FOX News, thinking the news would surely put him out of his misery. Thoughts of Shel kept banging around in his head, though, and he couldn't seem to get them nailed down in any manner that would let him know why he was thinking about him so much.

After a few minutes of watching the international news, Tyrel almost changed channels. Then he saw Shel's picture on the screen behind the anchorman.

The picture was a twin of one Tyrel had stuck in his wife's family Bible. It was where she'd kept all her important papers and memories.

The Bible still held pressed flowers from the first time Tyrel had courted her, along with baby pictures and report cards.

Tyrel sat up a little straighter and turned up the television's volume. He wasn't worried about waking Ramon. The boy had sacked out in Don and Shel's room. That was how Tyrel still thought of the bedroom at the back of the house.

Don and Shel's room.

Like they were going to be coming right back at some point.

At least their mama hadn't had to watch them move out, especially the angry way Shel had left. Tyrel knew that would have hurt her. And maybe it would have damaged their relationship. She'd always put a lot of store in her boys.

That was what she'd always called them. The boys, like they were the only two boys in the world.

Tyrel forced himself to focus on the news story. The anchor related how a young man named Bobby Lee Gant had killed one man and was about to kill a woman and maybe Shel when Shel had shot him.

The fact that his son had killed somebody didn't bother Tyrel. That was what soldiers did. He'd killed men himself. War was war, and killing enemy soldiers was what he'd been over there to do.

But one didn't deserve it at all.

Tyrel blinked back the pain of that stray memory and listened to the dead young man's name again. Something about it sounded familiar. Then again, in Texas there were a lot of Robert Lees and Johnny Lees. Bobby Lee couldn't have been so unique that he'd notice it.

Then the anchor started talking about another man, the boy's father. Evidently he was a criminal too. His picture appeared on the wall behind the anchor desk.

And Tyrel was slammed right out of Texas and back into Vietnam.

⊛ ⊛ ⊛

>> MECKLENBURG COUNTY MEDICAL EXAMINER
>> 618 NORTH COLLEGE STREET
>> CHARLOTTE, NORTH CAROLINA
>> 0357 HOURS

"I'm too drunk for this," Fat Mike said as he leaned against the wall near the building's back door. He belched, then cursed.

"Keep quiet." Victor spoke softly.

"We get caught, this could go really bad," Fat Mike said.

"You're worrying too much. We won't get caught." Victor stood. "You about got that lock?"

The skinny biker working on the lock raked his long hair back with a hand. "Almost. This ain't as easy as picking your nose."

"Get it done." Victor glanced around. He knew Fat Mike was right. They had no business being there.

But he hadn't gotten to tell Bobby Lee good-bye in a respectful manner. He owed his son that much, and he wanted to do it while he was still mostly intact. He knew the coroner would get around to gutting Bobby Lee at some point, even though everyone knew exactly what—and who—had killed him.

Victor didn't like thinking about that. He was of half a mind to steal his son's body and provide his own burial. Except that he had no place to put him, and he wasn't going to bury Bobby Lee out in the woods where the animals could have at him.

"You said there's only one security guard on duty?" Victor asked Fat Mike.

"Yeah." Fat Mike belched again. "But I really think this is a bad idea. If we get caught—"

"Ain't gonna be no 'we.' It's gonna be me. I'm going in there. And if *I* get caught, then I'm gonna make my new buddies at the FBI pull my fat outta the fire."

"They may let you get all nice and toasty before they do that."

"I'm doing this," Victor said in a cold, dead voice.

Fat Mike wouldn't meet his eyes. "Something else you should probably know."

"Well spit it out."

"I found out who rolled over on Bobby Lee."

"I already know that. His girlfriend."

Fat Mike looked at him in surprise.

"My FBI buddies told me that. She got caught holding by the Charlotte PD. She says she fell over on Bobby Lee because she's pregnant and don't want the baby born while she's in jail. I figure she just didn't want to do no slam."

"Yeah. You're probably right."

The biker at the back door stood.

"Give up?" Victor asked.

"Nah, bro." He grinned. "I got it. Even took out the alarm." He pulled on the door and it swung open almost soundlessly.

Victor nodded. "Way to fire. Gimme a few minutes. Wait here and I'll be back." He stepped into the morgue.

⊛ ⊛ ⊛

>> RAFTER M RANCH
>> OUTSIDE FORT DAVIS, TEXAS
>> 0306 HOURS (CENTRAL TIME ZONE)

Tyrel went back to his bedroom and switched on the light. As always, his bed was neatly made, the spread pulled tight enough that a quarter would bounce if dropped on it.

The bed had been one of the points of contention he'd had with his wife. No matter how hard she'd tried, she could never make it well enough to suit him. She'd finally given up in exasperation and let him do it. And he had, every morning they'd been together.

The Army had taught Tyrel how to make a bed. The Army had taught him a lot of things. Not all of those things had been good.

He went to the closet, stood on tiptoe, and slid away the secret panel he'd placed there. He'd built the ranch house for his wife. Every stick of it had been put there by his hand. He knew it completely, and he'd built it to be a fortress that would keep the rest of the world at bay.

But at the very heart of it, he'd hidden the darkness that consumed his soul.

Everything he'd brought back from Vietnam, other than the guilt, had been carefully packed away in the olive drab ammo box.

He carried the box back to the bed and sat down. He unlatched the lid, then slowly and meticulously began to take out things he hadn't seen in over forty years.

Medals, mementos, and photographs soon littered the bed. He'd never paid much attention to the medals. He didn't even know why he'd kept them. Except that his daddy had.

His daddy had kept his in an ammo box too, but he'd kept the ammo box out in his shop. Earl McHenry had been a carpenter by trade. He'd taught Tyrel everything he'd wanted to learn, which wasn't ever as much as his daddy had wanted to teach him. Thankfully it had been enough to build the house. And in doing that, Tyrel had taught himself other things.

He focused on the pictures. It didn't take him long to find Victor Gant.

Gant looked like the devil incarnate. He stood there smiling with his M14 on the ground beside him. He'd refused to give up his rifle for the M16 the Army had started bringing en masse into the war effort.

A pack of unfiltered cigarettes rode under his helmet band. He wore his uniform shirt open. His dog tags lay against his broad, naked chest. He'd been twenty-four or twenty-five.

Tyrel had been twenty-one at the time.

Victor Gant, already a veteran of ambushes and firefights, had seemed like a mythical hero when he swaggered through the jungle and the bars servicemen haunted in those days.

Tyrel had been swept under Gant's influence. But for whatever reason, Tyrel had never been asked into the inner circle.

Gripped by the old fear that had haunted him for over forty years, Tyrel sorted through the pictures. He dreaded finding what he was looking for, but he couldn't help searching for it.

Then, a couple dozen black-and-white photographs later, Tyrel found the one he was looking for.

Dennis Hinton sat on the prow of a PBR that was tied up in the Qui Nhon harbor. He was bare-chested and quiet and looked almost embarrassed in the picture. His hair was so blond it looked white against his tanned skin. Other rigid-hulled swift boats, designated Patrol Boat, River, and called Pibbers or Riverines, were visible in the bay waters behind him.

Even with all the military hardware around him and the M14 in his hands, Denny looked like a child. They all had.

Except for Victor Gant. Gant had been dark and virile, his eyes cold and merciless. When it came to killing, Victor had been one of the most efficient predators Tyrel had ever met.

This man isn't going to let the death of his son go unchallenged, Tyrel told himself.

If there was ever a man who lived to get his pound of flesh from anyone who crossed him, it was Victor Gant.

But that night Denny had died—*No. The night you killed Denny,* Tyrel amended—Victor Gant had become a savior. He'd gotten Tyrel out of the worst thing that had ever happened to him.

At least, that was what Tyrel had thought at the time. That was before everything he'd done had followed him home and staked out a piece of his hopes and dreams for the last forty years.

Without warning, Tyrel's hands started to shake. His vision misted. He wiped his mouth with the back of his arm and thought he was going to be sick.

CRIME SCENE
NCIS
NAVAL CRIMINAL INVESTIGATIVE SERVICE

26

E SCENE ✪ NCIS ✪ CRIME SCENE
NAVAL CRIMINAL INVESTIGATIVE SERVICE

>> MECKLENBURG COUNTY MEDICAL EXAMINER
>> 618 NORTH COLLEGE STREET
>> CHARLOTTE, NORTH CAROLINA
>> 0420 HOURS

Victor Gant walked fearlessly through the morgue. His boots thumped against the tiled floor. The red glare of the exit signs shone against the floor's surface and made it look like coals burned underneath. Almost as if he were walking above the pits of hell.

Victor's quick research had indicated that the offices closed down at five and that everyone went home shortly after that. An answering service picked up any after-hours calls.

Except for the lone security guard, Victor had the place to himself. They'd gotten a description of the layout from a Mexican janitor who'd worked there until he was busted selling weed. After the question was raised at the bar, Shaky Carl had come up with the ex-janitor's name.

In minutes, Victor was in the vault. The book listing the locations of the bodies—apparently nobody completely trusted the computer systems—was on the desk.

Victor plucked a pair of disposable surgical gloves from a box near the chemicals and equipment, then strode to the desk and flipped through the book's pages and found the latest entries.

Bobby Lee's name was there.

Stomach tight and temples pounding, Victor tossed the book back onto the desk and stepped over to the vault area. He took hold of the handle and pulled.

The table extended outward soundlessly.

There wasn't enough light to see clearly, so Victor took his Zippo from his pocket and spun the striker. The yellow and blue flame climbed upward and brightened the room.

Even though he'd steeled himself for what he was about to see, Victor's heart thudded to a stop inside his chest.

Bobby Lee lay on the table. Two bullets had punched through his face, leaving hideous wounds behind. His lower jaw was shattered and torn loose. The second bullet had punched through his cheek under his right eye.

Then Victor's heart restarted with an explosion that filled him to bursting and quickly subsided.

"I will kill the man that killed you," Victor whispered. "I never gave you any promises while you were alive, but I promise you that now."

He bent down and kissed his dead son's forehead.

A footstep scuffed the floor outside the room.

⊛ ⊛ ⊛

>> INTENSIVE CARE UNIT
>> PRESBYTERIAN HOSPITAL
>> CHARLOTTE, NORTH CAROLINA
>> 0423 HOURS

"Hey, Don."

Don rolled over on his side and pulled the blanket up over his shoulder. If he was lucky, Shel would forget about him for another ten minutes and he could get some more sleep. All he needed was a few more minutes and he'd be—

"Hey, man, come on. Wake up."

Don ignored Shel.

"Don." Shel's voice was louder now. He had always been the one more like their daddy. Shel and Daddy always got up at the crack of dawn, even if both of them had gotten to bed late the night before.

"Hey."

Exasperated, Don said, "Give it a rest, Shel. A few more minutes isn't going to kill anybody."

"Your phone is ringing. Wake up."

Worn to the bone, Don rolled over and looked up at the dark ceiling while he waited for his brain to make the necessary connections. Then he remembered; he was in the hospital in North Carolina with Shel.

"You awake?" Shel asked.

"Yeah." Don listened. "I don't hear a phone."

"That's because it stopped ringing."

"Oh." Don groaned as he sat up.

"So how's that chair for sleeping?" Shel taunted.

"Remember when we had to sleep out in the barn when the cows were calving?"

"Yeah."

"Those were good times by comparison."

"I remember. Me and Daddy would be awake all night, and you'd sleep most of it away."

Don heard the country accent come back into Shel's words. It was funny listening to it happen. Shel had cleaned up his diction a lot after he'd entered the Marines. A lot of the men he'd served with had been merciless about accents, and he'd had a bad one.

"Not my fault. I've always needed more sleep than you guys." Don rubbed the heels of his palms against his eyes.

"You going to see who called?"

"What time is it?"

"About four thirty."

Don thought about that. "Joanie and the kids won't be up by now." Then he factored in the time difference. "It's three thirty in Texas." Since it wasn't the family, that narrowed the possibility to a parishioner at his church. Don had a reputation for being a good counselor and a lot of people had his cell phone number.

He laid his head back and closed his eyes. All he needed was a few more minutes of sleep.

"Don," Shel said.

"Yeah."

"You need to check that phone?"

Don fumbled with his pocket. "Why are you awake?"

"The night nurse is cute. I didn't want to miss her."

"Thanks for that."

"You're too married to appreciate things like that."

Don peered at his brother. He could barely make him out in the darkness. "You sound better."

"I feel better. I'm ready to get out of here."

"I don't think that's going to happen."

Shel sighed. "This being laid up is going to be wearisome."

"You should enjoy the downtime."

"I wasn't made for downtime."

Don silently agreed with that. He didn't know who was more driven: Shel or their daddy. When he opened the phone and checked under recent calls, he was surprised at the number he found.

"So who was it?" Shel asked.

"Daddy," Don said. "I didn't even know he knew my cell phone number."

⊛ ⊛ ⊛

>> MECKLENBURG COUNTY MEDICAL EXAMINER
>> 618 NORTH COLLEGE STREET
>> CHARLOTTE, NORTH CAROLINA
>> 0423 HOURS

Howie Jernigan attended junior college and loved horror magazines. He needed money to go to college, and he intended to be a writer. Both of those things were parts of the reason he'd taken the job as night security guard at the county medical examiner's office.

The money thing was self-explanatory. The writing part was almost as easy to explain, but it was slightly twisted. When he sold his first horror novel, he wanted the About the Author page to mention that he'd once worked in a morgue.

That would get people's attention and boost up the cool factor. And it would be something he could talk about on Leno or Letterman.

The fact that the medical examiners did autopsies of murder victims there only added to it. He could claim he'd been part of big murder cases. *Instrumental,* he told himself. *I was* instrumental *in the solution of several big crimes.*

Unfortunately, during the four-month tenure of his employment, there had been no big murder investigations. There had been drunk drivers and heart attack victims, people who'd drowned and people who'd burned to death in fires.

There hadn't been a single murder of note.

At least, there hadn't been any until Bobby Lee Gant had gotten his head blown off at the tattoo parlor. Even then, Bobby Lee wasn't murdered. He'd been killed in self-defense.

But still, the shooting went down as a homicide. And that was what it would stay called too. If a person killed a person, no matter if that killing was justified, it was a homicide. A justifiable homicide, but a homicide nonetheless.

Howie had played high school football and remained in shape. The shirt of his security uniform was tight across his shoulders and chest. He was twenty-one years old and knew how to take care of himself. He was prepared for anything.

But during his employment at the medical examiner's office, there had never been any break-ins or even juvenile destruction of any kind. It had always been quiet. He'd sat in the office where he watched the security monitors in between reading books by favorite authors. Mostly he'd read.

But tonight the security cameras had gone down.

There hadn't been any real instruction on what to do if that happened. Howie didn't want to call the police department all freaked out if it was something as simple as plugging a wire back in somewhere or throwing a switch.

And he didn't want to look like he was scared being there alone. Being remembered as the wannabe horror writer scared of his own shadow wouldn't have been a good thing.

So he'd gone looking for the switch.

That was when he thought he'd seen a light in the autopsy room.

Going into that room pretty much guaranteed he'd be creeped out. Every time he went in there he was pretty much creeped out.

He'd only actually seen a dead body in there once. That had been when he'd gotten the tour during business hours. Seeing the wrinkled and withered body of the old man had almost been enough to put him off the job.

Standing outside the autopsy room, Howie told himself that the medical examiners went off the clock at five and he didn't come on till ten. That almost guaranteed that there'd be no dead bodies from ten till six in the morning Monday through Friday.

When the light flickered out in the vault room, Howie almost went for the police anyway. Only a deep fear of being ridiculed kept him from it. Despite his size, he was always the kid who'd gotten shoved into his own locker in junior high.

Some of the people who'd done the shoving had gone on to become police officers. Some of them had gone on to become the druggies and thieves in town too. That was just life after high school.

He wasn't armed. Protecting dead bodies didn't usually involve any kind of real danger. The only problem would be kids wanting to break in to look at bodies and challenge each other to touch one.

Kids, Howie reflected at the grand old age of twenty-one, did some awfully strange things and had truly weird ideas.

With his long-handled flashlight in hand, he approached the door of the vault. The beam fell over the open doorway. That was strange, because he'd been certain it was shut. He always liked to make sure this door was closed. Sometimes—actually more often than he liked to admit—he imagined some of those dead people in the vaults getting up off the tables and coming calling.

Those were definitely not happy thoughts.

As he held the flashlight on the door, he listened for any sound of movement inside. If it had been kids, he'd have figured they would have given themselves up by now.

But there were a few kids these days who wouldn't give up anything unless they had to.

Howie cleared his throat and said, "Come on out of there now. Come on out and we'll talk. We don't have to call the police if we can talk."

There was no response.

Getting aggravated, Howie rapped his flashlight against the doorframe. "Come on out. I mean it. If I have to come in there after you, we'll be calling the police—and your parents—for sure."

There was still no response.

Howie screwed up his courage. He heard nothing in the room. Of course, he reminded himself, zombies that weren't moving were quiet too. But he didn't really believe in zombies. They were just cool monsters.

He walked into the room and shined the light around for a second. When he caught sight of the body rolled out of the vault and hanging there over the floor, he froze. He couldn't even breathe.

Despite the fact that he hadn't been there when the doctors had gone home, Howie was fairly certain they never left the bodies hanging out in the open like that. His hand crept down for the cell phone he wore on his belt. The phone wasn't for use on the job. It was more to keep up with his peeps.

Before he could pull the phone from his belt, he heard someone breathe behind him. He wasn't alone in the room.

Just like that, he realized his mistake. He'd become *that* guy. In every horror movie, there was always *that* guy who became the sacrificial lamb. Usually he was the one who walked into a basement—or a medical examiner's morgue—when everyone else understood that you weren't supposed to do that.

He turned around slowly, but it was actually as fast as he could move. All of his muscles felt numb and dead. Although he didn't point the flashlight at the figure standing behind him, there was enough reflected glow to recognize that a man stood there.

In the darkness of the morgue, the man looked like some wild-eyed creature. Howie had just a moment to wonder if maybe zombies did exist after all.

Then the man swung something that caught Howie in the face and drove him backward. Darkness drank down his thoughts and took him away before he hit the ground.

CRIME SCENE
NCIS
NAVAL CRIMINAL INVESTIGATIVE SERVICE

27

E SCENE ✪ NCIS ✪ CRIME SCENE

NAVAL CRIMINAL INVESTIGATIVE SERVICE

```
>> INTENSIVE CARE UNIT
>> PRESBYTERIAN HOSPITAL
>> CHARLOTTE, NORTH CAROLINA
>> 0428 HOURS
```

Shel cranked the bed upward with the remote control taped to the side of the bed. Movement hurt, but hurting meant he was alive. It also meant that the doctor had cut back on the pain medication, but that was all right. Pain meds were a necessary evil in recovery. He'd been wounded enough times to know that. But he was just as glad to get over needing them.

Don just stared at the phone in his hand.

"Are you gonna call him back?" Shel asked.

"I'm thinking about it," Don said. He gazed at the phone like it was a coiled rattler about to strike.

"If Daddy called, it must have been important," Shel said.

"It could have been a mistake."

Shel snorted. "Wimp."

"Nope. Just thinking things through. The one thing that keeps coming back to mind is that Daddy has never—and I do mean *never*—called me on my cell phone."

"All the more reason to call him."

"He might have accidentally hit the buttons."

"And dialed your cell phone number?"

Don grimaced. "Does sound pretty weak when you say it like that."

"It is weak," Shel said. "Give me the phone and I'll call him."

Don started to hand the phone over, then pulled it back. He eyed Shel suspiciously. "If I give you the phone and you chicken out, Daddy's going to see my number on his caller ID."

"I didn't know Daddy even had caller ID," Shel said. His daddy was notorious for being against technological advancement, though he'd gotten satellite television once it became available.

"He's got it," Don said. "You can call him from the hospital."

"If I call him from the hospital, they'll mask the numbers. When he sees a number he doesn't recognize, he'll probably ignore it."

"Don't you have a cell phone?"

"Yes."

"Then why don't you use it?"

Shel tried to be very patient. He also tried not to think about his daddy having a heart attack and calling for help.

"Because Daddy won't recognize that number either. Give it up, Don. Your phone is the only one we can use."

Reluctantly Don handed his phone over. "Have you ever thought about how ridiculous it is that two grown men have trouble calling their daddy?"

"Not really," Shel replied.

"Well, maybe you should," Don said.

Shel found the number and hit Send. His breathing grew shorter and tighter, and he felt like he was going into combat. He hated the fact that the machinery connected to him revealed that rising stress level to Don.

Tyrel answered on the second ring.

"Don," Tyrel growled.

"It's not Don, Daddy," Shel said. "It's me."

"Where's Don?"

"Went to the bathroom. He left his phone on the nightstand. He'll be back directly." Shel was conscious of how his accent had crept into his words. "I figured I'd call you back and see if something was wrong."

"Nothing's wrong."

Shel listened to the slur in his father's voice. Tyrel drank every now and again, but he never let it get ahead of him. In all his years growing up on the Rafter M, Shel had never seen his daddy drunk. He suspected he was listening to that now.

"I called to talk to you," Tyrel said.

"Yes, sir," Shel said.

"I didn't come up there because I figured you were too mean to kill. You got too much of your old man in you for that."

Shel honestly didn't know whether to feel proud or angry about that comparison. Other people had always compared him to his daddy, but he'd never done it himself.

It was something he would never do.

"Yes, sir," he said.

"Are you doing all right?" Tyrel asked.

"I am."

"Nurses taking good care of you?"

"Yes, sir." Shel felt uncomfortable talking to his daddy like this. Tyrel wasn't one for talking about things. *It's the alcohol,* Shel couldn't help thinking. He braced himself as best he could because he knew the call could be as unpredictable as a roller coaster ride.

"I wouldn't . . . want nothing to happen to you, boy." Tyrel's voice cracked at the end.

Before he knew it, and without even understanding why, Shel had a lump in his throat. It wasn't just his father's admission that he cared about him, which wasn't something Tyrel McHenry had ever owned up to; it was the fact that his daddy was anywhere near to losing control.

The only time Shel had ever seen his daddy hurting had been at his mama's funeral. Even when Shel's mama had died in the hospital and they'd all been sitting in that hospital room listening to her gasp for her last feeble breaths, Tyrel McHenry had never shown weakness.

When she'd gone on, when the heart monitor had flatlined and the constant chirp filled the room, they'd watched as the nurses had disconnected everything. Then Tyrel had stood in those straight-legged jeans he always wore, taken his cowboy hat off, and walked over to his dead wife. He looked at her for a time, then bent down and kissed her gently on the forehead.

"Sleep easy, ol' gal. I got my hand on the wheel. I'll get your young'uns raised up right," he'd whispered.

Then he clamped his cowboy hat on and turned to Don and Shel with his face like stone.

"You boys tell your mama good-bye. I'll be outside waiting when you're ready." And he'd walked out.

That day, Shel had hated his father. It had been everything Don could do to keep him from forcing a confrontation right there in the hospital parking lot.

Then, days later at the funeral, Tyrel had stood at the back of the family area in the funeral home and listened to the preacher's words. Tears streaming down his own face, Shel had turned to watch his daddy. Only one time, and only briefly, Tyrel had sipped at a breath and hiccuped. His face had knotted up in agony. Then he'd forced it back to that harsh mask he'd always worn.

That was what Shel heard now, and it left him shattered and scared in ways he'd never felt even when he'd been under fire on the battlefield.

"I'm fine, Daddy." Shel was surprised by how tight his voice was. "I'm just fine."

"Well, you stay that way, boy. I won't put up with anything less."

"Yes, sir."

"The reason I was calling is this."

Shel waited.

"That boy you shot—"

Shel wanted to point out that Bobby Lee had been a full-grown man, but he didn't.

"—had a daddy," Tyrel continued.

Through the haze that swirled inside his head and muddied his thoughts, Shel tried to get a sense of what his father was trying to tell him. He felt like he was going to have to defend himself for shooting Bobby Lee.

Instead, Tyrel said, "I knew that boy's daddy. He's a vicious man, Shelton. He's one of the devil's own. You're going to need to watch your six for a while. And if there's a way you can punch Victor Gant's ticket for him, you might just be better off for the doing of it."

Shel barely breathed. He couldn't believe what his daddy was telling him.

"You hear me, boy?" Tyrel growled.

"Yes, Daddy," Shel whispered.

"You watch yourself for the next little while. And you take care of Don, too. He ain't like you and me. He looks more for the gentle side of things. He ain't gonna know how to look for somebody like Victor Gant. You hear me?"

"Yes, sir."

"It'd be better if you sent him on outta there and got him outta the line of fire," Tyrel said. "And tell them friends of yours to watch out for themselves too. If Victor Gant can't get at you, he'll take what he can."

Shel listened to the thud of his heart banging inside his chest. *How does my daddy know someone like Victor Gant?* Shel couldn't think clearly enough at the moment to reason that out.

"Well," Tyrel said, "I reckon that's all I got to say. Now that I said it, I'm gonna go to bed. If you had any sense, you'd do the same instead of lying awake at all hours of the night."

"Yes, sir," Shel said, but even before he got the words out of his mouth, Tyrel had hung up. Shel took the phone from his face and gazed at perplexedly.

"Shel," Don said softly.

"Yeah."

"What did Daddy want?"

"To tell me to watch my six," Shel said numbly.

"Your six?"

Shel tossed Don the phone. "My rear flank. He told me to look out for trouble."

"What kind of trouble?"

"From Victor Gant."

Don took a moment to reason that out and connect the dots. "The father of the young man you shot?"

"Yeah."

"Why would Daddy call you to tell you that?"

"He said Victor Gant is one of the devil's own. He said Victor Gant would come after me for killing his boy."

"I think Commander Coburn knows that," Don said.

"Probably. Will's a smart man."

Don looked puzzled for a moment. "How did Daddy know about Victor Gant?"

"He said he knew him."

"Daddy?"

Shel nodded.

"How would Daddy know a man like that?"

"That is the question, isn't it?" Shel lay back on the pillow, but he knew he wasn't going to get any more sleep that night.

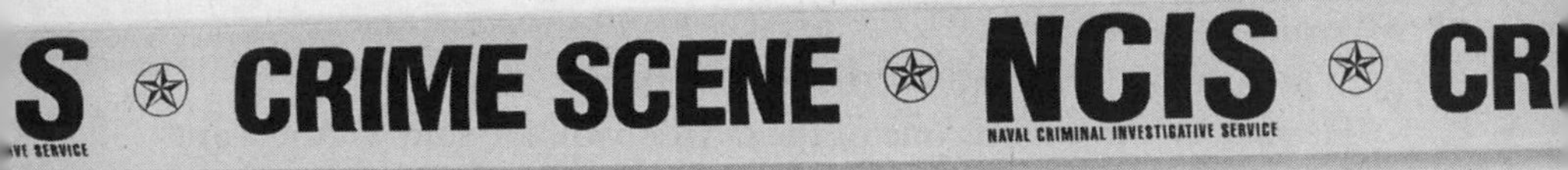
CRIME SCENE
NCIS
NAVAL CRIMINAL INVESTIGATIVE SERVICE

28

E SCENE ✪ NCIS ✪ CRIME SCENE
NAVAL CRIMINAL INVESTIGATIVE SERVICE

>> SHERATON HOTEL
>> CHARLOTTE, NORTH CAROLINA
>> 0639 HOURS

Will rolled over in bed and grabbed his iPAQ phone from the nightstand. "Coburn."

"Aren't you up yet?"

It took Will a moment to recognize Police Chief Tarlton's voice. The man sounded entirely too awake and happy for it to be the time that showed on the PDA's viewscreen.

"No," Will answered. He slitted his eyes against the weak sunlight hammering the eastern balcony windows. The drapes only blunted part of the brightness. "Is Shel—?"

"Everybody at the hospital is fine," Tarlton said. "Besides your people, I okayed some of my guys for OT."

"I appreciate that."

"No problem. Since you're going to help me stir up my favorite hornet's nest and rile the FBI, it's the least I could do."

Despite the lack of sleep, the worry, and the fatigue he felt, Will couldn't help but grin. "I'm going to do all that, am I?"

"Oh yeah. In fact, you're going to love the next little thing that dropped onto our plates during the night."

Will waited.

"That's the part where you're supposed to ask me what happened," Tarlton said. "Kind of a prompt."

"I'm patient," Will said.

"Guess what was broken into last night?"

"I don't have a clue."

"The county medical examiner's office."

Thoughts circled through Will's mind, and he didn't like how any of them were shaping up.

"Want to guess who broke in?" Tarlton said. "I'm discovering that you're lousy at prompts."

"Victor Gant," Will said.

"Yep."

"But that doesn't make sense."

"We're not exactly dealing with a logical person here," Tarlton said. "You need to keep that in mind."

"Was Gant caught on the premises?"

"No. That would have tidied up what we had planned for the day."

"If you could have sold the judge on it."

"I think I could have. But Gant breaking into the county medical examiner's office gives us a free move. So to speak."

"The medical examiner's office is under county jurisdiction."

"Yes." The smile was evident in Tarlton's voice. "Guess who's going to be riding shotgun with us today?"

"The sheriff."

"Yep. He's an old fishing buddy. After I got the particulars of this, we agreed that a joint effort by the city and county was required. We also decided that the NCIS could stand the heat too."

Will smiled. "Because you know that busting Gant today is going to irritate Urlacher."

"Nolan—that's the sheriff—and I figured you and yours could ride along. When it comes to matching up federal muscle, we thought maybe you could handle Urlacher and the FBI."

"Because Bobby Lee Gant's body is property of the NCIS as evidence."

"Exactly. How soon can you be down to Alice's Café?"

"I don't know where that is." Will stood and started grabbing clothing from his duffel bag.

Tarlton gave him directions.

"Why are we meeting there?" Will asked.

"Because we don't want the bad guys to figure out what we're going to do," Tarlton said. "And so Nolan and I can have a piece of pie while we're waiting on you. It'll take you ten minutes to get here."

⊛ ⊛ ⊛

>> 0643 HOURS

Will knocked on the adjoining room door and said his name, then used a key card to disengage the lock. Slowly he pushed the door open.

Remy was sitting up in bed with his pistol gripped in both hands. His eyes were red-rimmed with sleep. Max sat on the bed beside him. The Labrador's head was lifted, and his ears were pricked.

"Tarlton found a lever we can use to get over on Victor Gant," Will announced. "We're rolling in five minutes. You'll need your riot gear. Meet me in the parking lot."

Remy nodded and said, "I brought my gear with me. Never go anywhere without it." He pushed out of bed like he'd had eight hours of sleep and walked over to a duffel on the desk.

SEALs, Will thought in disgust as he went back to his own room. He figured he'd be lucky to beat Remy to the car.

⊛ ⊛ ⊛

>> 0647 HOURS

By the time Will was ready, Remy was leaning against the bumper of the gray Taurus with his arms folded and looking totally alert. Max lay in a black pool of fur at his feet.

Will opened the trunk, and Remy threw in his riot gear duffel. They moved to the front of the car and climbed in. Max took the backseat, then hung his head between them.

"Didn't know you got Max last night." Will started the car and let it idle for a moment.

"Swung by the hospital. Figured I'd get him out for a bit today. There's a park not far from here."

"I'm surprised Max left."

"Shel told him to."

"I'm surprised the nurses let him go. From what I've heard, they're practically ready to adopt Max as the hospital mascot." Will put the transmission in reverse and backed out.

Remy grinned as he adjusted his wraparound sunglasses. "This dog's got stealth ninja moves those nurses have never seen. I'd swear he's been SEAL-trained."

"How's Shel?"

"Groggy. Sore. Ready to get out of the hospital."

Will knew that would be true. He accelerated, halted at the parking lot's edge for a moment, then merged with traffic.

"Shel seemed a little distracted, though," Remy said.

"Did he?"

"Yeah. His brother was there. Sleeping. Shel and I talked, but he didn't say what was on his mind."

"He came close to getting killed," Will said. "That usually brings me up short."

"Maybe, but this is Shel. It didn't happen, so it doesn't matter."

"True." Will shot through traffic.

"We're in a hurry?" Remy asked.

"We are." Will tapped the brake, then accelerated around a delivery truck and briefly took the inside lane again. "So you think Shel has something on his mind?"

"Yep. On the way out of the hospital, I called Estrella and let her know. If anybody can get that jarhead to talk about the warm and fuzzy of his life, it's her."

Will silently agreed. Shel and Estrella had been close ever since Shel had been assigned to the team. They shared a bond that partly came out of the language they shared, but he knew it was more than that too.

"Where are we headed so early?" Remy asked. "The PD is back the other way."

As he drove, Will explained.

❂ ❂ ❂

>> ALICE'S CAFÉ
>> KINGS DRIVE
>> CHARLOTTE, NORTH CAROLINA
>> 0656 HOURS

"Well," Remy said a few minutes later, "nobody's going to miss them. It looks like a law enforcement convention."

Will had to agree. Police cars and sheriff's deputies' vehicles filled the small parking area around Alice's Café and spilled over into the surrounding neighborhood. There was a mix of sedans and off-road vehicles, and Will could see a mix of police uniforms and sheriff's uniforms on the men standing by the cars.

"Do you think there are enough of them?" Remy asked with a grin.

"Victor Gant's biker club is pretty deep in manpower too." Will pulled in behind Tarlton's car as the police chief flagged him down.

"Morning, Agent Coburn," Tarlton greeted. "This is Sheriff Nolan Greene." He indicated the tall, heavyset man in a sheriff's uniform.

Greene stood nearly six and a half feet tall and was built like a bear. He looked as though he was in his late forties. Gray brushed at his temples and robbed the color from his sandy-red hair. Freckles covered his round face. He wore a Sam Browne belt that supported a Desert Eagle .44 Magnum.

"Nolan's big enough to go hunting bears with a switch," Tarlton said, "but he still packs that hand cannon." He handed Will a white paper bag. "I figured you guys didn't take time for breakfast."

"No." Will dug into the bag and found it held biscuit sandwiches with sausage, breakfast steak, bacon, ham, and eggs. "Thanks." He took one of the biscuits and passed the bag on to Remy.

Tarlton handed him a tall cup of coffee.

"Benny's always had this thing for tea parties," Greene growled with mock sarcasm.

"Don't want to miss breakfast," Tarlton said. "Most important meal of the day."

Remy took a biscuit out and flipped it to Max. The Labrador caught the biscuit but didn't make it disappear until Remy gave him the command that it was all right.

"Army dog?" Greene asked.

"No, sir," Remy replied. "This is a Marine."

"Better-looking than some I've met," Greene acknowledged, with a quick glance at Tarlton.

⊛ ⊛ ⊛

>> 0701 HOURS

"Victor Gant is holed up in a closed warehouse," Tarlton said. He pointed at the location on the street map spread across the hood of his car. "This neighborhood we're in, Cherry, is an older one. I won't bore you with the history, but it's had its ups and down."

Will was vaguely familiar with the neighborhood's history. Cherry was one of Charlotte's older neighborhoods and had shuffled back and forth between affluence and poverty and between black and white and was currently being torn between private residences and strip malls.

"Factories and houses have come and gone around this neighborhood," Tarlton said. "Back in the 1960s, the building in question was a machine shop. Supplied the war effort over in Vietnam. Back in the day, it offered a lot of jobs and helped stabilize the economy. In the 1990s, it went bust. A few other businesses tried locating there. Mom-and-pop shops. Storage facilities. Nothing worked. Then the Purple Royals bought it."

"The motorcycle gang *bought* the building?" Remy asked.

Tarlton nodded. "Some of the biker gangs have put down legitimate roots. Set businesses up as fronts and even tax shelters. Hard to get popped on a vagrancy charge when you can prove you're employed somewhere."

"What do they do there?" Will asked.

"It's a machine shop, mostly. That's what the lower floors are. Victor Gant hired a company to broker jobs for these guys." Tarlton grinned. "They're so law-abiding there that they pay taxes."

"Anybody ever gone in there for a look around?"

"Yeah. Place is run well. It's legit. Never found any drugs or contraband there."

"They could use it as a chop shop," Remy suggested.

Tarlton nodded. "They could. But I've never found any evidence that they do. They've even got a speed shop in the northeast corner of the building. Custom headers. Rims. Tires. The works. All legit."

"The cover is tight," Will said.

"That's what I'm saying. We'll have to be careful inside."

"You're sure Victor Gant is there?"

"I know he is. After I talked to the kid at the medical examiner's office, I put one of my undercover guys on the site. He let me know Gant showed up there a couple hours ago."

Will took that in. "You've got a warrant for Gant?"

"I do. Judge Carson signed off on a warrant for Gant's arrest for assault and for breaking and entering. The lock on the ME's office was juked."

"Any evidence there?"

"Not yet. I've got a crime team looking for a matchup."

"But you have Gant solid on the assault charge?"

Tarlton nodded. "That's dead-solid perfect. The kid from the ME's office picked Gant out of a six-pack. Kid knew it was Gant by name before we gave him the pics."

"How did he know that?"

"He's been following the story."

"How's he doing?"

Tarlton shrugged. "He's still in the ER. He's got some bruises and a few stitches. The doc was talking about keeping him for a few more hours in case there's a concussion. But he's going to be all right."

"If it comes to it, will he testify?"

"Yeah. He's a stand-up kid." Tarlton smiled a little. "He has visions of being a hero."

"That's not a bad thing," Will said. "That's why a lot of men get into this business."

Will had come to the NCIS to get off shipboard duty and try to save his failing marriage. But he'd since learned a lot about the other law enforcement personnel and the passions that drove them.

"I always thought it was the cool uniforms," Remy said with a straight face.

"They don't come any cooler than the Marine Corps," Tarlton said.

"Marines can't touch Navy dress whites, Chief."

"When are we going to do this?" Will interrupted before the friendly banter could continue.

"Well," Tarlton said, "there's no time like the present." He folded the map. "Let's roll."

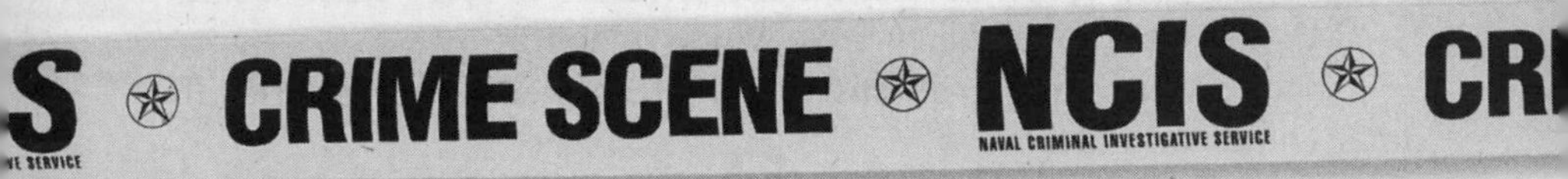
CRIME SCENE
NCIS
NAVAL CRIMINAL INVESTIGATIVE SERVICE

29

E SCENE ✪ NCIS ✪ CRIME SCENE
NAVAL CRIMINAL INVESTIGATIVE SERVICE

>> HAWTHORNE MACHINE SHOP
>> HAWTHORNE LANE
>> CHARLOTTE, NORTH CAROLINA
>> 0729 HOURS

Hawthorne Machine Shop sat back in a stand of old oak trees whose branches scraped the metal top of the two-story building. It was a rectangular cinder block building with a simple sign over the front of the north side that advertised Hawthorne Speed Shop. A black-and-white checkered flag hung above the doorway to the speed shop. A large window showed a selection of tires, rims, and other accessories in bright, gleaming chrome.

The west end of the building held another sign, announcing the presence of the Hawthorne Machine Shop. Both signs looked similar, standing on rectangular surfaces that were attached to the building by supports.

Both businesses were open.

"We got civilians on the premises," Tarlton announced over the radio headsets.

At the back of the Taurus, Will and Remy suited up in the riot gear. In addition to helmets and Kevlar vests with *NCIS Agent* stenciled on the back, they also wore shoulder and knee protective gear and gloves to protect against abrasions and impacts.

Will and Remy used the buddy system, each checking the other off on the prep list as they readied themselves. Will carried one XD-40 on his right hip and another under his left arm.

Remy carried two Beretta M9s in the same positions.

Both of them left their M4 assault rifles in the equipment duffels, but they picked up chopped-down Mossberg pump-action shotguns that held five rounds and sported skeletal folding wire stocks.

"You ready?" Tarlton asked.

Will nodded. Adrenaline flooded his body, but he was used to the feeling and concentrated on his breathing. Remy was as relaxed as if he were out for a Sunday walk.

Lord, Will prayed quietly, *keep us safe and let us do no harm.*

After a brief radio check, they followed Tarlton's SWAT team onto the premises.

Will's stomach clenched in anticipation of what was about to take place.

Trying to fight the police and sheriff's department would be foolish, and Victor Gant was no fool, but Will knew the man was ruthless.

He kept moving, the shotgun in both hands and canted forward and down so he could snap it up into readiness at a moment's notice.

⊛ ⊛ ⊛

>> ALLINGTON HOTEL
>> CHARLOTTE, NORTH CAROLINA
>> 0733 HOURS

When the ringing phone woke him, FBI Special Agent-in-Charge Scott Urlacher cursed. He wanted to ignore it, but he knew he couldn't. He hadn't gotten promoted to his present position by ducking trouble when it came his way.

He grabbed the phone and barked, "Hello."

"We've got a problem."

It took Urlacher a moment to recognize the voice as one of the men he had watching over Victor Gant.

"I don't want to have a problem," Urlacher replied.

"The local police, sheriff's deputies, and the NCIS are closing in on Gant's place over on Hawthorne."

"Why?"

"I don't know. But they've come loaded for bear. Riot gear and a lot of men."

"Find out," Urlacher ordered. "And get the team there." He pushed himself out of bed and grabbed for his pants. He wasn't about to let his plans for Victor Gant be thwarted by the likes of Will Coburn. Gant had managed to stay out of trouble for a long time. His son's death had put him up against the wall.

Urlacher intended to keep him there.

⊛ ⊛ ⊛

>> HAWTHORNE MACHINE SHOP
>> 0736 HOURS

Victor came up with a pistol in his fist. His dreams had been twisted and dark, taking him back to the jungle. He'd been turning over bodies after a rocket attack had taken out his unit. Every body he turned over had worn Bobby Lee's face.

The pistol sights settled on Fat Mike's round face, only inches out of reach.

"Friendly!" Fat Mike yelped and held his hands up over his head. "Victor! Friendly!"

Fat Mike's words and voice soaked through the old terror and frustration that gripped Victor. He eased the pistol's hammer back down and dropped his hand and the weapon to the bed again.

He gazed around the simple room. It took a moment for it to click in; then he realized he was on the second floor of the machine shop. Those rooms had been turned into crash pads for the chapter.

"What's going on?" Victor grated.

Fat Mike stood to the side of one of the windows. He peered out at the rising sun.

"Cops," Fat Mike said. "They're all over the place, bro."

That woke Victor. He sat up in bed and started coughing. Cursing his smoking habit, he reached for the pack of cigarettes beside the bed, shook one out, and lit up. He joined Fat Mike at the window.

Looking out, he saw that the police had congregated on the premises en masse. He cursed again.

"I told you not to break into the ME's office," Fat Mike said.

"It had to be done," Victor said. "They weren't going to let me tell Bobby Lee good-bye otherwise."

"Didn't say it wasn't the *right* thing to do," Fat Mike agreed. "I just don't think it was the brightest thing."

"Done is done. Can't go crying over spilt beer." Victor reached into his pants pocket and dragged his cell phone out. He'd put Agent Urlacher's number on speed dial.

⊛ ⊛ ⊛

>> 0737 HOURS

Will followed Tarlton's people. For a locally trained police unit, they moved well. They also kept quiet and didn't talk much, which was another plus. A lot of guys got the idea they should dialogue during an op like the men featured on *Cops* and other television shows.

The bikers in the machine shop saw them coming. They were hard-eyed men in jeans and sleeveless shirts, with tattoos all over their arms and bandannas tied around their heads.

Tarlton's people and Greene's deputies put bikers and customers up against the wall as a matter of course. The same question kept cropping up.

"Where is Victor Gant?"

Only a few of those asked knew. They told them the outlaw biker leader was upstairs.

⊛ ⊛ ⊛

>> 0739 HOURS

"Look, Victor, don't panic," Special Agent Urlacher said.

"I'm not panicked," Victor replied as he watched the police invade the premises. That was the truth. He wasn't panicked. He was angry.

"Good."

"You said these men couldn't touch me. You said you were gonna handle that. We had an agreement."

"Based on what I knew of you when I cut the deal with you, they couldn't touch you."

"And now they can?"

"I don't know," Urlacher told him. "I'm working that out now. Why are they coming after you?"

"I don't know," Victor lied. He couldn't help himself. Lying was a reflex action when dealing with cops. He'd done it all his life.

"I don't think they have a leg to stand on," Urlacher said. "But I'm headed there. Don't say anything to these people until I do."

"I won't," Victor agreed.

"And tell your men to keep their weapons holstered. Any shooting starts, this thing gets complicated really fast."

"Sure." Victor cursed. "Just you get here. Fast." He hung up and shoved the phone into his pocket.

⊛ ⊛ ⊛

>> 0741 HOURS

Tarlton almost died at the third door of the individual rooms along the second floor. The law enforcement group stood out in the oval hallway only a short distance from the steps they'd come up. Three other sets of steps mirrored the points of a compass.

Will stood behind Tarlton and saw the woman with the man in the room. Both of them were getting dressed hurriedly. The man held a Baggie of drugs that he was frantically trying to pour down the sink at the back of the room at the same time.

"Police!" Tarlton yelled. "Put the Baggie down and step back with—"

At that time, the young woman brought up the Colt .357 Magnum she'd been holding. She had a good hold on the pistol and appeared to know what she was doing with it. She had Chinese tattoos inked along her forearms.

Will hooked a hand into the collar of Tarlton's Kevlar vest and yanked the police chief back as he started to backpedal. Tarlton hadn't seen the threat the woman offered until it was almost too late. Muscling the man out of the doorway smoothly and efficiently, Will pressed Tarlton into the wall just as the woman started firing.

The Magnum hollow points fragmented against the doorframe and blew splinters out into the hallway. The reports in the enclosed space were deafening. They punctuated the long scream the young woman loosed.

Will knew she was on drugs and stoned out of her mind. He'd noticed the wildness in her eyes. She wasn't even totally aware of what she was doing.

Pressed up against the wall, Will gave silent thanks to God for allowing him to see the young woman's movements. He'd been just as focused on the man at the back of the room as Tarlton was.

One of the deputies spun around the doorframe and lowered his semiautomatic into position. "Sheriff's department!" he bellowed.

The young woman turned toward him.

The woman was out of bullets. Will knew that. The wheel gun she grasped so tightly only carried six rounds. She'd fired all of those into the doorframe. He'd counted out of habit.

The deputy reacted anyway. He looked young, eager, and afraid, which was always a bad combination.

"No!" Remy said and reached for the man. Evidently he'd counted the shots as well. "She's out of—"

The young woman fired her weapon. Only the dry snap of the hammer striking the firing pin came out of the room.

Mesmerized by his own imagined brush with death, the deputy fired at the woman twice before Remy was able to grab his hands and pull the pistol up. The deputy fired two more shots into the ceiling. Remy body-checked the man and took the weapon away.

But it was too late. Both bullets had struck the young woman. She stutter-stepped back and whipped around in a quarter turn. Blood poured down her right side.

"Stand down!" Tarlton roared. "Hold your fire!"

The biker at the back of the room dropped the Baggie and ran to the woman's side.

Tarlton led the way into the room. He held his pistol before him and aimed at the biker. "Down on the floor!"

"You shot her!" The biker was young, probably in his early twenties. "Man, you didn't have to shoot her!"

The biker was high enough that Will had to wonder if he'd even registered the fact that she'd shot at them first.

"Down!" Tarlton grabbed the man's jacket collar and dragged him to one side. The police chief held the pistol back so it was out of reach. "Get on your face!"

"You killed her!" The biker cursed again in a voice loud enough that Will had no doubt the accusation carried around the oval hallway. "She's dead!"

Remy dropped into position beside the woman. Blood soaked her side as Remy pulled on a pair of surgical gloves from the medical supplies in his combat harness. He put two fingers against the side of her neck and waited.

Then he looked up at Will. "I got a pulse." He reached into other pockets and pulled out compresses.

Tarlton called in the shooting, then snapped handcuffs on the man whose back he was kneeling on. "They got an ambulance and the fire department rolling."

"Anybody here got any medical training?" Remy asked.

One of the policemen raised his hand.

Remy tossed him a pair of surgical gloves. "Put those on. Let's see if we can get the bleeding to stop."

"You got this?" Will asked.

Without looking at him, Remy nodded. Max hovered at his side, gazing around anxiously. The Labrador had already set up a perimeter guard.

Will stepped back out into the hallway. Tarlton, finished with his prisoner, was at his heels.

Bikers emerged from the other rooms. Evidently a lot of them hadn't awakened yet. They came out with guns and shotguns in hand.

"Police!" Will yelled with all the authority he could muster. Since he'd been one of the youngest XOs on an aircraft carrier, he'd learned to project his voice. "Put your weapons down immediately!"

The bikers didn't follow his orders, and Will was certain the hallway was about to turn into a bloodbath.

Farther down, Victor Gant stepped into the hallway with a pistol in his fist.

"Gant!" Will yelled. "Tell them to put the guns down or this is going to go very badly."

"For who?" Victor grinned at him with cold maliciousness. "Seems to me we got you outnumbered up here."

"It's not going to play out like that," Will promised. "And you know it. We're ready for this and your men are still getting it together. If this starts on your word, you're the first man to go down."

Victor hesitated for a moment. Will saw the indecision on the man's face. Victor wanted to push the situation into a violent confrontation.

Will centered his shotgun's sights over the man's chest. He still wasn't certain he'd gotten his point across. His finger curled over the trigger.

"You heard him," Victor said without looking at anyone. "Put your weapons down and plant your faces on the floor."

After he issued his command, Victor dropped to his face on the floor and waited quietly to be taken into custody.

Will went forward and cuffed him.

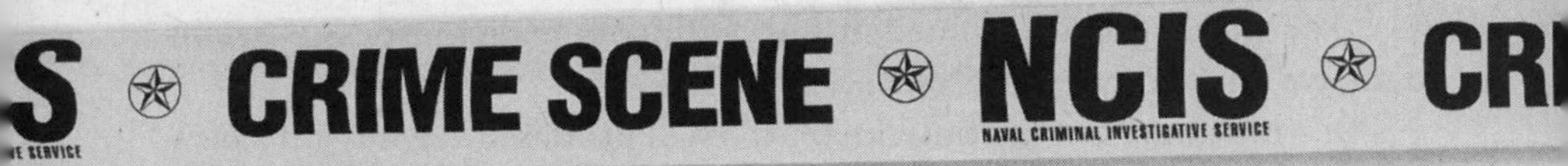
CRIME SCENE
NCIS
NAVAL CRIMINAL INVESTIGATIVE SERVICE

30

E SCENE ✪ NCIS NAVAL CRIMINAL INVESTIGATIVE SERVICE ✪ CRIME SCENE

>> HAWTHORNE MACHINE SHOP
>> HAWTHORNE LANE
>> CHARLOTTE, NORTH CAROLINA
>> 0801 HOURS

"Why are you here?" Victor Gant demanded.

Will hauled the man to his feet and pushed him face-first into the nearest wall. The man reeked of sour sweat, alcohol, and reefer smoke.

"Because you made it personal," Will answered.

Victor cursed. "Your people did that when they killed my boy."

"Bobby Lee brought what happened to him on himself."

"Yeah, well so did your gunnery sergeant."

Will grabbed a handful of the man's hair and yanked his head around so he could face him. "Now I'm making it personal. I'm going to put you away, and when you get out, I'm going to put you away again. You're not going to be able to breathe without me standing in your shadow as long as I feel like you're a threat to one of my people."

Victor glared at him. "You don't have that kind of time, cap'n."

"You'd be surprised at the kind of time I have," Will stated.

A lazy smile pulled at Victor's cruel mouth. "Don't know what you think you got on me, but you ain't gonna make it stick."

"We're going to start with breaking and entering at the ME's office," Tarlton said as he cuffed a man next to Victor. "That's just to get you in a cage. Then Commander Coburn is going to bring up charges of tampering with evidence in a homicide investigation."

"What evidence!" Victor tried to push off the wall.

Will dropped a knee into the back of Victor's knee and caused it to go out from under him. He put an elbow into Victor's back and bounced him off the wall.

"Stay," Will growled.

"Your son was killed," Tarlton said. "Until Gunnery Sergeant McHenry is cleared of any wrongful charges—and he will be—Bobby Lee's body is evidence in the investigation. We have a witness who says you broke in and touched the body."

"I was saying good-bye to my son!" Victor roared.

Will heard the pain in the man's voice and couldn't help feeling it as a father himself. He couldn't imagine how he would act or how he would go on if something ever happened to Steven.

Put that away, he told himself. *You've got a job to do here. You're not Victor Gant, and Steven is never going to be Bobby Lee.*

Will prayed for that to be true with all his heart.

"Chief Tarlton," someone called over the radio.

"Yeah," Tarlton responded.

"I got an FBI agent here, name of Urlacher. He says he wants to talk to you about Victor Gant."

"Tell him I'm busy." Tarlton pulled the biker he'd cuffed from the wall and started walking him down the hallway.

"Yes, sir. I did. But he's waving some kind of legal paper at me that he seems right proud of."

"It's a court injunction," Urlacher bellowed loud enough to be picked up by the radio. "You're interfering in a federal case."

Tarlton glanced at Will. "Sounds like Urlacher went directly to the nuclear weapons. You got enough muscle to handle this?"

"I don't know," Will answered.

"Man," Victor said, grinning now, "you guys ought to know you can't screw with the FBI."

⊛ ⊛ ⊛

>> PARKING LOT
>> HAWTHORNE MACHINE SHOP
>> 0824 HOURS

"Let me translate the big words for you, Commander Coburn, Chief Tarlton," Special Agent-in-Charge Urlacher growled. "You can*not* usurp control of my informant. He's under my protection. More than that, he's under the protection of Judge Terri Watson. You have no right to arrest him."

Tarlton leaned against the police car and eyed the FBI agent with grave distaste. "Actually, I have every right to arrest your *informant*. He's been interfering with an ongoing homicide investigation."

"He went to say good-bye to his son." Urlacher looked apoplectic.

"Then," Tarlton said evenly, "we agree that he broke and entered."

"Even if he did," Urlacher said, "here's his get-out-of-jail-free card." The FBI agent waved the injunction that prevented the detainment of Victor Gant.

Will wasn't happy. He stood at the rear of the police vehicle where the motorcycle leader had been stashed. On the other side of the parking lot, Remy worked with EMTs to stabilize the woman the sheriff's deputy had shot.

"Give Gant to me," Urlacher stated in a harsh voice, "or you're going to be in contempt of Judge Watson's court."

Since Judge Watson presided over a federal court in Washington, D.C., Will knew that Tarlton—and he—could be buried in a mountain of red tape and possibly face criminal charges.

Still, Tarlton didn't seem to be impressed. He leaned a hip against the car and smiled. "You know, Will, I've had a lot of people threaten me during the time I've been chief here. You probably have too."

"I have," Will agreed. He didn't always play nice with people outside the military's rank and file either. The military was a different matter, though. Everything had a chain of command, and that was obeyed first.

"You ever been threatened by the FBI?" Tarlton looked as though he was really interested in the answer to his question.

"Not threatened, exactly."

"They threw the big intimidation cloud, didn't they?"

"Pretty much."

"Offered interdepartmental assistance, then hosed you the first chance they got and got all offensive when you called them on it."

Urlacher turned redder.

Despite the situation, Will found he was taking a perverse satisfaction at digging his heels in. He wasn't going to let Tarlton swing by himself if things went south.

"That sums it up," Will agreed.

"We found a lot of weapons in that warehouse, didn't we?"

The Purple Royals, as it turned out, had had quite a cache of weapons on hand. Tarlton and Will were guessing that they'd been planning on a big trade-off somewhere. Weapons were better than cash in a lot of third world countries.

"We did," Will agreed.

"Do you think we could make a case for Homeland Security?" Tarlton asked.

"It's possible."

Urlacher had reached his limit. He took a step forward and jabbed Tarlton in the chest with his forefinger. "You listen. If you don't let that man go this instant, I'm going to—"

"What?" Tarlton interrupted. "Run and tell? And if you poke me with the finger again, I'm going to snap it off and shove it up your nose."

Urlacher withdrew his hand. "Give me Victor Gant." He pulled his phone off his belt. "Now."

In the end, Will knew they had no real choice.

Tarlton nodded at the police officer manning the vehicle's rear door.

The policeman opened the door and hauled Gant out.

The biker grinned. "Special Agent Urlacher," he acknowledged. "Good to see you again."

Urlacher didn't say anything.

Gant turned to Will. "And you tell your gunnery sergeant that I'll be seeing him soon. Maybe not as soon as I'd hoped, but I'm a patient man."

Will struggled with his temper. He tried to play it cool, but he was tired and stymied. More than that, he was protective of his team. They were family to him, and a man didn't let his family get threatened without drawing a line in the sand. He'd tried to do that here today, but Urlacher had yanked the fangs from that.

Walk away, he told himself. *Just let it go.* But he didn't like feeling powerless, and he didn't like having his team exposed to predation.

"And since you've gotten so swollen up over this thing," Gant said, "maybe I'll pick off another one of your people while I'm—"

Nothing human could have held Will in check at that moment. He'd turned the other cheek and tried to work within the law. That hadn't worked out. His anger exploded. He stepped forward and threw an eight-inch punch into the center of Gant's stomach.

The biker's breath shut down immediately. Will hit him again with a hook that caught him in the side of the jaw.

Gant's legs turned to rubber, and he dropped to his knees. His shaggy hair fell over his shoulders.

Then Tarlton was there, wrapping his arms around Will and butting Will back with his chest.

"Easy, champ," Tarlton said. "You've made your point."

Will let himself be led away. He felt guilty at once, but there was a savage need to protect his people that still demanded to be fed.

"It's all right," he said calmly. "I'm good."

Tarlton stepped away from him but remained between him and Gant.

"Urlacher," Tarlton said without turning around or taking his eyes from Will, "pick up your trash and get out of here before I decide to run you in for littering."

Gant hacked and spat and gagged as he tried to regain his breath.

"You can't do this," Urlacher said to Will. He caught one of Gant's arms and helped the man to his feet. "I'll arrest you myself for assault."

"You're out of the FBI's jurisdiction," Tarlton said. "And if you try to press any charges, I'll bury you and your new pet ape on the court docket. You can expect a nice long stay in town if you want." He turned to face Urlacher. "Do we understand each other?"

Urlacher bit back a reply, swallowed, then nodded.

"Get him out of here," Tarlton ordered. "Before I decide to find out if Judge Watson is really interested in backing your play by sending somebody here."

"Get these cuffs off me," Victor Gant growled. His dark eyes lasered into Will's.

"I don't think that's a good idea." Urlacher pulled on Victor's arm.

Victor whipped his arm free of the FBI agent. He spat blood at Will's feet.

"You got a guy on your team who likes blowing up kids that don't know better," Victor snarled, "and you're mighty big on hitting guys who got their hands cuffed."

Will felt bad about that. As much as Victor Gant had had it coming, Will still didn't like taking advantage of the situation. At the time, though, he hadn't even thought about it.

"You Navy boys never was all that tough back in the jungle," Victor said. "You guys never stayed till the water got hot."

"I'll be here," Will said.

"We'll see, Navy man." Victor showed him a mirthless, scarlet grin. Then he let himself be led away by Urlacher. His mocking laughter sounded even after the FBI agents put him in the car.

Will watched the FBI vehicles drive away.

"You know," Tarlton said, "I think that went really well."

Will watched the cars make the corner and disappear. "That's sarcasm, right?"

"One of my best things. Totally underappreciated if you ask me, though."

"I can see how that would happen." Will let out a tense breath. "About hitting him—"

"If you hadn't, I would have."

"Not a good thing to do."

"I forgive you. It's not like Victor Gant asked anybody's permission for killing those men."

"We don't know that he killed anybody," Will said.

"We haven't *proven* he's killed anybody. I don't have a single doubt about his guilt. And I intend on trying to pin him to one of those murders we *suspect* him of."

"It would be interesting to see if we can put that together."

"Kind of like a hobby," Tarlton said.

"I like the occasional hobby," Will said.

"The problem is, if you make Victor Gant a hobby, he's going to come back on you."

Will didn't say anything. He'd gotten that feeling as well.

"He'll probably try for that sergeant of yours first," Tarlton said. "But you can bet he's marked a spot on his dance card for you as well."

"Yeah." Will took another breath. "In the meantime, Urlacher will keep him locked down. That's almost as good as putting him in jail."

Tarlton nodded. "It would be interesting to know what Urlacher's working on."

"The heroin supplier."

"You got all that NCIS equipment and those international contacts."

"I do."

"You might want to broaden your new hobby and take a look into that end of things."

Will smiled. "I was thinking about that myself."

"I'm thinking that Sheriff Greene and I can shake up the Purple Royals while Victor Gant is MIA. We can send you a few more heroin samples. Maybe get you some names you can run through those fancy computers you have."

"You have computers."

"I'm betting your computers are better than our computers," Tarlton said. "I'm also betting if anyone can trace that heroin back overseas, your agency is going to have a better shot at it than the Charlotte police department."

"I'll let you know," Will said.

31

SCENE ✪ NCIS ✪ CRIME SCENE
NAVAL CRIMINAL INVESTIGATIVE SERVICE

>> INTENSIVE CARE UNIT
>> PRESBYTERIAN HOSPITAL
>> CHARLOTTE, NORTH CAROLINA
>> 1208 HOURS

Shel held his cell phone to his ear and listened to the phone ring at the other end. He watched the news footage of the raid on the warehouse that Will and Remy had gone on. Seeing the news story made him feel guilty. He belonged out in the field, not in a hospital bed.

"Shel?" Estrella answered in a friendly and surprised voice.

Shel muted the television. All that was left was the hum of machinery and Don's light snoring as he slept in the chair next to the bed.

"Hey, Estrella," Shel replied. He continued the conversation in Spanish because he wanted privacy and he hadn't seen a Hispanic nurse in the ICU yet. "Did you decide to take the morning off since Will's out of town?"

"Ha," Estrella responded. "I only took the morning off because I worked all night helping Will track information regarding Victor Gant. Now I find out that it only half worked."

"Yeah, well, the Feds got involved." Shel scratched his nose. There was still enough morphine in his meds to make his nose itch.

"Will's got me looking into Special Agent-in-Charge Scott Urlacher's caseload now."

"Under the radar, of course."

"Of course. So how are you?"

"Bored. Ready to get out of here."

"Bored, huh?" Estrella said. "I can't believe you're still slacking."

"Now that I know they make you lie in bed this long, I'm gonna make it a point never to get shot again."

"Good plan. Did you think that up all by yourself?"

"I did."

"Head hurt much?"

"Don't worry about it. They've got me on pain meds."

Estrella laughed.

"Has Will given you any clue what he's wanting now?" Shel asked.

"Will thinks Urlacher wants Victor Gant's heroin supplier."

"It's not somebody local?"

"Judging from the purity of the drugs Victor Gant's people have been caught handling, I'd say it's not local."

"Then where?"

"Probably out of the country. Heroin's being traded in Central America, then getting brought into the United States through those supply channels. Usually up Interstate 35."

"But along the way, it gets stepped on," Shel said.

"Usually pretty hard," Estrella agreed. "So everybody along the way can take their cut. The stuff the Purple Royals are running is almost pure."

"They have a direct route."

"I think so."

"And that's why the FBI is so hot and heavy after the source."

"It would be a nice bust," Estrella said. "But you didn't call to talk about that. You're just covering ground that you know Will has already covered."

Shel didn't say anything.

"Why did you really call?" Estrella asked.

"I'm getting the feeling you know me too well," Shel said.

"I do. So fess up."

Shel hesitated. "This is about my daddy, Estrella."

Estrella waited and didn't say anything. He knew she was aware that he didn't talk about his father much.

"I got a phone call from him in the middle of the night," Shel said. "He was drunk. Or had been drinking. Not enough to get totally skunk-faced, but drunker than I've ever heard him."

"All right."

Shel hesitated, knowing that once he pressed forward there would be no going back. "You know I don't have a good relationship with my daddy."

"Yes."

"For him to call out of the blue like that?" Shel shook his head. "Something's going on."

"What do you want me to do?"

"Victor Gant was a career Army man. He pulled tours in Vietnam. So did my daddy."

"You think Victor Gant served with your father?"

"That's the only way Daddy could have gotten to know someone like Victor Gant. Gant's from North Carolina. Daddy grew up in west Texas. Except for the Army, Daddy's never been out of the state. Never off the ranch much either."

"I can pull records from the United States Army," Estrella said. "But this is something that's going to take a while. The military is still archiving some of that information."

"It's a needle in a haystack," Shel agreed. "I knew that before I decided to ask you to take a look."

"I'm glad you appreciate the effort."

Shel hesitated a moment, then knew he had no choice if he wanted to keep his privacy. He cleared his throat. "One other thing."

"Sure."

"While you're poking around in those files, I'd appreciate it if you kept this below the radar." Shel hated asking her to do that. It was almost like he was saying he didn't trust Will or the others.

"I can do that," Estrella said.

"It's just that it might not be anything. And if it isn't—if it's just that Daddy was around something Victor Gant did in the military and knows him from that—it's not going to help Will track the heroin."

"I agree," Estrella said. "Personal business is personal business."

"Thanks, Estrella. How's Nicky?"

"Off sailing with Joe and Celia."

"Well," Shel said, gazing out the window, "that sure beats lying in this bed." *And wondering how Daddy knows a man like Victor Gant.*

⊛ ⊛ ⊛

>> RAFTER M RANCH

>> OUTSIDE FORT DAVIS, TEXAS

>> 1236 HOURS (CENTRAL TIME ZONE)

"Do you have a headache, Senor Tyrel?"

Even though he was wearing his hat to shade his eyes against the bright noonday sun, Tyrel squinted to look at Ramon.

The youngster sat astride a paint mare. Red west Texas dust covered him like powder that had been sifted on. His black hair gleamed in the bright sunlight.

"I'm fine," Tyrel said sourly as he continued to lean on the corral. But he wasn't. He had a headache that felt like it was going to suck the top of his skull in and pour it out through his ears. It had been years since he'd had one like that.

The newborn colt frolicked in the sunlight. Although he wasn't anywhere near coordinated enough yet, the colt tried to kick his heels as he ran around his mama.

"That little horse is going to be a dickens," Ramon said. He grinned at the colt's antics.

Despite the way he felt, Tyrel grinned a little at that. The word was his and he knew it. Hearing Ramon say it just sounded funny.

"You don't look so good." Ramon dismounted and tied the reins to the corral.

"I feel better'n I look," Tyrel growled. "I can still set a horse longer than there are hours in the day."

Ramon shrugged. "I didn't say you couldn't. I was just wondering if you should get in out of the sun."

Irritation flared inside Tyrel. He reined it in because he didn't want to visit any of it on the boy.

"I suddenly look old to you, Ramon?" he asked.

"No, senor. You looked this old yesterday too." The answer was earnest and innocent of rancor.

"You know," Tyrel said, "now I'm kinda wishing I hadn't asked that question."

"Why?" Ramon looked confused.

"Never mind, amigo. The fences all look good?"

"*Sí.*" Ramon reached into his shirt pocket. "There are a few places we need to mend soon. I made notes." He passed over the small notebook Tyrel always sent him with.

Tyrel glanced through the notes, then pocketed the notebook. "You eat yet?"

"I had a burrito I took with me. I'm all right."

"You're young, amigo. You can eat again. Come on inside the house. I got a pot of beans on."

Ramon looked troubled. "Are you sure?"

"I wouldn't have asked if I hadn't been." Tyrel threw the dregs of the coffee into the corral and spooked the little colt into jumping and nearly getting tangled up in his spindly legs.

Even with the hangover plaguing him, the colt's surprise pleased Tyrel. He laughed a little. That kind of innocence, where everything in the world was surprising, was hard to come by. He missed it.

⊛⊛⊛

>> INTERVIEW ROOM
>> FEDERAL BUREAU OF INVESTIGATION FIELD OFFICE
>> CHARLOTTE, NORTH CAROLINA
>> 1348 HOURS

"I'm in a real bad mood here, Victor."

"Maybe you should try a nap," Victor said. "I hear a lot of people put store by them."

Urlacher sat on the other side of the table. "You think you're smart, don't you?"

"Maybe so, but it seems like you're the one with all the questions," Victor said. He sipped the Gatorade someone had gotten for him. He'd turned down the offer of coffee, water, and a soft drink to be difficult and to prove that the FBI agents were going to do whatever it took to make him happy.

As long as they thought he was going to rat out his connection.

"Let me give you a few answers for a change," Urlacher said. "I'm protecting you at this point. That protection's not going to last long. And I'm betting that NCIS commander can put something on you that the local cops haven't been able to find. He'll find a body you didn't quite bury enough or buried in the wrong place. Then you're going to be looking at a fall for murder one."

Victor sipped his Gatorade. He didn't feel quite as confident as he had a moment ago, but he wasn't going to let on.

"In fact, I'd be willing to bet that if I let you go, you'll do something stupid about that big Marine who shot Bobby Lee," Urlacher said.

"You can bet the farm on that," Victor grated.

"Even if you manage to kill that man," Urlacher said, "NCIS will hunt you down for it and you'll go away forever anyway."

"They won't find me."

"We found you."

Victor laughed in derision. "I wasn't hiding."

"You know, Victor, that's the first truly stupid thing I've heard you say."

Victor leaned across the table. "If I decide to disappear, I'll disappear. I was trained by Uncle Sam in one of the hardest-fought ground wars the

United States has ever been in. In my time, I've been a ghost. I've walked into camps at night, with armed men everywhere, found the officer in charge, dropped a hand over his mouth, and slit his throat. Then I held him like a baby while he fought and kicked and drowned in his own blood."

Urlacher didn't say anything, but Victor saw that his words had left an impression on the man.

"Don't make the mistake of thinking that just because that Navy guy hit me this morning I can't take care of myself," Victor said.

"I want your connection," Urlacher said.

"You can't have him," Victor said.

"Hanging on to him is foolish."

"Says you."

Urlacher shook his head. "You can't go back to that life, Victor. Whether you're willing to admit it or not, everything you've had up till now is gone. The heat's going to be on your gang. Tarlton will take Fat Mike and the others apart; then they'll break the pieces."

"I don't believe that."

"Then I should just give you back to Coburn and let you take your chances."

"No," Victor said. "You gotta learn to be happy with what I'm willing to give you."

"What you're giving me isn't enough."

Victor finished the Gatorade and set the plastic container aside. "Get a pen and paper. I'll give you the local MS-13 dealers."

Urlacher gestured, and one of the younger agents brought over a legal pad and a pen. The FBI special agent-in-charge slid them over to Victor.

"Get me something to eat," Victor said.

Urlacher just stared at him.

Victor didn't move to take up the pen.

Angrily Urlacher gestured at one of the younger agents.

"Ribs," Victor said. "Falling off the bone. Potato salad and coleslaw. And it better be hot when it gets here. And I want a gallon of tea."

Urlacher nodded, and the young agent stepped out of the room.

Victor pulled the pad to him. Then he picked up the pen and started to write. Despite his bravado, he knew he was working on borrowed time. The FBI would protect him only as long as he kept the pump primed. The minute he shut down entirely, they would too.

You know enough, he told himself. *You stretch it out, give it to them a piece at a time, you're gonna be fine. Fat Mike or Tran will come through for you.*

And then he was going to find that Marine sergeant and blow his candle out.

32

E SCENE ✪ NCIS ✪ CRIME SCENE
NAVAL CRIMINAL INVESTIGATIVE SERVICE

>> INTENSIVE CARE UNIT
>> PRESBYTERIAN HOSPITAL
>> CHARLOTTE, NORTH CAROLINA
>> 1402 HOURS

"What are you doing?"

"I'm getting out of bed," Shel said. "It's what you do when you choose not to sleep all day. Like some people I could name." He pulled the IV stand toward him.

"I don't think you're supposed to get out of bed." Don pushed himself up from the chair.

Suddenly light-headed, Shel hesitated for a moment. He breathed slowly and steadily till the feeling passed. Then he disconnected the sensors attached to the adhesive pads stuck to his chest and pulled off the finger sensor.

The machines immediately chirped for attention.

"The nurse is going to know," Don said.

"If you would stop being such an Eeyore," Shel complained as some of the pain hit him, "we might be able to make an escape before the nurse comes to investigate."

"You're going to get into trouble."

"Not if we hurry. And they don't build Marine-size trouble here."

"*I'm* going to get into trouble."

Shel chuckled. "If I hadn't gotten you into trouble when we were kids, you would have turned out boring. You wouldn't have anything to talk about in church."

"We didn't get into any real trouble."

"*This* isn't any real trouble."

"Says you," Don told him. "All you have to do is fake being in pain and they'll leave you alone."

"Tell them you came after me as soon as you found out I was gone. I'll back you up."

"You're not going to be able to escape. You're decrepit."

"I'll warm up." Shel used the IV stand as a crutch and got to his feet. He was actually amazed to find that he could stand on his own.

"You're going to fall flat on your face."

"When I do, you can tell me that you told me so then. At the moment, a little more help with the escape, please." Shel started to shuffle off.

"Hey," Don called. "Wait."

"I don't have time to wait. Escaping's more of an active thing."

"Yeah, well unless you intend to moon the rest of the people in ICU, you'd better put this robe on."

Shel turned to find Don standing there with a robe. "Thought I noticed a draft." He held his good arm up, and Don slid the robe's sleeve over it. Then, with his good arm over Don's shoulders and Don holding on to the IV stand, they were off.

"Do you have any idea where you're going?" Don asked.

"Yeah. To see my dog."

"Max left with Commander Coburn and Remy last night."

"Yeah, well he's back now."

"How do you know that?"

"I'm a Marine," Shel said. "We know things."

✪ ✪ ✪

>> RAFTER M RANCH
>> OUTSIDE FORT DAVIS, TEXAS
>> 1307 HOURS (CENTRAL TIME ZONE)

Tyrel dished up bowls of pinto beans flavored with jalapeños and onions, then put them on the table at the same time the oven timer went off. He used a dish towel to fetch out the pan of corn bread.

Before he reached the counter, he knew he should have gotten an oven mitt. The towel was damp enough to conduct the heat. Still, he managed to get the pan to the counter without dropping it. The distraction provided by the hangover helped.

He waited a few minutes for the corn bread to cool while he watched ESPN. Watching baseball was only a habit, though. His thoughts were on Shel and Don. And the danger they faced.

Victor Gant was probably the most dangerous and cold-blooded man Tyrel had ever had the misfortune to meet. He could remember that night in Qui Nhon like it was yesterday. The metallic odor of blood filled his nostrils.

"Don't you worry none about this, Private McHenry. You're Army. We're Army. We'll take care of this. Ain't nobody never gonna know. This'll be our little secret."

But that little secret had gotten bigger and heavier to carry every year. Tyrel sometimes thought it was amazing that his back and shoulders weren't bent under the weight of it. Back when the boys' mother had still been alive, it hadn't weighed as much. Being alone had made the burden worse.

❂ ❂ ❂

>> 1322 HOURS (CENTRAL TIME ZONE)

Ramon entered the small kitchen and looked a little apprehensive. Tyrel knew the boy wasn't completely at ease around him even though they'd known each other for years. Most people, Tyrel reflected, hadn't been at ease with him.

He didn't regret it. That was just how things had been. With the hand that God had dealt him, that was just the best that things could be.

Don was always at him about seeking God's help for one thing and another, but Tyrel knew the truth. That one evil thing he'd done in Qui Nhon had pushed him right out of the Lord's sight.

No sparrow fell without God knowing, but he still let them sparrows fall, didn't he?

"Did you get your hands washed?" Tyrel asked.

"*Sí*, senor." Ramon stood awkwardly.

"Pull out a chair and have a sit."

Ramon did.

Tyrel cut the corn bread into large hunks and put them on a plate. He put the plate on the table, then got the butter—fresh-churned, none of that store-bought stuff—from the refrigerator. His wife had always made it before she died, but he did now because it reminded him of her.

"What would you like to drink?" Tyrel asked.

"Anything will be all right," Ramon said.

Tyrel opened the refrigerator and peered inside. He ran on coffee all day, but he kept milk and some juice and soda pop for Don and Joanie's kids.

"I got juice and pop," Tyrel said.

"Either will be fine," Ramon said. "Thank you."

"I got strawberry pop," Tyrel offered. "Don and Joanie's kids seem to like that."

"I like strawberry."

Tyrel took a can of pop from the refrigerator and stopped himself short of just plunking it down on the table.

"You want a glass?" Tyrel asked.

"The can is fine."

Tyrel handed it to the boy, then poured himself a tall glass of buttermilk. He sat at the table and took his hat off.

"Do you want to give thanks, senor?" Ramon asked.

The question caught Tyrel off-stride. Normally he and Ramon didn't take meals together. Tyrel provided food, but generally food was eaten on the run, microwaved from the refrigerator, and eaten out of hand or alone.

Tyrel blinked at the teenager and felt increasingly uncomfortable. He didn't give thanks for meals. There hadn't been much in his life to give thanks for in a long, long time.

"If you don't want to . . . ," Ramon said.

"No," Tyrel said. "Giving thanks is all right. Your mama and daddy raised you up right. I was just forgetting myself, is all. I'm not used to eating with somebody and saying it out loud." He hesitated. "You know the words?"

"*Sí*, senor."

"Then why don't you say 'em?"

"If you wish, but my father always reserves the right to lead prayer at his dinner table. He says it is a father's duty to show the way to God and all things in the world."

"Well," Tyrel said, "I've always thought your daddy was a smart man. One of the smartest I've ever known. Now and again, I've told him that."

Ramon smiled, more at ease now. "*Sí*, senor. Very smart."

"But this here's my table, and I do things a little differently. Don was always the one to give thanks."

"Pastor Don?" Ramon grinned. Don was well liked by most of the community.

"Since he ain't here, why don't you do it?"

"Of course, senor. I will be glad to." Ramon put his hands together, closed his eyes, and bowed his head.

Even though he felt like a hypocrite, Tyrel put his hands together too.

He didn't close his eyes or bow his head, though. He wasn't that much of a hypocrite.

Ramon prayed in a strong, steady voice. All of the insecurity he had shown was gone. "God, we give our thanks for this meal and for your blessing. Thank you for the fine young horse you gave to Senor McHenry. He is beautiful. Thank you for our chance to be together today. Keep us in your sight and always guide us in your ways. Amen."

Tyrel took a deep, slow breath and tried not to think too hard on the fact that he didn't feel the trust the boy obviously did. God had turned away from him a long time ago. He'd accepted that.

⊛ ⊛ ⊛

>> 1328 HOURS (CENTRAL TIME ZONE)

Tyrel and Ramon ate in silence. Tyrel was never moved much to talk while he ate. Eating was a chore, something to be done so he could move on to his next thing to do. But he remained conscious of the boy, and he was beginning to think he'd made a mistake to ask Ramon to stay. Tyrel still didn't know why he'd done that.

As Tyrel had watched the boy praying, still clad in his dust-covered clothes, he'd been reminded of how many times he'd seen Shel and Don sit across that table from him. He'd watched them grow up at that table, had talked with them about the ranch and chastised them there too. But he'd missed a lot of dinners with them because there was always something to do around the ranch.

Had he attended more dinners than he'd missed? Tyrel honestly couldn't remember, and it hurt him that he didn't know. Then he got angry because he hadn't been the one to choose to be away from the table on those evenings. He would have liked to have been at dinner instead of chasing cows, mending fences, or working on the equipment.

His life hadn't gone the way he'd wanted it to in a long time. Still, the guilt even at this late date was sharp and jagged-edged. It cut especially deeply today, and he didn't know what had caused that.

Looking at Ramon in his work-stained clothes, Tyrel remembered how Shel had been as a boy. Quiet and methodical, always giving himself to everything he'd ever wanted to do. He had constantly challenged himself and everything around him, like he could throw a saddle on the world and ride it till he had it in hand.

But listening to Ramon's words had made Tyrel think of Don. Like his mama, Don had always been pulled toward the church and God. When he'd been young, Tyrel had been like Shel, but he'd given his Sundays to the Lord. That was how he'd met the boys' mama. They'd gotten to know each other at Sunday school, then started dating at church socials.

When he'd gone away to Vietnam, Tyrel had known she might forget about him or give up on him. A lot of women during that time did. After the events that night at Qui Nhon, he hoped she had forgotten about him. He stopped writing her back; he started drinking and just put in his days on patrol, expecting the bullet that would cut him down and balance the scales that he owed.

But that bullet never came. And when he'd gotten back to the States, she was waiting. Despite his best intentions to turn away from her because he knew he wasn't the man she thought she knew—and definitely not the man she deserved—he'd been drawn to her.

"Senor?"

Tyrel looked up at Ramon. "What?"

"Are you going to call Pastor Don and his family?"

"Why?"

"To tell him about the colt. You promised him you would call."

Joanie and the kids wanted to know when the colt was born. Tyrel had forgotten that.

"The children will want to see the baby horse," Ramon went on.

"I'll give 'em a call when we finish up here," Tyrel said. He felt resentful about having to do it, though. Don and Joanie knew how to keep their distance from him, but their kids didn't. They kept trying to treat him like a grandpa.

"Good." Ramon smiled. "They'll like the colt."

Looking at the boy, Tyrel suddenly missed Shel and Don when they were that age. Shel had been the fireball of the two, always in the middle of something and always pushing himself to go faster and higher. Don had been more quietly contemplative, but he'd let Shel talk him into trouble more than a few times. They'd never gotten into bad trouble, but often enough they'd gone and done when they shouldn't have been going and doing. It was just how boys became young men.

He pushed those feelings away. He had no place for them. More than that, he didn't deserve them. Their mama had been the real parent in the family. Not him.

He turned his attention to eating and walled away from the past like he'd done every day since Qui Nhon. He'd lost his past the night he shot that soldier, and he had denied the future every day he'd lived since.

That was the best he could do.

He'd held up for forty years doing that. If Victor Gant's name hadn't come at him, he was sure he could have finished out his tour on this world and been done with it. He concentrated on that and thought about the work he had ahead of him.

⊛ ⊛ ⊛

>> VISITORS' ROOM
>> PRESBYTERIAN HOSPITAL
>> CHARLOTTE, NORTH CAROLINA
>> 1432 HOURS

"See? I told you he was here."

Don gazed across the room and saw Max lying at Remy Gautreau's feet. Remy was busy chatting up a young woman in a neighboring chair.

"I still don't understand how you knew that," Don said. Over the years that Shel had been paired with Max, he'd often been amazed at the connection between the two.

"Part of being a Marine," Shel responded. "I couldn't explain it to you if I tried."

Max's ears pricked when he recognized Shel's voice. Still, the Labrador didn't move from where he was. His pink tongue snapped back into his mouth and he tensely waited.

Shel made a signal. It was so fast and so small that Don, who was watching, didn't see it.

Immediately the dog hurled himself up and sped across the intervening space. Other people in the waiting room pulled back, but two small boys laughed and pointed at Max. His attention yanked from the pretty woman sitting beside him, Remy made a frantic grab at Max, but he was way off the mark. Then he saw Shel and relaxed.

Max immediately sat on his haunches in front of Shel. He nosed Shel and sniffed the offered palm.

"Hey, buddy," Shel said in a low voice. Carefully, using the IV stand, he knelt beside the dog. Max licked his face in obvious excitement. "It's good to see you too." Shel patted the dog.

"Well, look who came back from the land of the dead," Remy said as he joined them.

Shel looked up. "Don, this is Remy Gautreau. Remy, my brother, Don."

"Are you supposed to be out of bed?" Remy asked Shel as he shook Don's hand.

"Sure," Shel said.

"No," a stern feminine voice said from behind Don. Dread filled him immediately. "He's not supposed to be out of bed."

Busted, Don couldn't help thinking.

Shel reached for Don, who helped pull him to his feet. At the same time, Max stood and took a defensive posture in front of Shel.

The nurse was in her fifties and obviously liked the position of power she had. She had a clipboard in one hand, and her other hand was braced on her hip. Her hair was permed, and she wore pale pink glasses.

"You're not supposed to get out of that bed, mister," the nurse said disdainfully. "You're going to be in big trouble with the doctor."

Doctor, Don thought. The woman used the term like she was addressing a recalcitrant five-year-old.

"Yes, ma'am," Shel said.

"Don't 'yes, ma'am' me. You've got my whole nursing staff in a tizzy." The accusation came out hard and high-pitched.

Don cringed a little. It was the type of voice that bullied other people into submission.

A deep, low growl came from Max's chest.

The nurse peered at the Labrador. "Is that a dog?"

"No, ma'am," Shel said immediately. "That's a Marine."

"That's a dog," the nurse argued. "What is a dog doing in the hospital? And why is he growling at me?"

"He doesn't care for your tone of voice, ma'am," Shel said. He talked more softly. "If I was you, I'd use my inside voice right now."

Don knew that Shel could stop Max's growling with a single word, and he knew there was no threat from the Labrador. But the nurse didn't.

"I'm going to get security," the nurse said defiantly. She backed away; then—when she felt like she'd reached a safe distance—she turned and fled.

"Man," Remy said, "you are gonna be in so much trouble."

"Nah," Shel said.

"Yeah, you are," Don said.

"Is he like this all the time?" Remy asked Don.

"I can't take him anywhere," Don said.

"You guys are funny," Shel said. "Maybe you should think about getting an act together."

"Are you supposed to be out of bed?"

Don turned and saw Commander Coburn coming up the hallway.

"No, sir," Shel said. Despite everything, Don noticed that his brother stood a little straighter.

"Now," Remy whispered, "you're a dead man walking."

At that moment, the head nurse returned with three large security guys in tow. She pointed at Shel and Max.

Smoothly the commander stepped up to intercept the group. He opened his badge case and froze the security guys in place.

"Who's in charge?" the commander asked.

The three security guys looked at the nurse.

"We won't need you," the commander said.

The three security guys faded like morning mist.

Suddenly alone, the nurse looked around nervously.

"I'll need to speak to the doctor in charge of Gunnery Sergeant McHenry," the commander said.

"Doctor is busy."

"Then get someone else who can sign Sergeant McHenry out."

"Only the doctor can do that."

The commander sighed. "Then find the doctor and get him here."

The nurse looked like she was going to protest, but there was something in the commander's steely gaze that broke her in an instant. She turned and hurried away.

The commander walked back to Shel. "Are you ready to get out of here?"

"Yes, sir."

"Then let's get your kit packed. I've got a bed and a doctor waiting for you back at camp."

Shel grimaced.

"I'm pulling rank on this doctor only to get you clear of the situation so we don't endanger civilians," the commander said. "We took Victor Gant down this morning, but that doesn't mean all the Purple Royals are going to stay clear. Do you read me?"

"Five by five, sir." Shel saluted.

"Then let's get a move on. We're burning daylight."

Shel took a step and almost fell. Even though he'd been prepared for the eventuality, knowing Shel would push himself past the point of endurance, Don couldn't get to him in time. But the commander shifted so quick Don almost didn't see the movement. He slid under Shel's arm and supported him.

"I've got you," the commander said. "Do you want a wheelchair?"

"No, sir. I got out here on my own two feet. If you don't mind helping me, I'll get back the same way."

"All right."

Amazed, Don watched them go. Max walked on the other side of Shel.

"Your brother's a tough man," Remy said.

"He always has been," Don said.

"Give him a couple of weeks, he'll probably be good as new."

"I know." Don took a breath and let it out. "I worry about him, though."

"It's okay to worry," Remy said. "It's good to worry. But you have to realize that he's going to chart his own course no matter what you say or do."

"I know that."

"Brothers are special," Remy said in a wistful voice.

The tone caught Don's attention immediately. Whenever someone said cryptic things like that, sounding as if they were halfway in the present and halfway in the past, he knew there was a story. There was always a story.

"You have brothers?" Don asked.

"One," Remy said but didn't turn to look at Don. "I had one."

"I'm sorry," Don said.

"Yeah," Remy said. "Me too." He glanced at his watch. "I've got to get going if I'm going to stay up with the commander. It's been a pleasure meeting you, Don."

Don took the hand Remy offered. "It's been a pleasure meeting you, Remy. And if you ever feel the need to sit down and talk about brothers, I'm here."

Remy held his gaze for a moment. Don saw the pain in the other man's eyes.

"I appreciate that," Remy said. "Maybe someday." Without another word, he took his hand back and walked away.

Don watched him go and wondered at the pain and confusion he'd seen in Remy's gaze. But Don knew from years of experience that whatever the story was, it was meant for another time.

33

E SCENE ✪ NCIS ✪ CRIME SCENE

NAVAL CRIMINAL INVESTIGATIVE SERVICE

>> BRADDOCK ROAD
>> LAKE BARCROFT, VIRGINIA
>> THIRTY-TWO DAYS LATER
>> 0717 HOURS

Death struck without warning on Braddock Road.

Seated in the back of the Suburban, Victor Gant stared through the dust-covered windshield between the two FBI agents. He was cuffed at the ankles and wrists, and the chains from both of those were secured to the thick leather belt around his waist.

Hospitality since he'd been among the FBI under Urlacher's care had dropped tremendously. Victor no longer received much in the way of preferential treatment. In fact, he was convinced that any day Urlacher would send him back to Charlotte and let them prosecute him.

Victor stared at the forest on either side of the two-lane asphalt road. The early morning sun had barely started to penetrate the tightly packed trees.

"You know," Special Agent Ralph Pittman said from the seat beside Victor, "this game you're playing with Urlacher has about run its course."

Victor ignored the man. Pittman was in his late thirties, old enough to talk with some experience but still too young and too full of himself to know when to shut up.

"Urlacher's getting tired of bagging small fish," Pittman said.

The MS-13 connection Victor had given the FBI wasn't small. Victor knew that. It had been a major coup locally, but it wasn't the international connection Urlacher wanted.

Victor also knew that not giving Urlacher that information was the only thing keeping him alive at the moment. If he ratted Tran out and Tran found out about it, his life would be over.

But he could hold out only so long.

When the driver's side window suddenly cracked and the driver's head jerked sideways and blossomed crimson, Victor thought the sniper had been after him. He realized what the danger was before any of the FBI agents in the car did. After all, none of them had ever had to deal with Charlie shooting at them from the brush.

Victor ducked his head into his lap and wrapped his hands over the back of his head. He'd seen guys who had lost a finger or two in an attack but had kept their heads intact.

The Suburban swerved out of control. The agent in the passenger seat grabbed the wheel and tried to keep the vehicle on the road. Despite his efforts, the vehicle swerved across the oncoming lane.

Two blocker vehicles, one in front and one in back, accompanied the transport Suburban. Instead of keeping Victor in lockdown at FBI headquarters in Quantico, Urlacher had demonstrated control by having Victor roused at 5:30 each morning he was going to be interviewed, then driven from the safe house near Lake Barcroft.

For the last two weeks, Victor had been out of ideas. The only thing that had kept him going was his stubborn refusal to give up and give in.

Now he was going to die.

Explosions sounded all around him.

Pittman cursed and pulled his pistol from his hip.

For an instant, Victor thought about attacking the man and taking the pistol from him. The chains were too short to allow that, though.

Without warning, the Suburban slipped off the road and flipped over onto its side. The ground scraped by only inches from Victor. Then the window hit a rock or stump or root embedded in the ground and shattered. The safety glass broke into tiny cubes and trickled away.

Victor slammed into the door and rattled against the exposed ground for a moment as Pittman's body hammered his. Then he felt the Suburban flip completely upside down and continue skidding.

All around Victor, the world seemed to have gone into slow motion. The Suburban spun slightly as it careened across the ground. He caught a glimpse of the rear blocking car stopped in the middle of the road. The vehicle was already wreathed in flames. Judging from the damage, Victor thought it had been hit by a rocket launcher.

Then the Suburban slammed into the trees at the side of the road. The windshield gave way as branches and underbrush invaded.

As Victor hung upside down in the seat, held in place by the belts, his head slammed into the window frame. He tried to hold on to his swirling senses, all too aware that gunfire was coming closer. He thought he heard footsteps outside the vehicle.

Then his vision and hearing splintered. He surrendered to the darkness.

⊛ ⊛ ⊛

>> 0723 HOURS

Pain strobed Victor's head even before he snapped his eyes open. The bright light made him close them again, then blink till he could stand it. His ears felt like they were packed with cotton; sounds seemed far away.

Beside him, Pittman flailed weakly and cursed. Blood spooled from his mouth and ran up his face, which was actually down because he was inverted as well. His pistol lay loose on the Suburban's ceiling. He flailed weakly for the weapon.

Concentrating, Victor reached for the pistol. There was just enough slack in the seat belts and the chains that held him for him to reach the pistol. He curled his fingers around it, then brought it up and pointed it at Pittman.

The FBI agent suddenly looked scared.

"No. Please," Pittman said hoarsely.

Victor's heart held no pity. While he'd been held by the FBI agents, he'd been aware of how much they all hated him. When he'd had some control over the situation, that had all been all right. But when that control had evaporated, they had stopped playing nice with him.

But now he had control again.

He pointed the pistol at Pittman's face and squeezed the trigger. The FBI agent stopped in mid-scream. He slumped, relaxed in death.

"Here," someone said.

Feet outside the Suburban tromped through the underbrush around the trees the vehicle had smashed up. The smell of gasoline drenched the area.

Victor shifted as quickly as he could and aimed the pistol toward the broken window. When he saw the man's face, he almost pulled the trigger out of reflex.

"Easy, Victor," Fat Mike said. "We come to get you out."

Although he moved the pistol out of Fat Mike's face, Victor didn't relax. His body hurt from the impact and his senses still spun.

On his knees, Fat Mike pulled out a switchblade, flicked it open, and put a big hand behind Victor's head, cradling it protectively.

"You're gonna fall, bro," Fat Mike said. "Try not to break your neck."

"I won't break my neck," Victor growled. "Just get me out of here."

Fat Mike sawed at the seat belts with the knife. The belts parted without warning. Victor dropped but managed to catch most of his weight on a shoulder. For a moment, though, he thought he'd broken his collarbone.

Another biker came over and helped Fat Mike ease Victor from the Suburban. They pulled him to his feet.

"Dead guy in the backseat has the keys to the cuffs," Victor said.

Fat Mike crawled into the Suburban.

Throbbing pain filled Victor's head as he gazed around the battlefield. When he saw all the violence that had been wrought, he knew no other term would adequately describe the scene.

One of the Suburbans sat in the middle of the road. Black smoke swirled up from the flames that wreathed the vehicle. The other Suburban was two hundred yards farther on. It lay on its passenger side on the other side of the road.

As Victor watched, one of the bikers tossed a Molotov cocktail into the vehicle and ran. Almost immediately, the Molotov cocktail caught fire and the Suburban began to burn.

Someone was still alive in the vehicle. Victor heard fear-filled screams of pain.

"Idiots," Victor said.

"Why?" Fat Mike stood up in front of him and started working on the cuffs with a key ring.

"Smoke's going to mark our twenty." Victor felt the weight of the cuffs drop away. Fat Mike knelt and started on the ones around his ankles.

"These guys carry GPS devices everywhere they go," Fat Mike said. "They probably already got ground units and air support closing on us."

The ankle cuffs dropped away.

"Then we'd better fade the heat," Victor said.

"Already taken care of." Fat Mike swept a small radio from his hip. "Move in."

"Roger that," someone said.

A moment later, the thunder of Harleys filled the area.

"How did you find me?" Victor asked.

"Wasn't us," Fat Mike replied. "It was Tran."

"How'd Tran find me?"

"You'll have to ask him. He gave me a number for you to call once we're clear of this."

A moment later, motorcycles poured out of the woods. The Harleys weren't trail bikes and were too heavy for soft ground, but evidently Fat Mike had found suitable places to go to ground.

"Tran sent you?" Victor asked.

"Yeah."

"What if you hadn't gotten me?"

Fat Mike met Victor's gaze dead-on. "We ain't gonna talk about that, bro. We did get you."

Victor knew that if Tran was concerned about him rolling over for the police, he would have had him whacked. He didn't blame Tran. It was just business.

"You okay to ride?" Fat Mike asked.

"The day I can't ride," Victor said, "you just drop me in a hole and cover me over."

One of the bikers rode toward him. Victor threw a leg over the bike, wrapped an arm around the man's midriff, and sat behind him.

"We got a place near here we can hole up," Fat Mike said.

Victor nodded. "What about that Marine who killed Bobby Lee? Did you find out anything about him?"

Fat Mike frowned.

"Do you know where he is?" Victor demanded.

"Yeah. They went back to the Marine camp at Lejeune." Fat Mike scratched his shaggy beard. "I think that's one beehive you ought to leave alone, bro."

Victor stared his friend in the eyes. "And you know that's the one I can't leave alone."

Slowly Fat Mike nodded. "I know, bro. We'll just have to be careful."

CRIME SCENE

34

E SCENE ✪ NCIS ✪ CRIME SCENE

NAVAL CRIMINAL INVESTIGATIVE SERVICE

>> OBSTACLE COURSE
>> CAMP GEIGER, NORTH CAROLINA
>> NINE DAYS LATER
>> 0734 HOURS

"You ready to give up yet, gunney?"

Drenched in sweat, feeling the burn of hard-used muscles in his legs and back, Shel concentrated on running. Running shouldn't be hard. It was one of the easiest things to do in the Marines. Even green recruits could run.

"No," Shel gritted. His shoulder still pained him, but it was healing faster than everyone—but him—expected it to heal. "I got more."

"I don't think you have any more, gunney," the young Marine beside him taunted. "I think you're old and you're used up. I think you're scraping the bottom of the barrel. I think you're just holding back, trying to save something for whatever you think will be the end of this little walk before breakfast."

His voice was nasal and full of flat *a*'s. It definitely marked him as a Yankee. Shel was certain the drill instructor who'd paired the man with him this morning had done so on purpose.

"If you need me to slow down," the young Marine offered, "you just bleat in pain."

Ignore him, Shel told himself. *He's just trying to get you off-stride.*

He stared straight through the countryside ahead of them. He wore aviator sunglasses that diffused the morning sun. His gray USMC shirt had turned dark with sweat.

Max loped at his side, barely even out of idle.

That's fine, Shel told himself. *The dog can run you into the ground, but you're not going to give in to this guy with the mouth.*

The Marine pacing him was in his midtwenties, nearly ten years younger than Shel. Not only that, but he must have been some kind of track star when he was in high school, which hadn't been that long ago. His name was Barry Garrick.

"They told me you were a great Marine back in your day," Garrick said.

"I'm a great Marine now," Shel replied.

"That's not what I'm seeing. What I'm seeing is old and used up. They tell me you got hurt and it broke your spirit."

"I got all the spirit I need, junior."

"We'll see, grandma." Garrick increased his stride and started to pull away.

Breathe out, Shel told himself. *You need oxygen. Get all the carbon dioxide out of your lungs. Breathe deep and keep breathing.*

He lengthened his stride, pushed away the fear and pain and uncertainty, and gave himself to the run. For the last five weeks, ever since he'd been cleared for light duty, he'd gone to the various satellite camps around Lejeune and trained. It hadn't been light duty. He'd punished himself, pushing his body back into the condition he was used to.

Remy had offered to work with him, but Shel had wanted to do it on his own, away from the NCIS personnel. He needed to be a Marine again, and the only place he could do that was with other Marines.

Shel reached inside himself for the iron strength that had always been his. There was a part of him that would never bend to anyone or anything as long as his heart still pumped. He'd created that for himself when he realized his daddy would never truly be there for him. He'd started building that strength when his mama had sat him down and told him about the cancer. He'd been fifteen then. His mama had lasted almost three years before she'd lost her battle.

Shel had never understood his daddy's distance from his sons, but he'd been constantly aware of the emptiness he felt where his daddy's love and affection should have been. When he'd no longer been able to stand that emptiness, he'd filled it himself. He had forced himself to be invincible and indomitable, and—for the most part—he'd been successful.

But that distance from his daddy wasn't working now. That phone call about Victor Gant while he'd been in the hospital haunted Shel. He hadn't found any answers. Estrella's research into his daddy's military career had only turned up more questions.

According to what she'd found, Victor Gant and his daddy had never served together. The only thing they had in common was an overlap in Qui Nhon.

So how had Tyrel McHenry gotten to know a proven scumbag like Victor Gant? That was the question. Actually, it was only one of the questions. Why would his daddy have made that phone call? Why had he gotten drunk that night?

Not knowing was frustrating. Not being able to ask was even more so.

Shel squeezed everything out of his body and reached for more. His body became a machine, inflexible and relentless. That was the kind of man he'd driven himself to become, the same kind of man he saw in Tyrel McHenry. Even though he didn't understand his daddy, Shel respected the quiet strength and steel of the man when he'd buried his wife and gone on working. Those had been the things Shel had chosen to emulate from his father.

Even when Shel became those things, though, his daddy had never seemed to notice. No matter what, Shel just hadn't been able to win his daddy's affection.

Those memories worried at his thoughts. Since he'd returned to Camp Lejeune, he'd tried to talk to his daddy a handful of times. But the man had been quieter than ever, and he'd refused to talk about Victor Gant. During their conversations, Shel had dropped plenty of hints that he'd be open to talking about the Purple Royals leader, but his daddy had shut that down.

Shel leaned forward a little more and pushed himself. Inexorably he gained on the younger man. In twenty more strides, he drew abreast of Garrick.

"You're breathing hard, junior," Shel said as he powered past the younger man.

Garrick tried to keep pace. Strain etched his features. Then his legs gave out on him. He cursed as he couldn't even maintain the pace and suddenly fell behind by a wide margin.

Shel kept running. He was deep into the runner's high now, lost in the charge of endorphins and adrenaline flooding his body. He stayed locked on the terrain ahead.

"Gunney," Garrick cried from behind him. "Wait up."

Shel went another twenty paces before he stopped and turned back to Garrick. The younger Marine walked along the trail with his hands on his head to best get oxygen to his lungs.

"You okay, youngster?" Shel asked as he pulled his arm over his head.

"Yeah," the younger man growled.

"I'm not going to have to carry you back, am I?"

"No." Garrick shot him a sour look.

"We could always run back to barracks."

Garrick laced his fingers over his head as his chest heaved. He grinned ruefully. "Maybe in a minute."

"You just trying to make me feel good?" Shel asked.

Garrick shook his head. "Nope. I'm maybe a little embarrassed."

"Nothing to be embarrassed about, Marine. You just ain't put on your full growth yet."

"Is that how you're going to tell it when we get back?"

Shel gave the younger man a lopsided grin. "There ain't anything to tell. What we do out here, it stays out here."

Garrick kept pacing with his arms over his head. "Where are you from, gunney?"

Shel knew his west Texas accent was showing. He'd heard it himself. It wasn't from hanging around with Don for the few days his brother had stayed at camp to get him out of Lejeune's Naval hospital. It came from thinking about his daddy so much.

"West Texas," Shel said. "Born and raised."

"I thought I heard that in there. I'm from Boston."

"I thought I heard that in there," Shel said.

Garrick grinned. "There are some things you just can't get past."

"I know," Shel said.

⊛ ⊛ ⊛

>> 0917 HOURS

Showered, shaved, and breakfasted, Shel took his place on the firing line. He'd changed into camo pants, combat boots, and a brown USMC T-shirt that fit his body like a second skin. He wore amber-tinted aviator sunglasses and ear protectors.

Other Marines lined the range, all of them awaiting orders.

Max stayed back inside the observation building with Garrick. After breakfast, the young Marine had been free. He'd elected to spend his morning with Shel. Although he wouldn't have admitted it, Shel was glad for the company.

It was Marine company. Garrick wouldn't talk unless Shel wanted to talk. Remy would have talked the whole time, and if he hadn't talked, he would have been hitting on the female support personnel. That was just Remy.

"Load your weapons," the shooting-range drill instructor ordered.

Shel slammed a full magazine into the pistol and racked the slide to strip and seat the first cartridge. He settled into an easy combat stance, pistol framed and held so his elbows formed 90-degree angles. The fingers of his left hand wrapped around the fingers of his right to provide the push-pull force that allowed the semiautomatic's action to operate without hanging up.

He didn't use the sights. He just imagined the pistol was part of his body. All he had to do was point it at the target like he'd point his finger.

The order was given to fire.

Shel focused on the silhouette downrange. They were shooting at fifty feet. Most gunfights in urban areas took place at less than ten feet. MOUT—Military Operations on Urban Terrain—focused on that kind of shooting.

Without hesitation, Shel fired. He aimed for the center mass and saved the last three for head shots. He laid his weapon down, cocked and locked, and waited for the DI's order to roll the targets in.

When the target came in, Shel saw that all the bullets had pierced the ten-ring in the heart of the silhouette, so close together that they made one hole in a two-inch group. The three head shots had caught the head exactly where the nose would be. They were hardly wider than a quarter.

"Gunney McHenry," the DI barked as he came to stand behind Shel and inspect the target.

"Yes, Sergeant," Shel responded. On the gun range, the DI was in command.

"Where were you directed to shoot?"

"Center mass, Sergeant," Shel said.

"Center mass," the DI repeated. "Yet I see this target's head has been air-conditioned."

Shel barely kept a grin from his face. "Yes, Sergeant."

"That looks like two bullets passed through that target's head."

"There were three, Sergeant."

The DI peered over Shel's shoulder. "Well, bless my soul, gunney, it appears *three* bullets did miss the center mass ten-ring."

"Yes, Sergeant."

"Did you miss your target, gunney?"

"No, Sergeant."

The DI clapped Shel on the shoulder. "This is my firing range, gunney. We do things my way."

"Yes, Sergeant."

"I say you missed your target and you owe me a beer for each one of those stray rounds. Just in case you can't add any better than you can shoot, that means you owe me three beers."

Shel grinned. "Yes, Sergeant. I can live with that."

⊛ ⊛ ⊛

>> 1142 HOURS

"You're not a tank, gunney. You're not designed to take damage. You're supposed to float like a butterfly and sting like a bee."

Shel tried to move more quickly, but even at his best he wasn't matched in skills with his opponent. During his military career, Shel had never formally taken martial arts the way some of the Marines had. There were sergeants who taught hand-to-hand combat that he wouldn't have willingly taken on without a baseball bat.

Over the years, Shel had tried to learn the combat systems, but they were too disciplined. He didn't like thinking that much about responding to a threat. He concentrated on reacting, picking up what he needed as he learned from experience.

Martial artists were deadly when everything went their way. The problem was that things didn't always go their way. Systems and training failed at some point when things jumped the tracks. Especially when they were pounding away at someone who could take punishment.

Shel could. He blocked punches and kicks with his forearms and legs and kept his gloved hands up close to his face. The Asian guy he faced now was a power lifter in addition to being a martial artist. He was almost as big as Shel, and he was *fast*. Man, he was fast.

He kept kicking and feinting with kicks, then driving his gloves into Shel's face. The punches hurt. Shel tasted blood and his nose leaked more.

"Get your hands up, Gunney McHenry," the DI squalled.

Shel had his hands up. His opponent just had so much raw strength that he occasionally punched through Shel's defense. His opponent grinned, obviously pleased with himself.

"You're not a tank, gunney," the DI bellowed. "He's turning you into hamburger."

Shel knew that was true. He wouldn't be able to handle much more punishment. Without warning, the Marine punched Shel in his wounded shoulder. Bright, hard pain flared through Shel. Before he could recover, the Marine hit him in the shoulder again.

He knows, Shel realized. *Someone told him about the wound.*

When the man attacked again, Shel tried to defend his shoulder. While trying to protect his injury, Shel left himself open for a left cross that almost put him down. Black comets whirled in his vision. He took a step back and lifted his hands.

His opponent came at him again, trying for the shoulder once more. This time Shel ducked beneath the blow, shifted, and twisted in an explosion of effort that sent his right hand into the man's stomach. Shel hit with everything he had. His fist sank into the man's body and took the wind out of him.

Semiparalyzed by the blow, the young Marine tried to step back. Shel moved with him, following up with another body blow with his left hand. Then he hooked the man twice in the side of his face with his right. The Marine's eyes started to glaze. Fired up now, Shel brought his left hand up in an uppercut that caught his opponent under the chin.

The man's eyes rolled back into his head and he fell to the mat.

Shel looked down at the man and felt proud. He'd been thinking the younger man was going to beat him. He could have lived with that in a combat exercise. He'd been beaten before. But in a real encounter, losing wasn't an option.

The DI knelt beside the man and placed two fingers on his jugular. Shel breathed out, his hands above his head, as he tried to get his respiration under control.

"He's got a pulse," the DI said.

"I didn't try to hurt him any more than I had to," Shel said.

"I saw that," the DI responded as he stood. "I also saw that he went for your shoulder."

"In a fight, I would have done the same thing."

"Maybe," the DI said, "but this wasn't a fight. This was a controlled exercise. When this young soldier comes to, I'm going to make sure he understands that." He paused. "How's the shoulder?"

Shel moved it. The pain was there, but it was tolerable. He smiled. "Better and better every day."

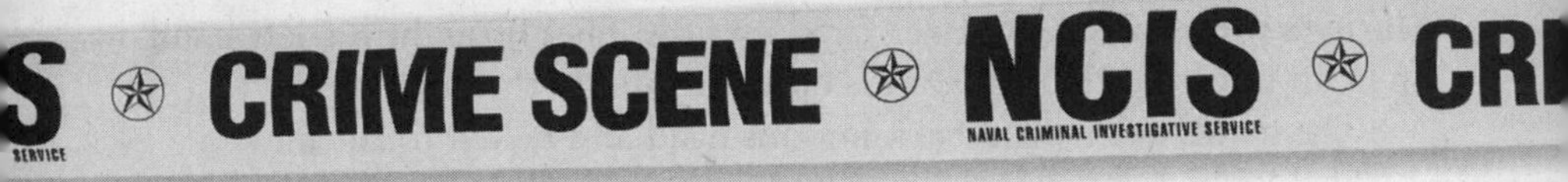
CRIME SCENE
NCIS
NAVAL CRIMINAL INVESTIGATIVE SERVICE

35

E SCENE ✪ NCIS ✪ CRIME SCENE

NAVAL CRIMINAL INVESTIGATIVE SERVICE

>> MOONEY'S TAVERN
>> JACKSONVILLE, NORTH CAROLINA
>> SIX DAYS LATER
>> 1318 HOURS

Shel parked in the gravel parking lot in front of the tavern and got out. The day was too hot to wear a jacket to hide the pistol at his hip. He fished his NCIS ID from his pocket and draped it around his neck. He curved the bill of his NCIS hat over his sunglasses and signaled to Max to leave the Jeep.

The Labrador dropped to the gravel and joined Shel.

When he didn't see Remy immediately, Shel tracked the loud hip-hop music to the SEAL's car. Remy sat with his arms folded in the front seat. He had his eyes closed and his head bobbed with the beat.

Shel stood at the side of the car. His shadow had just covered the window when Remy cracked his eyes open and looked up at him. One of his hands had slid smoothly to the pistol on his hip.

Then Remy grinned and the window powered down. "Hey, jarhead. It's been so long I thought maybe you'd forgotten your way here."

"Not hardly." Shel smiled a little.

Remy uncoiled, opened the door, and slid out of the car. "As I recall, it's your time to buy."

"It isn't," Shel said, "but I'll buy anyway."

"What's the occasion?" Remy fell into step with Shel as they walked toward the tavern.

"Docs just cleared me from light duty. No more desk jockey."

"Cool." Remy yawned. "Now maybe I can start getting some sleep on that stakeout."

Even while on the desk, Shel had kept track of the team. Remy was currently assigned to follow up on leads dealing with a local loan shark who specialized in taking advantage of military men. Alcohol, drugs, sex, and loan sharks were always problems around military installations. Temptations were everywhere, and the young Marines and sailors were prime targets.

"Will didn't hang with you last night?" Shel asked.

"He tried to." Remy frowned. "A young Marine got into a bar fight with his wife's boyfriend."

"Didn't hear about that."

"That's because you were probably sleeping."

Actually Shel hadn't been. Lately he'd been poring over the information Estrella had gotten regarding his daddy. He was also monitoring the FBI's manhunt for Victor Gant.

So far the FBI hadn't picked up the man's trail. It was as if Victor Gant had vanished from the face of the earth. There was even some speculation that he'd left the country.

Shel didn't think that had happened. Victor Gant wasn't the sort of man to walk away from the game when there were still cards on the table.

"So Will covered the bar fight, and I stayed on the loan shark," Remy said.

"A bar fight? Doesn't seem like anything we'd be interested in."

Remy frowned and shoved his hands in his pockets. "Before morning, it turned into a homicide investigation."

Shel shook his head.

"Twenty-three-year-old Marine," Remy said softly. "Just got back from Iraq."

"He was still jacked up from being over there," Shel said.

"Yeah. Made it worse, him finding his wife out with her boyfriend."

"The military and marriage don't go together easily."

"Is that why you never married? 'Cause I was thinking maybe you just couldn't find somebody that would have you."

Shel knew both of them just wanted to avoid the heaviness of the murder. They saw too much of that kind of work, and the violence that led up to it. "I thought that was your excuse."

"No, man," Remy said. "I'm just selective. Haven't found the right one yet."

⊛ ⊛ ⊛

>> 1331 HOURS

Minutes later, Shel and Remy sat at a back booth with plates of fajitas and iced tea. Max lay at Shel's feet and watched them eat. Shel dropped food to the dog on a regular basis.

"You know," Remy said, "that dog doesn't look Mexican."

Max cocked his head and looked at Remy.

"It's an acquired taste," Shel said.

Remy dropped a piece of fajita meat. Effortlessly Max caught the meat between his teeth. But he made no effort to eat it. Instead, he turned his liquid brown eyes on Shel.

Shel signaled the dog to eat.

Max tossed the meat up into the air and gulped it down with noisy chewing.

"So it's like that, is it?" Remy admonished Max. "You're not going to eat for me unless Shel okays it."

Max just stared at him.

"He's a one-man dog," Shel said. He dropped a hand to Max's head and patted him.

"I guess so. Must make a great partner."

"He doesn't talk as much as some I've had," Shel agreed.

"Oh," Remy groaned in protest, "you did *not* just go there."

Shel grinned. "I've missed this."

"Yeah. Me too." Remy doubled his hand into a fist and offered his knuckles.

Shel met Remy's fist with his own; then they returned to eating.

"Scary stuff in the tattoo parlor," Remy said.

"Yeah." That was the first time either of them had mentioned the shooting. Shel knew neither of them would speak of it again. Being in special forces, both men acknowledged that death potentially lay in wait for them at all times, but they didn't dwell on it. They couldn't. If they did, it made the job impossible to do.

"If Will pairs us up tonight," Remy said, "you remember that you owe me."

"Do you really think Will will assign me to something as lame as a stakeout on a loan shark?"

"Now you're hurting me," Remy said.

Shel smiled. He *had* missed the camaraderie.

"So where have you been?" Remy asked.

"With the Marines," Shel said. "Getting my head together." He paused. "It's nothing against you, Remy. But you're not a Marine. I'm not knocking the SEALs, and I'm especially not knocking you. But a Marine's place when he's rebuilding himself is among Marines."

"No prob," Remy said. "Whatever it takes. At least you're back."

Shel nodded. "I am."

⊛ ⊛ ⊛

>> 1417 HOURS

Victor Gant sat astride his motorcycle in the trailer. He could hear the rumble of the big 18-wheeler's engine as it pulled the bike trailer. A small floodlight at the front of the trailer barely broke the darkness.

"Coming up on the stop," Fat Mike said over the headset radio Victor wore.

"Copy that," Victor said. He wore road leathers and had a Kevlar vest under his colors. Normally he didn't wear a helmet, but he did today. It was a full-face helmet that covered his jaw and chin too. A cut-down Mossberg shotgun was slung over his left shoulder. He wore his .45 in a shoulder holster under his colors. The chill calm that had always filled him before a hop through the jungle in Vietnam filled him now. Out of habit, he glanced at his watch.

"Spotter confirms the Marine at the tavern," Fat Mike said. "He's headed out the door now. He's got company."

"Who?" Victor hoped it was Coburn. His anger against the commander had sharpened over the past few weeks.

"The black guy that was with the Marine at Spider's."

Well, Victor said, *that'll have to be good enough.* The black man had been there the night Bobby Lee was killed. Bagging the Marine and his friend would feel good.

"Ready," Fat Mike said.

Immediately Victor flicked his thumb over the electric starter. The motorcycle's big engine throbbed to life. Nine other engines did the same. Thunder filled the trailer.

The 18-wheeler slowed. Victor felt the gradual reduction of speed. He grew even more calm. *Let's do this,* he growled to himself.

"All right," Fat Mike said. "Your target's on your left."

The truck stopped. The air brakes chuffed loudly enough to be heard over the warbling motorcycle engines.

"I'm coming around," Fat Mike advised.

Victor glanced around at the men who were riding with him. All of them were seasoned criminals. Most of them had killed before. Some of them had been to prison before. Going back didn't scare them, but they didn't intend to do that.

A moment later, Fat Mike pulled the trailer's back door down. Bright sunlight cut into the gloom.

"All right," Victor said over the headset that connected him to the rest of his men. "Let's ride." He twisted the accelerator and let the clutch out.

Victor took the lead and roared down the inclined ramp leading out of the trailer. When he reached bottom, he brought the motorcycle around and headed into the gravel parking lot. The other motorcycles trailed only a short distance behind him and flared out in a phalanx of thundering metal.

Shel McHenry, the other man, and the dog were caught out in the open. Victor grinned as he saw the Marine look in his direction. With one quick grab, Victor yanked the shotgun from the shoulder scabbard and pointed it at the Marine. As cut-down as it was, the shotgun was more pistol than anything else.

He squeezed the trigger. Double-ought buckshot exploded from the shotgun's throat and sped toward Shel McHenry. The abbreviated weapon jumped erratically in Victor's grasp, but the semiautomatic function fed a new shell into place.

CRIME SCENE
NCIS
NAVAL CRIMINAL INVESTIGATIVE SERVICE

36

SCENE ✪ NCIS ✪ CRIME SCENE

NAVAL CRIMINAL INVESTIGATIVE SERVICE

>> MOONEY'S TAVERN
>> JACKSONVILLE, NORTH CAROLINA
>> 1417 HOURS

"Max!" Shel roared as he slapped his thigh to bring the dog in close to him. By then Shel was already in motion. The Purple Royals' colors stood out and identified them at once.

Remy broke for cover at the same time but in a separate direction to split the attention of their attackers. That was how they'd been trained for urban area action. Split, but not far, and regroup as needed. It made them harder to hit, more difficult to cover, and gave them overlapping fields of fire.

A cloud of double-ought buckshot punched through the windshield of a parked Ford pickup. The loud report almost drowned out the noise of the breaking windshield, barely audible anyway over the rumbling Harley engines. Cube-shaped glass crunched under Shel's feet as he beat a hasty retreat. He drew the SOCOM .45 from his hip and took a two-handed grip as he crouched behind an SUV.

Bullets peppered the vehicle.

Shel felt Max braced at his knees, ready to take action. The SUV sagged suddenly as the front tire blew. A quick step put Shel at the rear of the SUV. Pistol held high, he peered around the vehicle, then singled one of the bikers out of the pack. He aimed for the man's center mass and fired twice.

The first bullet took the mirror off the motorcycle's left grip. The mirror had slid over in front of the biker's chest. The second bullet hit the biker in the chest. He lost control of the motorcycle but didn't let go of the handlebars.

Before he could recover, the motorcycle ran into a parked car. The bike flipped onto its side and threw the rider to the ground. The biker pushed up on his hands and tried to get to his feet.

Body armor, Shel realized. Their attackers had come loaded for bear, as his daddy would say.

Remy wheeled from cover and took deliberate aim. One of his bullets struck the man's helmet. The 9 mm round ricocheted off the helmet's hard surface. The next two struck the biker in the neck. He struggled for a moment, then slumped to the ground.

As he watched the man die, Shel hardened his heart. The way they were outnumbered, he knew they couldn't afford to leave their enemies able to fight.

Another biker brought his Harley around and planted his feet. He lowered an Uzi and unleashed a torrent of rounds in Remy's direction. Remy ducked back immediately. Bullet holes chased him.

Shel shifted and fired two shots into the man's back without hesitation. This wasn't one of the Louis L'Amour stories where two men faced each other and slapped leather like the books Shel had grown up on as a kid. This was war. In war, a warrior didn't always call another man out and take him on face-to-face.

The biker jerked and fell sideways. The fact that there was no blood reinforced to Shel that the men wore body armor.

A Harley engine blasted to Shel's left and raced closer. He turned and watched as the biker lifted a machine pistol in one big, hamlike hand. Shel stood his ground and fired instinctively. Running was only going to get him killed a heartbeat later, and by then the biker could have taken cover.

Bullets cut the air only inches from Shel's head and face. He didn't hear them passing, but he felt the heated wind tug at his hair and pulse against his jaw. Two of his bullets caught the biker in his helmet. One of the rounds glanced from the rounded surface of the helmet, but the other crashed through the faceplate.

The biker, suddenly slack, toppled. The motorcycle dropped with him, momentarily engaged gears, and spun out. The rear tire threw gravel like shrapnel. Then the engine sputtered and died.

Down to five rounds in his pistol's magazine, Shel took the opportunity to reload. He shoved the partially spent magazine into his back pocket so he could find it if he needed it. Then he ducked and ran around the SUV in order to change his position.

Three attackers were down. Shel pulled up a mental image of the bikers. There had been ten of them when the shooting started.

Shel stayed hunkered down behind the pickup while two motorcycles zipped by. The bikers sprayed the truck.

Shiny chain links draped over the side of the pickup's bed grabbed Shel's attention. Judging from the mud caking the vehicle, the driver spent considerable time off-road. Moving quickly, Shel yanked the chain down with his free hand, then underhanded it at the next motorcycle.

The chain struck the motorcycle's side and wrapped up in the rear wheel. Before the biker knew what was happening, the motorcycle's rear tire locked up. The rider flew over the handlebars and managed an inelegant face-plant.

Conscious of everything around him, Shel watched as the downed biker forced himself up to his knees and halted there for a moment. Before he could move again, Shel took aim at the man's neck and fired. The man rolled over and was still.

In less than a minute, the parking area was riddled with bullets and spent brass. And nearly half of Victor Gant's would-be murderers were down.

Victor himself sat almost seventy yards away calmly reloading his cut-down shotgun. Shel took a bead and fired. The round slapped against Victor's helmet and rocked his head back. Then he engaged the clutch and the accelerator and shot forward. He raised the shotgun before him and fired.

Shel ducked the blast and felt the vehicle behind him shiver with the impacts. Victor Gant roared past him, followed quickly by the other survivors of the attack. When the last of the five went past, Shel stepped out and took aim at the last motorcycle's rear tire.

The tire exploded. Rubber came loose and flapped against the wheel housing. Out of control, the biker slammed into a twentysomething-year-old Trans Am. He didn't get back up.

Gun in hand, forcing himself to move, Shel crept toward the last man they'd downed. As Shel kept watch, Victor Gant's bikers roared out onto the street. Shel reached into his pocket and took out his cell phone.

Remy maintained his cover with his pistol extended and ready to use.

Shel called NCIS headquarters and got Will on the phone. Briefly he outlined what had just taken place. Beneath his fingertips, the biker's pulse was fast and weak.

"Stay there," Will advised. "Secure the site. Estrella's already notifying

Jacksonville PD and the sheriff's department. They can get out roadblocks. We'll be there in a minute."

"Copy that," Shel said. Then he broke the phone connection and walked back to his Jeep to get a pair of disposable cuffs. He knew Victor Gant wasn't going to let this go.

❂ ❂ ❂

>> 1423 HOURS

As he tightened the cuffs on the unconscious biker's hands, Shel's cell phone rang. He answered without checking caller ID, figuring it was Will or one of the team.

Instead, it was Victor Gant.

"You got more lives than a cat, jarhead," Gant snarled. "Thought I had you cold."

Calmly Shel stood and signaled to Remy, who was already getting portable barricades from the local PD who were just then starting to arrive. Remy looked at him. Shel pointed at his phone and mouthed, *Gant.*

Understanding, Remy used his own phone to call NCIS headquarters and initiate a GPS lock on Gant's phone.

"Well," Shel drawled, "you got high marks for effort. And it only cost you five of your guys to find out that you weren't good enough."

Victor cursed.

Shel dragged the handcuffed biker to shelter under a 4x4 pickup. He checked the surroundings. It wouldn't have surprised him to learn that Victor had another team in waiting or had doubled back.

"I'm still here," Shel said. "Still standing. If you decide you want to take another run at me, I'll be here waiting."

Remy had taken up a support position too. But he'd switched his pistol out for the M4 assault rifle he carried as part of his traveling equipment. The commands he'd yelled earlier hadn't kept the locals back, but they were staying back now that the rifle had come out into the open.

"I think I'm going to pass on that," Victor said. "I've got things to do."

"There's a big score between you and me," Shel said. "You didn't strike me as the type of man to leave something like that standing."

"I'm not," Victor promised. "I'm purely an Old Testament kind of guy. If you know anything about me, you know that."

"Your son shot me," Shel said. "He took me on while looking me in the eyes. Takes a real man to do that."

Victor laughed bitterly. "You sure like to push buttons, don't you, boy?"

"If we went at it one-on-one, I'm just saying this thing might end up differently. You want me. I'm willing to meet you. Just name the time and place." Shel glanced at Remy.

Remy spoke into his cell phone, waited a moment, then shook his head.

"How do I know you'd show up there?" Victor asked.

"I'll give you my word," Shel replied. But he knew he wouldn't do that. There was no way Victor would meet him under such circumstances. Not willingly.

"Your word." Victor snorted. "Your father teach you to stand by your word, jarhead?"

Shel felt a pit open up beneath him, and he knew he was playing with fire. His daddy's life—especially what had gone on in Vietnam—was never spoken of.

"I knew your father," Victor said. "Back in the jungle. Back when the government gave us an even harder war we couldn't win."

Shel steeled himself to make no rebuttal. The most onerous thing about this conversation was that Victor Gant knew things about Tyrel McHenry that Shel didn't.

"Cat got your tongue, jarhead?" Victor taunted.

"I've been listening," Shel said. "And I've decided that you ain't fit to breathe my daddy's name."

"Is that right?" Victor laughed. "You got a mighty high opinion of your father."

"He's a good man." Shel knew that was so, even though he couldn't explain why his daddy had kept his sons—and the rest of the world—shoved away.

"Did he ever mention me?" Victor asked.

"No."

"Probably not. He had plenty of reason not to."

Shel wanted to shout the man down, and it took everything in him not to do that. If he angered Victor too much, the biker leader might break the phone connection. Instead, Shel glanced at Remy again.

After a brief conversation, Remy shook his head. He took his phone away from his ear and made a circular motion, mouthing, *Keep going.*

Shel knew the fact that Victor was in motion, running through overlapping cell-phone towers, was making the trace more difficult. Breathing out, Shel held on to his focus and tried his best to push all the anger away from him.

"Did your father ever tell you about the man he murdered?" Victor asked.

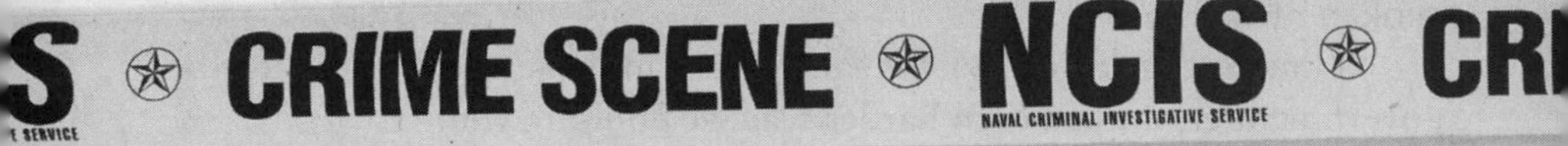

CRIME SCENE
NCIS
NAVAL CRIMINAL INVESTIGATIVE SERVICE

37

E SCENE ✪ NCIS ✪ CRIME SCENE
NAVAL CRIMINAL INVESTIGATIVE SERVICE

>> MOONEY'S TAVERN
>> JACKSONVILLE, NORTH CAROLINA
>> 1432 HOURS

Shel exploded as the biker leader's words slammed into him. "You're a lying sack of—"

"Your father has a lot of secrets, jarhead," Victor interrupted. He spoke slowly, calmly, mockingly. "I helped him bury the soldier he killed that night in Qui Nhon. And when we finished covering him over, your father prayed over that dead man and gave up on God in his next breath."

Fear and anger throttled Shel. He tried to speak and couldn't. His throat felt like it had swelled nearly shut. He forced himself to breathe, and even that was difficult.

"When you see your father again, maybe you ought to ask him about that," Victor suggested. "Remind him that there ain't no statute of limitations for murder. And that the Army still hangs war criminals."

Get me a twenty, Shel thought desperately, looking again at Remy. He knew Estrella would be the one running the phone search. *Find this jerk for me.*

Remy shook his head.

"I'll tell you something else," Victor said, "if you people find me again, I'm going to tell everything I know to the newspapers. Maybe catch one of those guys at *60 Minutes* or something. They like stories that have a history. Maybe you'll get to see your father swing from a gallows."

Cold anger replaced the heat inside Shel. When he spoke, his words were calm and measured. "You'll never live to see that happen."

Victor laughed. "Touched a nerve, did I? What is it, jarhead? You got some kind of hero worship about your old man? When I saw you, I figured you for the type. I hate to be the one to bring it up, but he didn't come see you in the hospital, did he? Just stayed down there at that ranch in Texas. Is he too old to travel these days?"

Shel didn't say anything.

"I'll be seeing you, jarhead," Victor said. "I ain't gonna forget about this little dance we got going on between us. I ain't the forgetting kind. I'm just gonna put it on a back burner for a while. Catch you on the flip-flop."

Before Shel could say anything, the phone connection ended. He turned to Remy. "Tell me Estrella found him."

Remy talked for a moment, then shook his head. "He was moving too fast. She got a general location. Jacksonville PD's already covering it."

"Where?"

Remy hesitated.

"*Where?*" Shel demanded. He didn't know what he'd do if he caught up with Victor Gant. He knew he wasn't truly in control of himself. But he couldn't sit back and do nothing.

"South side," Remy said. "When she lost the signal, Estrella said Gant was rolling south."

Shel closed his phone and started for his Jeep.

"Shel," Remy called.

Shel ignored him. Anger pooled inside him like bubbling lava.

"The PD's not going to let you leave," Remy said. "They want us to stay here."

Shel stepped into the Jeep and slid behind the steering wheel. Max vaulted through the passenger window and settled into the seat. The Labrador was alert and pensive.

"You're making a mistake," Remy said.

Without answering, Shel put the Jeep in gear and backed out into the parking lot. He threaded through the wrecked motorcycles and bodies toward the street exit. One of the policemen started for him.

"Sir," the officer said as he held up a hand and kept the other on his gun butt, "I'm afraid you're going to have to stay with the scene."

Shel ignored the man and rolled on by. He knew the policemen weren't going to fire on him. They might not like the fact that he had disobeyed them, but they weren't going to shoot him.

One of the police cars pulled out of the parking lot and followed Shel with his lights on.

Shel didn't care. Victor Gant was headed south, so south was where Shel was going to head. He just hoped he found the man, but he didn't know what he was going to do with him when he caught up with him.

Shel was so focused on the idea of finding Victor Gant that he didn't see the police car swing out in front of him until it was almost too late. He jammed on the brakes and managed to bring the Jeep to a stop moments before it would have slammed into the squad car. Before he even had a chance to put the Jeep in reverse, the cop was out of the car, gun drawn.

"Stand down, Gunnery Sergeant," the cop yelled. "I am placing you under arrest."

Fuming, Shel realized he had no choice. He put the vehicle in park and resigned himself to the fact that Victor Gant was most likely going to escape—again.

⊛ ⊛ ⊛

>> NCIS OFFICES
>> CAMP LEJEUNE, NORTH CAROLINA
>> 1843 HOURS

When Will entered his office, he found Shel waiting for him.

The big Marine stood impassively at the window and stared out at the camp. His sunglasses covered his eyes. Max lay at his feet. After being remanded to NCIS custody by the Jacksonville PD, Shel had returned to camp. He now wore Marine cammies, complete with the uniform hat. Evidently he'd taken time to shower, shave, and get his kit together. A duffel bag sat beside one of the chairs in front of Will's desk.

Like an automaton, Shel spun expertly and saluted Will. He held the salute until Will returned it.

"At ease," Will said.

Effortlessly Shel relaxed into parade rest.

Will pointed at the chairs in front of his desk. "Take a load off."

"Thank you, sir," Shel said. "But I'd prefer to stand."

"I'd like to sit," Will said, feeling a little irritable, "and I'd like not to have to twist my head off to look at you."

Shel moved to the front of the desk and stood silently.

"That's not a whole lot better," Will said.

"I was thinking we could make this a short conversation," Shel said.

Will studied Shel. They'd been friends through their work at the NCIS for years. Will had trained Shel in a lot of the crime scene investigation techniques. Shel had helped Will work on his fighting skills and pistol marksmanship, neither of which was imperative aboard an aircraft carrier.

"You left a crime scene today." Will flipped open a yellow legal pad to the notes he'd taken earlier.

"Yes, sir. I was in pursuit of the men from that scene."

"The pursuit was already in hand. We'd coordinated that aspect of the operation through the Jacksonville PD."

"I understand that, sir. Remy had control of the crime scene. Only one of us was needed."

"In your opinion, Gunnery Sergeant," Will said, responding to the military slant Shel was insisting on keeping. "I gave orders for you to stay there."

"I disobeyed those orders," Shel said. "I'd appreciate leniency."

"Do you want to tell me why you left?"

"I didn't want Victor Gant to get away."

"One man wasn't going to make a difference," Will said.

"Sir, I am a Marine. As a Marine, I'm trained to believe that one man *can* make a difference. I'm trained to be that man."

Will leaned back and studied Shel. Max whined a little, obviously distressed over his partner's emotional state.

And what is that emotional state? Will wasn't sure. Over the years of their association, he'd seen Shel under all kinds of stress. But he'd never seen the man as he was now.

"I don't want to argue the validity of Marine training—," Will began.

"Thank you, sir," Shel interrupted.

"—but I'm also going to have to finesse this with the Jacksonville PD," Will went on. "They're not very happy with you."

"The feeling is mutual, sir," Shel said. "They were already mobilized. Catching Victor Gant and his people should have been simple."

It hadn't been, though. Victor Gant and his surviving team members had dumped their motorcycles in an alley and fled the city with some other transportation. Even the 18-wheeler they'd used to arrive at the scene had been recovered. The tractor-trailer had been stolen. The long-haul driver had been found dead on the highway nearly an hour from Jacksonville.

"Do you want to tell me about this, gunney?" Will asked.

"About what, sir?"

Will's irritation deepened. "How Victor Gant got up inside your head."

"No, sir."

Will hadn't been expecting that response. He hadn't expected a direct answer either. Now that he'd asked the question so directly and gotten such a direct reply, he didn't know how he was going to move forward.

"What did Gant tell you while you were talking to him?" Will asked.

"He threatened me, sir," Shel said.

Will thought about that. He'd been through hard and dangerous times with Shel. A threat wasn't going to ruffle the Marine's feathers.

"Threatened you?" Will repeated.

"Yes, sir."

"I'm not convinced that's the reason you left that crime scene."

"I wasn't aware I had to convince you in any way regarding my actions, sir."

"I would like an explanation."

"I wanted to apprehend Victor Gant, sir. I thought one more car in the search might help. I judged that a better use of my time."

"Than staying behind to secure the crime scene."

"Yes, sir."

"Victor Gant got away."

"I'm aware of that, sir. I did what I could do."

Will sighed. "I'm not blaming his escape on you."

"Yes, sir. Thank you, sir."

"I don't believe Victor Gant threatening you would be enough to make you disobey an order."

Shel looked troubled for just a moment. "I don't know how to get you to believe in my disobedience, sir."

Frustration chafed at Will. Shel had closed down on him—lock, stock, and barrel—and Will didn't know why.

"About my punishment, sir," Shel said.

"I didn't say there was going to be punishment," Will replied.

Shel nodded. "I just figured—"

"You figured wrong, gunney," Will said sharply. "Maybe you need to realize that you're not the only one who can throw away the playbook when it doesn't suit you."

"Yes, sir."

Will let out a pent-up breath. "The issue at hand is what to do with you."

"Permission to speak freely, sir?"

Thank God, Will thought. "Yes."

"In addition to myself, Victor Gant also threatened my family. I've got some leave coming—"

That was an understatement. Shel was a Marine 24-7. There wasn't a person on the NCIS team who logged more hours or had more leave coming.

"—and I'd like to use some of it," Shel went on. "I want to go back home. For a little while."

"We need you here," Will said.

Shel was silent for a moment. "I understand, sir. But I think maybe I was too hasty in coming back to full duty. Today, during that fracas, I hurt my shoulder. I think maybe I should rest it."

"I can put you on a desk for that," Will pointed out.

"There are plenty of desk jockeys," Shel replied. "So there shouldn't be any reason to stand in the way of my request for leave. Sir."

Will knew he'd been neatly outmaneuvered. He didn't feel like being civil about it. Nor did he want to let Shel go when he was obviously dealing with harsh circumstances.

The fact of the matter was, though, Will didn't have a viable reason to deny the request.

"You'll need to fill out leave papers," Will said.

Shel reached into a pocket and took out a folded mass of papers. He handed them over.

Will took them and dropped them onto the desk without looking at them.

"Shel," he said, "I'm your friend."

"Yes, sir. I've always thought of you that way."

"As your friend, I'm asking you what's going on."

For a moment, uncertainty wavered on Shel's face. "I appreciate that, sir. I do. But I don't have anything to say that I haven't already told you."

Will looked at the dark lenses of Shel's sunglasses. No answers lurked there. And in the end there was nothing else he could do.

"You're dismissed, gunney," Will said.

"Thank you, sir." Shel fired off a crisp salute. After Will returned it, Shel pivoted a perfect 180 degrees and left the room.

Godspeed, Will thought. Then he offered up a small prayer and asked God to watch over his friend while he was gone. Letting people go when they were determined to walk into the jaws of trouble was always one of the hardest things to do.

38

SCENE NCIS CRIME SCENE
NAVAL CRIMINAL INVESTIGATIVE SERVICE

>> NCIS OFFICES
>> CAMP LEJEUNE, NORTH CAROLINA
>> 1909 HOURS

"Did I just see Shel leave carrying a duffel?" Maggie asked.

"Yeah," Will said as they walked through the hallway toward the main computer area.

"Where's he going?"

"Home."

"Why?" Maggie sounded unbelieving.

"He asked for leave to go home."

"Why would he want to go home? He never asks for leave."

"I'm aware of that," Will said.

"Did he give you a reason?"

"I asked."

"And?"

"He said he had leave coming. He said he hurt his arm today. He said he felt like going home. He said Victor Gant threatened his family."

"Do you believe any of that?" Maggie asked.

"Yeah. My answer would be all of the above."

"No."

"No?"

"You're smarter than that."

"Am I?"

"Shel will always have leave coming," Maggie said. "If he hurt his arm, Shel would rather cut it off than let you bench him to a desk under a medical restraint."

Will had to admit that was true.

"Shel is conflicted about going home," Maggie said.

Since she was the team profiler, Will was certain Maggie knew what she was talking about.

"And if Victor Gant threatened his family," Maggie went on, "he'd definitely stay with us. We offer the best chance at finding out where Gant is."

Will nodded. He couldn't argue the logic. He'd been chasing the same conjecture.

"So what's changed?" Maggie asked.

"I don't know. That's why I thought I'd ask Estrella."

⊛ ⊛ ⊛

>> 1919 HOURS

"Shel didn't mention anything to me about going home," Estrella said. She sat in the ergonomic chair at her station and looked worried. "Usually he tells me everything that's on his mind."

"Not everything," Maggie said. "I don't think Shel tells anybody everything." She glanced apologetically at Estrella. "Though he tells you more than most."

Will looked out over the workroom. Several other NCIS agents were in their cubicles, striving to clear their caseloads.

Estrella looked troubled. "There is one thing that he talked to me about that I haven't told you."

That drew Will's instant attention. "Now would be a good time to discuss that."

"It doesn't seem like it connects anywhere." Estrella turned her attention back to the computer. Her fingers glided across the keyboard in swift syncopation. "Shel asked me to look up his father's service record."

"His father was in Vietnam," Will said.

"I know."

"Shel doesn't talk much about his father," Maggie said.

"No," Will agreed.

"How did you know he was in Vietnam?"

"Because I know that Shel's father is a sore point with him. When Shel mentions him, I listen."

"Have you ever asked him about his father?"

"No," Will said. "Men try not to do things like that to each other."

"Right," Maggie said. "But you're not just a man. You're also his commanding officer."

"I play the counselor role when a man needs me to. But I wait for him to make that decision. I don't make it for him." Will stared at the computer screen. "What was Shel looking for concerning his father?"

"I don't know," Estrella said. "Not exactly. I know he was interested in finding out if Victor Gant was ever in Qui Nhon."

"What's Qui Nhon?" Maggie asked.

"A key port for American forces in the Vietnam War," Will answered. "A lot of people passed through there."

"'A lot of people' included Tyrel McHenry and Victor Gant," Estrella said.

Maggie moved in closer as well. "Both of them were there?"

Estrella nodded. "It looks like they were there for a time together."

"Same unit?" Will asked.

"No. Different units. But both of them were assigned to units that patrolled the roads in and out of Qui Nhon. Those roads were regularly attacked."

"Because they were major supply lines for the American offensive," Will said. "They drew a lot of heat. And the PBRs—"

"Sorry," Maggie broke in, "what are PBRs?"

"It stands for Patrol Boat, River," Estrella answered. "They were fast-attack watercraft used for attacking North Vietnamese boats and ships and for attacking ground units within striking distances of the rivers."

"And they were a big threat to the North Vietnamese," Will finished.

"If Victor Gant and Shel's father were both there at the same time," Maggie said, "you have to ask yourself if they knew each other."

"I think that's what Shel wanted to know," Estrella said.

"Did he ask you to find out?" Will asked.

"No. But he did ask me to match up his father's time there with what we knew about Victor Gant."

"Does Shel know they were there at the same time?"

"He does."

"When did you tell him?"

"Shortly after his return to Lejeune."

"If Shel's known about that this long," Maggie said, "why is it so interesting to him?"

"Because Victor Gant threatened Shel's family," Will said.

"Do you think it has something to do with what happened back then?" Estrella asked.

"Did you find anything to suggest there's a link?"

"Other than the fact that Tyrel McHenry and Victor Gant could have known each other, nothing."

"Even if they did know each other," Maggie said, "they'd have been, what, twenty or twenty-five years old? Suddenly, forty years later, that's going to matter?"

Will stared at the photograph of a young Army private. Tyrel McHenry had been little more than a boy, not much older than Steven when he'd been dropped into Vietnam. Thinking back on that war, thinking about the one in Iraq, Will realized again that war often ran on the lives of the young.

"Did you talk to Shel about this?" Will asked.

"A little."

"Did he give you any idea what he was looking for?"

"No. He just asked about the time frames."

Will considered that. "As I think back on it, until today Shel hasn't had any contact with Gant. Anybody remember it any differently?"

Maggie and Estrella answered negatively.

"But if Shel asked about the time frames while he was in Charleston," Will said, "someone had to have told him. And only two people would have known whether Tyrel McHenry and Victor Gant knew each other."

"I talked to Don," Maggie said. "Shel was agitated one day. He didn't talk much. I asked Don about it, and he said that they'd gotten a phone call from their father in the middle of the night."

Will turned that over in his mind. Although he hadn't said anything when Shel's father didn't put in an appearance at the hospital after Shel was so grievously wounded, he'd wondered.

"What was the phone call about?" Will asked.

Maggie shook her head. "Don didn't know. But he said ever since he'd gotten the call from his father, Shel had been agitated."

"I didn't notice it."

"You," Maggie said, "had your hands full dealing with getting Bobby Lee Gant's body back here and leading the investigation there."

Will took in a breath and let it out. He had been busy. He was still busy. But he got the distinct feeling that Shel McHenry was taking a long stride toward trouble.

Maybe big trouble.

"How much time have you spent on these files?" Will asked.

Estrella shook her head. "Not much. Shel only wanted me to confirm any overlap. I did that."

"We need more." Will rubbed his tired eyes. "Prioritize this and dig into it like it was an ongoing investigation."

"All right."

"But keep it quiet."

Estrella nodded. "How quiet?"

"If Shel calls and asks, don't tell him we've got an interest in it."

A troubled look twisted Estrella's features. "I don't like doing that."

"I know. Neither do I. But whatever's inside pushing Shel has got him in a death grip. If he finds out we're digging into his turf, he's not going to handle it well. I don't want his distraction with what we're doing to get him killed. Victor Gant tried to kill him today. I don't think he's finished."

"Understood."

"Good." Will nodded at the file Estrella had open on her computer. "Send me whatever pertinent data you've turned up. I want to take a look at it."

"All right," Estrella replied.

"Maggie," Will continued, "maybe you should background the people involved in this."

"I will," Maggie responded.

"Good. As soon as you get everything together, let me know."

⊛ ⊛ ⊛

>> 2038 HOURS

The phone rang while Will was working on the paperwork from the previous night's homicide. He was running on fumes and he knew it. He lifted the handset and answered.

"Commander," a gruff voice with a heavy accent said, "this is Sheriff Dale Conover. I got a message says you called me."

"I did," Will said. "Thanks for getting back to me. I've got an agent who lives outside of Fort Davis."

"Shelton McHenry. Tyrel's boy."

It seemed funny that anyone would call Shel somebody's boy. Will grinned a little at that but tried to keep it out of his voice.

"That's right," Will said. "Do you know Shel?"

"A little." A hint of a smile crept into the sheriff's voice. "When Shel was a pup, he didn't exactly go along to get along. He liked fast cars, faster motorcycles, and fighting."

That surprised Will.

"Don't get me wrong," Conover said. "Shelton was a good boy. Just had some waywardness in him. Came by it honest. Tyrel McHenry has always been known to throw a saddle across a wild bronc, and he never walked away from a fight. But I suppose the Marine Corps gentled Shelton down some. I heard from his brother, Don, that Shelton's doing good for himself."

"He is," Will replied. "Shel's one of the finest men I know."

"Well then, what can I do for you, Commander?" Conover asked.

"We've had some trouble here," Will said. "There's a biker gang called the Purple Royals."

"I've heard of 'em," Conover said. "Bunch of outlaws and one percenters."

"That's right. They're led by a man named Victor Gant. Does that name mean anything to you?"

"Nope. Should it?"

Will hesitated, then decided he had no choice about proceeding if he wanted to help Shel and his family. "I think there's some history between Victor Gant and Tyrel McHenry."

"Well, I don't know where you're getting your information from, Commander, and I wouldn't be one to tell you your business, but I got to tell you that I don't see how that could be. Tyrel McHenry won't ever win no awards for being the friendliest man in these parts, but he's one of the most law-abiding I know of. He wouldn't have nothing to do with the likes of the Purple Royals."

Will leaned back in his chair. "Shel's coming home for some leave."

"Don't see what you need me to do, Commander. If you need something, you're gonna have to just up and ask."

"Victor Gant had a son who was guilty of attacking a Marine," Will said. "Shel went to arrest him. The bust went south, and Shel ended up killing the son. Shel nearly got killed doing it."

"I take it Victor Gant ain't the forgiving type."

"No. He and his men made an attempt on Shel today. Shel and another one of my agents left three of the bikers dead."

"None of them was Victor Gant?"

"No."

"That there's a shame. Probably would have saved you some trouble."

"I think so too," Will agreed. "Now here's the interesting part. When we investigated Victor Gant's background, we found out he was in Vietnam at the same time Tyrel McHenry was."

"They knew each other back then?"

"We don't know that for sure. But we're confident Gant has made the tie to Shel's father."

"And you're thinking Gant and his boys might take a run at Tyrel McHenry?"

"I have to wonder why Shel decided to take leave suddenly and go back home."

"Well, I'll tell you one thing," Conover said, "and I'll guarantee it. If Gant decides to take on Tyrel McHenry, you might not have any more worries. In this county, there ain't many that come any tougher than Tyrel McHenry. That man's harder than a pawnbroker's heart and rougher than tree bark."

Will smiled at that. "I guess Shel didn't fall far from the tree."

"Maybe not in some ways," Conover agreed. "But Shelton—for all them daredevil ways of his—has got a good heart. And Don? Why he's the salt of the earth. Good people. Tyrel McHenry's a horse of another color."

"What do you mean?"

"There's something soured inside that man," Conover said. "That's the best I can explain it. He's hard and distant. Never got too close to his family. I think that's one of the reasons Shel was such a challenge to the straight and narrow. He was just trying to earn his daddy's respect. Or maybe get his attention."

Will remembered the gentle face of the young Army private that Tyrel McHenry had been.

"Some think it was the Vietnam War that changed Tyrel McHenry," Conover said. "Ever since he came back from there, folks who knew him said he'd changed. When he was younger, he was something of an outgoing man. A lot like Shel, I've been told. And he cared about people. Went out of his way to help them and get to know them a little. While his wife was alive, he was more sociable. You couldn't exactly warm up to him, but at least he was around. Nowadays, he's pretty much a hermit. Don't nobody go out to the Rafter M that don't have business there."

"How isolated is the ranch?" Will asked.

"Sets off to itself, that's a fact," Conover said. "And Tyrel runs it pretty much by himself."

That didn't sound good.

"If Victor Gant does come gunning for Tyrel, that could be a problem." Conover paused. "Tell you what I can do. I'll have a couple of my deputies take regular runs out that way. Maybe keep an eye on things. If something comes up, what's the best way to get hold of you?"

Will gave the man his cell phone number.

"Very good, Commander. Though I hope I don't have to use this," Conover said.

"Me too," Will said.

CRIME SCENE

NCIS
NAVAL CRIMINAL INVESTIGATIVE SERVICE

39

SCENE ✪ NCIS ✪ CRIME SCENE

NAVAL CRIMINAL INVESTIGATIVE SERVICE

>> RAFTER M RANCH
>> OUTSIDE FORT DAVIS, TEXAS
>> 1646 HOURS (CENTRAL TIME ZONE)

Even at a distance, Shel could pick out the Rafter M property lines.

There was something about the land that tied a man to it. No matter how determined a man was, he couldn't fully escape the area where he grew up. Men Shel had met in the service who'd grown up in metropolitan areas were often marked by those environments as well. Even before Shel had joined the NCIS, he'd learned that if a man knew what to look for, he could tell a lot about where another person grew up just by watching.

He stopped the rental car a quarter mile from the turnoff to the narrow rutted road that led up to the ranch house where he'd grown up. He told himself that he was just getting out to stretch from the long drive and from all the hours spent in airplanes and airports. Given that he'd made the trip so suddenly, he hadn't been able to secure a straight shot home. He'd also had two long layovers waiting on standby for last-minute flights.

He wore jeans, a pair of his favorite cowboy boots that were worked in and comfortable, a Texas Rangers ball cap he'd bought to knock the sun off, a brown USMC T-shirt, his pistol on his hip, and sunglasses. He'd shaved in the airport bathroom to keep himself clean-looking but also just for something to do.

Max got out of the car and put his nose to the ground. It didn't take the dog long to find a jackrabbit lazing in the shade and avoiding the blistering heat. Max slowly closed on the rabbit, and it waited until the last minute to make its break. The rabbit exploded from the ground, kicked out at Max with its powerful back legs, and zipped across the countryside in a broken field sprint. Max tried to follow, but he had too much mass and kept overrunning his target.

In spite of the tension he felt, Shel grinned at the sight. There weren't many things that could catch a Texas jackrabbit.

Less than a minute later, the rabbit came to a stop atop a hill in the shade of a thicket of Indian paintbrush. The bright red blossoms stood out against the dry brush. The plant was also called prairie fire, but Shel had always known it as Indian paintbrush. His mama had loved it.

For a moment he got caught up in his emotions. Losing his mama had been hard. But it hadn't been hard just on him. Don and their daddy had suffered as well. Their daddy had never talked about it though. Shel had sometimes wondered if his father had just accepted his mama's death as something to be expected.

Tyrel McHenry had never been a man to expect much out of life. Or at least he'd never given the appearance of being one.

Shel looked up at the bright blue sky. The cap's bill shaded his eyes.

Did you know Daddy was a murderer, Mama? Shel asked. *Did he tell you? Or did he keep that secret from you too?*

He knew there was no way of knowing. His mama had kept secrets when there was a need. She'd kept a few of Shel's. At the time he'd been grateful. She'd had to come get him out of jail once, and she'd paid a handful of speeding tickets for Shel without ever telling her husband. Things had been hard enough at home with Tyrel McHenry keeping the distance from his boys. Having those scrapes with the law would have only fanned the fire.

But even as he asked that question and got no answer, Shel understood that he didn't know whether his daddy was a murderer. He just had Victor Gant's voice in his head saying that. Over and over again. Those words had haunted Shel since he'd left Camp Lejeune.

How could you be raised by a man and never know enough about him? Shel wondered. In the end, though, he suspected that's the way it always was between daddies and sons. Probably between mamas and daughters, too. Sons and daughters just assumed they knew everything, and parents didn't reveal everything in their lives because they didn't want to be vulnerable in the eyes of their children.

Max sidled up the hill like he was just wandering around, then made another run at the rabbit.

As trained as he was, the Labrador couldn't give up being a dog.

Shel figured that no matter how much Marine he was, he couldn't give up being his daddy's son either.

After a few more minutes, he knew he couldn't put off getting there any longer.

He called Max to him and clambered back into the SUV. Then he started the engine, put the transmission in gear, and headed back home.

⊛ ⊛ ⊛

>> 1706 HOURS

When Shel pulled in beside his daddy's Ford F-150 pickup, some of the tension had gone away. He was into it now, whatever happened, and adrenaline buzzed through his system.

He got out and noticed that Joanie's minivan was parked there as well. Shel hoped Don wasn't there. If anybody could see the shape he was in mentally, it would be Don. Shel really didn't need that now.

Instead of going into the ranch house, Shel walked around back toward the corral and barn. It was daylight hours and after lunch, too early for dinner. No one would be inside the house.

"Hey, Uncle Shel!" an excited girl's voice screamed. "Hey, everybody, it's Uncle Shel!"

The five-year-old girl raced from the corner of the house in a flurry of arms and legs. She was thin and as dark-skinned as a Native American. She got her black hair from her mother, and it flowed behind her as she ran.

Shel knelt and caught her up easily. She hugged his neck so fiercely and honestly that it caused a lump to form in the back of Shel's throat.

Gently he patted her back. "Hey, Rachel, it's good to see you."

"I've missed you, Uncle Shel." The little girl leaned back, then leaned forward again and kissed his cheek. "You've been gone a long time."

"I have," Shel admitted. "But I'm here now."

"I'm glad."

Joshua and Isaac ran up next and threw their arms around Shel. Joshua was ten; Isaac was about to turn eight. Both of them favored Don.

Shel tousled their heads and returned their hugs. He couldn't help grinning like an idiot. Don's kids always had that effect on him. He didn't know why he didn't come around more often.

Then he saw his daddy standing at the corral with a cup of coffee in one hand. Tyrel McHenry didn't look like a happy man. Shel knew for a fact that he didn't like a lot of company.

Joanie, beautiful as ever, leaned against the corral. She smiled and waved at Shel.

"I'd come over," she called out, "but I don't think I could get through the mob."

"Probably not," Shel agreed. He looked back at Rachel. "So what are you doing here?"

"We came to see Grandpa's new pony," Rachel answered.

"It's a colt," Isaac said. "A pony's a small horse. Not a newborn." He loved words and being exact about things. Neither Don nor Joanie knew where that trait had come from.

Rachel ignored him. She did that a lot with her older brothers. "I always wanted a pony. Grandpa said I could have the baby pony."

Isaac groaned.

"Only because you kept whining for it," Joshua said.

"Yeah," Isaac agreed. "She wouldn't be quiet about it."

"Do you want to see my pony, Uncle Shel?" Rachel's gaze was open and innocent.

"Sure I do," Shel answered. He shifted the girl to his hip and walked toward the corral. "Where's your daddy?"

"Dad's at the church," Joshua said. "He's counseling Bill and Mary. They're going to be getting married at the end of the month." He looked up at Shel. "Did he know you were coming?"

"Nope. This was a surprise." Judging by the scowl on his daddy's face, Shel figured Tyrel McHenry was the most surprised of them all.

"Daddy's going to be glad to see you," Isaac said.

"Where's your boo-boo?" Rachel asked.

Shel looked at her, trying to comprehend what she was talking about.

"Daddy said you were hurt," Joshua said. "Then I heard him tell Mom you were shot."

"I was," Shel said.

Rachel's eyes rounded as she stared at Shel. "Oooooh, scary."

Shel smiled at her. "I'm better now."

"I'm glad." Rachel hugged him again.

For a minute as he held her, Shel thought about what it might be like to have a child of his own. It wasn't something he often considered. But the idea, as tempting as it sometimes was, scared him more than anything.

Having a marriage, even without a child involved, was a big commitment. Shel couldn't see trying to divide his time between the military and a relationship. He often dated but never got serious. If he tried to commit to both, both would have suffered. If he chose one over the other, it wouldn't be fair to the one that he didn't choose.

And he loved being a Marine.

But the biggest fear was that he would be the kind of father his daddy had been. He couldn't bear that. Somehow Don made it all work, but Shel couldn't see himself managing to do that.

Shel caught his daddy's eye as he reached the corral. "Hello, Daddy."

"You're looking fit," Tyrel said.

"Yes, sir. I've been working on it." As Shel stared at his daddy, he noted the dark circles beneath Tyrel McHenry's eyes. Shel had never seen circles like that before, not even when his daddy had gone sleepless for days. He looked like he'd lost weight as well, and his skin held a little gray.

Shel couldn't help thinking of men he'd brought into the NCIS office who'd had guilt working on them for months. They'd always been ready to confess just to get out from under their own personal demons.

"My phone works," his daddy said.

"Yes, sir." Shel suddenly felt like he was twelve again and had just gotten busted for sneaking out of the house at night. "I should have called. I apologize."

"Nonsense," Joanie said as she looped her arm through Shel's. "It's always good to see you. In fact, I know the kids love having you over, so why don't you plan on spending at least part of your time home with us?"

That was Joanie, Shel realized. Don couldn't have found a better woman if he'd tried. In that simple invitation, she'd given Shel and his daddy all the wiggle room they needed to get out of seeing each other any more than they had to.

"Sounds fine, Joanie," Shel said. "Thank you."

"You're always welcome. I know Don would like to spend some time with you that doesn't involve hospitals."

"See my pony?" Rachel pointed at the young foal in the corral.

"I do," Shel said.

"I'm going to name her Petunia," Rachel declared.

"Petunia's a dumb name," Joshua said.

"It's a girl name," Isaac said. "That's a boy."

Max placed his front paws on the corral railing and barked. The colt shied away and nearly fell over his too-long legs.

"Don't bark at Petunia, Max," Rachel said. "She's just a baby."

"He," Isaac said with a put-upon air. "He. He's a boy."

Shel leaned against the corral and tried to think good thoughts, but Victor Gant's accusation about his daddy remained uppermost in his mind.

CRIME SCENE
NCIS
NAVAL CRIMINAL INVESTIGATIVE SERVICE

40

SCENE ✪ NCIS ✪ CRIME SCENE

NAVAL CRIMINAL INVESTIGATIVE SERVICE

>> RAFTER M RANCH
>> OUTSIDE FORT DAVIS, TEXAS
>> 1813 HOURS (CENTRAL TIME ZONE)

Later, when Joanie declared it was time to go home, Shel kissed his niece and nephews good-bye and helped bundle them into the minivan. From the corner of his eye, he noticed his daddy submitting awkwardly to hugs from the children.

Try as he might, Shel couldn't remember a time when his daddy had held him. Even at his mama's funeral, Tyrel had clapped him on the shoulder and told him he was strong enough to survive it. Then he'd dropped a single rose onto his wife's casket and walked away.

When Shel had found his daddy later, after spending the brief time to talk with his friends and friends of the family that his daddy hadn't, his daddy had been working the livestock. Work was one thing that Tyrel McHenry did every day of his life.

Once Joanie's minivan was on the highway and out of sight, Tyrel turned to Shel. "Well, I got work to do. What are you gonna do?"

"Could you use some help?"

"Just putting up some hay in the barn. Got winter coming on. I want to be ready." Tyrel fished a pair of work gloves from his back pocket and headed for the barn.

"Could you use some help?" Shel asked again. He hated having to ask again.

"I can get it done. You just go ahead and do whatever it is you come out here to do." Tyrel kept walking.

I came out here to talk to you, Shel thought. But he couldn't get the words past his lips.

"Is it all right if I stay here, Daddy?" Shel asked.

"Whatever you want to do. You know where your room is."

"Yes, sir." Shel watched his father walk to the barn and tried to let go of some of the anger that filled him. He had questions on his heart that demanded answers. Finally he followed his daddy into the barn.

❂ ❂ ❂

>> 1819 HOURS

A large flatbed truck was parked in the middle of the barn. Rectangular bales of hay were stacked all over it. Only a few bales had been moved.

"Joanie and them kids interrupted my work," Tyrel said as he pulled his gloves on. "'Course, I knew they was coming. They called."

"Yes, sir. I'll remember."

"Don't cost much to be respectful," Tyrel said, as he'd done thousands of times before, "but it costs too much if you don't show respect."

"Yes, sir." Shel took a deep breath. The barn reeked of hay, mildew, animal sweat and spoor, and leather from saddles and tack hanging on the wall. He grabbed the cords that held a bale of hay together and lifted it from the truck bed.

"You bring any gloves?" Tyrel asked as he tossed the bale on the big stack against the barn's back wall.

"No, sir."

Tyrel scowled. "You give any thought to this trip? Or did you just light out?"

"Just lit out," Shel said.

Tyrel looked at him a little more closely then. "There's gloves in the front of the truck."

"Yes, sir." Shel put his bale of hay on the stack and headed for the truck cab. He opened the door and found a pair of well-used leather gloves on the seat. He pulled them on and returned to the rear of the truck.

Tyrel had continued working. His boots thumped across the floor.

Shel grabbed a bale of hay in each hand and carried them to the wall.

"Shoulder come back together all right?" his daddy asked.

"Yes, sir."

"Figured it would. You've always been tougher'n a boot."

"Yes, sir."

They worked in silence for a while. The work was hard in the heat, but it was something Shel had done for years. After the first few minutes, he was covered in sweat. His daddy was too, but he showed no signs of slowing down. He moved as effortlessly as a machine.

"You got a reason for wearing that pistol?" his daddy asked.

"Yes, sir." Shel grabbed two more bales of hay. They were light, dry, and packed. Alfalfa would have weighed over twice as much. But alfalfa was expensive. "Yesterday, Victor Gant tried to kill me and a buddy."

Tyrel looked at Shel then. "And you come out here?"

"Yes, sir."

"Ain't like you to run from trouble."

Anger stirred within Shel and he tried to get a grip on it. "I didn't come here running, sir."

"Gant threatened your family, did he?"

Shel barely curbed the heated response that was inside him and fighting to get out. "Yes, sir. He did."

"You killed his boy," Tyrel said. "He's gonna want blood for that."

"Yes, sir."

"You shoulda killed him."

"I tried. Man's hard to kill."

Tyrel nodded. "They tried to kill him in Vietnam, too."

"Who?"

His daddy shook his head. "Charlie. Who else would have tried to kill him over there?"

"I read Gant's service jacket," Shel said. "Man didn't exactly walk a straight line while he was over there. The Criminal Investigation Command checked him out several times."

"Those were hard times over there, boy. Today's the same. This war over in Iraq, it's plenty bad. Got kids over there doing things they shouldn't do. Rape, theft, black market, and drugs."

"I know. I've been over there in it."

"You put young, innocent men in a war zone, they don't come out the same way. Anybody who thinks they'll come out the same is a fool."

"Yes, sir."

"Victor Gant, he was probably a bad one even before he went over there." Tyrel picked up another bale of hay and headed for the stacks.

"I think so too," Shel said.

"What kind of shape is that shoulder in?"

"I'm a hundred percent."

Tyrel nodded. "Let's see if it is. Throw me them bales down from that truck bed."

"Why don't you throw them down?" Catching the bales was harder than throwing them, and Shel was bigger and younger than his daddy.

"Because I told you to."

"Yes, sir." Shel turned and vaulted up onto flatbed without strain. He plucked at the sweat-soaked T-shirt and tried to create a gust of cooler wind. Then he picked up a bale of hay and tossed it down to his daddy.

Tyrel caught the hay bale as if it weighed nothing. He walked it over to the stacks and climbed up the makeshift stairway made of bales. At the top, he stacked the bale.

"Can you throw those bales over here?"

"Yes, sir." Shel bent down, caught up a bale, and threw it onto the stack where his daddy stood.

Tyrel managed the bale easily and motioned for another. "Keep 'em coming. I want to get this done before I go to bed tonight. We get done early, there's a ball game on."

"Yes, sir." Shel bent to the task and began shoveling bales across the distance.

⊛ ⊛ ⊛

>> 1926 HOURS

The work took Shel back years. He remembered when his daddy had first trained him to stack hay, then when he'd trained Don.

He recalled the first time he and Don had done it by themselves; they'd done it while their daddy was preoccupied with the cows and the veterinarian. They'd stacked the bales as quickly as they could. As a result, by their daddy's standards, the effort had been slipshod. He'd made them take the stacks apart and restack the whole load while he'd watched.

At the time, Don had been disappointed because he hadn't gotten to go somewhere he'd wanted to. Shel couldn't even remember where that was now. As for Shel, he'd been angry—and embarrassed. Those emotions were always a bad combination for him.

Shel had wanted to do the hay as a surprise for his daddy. He'd thought maybe he could get his daddy's attention. He'd been thirteen. It had been a lot of work for a thirteen-year-old, and having to convince Don to help him hadn't been easy.

Even now that old anger rolled over him as he worked. He grabbed the bottom of his T-shirt and mopped the sweat from his face.

"You ain't slowing down on my account, are you?" his daddy called.

Shel looked at the man. Tyrel looked as relaxed as if he'd been taking life easy. Sweat stained his shirt, but he wasn't breathing hard and didn't appear tired. At times like this, Shel didn't think the man was human.

Bending to the task again, Shel got into the rhythm and focused on moving through the bales. His shoulder ached a little from the repetitive lifting, swinging, and throwing, but he wasn't going to quit. He let his anger feed his adrenaline, strength, and endurance.

And he still couldn't bury his daddy in hay bales. Every one he threw was quickly stacked before he could throw the next. The effort became an exercise in futility. Frustration chafed at him until he'd thrown the last bale. Then, when he looked and found his daddy putting the bale away like it was nothing, he cursed.

That drew his daddy's attention immediately.

Cursing wasn't something Shel was given to. His daddy had brought him up to watch his mouth, especially around women and children. Even the loose swearing so prevalent in the military hadn't stuck on him.

Shel's immediate impulse was to apologize. He stopped himself just short of that. Instead, he didn't look at his daddy and jumped from the back of the truck.

His daddy joined him a moment later. Without a word, Tyrel stripped the gloves from his hands and shoved them into the back pocket of his jeans.

"You got something on your mind, boy?" Tyrel's voice was hard and carefully measured.

"Just forgot myself is all," Shel said.

Tyrel eyed him. "That's just a word. Me and you both have heard that word more'n a few times. Probably used it too."

Shel felt ridiculous. He was taller and bigger than his daddy. He was a Marine. He was wearing a pistol on his hip.

And still he felt like a ten-year-old standing there.

"It ain't the word I'm bothered about," Tyrel said. "You come here to this house with a chip on your shoulder the size of a Clydesdale, and you ain't keeping it together. I want to know what's going on."

Shel tried to speak and couldn't. Helpless, he shook his head.

"Is it Victor Gant?" his daddy asked.

"I don't know." Even as he said it, Shel knew he'd made another mistake. The last thing Tyrel ever wanted to hear one of his sons say was *I don't know.*

Tyrel's voice hardened. "Well, that's an outright lie, boy. If there's anybody in this world who knows what he's mad at when he's mad, it's you."

Before he could stop himself, Shel said, "Maybe I'm a better liar than you gave me credit for, Daddy. The way I understand it, I come by it honest enough."

Tyrel's face tightened and his voice became a hoarse rasp. "What are you talking about?"

"I'm talking about that soldier you killed over at Qui Nhon." Even though he'd been in hundreds of fights and was amped up on adrenaline, Shel didn't see his daddy move till just before the hard-knuckled fist exploded against his jaw.

41

E SCENE ✪ NCIS ✪ CRIME SCENE

NAVAL CRIMINAL INVESTIGATIVE SERVICE

>> RAFTER M RANCH
>> OUTSIDE FORT DAVIS, TEXAS
>> 2004 HOURS (CENTRAL TIME ZONE)

Caught almost flat-footed by the blow, Shel rocked backward. For a moment he thought his head had come clean off his shoulders. Black spots exploded in his vision.

Half-dazed, Shel threw a punch of his own.

Either his daddy hadn't been expecting it or he'd thought Shel was going to go down. Shel's fist caught him full in the face and drove him backward. Tyrel's head snapped around. Something popped.

Horrified at what he'd done out of reflex, Shel hesitated. Then he caught another punch on his chin that knocked him back.

Without another word, Shel and Tyrel fought. Max started to come forward, but Shel called the Labrador back. Whining, Max subsided and lay flat on the hay-covered ground.

Pain flared Shel's senses. Despite the blows he landed on his daddy, Tyrel refused to go down. For every punch Shel threw, his daddy came back with one.

Tyrel McHenry knew how to fight. He'd boxed before he'd gone into the Army and been sent to Vietnam. After he'd gotten back, there'd been more fights. And he never held back.

Blood filled Shel's mouth and made breathing difficult. He stepped back and spat blood. His chest heaved.

His daddy hit him again.

Tyrel wasn't faring much better. He breathed liked a bellows pump. His nose was no longer straight. Blood leaked down over his chin.

Shel stepped back again, then gave ground as Tyrel came at him. There was no mercy in his daddy. Something fierce rode him, drove him to the fight with everything he had. Blocking blows that came just as hard and as fast as the first one, Shel punched and fought back. He spotted an opening and clubbed his daddy on the side of the head with his fist.

Stumbling back, Tyrel lost his footing for just a moment. He sat down heavily, almost out on his feet.

Bending over, Shel rested his bruised hands on his knees. He didn't have the stomach for fighting any more. He wanted to be done with it. He wanted to walk away.

But the question remained.

"Is that what you are, Daddy?" Shel asked hoarsely. "A murderer?"

Tyrel flailed an arm out for a paddock wall, caught the planks, and tried to pull himself up. But he didn't have enough strength or focus to do that.

"Who did you kill over there?" Shel demanded.

"I killed a lot of people," Tyrel growled. "That was my job. Just like yours. Just like when you killed Victor Gant's boy. Does that make you a murderer?"

"No," Shel said. "No, it don't. But Victor Gant told me you killed an American soldier. He said he helped you bury him."

Using both hands, Tyrel pulled himself into a standing position. "You gonna believe that man?"

Shel stared at his daddy. "If he's lying, tell me that, Daddy."

Tyrel refused to meet his gaze. His chest rose and fell.

"Tell me that Victor Gant was lying, Daddy," Shel said. "Just tell me that. I won't even wonder why you hit me."

His daddy's breath roared in the silence of the barn.

"Can you do that, Daddy?" Shel whispered. He no longer had the strength to speak in his full voice. His arms and legs felt weak. If his daddy attacked him again, he didn't know if he could defend himself.

"You get on outta here, Shelton." Tyrel swiveled his head to stare at Shel. "You hear me? You get on outta here."

"Daddy—"

Crying out like a trapped animal, Tyrel reached for a pitchfork and yanked it from a hay bale. He swung it around to point the tines at Shel. "You get offa my property. *Now!*"

Tears filled Shel's eyes and that embarrassed him too. "Daddy—"

"You get on outta here, Shel," his daddy ordered, "or one of us is gonna get killed in the next minute."

Shel knew his daddy meant every word he said. If he tried to stay, his daddy would try to make him leave. And one of them would most likely end up dead. Without a word, he backed away till he felt he had enough distance between himself and the man he'd never truly known.

Then Shel turned and walked out of the barn. He called Max to his side. Without turning back to look, he walked to the rental SUV and crawled inside. When he finally did look back at the barn, he couldn't see Tyrel. Shel couldn't believe what had happened.

Reluctantly, but knowing he had no choice, he keyed the ignition and drove away.

⊛ ⊛ ⊛

>> 2051 HOURS

For a long time after Shel had gone, Tyrel stood in the quiet of the barn. He forced himself to be calm after he heard Shel drive away. The pain from the blows Tyrel had received during the fight hurt, but not nearly as much as what he felt inside.

He didn't think he'd ever hurt so bad in his life. Not even when Amanda had died. She'd slipped away, little by little, over months. Sad as it was, he'd been able to adjust as he went along, although it was still hard.

But Shel . . .

A ragged cry of pain escaped Tyrel's bloodied lips. He couldn't believe it when he heard it. The sound was more that of an animal than anything human. He couldn't remember the last time he'd hurt so badly. Even not being there when Don's kids were born hadn't hurt as much as the look of disbelief on Shel's face.

He was waiting on you to deny it, Tyrel told himself. *He came out here all this way not because he wanted to confront you about it but because he wanted you to tell him it wasn't true.*

But it was. All of it was true.

When he finally had himself a little more under control, Tyrel walked back to the ranch house. The sun was finally starting to wane. Darkness crept in from the east, sliding across the land and sticking long black fingers into the red orange sunset.

In the house, he stood over the sink and washed his face. The washcloth he used came away smeared in blood. His lips had swelled and he couldn't breathe through his nose. When he cleared his sinus passages, bloody mucus filled the paper towel. He was pretty sure his nose was broken.

You had it coming, he told himself. *You had a lot worse coming. You still do. What you shoulda done all them years ago was turn yourself in.*

He hadn't been able to, though. He'd been too scared. Victor Gant had assured Tyrel that no one would ever know. He hadn't realized how much of a difference knowing himself would make. There hadn't been a day in his life since that Tyrel hadn't thought about Dennis Hinton.

The young man's name was haunting in itself. It had taken Tyrel months to figure out why. Then, when he looked at it one day, he'd realized that Dennis spelled backward was *sinned*.

It had been a sobering discovery.

Somewhere out there, in a grave near Highway 19 only a few miles outside of Qui Nhon, Dennis Hinton lay moldering and unclaimed by his family. Nightmares about Hinton rising from his grave had tormented Tyrel's dreams for almost forty years.

Now they'd come home to roost. Tyrel just hadn't expected Shel to be the messenger.

With a shaking hand, Tyrel turned the water off and stepped back from the sink. Fearful yet calm, he gazed around the kitchen.

You knew it was going to come down to this, he told himself. *This ain't no surprise, and you're a fool if you pretend it is. Sooner or later, you knew you'd have to decide to run for your freedom or stay and get arrested.*

He'd lived in denial so long that it was hard to think he wasn't going to live out his life unnoticed. He'd lived such a small life. He hadn't reached for much. When he was younger, there had been so much more that he wanted. But he hadn't taken on a thing he couldn't walk away from if he had to.

Except for Amanda and the boys, he told himself. He'd kept them at a distance, though. All of their lives and most of his, he'd forced them to be strong and independent. Shel had gotten that message and had stayed away a lot. Only Don, with his church ways and belief in God, had continued to try to work on their relationship. The grandkids were the hardest, though. When they were born, Tyrel couldn't help but feel—partly—that he'd gotten a chance to do things over.

He hadn't allowed himself to feel that way for long, though. That was a loser's wager. He wasn't nearly the kind of man they all thought he was.

Still hurting, Tyrel went to his bedroom and took out the bottle of Jack Daniel's he'd bought a few days ago. Since that drunken call he'd made to Shel in the hospital, he'd stayed away from the booze. It was too easy to get lost in the strong drink.

He retreated to the living room and sat in the easy chair. He drank straight hits from the bottle. The whiskey hit his stomach like napalm. He felt the pain in his face and his heart lessening with each drink.

Then he felt something else.

The sensation of being watched by a predator was unmistakable. Tyrel had learned it in the jungles of Vietnam, and he'd returned home with it. He'd had times when he was out on the streets of big cities when that singular ability had manifested again.

Sometimes, out in the far pastures, he'd gotten the same feeling when he'd been spied on by coyotes.

And from time to time, he'd gotten that feeling from other men while in bars or sale barns.

Tyrel had that feeling now. He took another hit off the whiskey bottle and looked through the nearest window. Full dark had fallen. No lights were on in the living room. He hadn't turned any on in the kitchen either.

Whoever was watching him had the benefit of anonymity in that darkness.

Tyrel took a final sip from the Jack Daniel's bottle and placed it beside the chair. Then he got up and walked to the master bedroom.

Heavy drapes blocked the window there. Even though they lived miles from neighbors, Amanda had always covered the windows in dark, hard material. Tyrel was certain he couldn't be seen.

He walked to the closet and removed the false flooring that covered the hidden area below. Even Amanda hadn't known about this, and he'd felt bad about that the whole time. But he couldn't just give himself up to be hanged or shot, whichever the military courts would decide. Not even the idea of living out the rest of his life behind bars was acceptable.

He pulled out the cash he'd saved up over the years. There was fifty thousand dollars in nonsequential hundred dollar bills. All of them were well circulated. They made a solid brick in his hands. Rubber bands held the bills together.

He shoved the money into a carry-on bag and added clothing. He didn't need much. He could buy more once he reached Mexico. Once he got into Juárez, he could disappear. There were places he could go and take up another identity he'd set up years ago.

All he had to do was escape whoever was out in the night.

He went to the gun rack by the bed, took out the Colt .45 Peacemaker, and strapped it around his lean hips. He had a little trouble buckling the belt due to the swelling in his hands, but he cinched it up and used the leg tie-down to secure the bottom of the holster. He added two speedloaders filled with extra ammunition, then dropped four boxes of extra bullets into the carry-on.

Outside, the mare whickered.

Shoulda got a dog, Tyrel thought. *A dog would let me know more which way they're coming from.*

But when his last dog had died three years ago, he just hadn't had the heart to get another. Losing the old hound had bothered him more than he'd guessed it would, and he knew he was starting to get too attached to things.

It's okay, he told himself. *They're coming at you in your territory. Nobody knows that land out there better'n you. Especially not in the dark.*

He figured he knew who was out there. Shel had confirmed that Victor Gant had threatened the family. At least the man had come after him, not Don and Joanie and the grandkids.

It surprised Tyrel that he thought of the children as that instead of Don and Joanie's kids. He had no right to claim them.

He shut the extraneous thoughts from his mind and concentrated on getting prepared. He took the .30-30 lever-action carbine from the gun rack on the wall. He didn't bother to check if the rifle was loaded. It was a tool, just like any other on a working ranch. The magazine was filled to capacity. He tossed four extra boxes of ammunition for the rifle into the carry-on.

Then he was ready.

Rifle in hand, he walked to the light switch and turned it off.

All right, he thought grimly. *Y'all bring it.*

42

SCENE ✪ NCIS ✪ CRIME SCENE

NAVAL CRIMINAL INVESTIGATIVE SERVICE

>> FORT DAVIS, TEXAS
>> 2113 HOURS (CENTRAL TIME ZONE)

"Aren't you going to come into the house?"

Shel sat in his rental SUV in Don's driveway and didn't look away from the basketball goal bolted to the garage. He and Don had hung the goal last spring. He could remember the first game they had played with the kids afterward. He didn't look at Don, but he knew his brother stood on the porch of the small house.

"In a minute," Shel said. He absently stroked Max's head. The Labrador had been tense ever since they'd left the Rafter M.

"There can't be anything that interesting out there," Don said.

Shel didn't speak. He couldn't. He didn't know what to say. He was also aware of the faces of the three children pressed against the living room window. Evidently Don or Joanie had made them stay in the house.

Don stepped down off the porch and crossed the neatly kept lawn. He wore slacks and a shirt. He probably hadn't gotten home from the church more than a few minutes ago.

As his brother closed on him, Shel felt that coming there was a mistake. He should have just taken a room at a motel, then got gone in the morning. He wouldn't have had to answer questions from Don.

And he could have put it all behind him that much sooner.

Except that running away wouldn't solve the problems he had now. Even if there was no proof that his daddy had killed a fellow soldier in Vietnam, Shel didn't know if he should open an investigation anyway.

What good would that do? he asked himself as he sat there.

"Shel?" Don stopped at the window and stared at him. "You okay?"

"Yeah," Shel whispered hoarsely. "I'm fine."

"What happened?"

Shel tried to speak and couldn't. His eyes burned and he knew he was about to cry. He felt angry at himself for being so weak and foolish. He knew he hadn't done anything wrong, but he felt like he had.

"Shel?" Don came closer and leaned on the door.

"I had a talk with Daddy," Shel said. His voice cracked. "Had something I needed to work out with him."

Don was silent for a time. From the corner of his eye, Shel saw the tight lines of fear on his brother's face as he took in the damage to Shel's face. He knew instantly what Don feared the most.

"Is Daddy all right?" Don asked in a quiet voice.

"Yeah." Shel tried to grin a little, but his pulped lips and swollen face made it hard. "Man hits as hard as a mule kicks, but he's definitely got the mule beat when it comes to stubbornness."

Don didn't smile. "Why did you get into a fight with Daddy?"

"He didn't like what I asked him."

Don shook his head. "I can't even begin to guess what you asked him."

"It's a long story, Don. I ain't yet decided what I'm going to do about it."

"You're going to tell me what's going on."

"I don't know if that's the right thing to do."

"Shel." Don's voice held more force in it now. "All the time I was growing up, I've seen you and Daddy argue and get mad at each other. When Mama was alive, God rest her soul, I think she kept you two from killing each other. Later, after she was gone, I tried my best to do the same."

"I think you probably did," Shel said.

"As much as I hated to see you go, I think it was the best thing you could have done at the time."

"I know." Shel took a deep breath. His ribs burned with pain.

"That's why you're going to tell me what's going on. Because that's the best thing you can do right now."

"You're not going to like it."

"I expect not, but I'd like not hearing it even less."

"Get in. I don't want to tell it here."

"Let me tell Joanie I'll be back." Don turned and walked back to the house.

Tired and hurting, Shel leaned his head back against the seat and tried to relax. He wished he hadn't come. He wished he'd just stayed at Camp Lejeune and left this part of his life alone.

More than anything, he wished that Victor Gant hadn't made a believer of him.

❂ ❂ ❂

>> RAFTER M RANCH
>> OUTSIDE FORT DAVIS, TEXAS
>> 2127 HOURS (CENTRAL TIME ZONE)

Deputy Sheriff Wayne Hayscott sipped his coffee as he drove the farm-to-market road that went by the Rafter M Ranch. Fifty-three years old, he'd already spent over half his life as a sheriff's deputy. The county was easy to patrol, and there was little trouble that went on in the area.

He didn't see the need to cruise by the ranch despite what the sheriff said. Tyrel McHenry was the meanest and orneriest man Hayscott had ever met. Tyrel was an old boar coon. Nobody in their right mind would try to tree him.

The cold coffee tasted bitter. Hayscott hated it even more because he was at least thirty minutes from another warm-up back at the quick stop.

Just be a minute, he told himself. *There and back out. No muss, no fuss.*

In the distance, he spotted the ranch house. It was dark. That wasn't a surprise. From what he knew of Tyrel McHenry, the man was up before the sun every day. That meant he'd be early to bed.

Hayscott put the coffee cup back in the holder; then he slowed and pulled the wheel around in a tight U-turn. His headlights swept across the scrub grass and cactus clinging to the side of the hill leading up to the Rafter M.

He was yawning when he saw the light glint on metal. Intrigued, he stopped the car and backed around to use the spotlight mounted by the window. The bright halogen beam pierced the dark night that almost hid the motorcycle that had been left there.

Upon closer inspection, Hayscott saw there were at least three motorcycles there. Warily he reached under the seat and pulled out the sliding rack that held an M4 and a 12-gauge shotgun. He also pulled his sidearm from its holster and dropped it onto the passenger seat in case he had to get to it quickly.

He reached for the handset and pulled it up to his mouth. "Dispatch, this is X-ray 46."

"Hey, Wayne," Jenny Wilcox's silken voice answered. She was a recent college grad who had returned to the town. Her daddy had been a police officer. Now he was a full-time fisherman and she called dispatch on the night shift. "Slow night?"

"It was," Hayscott said. "I'm at Tyrel McHenry's ranch. The sheriff said he wanted us to keep an eye on the place for the next few days."

"I know." Jenny sounded immediately more interested. "I saw the handout. Supposed to be a threat from some biker gang?"

"The Purple Royals," Hayscott answered. "I think I'm looking at some of their motorcycles right now."

"Are you sure?"

"Let me get a little closer and send you some of the tag numbers. We'll match 'em up and see what we get."

"Okay, but be careful. Those men are dangerous."

Hayscott took his foot from the brake and let the cruiser roll forward. He twisted the spotlight and tried to focus on the motorcycles.

"You know me, Jenny," Hayscott said. "I'm always careful."

Hayscott was almost on top of the motorcycles. For a minute he thought he was going to have to get out of the car and go have a look. Then the numbers came into focus.

You got old man's eyes, he chided himself.

"Okay, I got a plate," Hayscott stated. "And it's from North Carolina." He wasn't happy about that. On the other hand, maybe a group of hunters was out deer hunting or running coon dogs. Just because the plates were from North Carolina didn't mean that the motorcycles belonged to Purple Royals.

"Let me have the plate number," Jenny said.

Hayscott started to read the numbers and letters off, but he noted movement on his left side. He swiveled his head around and stared down the length of a silencer-equipped pistol.

"Sorry, bro," a deep voice said. "You picked the wrong night to come down the wrong road."

Hayscott started to reach for his handgun; then white light belched from the muzzle of the offending weapon. Heat hammered his head and he suddenly couldn't sit upright anymore. He started falling forward, but he never felt himself hit the steering wheel.

❀ ❀ ❀

>> MAUDE'S TRUCK STOP & ALL-NITE DINER
>> OUTSIDE FORT DAVIS, TEXAS
>> 2127 HOURS (CENTRAL TIME ZONE)

Shel sat in the SUV outside the diner. He'd started talking to Don along the way. Despite his best efforts, Shel hadn't been able to wait. He'd finished up about the time they'd pulled into the parking lot.

Three 18-wheelers, two sheriff's cruisers, and a handful of through traffic parked there. He stared at the bright light of the diner. For a moment, Shel resented how the lives of the people inside the diner hadn't been affected by the events of the evening. They ate and talked, and he felt like he'd been turned inside out.

"Do you know if there was a murder committed over there?" Don asked finally. "Do you know who Daddy was supposed to have killed?"

"No."

"That was forty years ago. I know there's no statute of limitations on a murder, but you'd have to have a body first, wouldn't you?"

Shel looked at Don. "This isn't about prosecuting Daddy."

"You said Victor Gant threatened to tell everybody."

"So what? The likelihood of finding that body—or a witness who could be trusted—is small."

"Then Daddy is going to be all right." Don sounded relieved. "Daddy will—"

"Go straight to hell for murder?" Shel asked.

Don looked at him.

"We're stuck," Shel said. "Me and you. I need to tell the military. And you gotta work this out with God. Both of us are where we never wanted to be over a man neither of us feels like he knows. You can't hide this from God any more than I can hide it from the military."

Don seemed overcome for just a moment. He stared at the large diner windows. "How can we help Daddy?"

"Would you listen to yourself? This isn't something we can fix. Even if I didn't say a word, do you think you can square this up with God and make it good in his book?"

Silence filled the SUV's interior for a moment. Then Max stood and put his head on Shel's shoulder.

"Is that what you're worried about?" Don asked, turning to look at Shel. "What God's going to think about all this?"

Shel felt suddenly uncomfortable. He didn't like talking about God. He never had. God had always been Don's thing.

But his daddy's damnation was what he was worried about the most. That surprised him. In the end, he supposed that was why he'd gone to Don's instead of just leaving town. Shel knew he didn't have any answers, and he was pretty sure the military didn't have anything he wanted to hear.

That left only Don.

"I'm going to be sick," Don said quietly.

"No," Shel said. "You're not."

But Don was. He turned suddenly and opened the door. He'd barely cleared it when he started heaving.

43

E SCENE ✪ NCIS ✪ CRIME SCENE
NAVAL CRIMINAL INVESTIGATIVE SERVICE

>> MAUDE'S TRUCK STOP & ALL-NITE DINER
>> OUTSIDE FORT DAVIS, TEXAS
>> 2131 HOURS (CENTRAL TIME ZONE)

Shel reached across and put his hand on his brother's back, just letting him know he was there. He wasn't feeling very good himself.

After a minute, Don's sickness passed. He flopped weakly back into the seat. Shel handed Don a disposable towelette from the kit he carried to deal with Max.

Don took it and wiped his mouth. "Thanks."

"You okay?"

"No." Don took in a deep breath and let it out. He looked at Shel. "Did Daddy say he . . . he . . . that he did what you think he did?"

"No."

"Then maybe he didn't. Maybe this is all just a—"

"He did it, Don," Shel stated. "I saw it in his face right before he hit me. I've seen guilty men before. And Daddy's guilty." Now that he'd seen that in his daddy's face, he realized he'd been staring at it his whole life. But he'd never recognized it before now.

The silence in the SUV stretched out lean and hard. Shel didn't know what to say. He knew he'd thought everything that must have been on

Don's mind. He just had to wait till Don caught up with him. Then they could talk about what they were going to do.

What you're *going to do,* Shel told himself. *You're not hanging this on Don. You're just letting him know what's going down before you do it. And you know what you have to do. Somebody out there, somewhere, deserves to know what happened to their son or husband or father. There are too many who didn't come back from that war. Even one more is going to make a difference.*

"Can you imagine what that must be like?" Don asked. "Living with a secret like that for over forty years?"

"I can't," Shel said. "Mostly I can't because I'd never do what Daddy did."

"You've killed people, Shel."

Shel didn't respond. He had killed people. There was no reason to contest it or point out that every time he'd ended a life it had been to save another that was hanging in the balance.

"Did you ask God's forgiveness for those deaths?" Don asked.

"No. Taking those lives in those situations was what I was trained to do."

"That doesn't mean you shouldn't seek God's forgiveness."

"I figured God forgave me when he kept me from getting killed," Shel said.

Displeasure tightened Don's face. "This isn't something you should take so lightly. You should always—"

"Don," Shel interrupted gently but firmly, "this is about Daddy. Not about me. Save your sermon for Sunday."

Don breathed in and out. "I know. You're right. The first thing we need to do is talk to Daddy."

Shel touched his bruised face. "Trust me when I say he's not exactly in a talkative mood over this particular subject."

"I don't mean any offense, Shel, but you're not the most tactful person on earth."

"Probably not. But I don't know many ways to ask someone if they killed somebody."

"That's exactly the kind of attitude I'm talking about."

Shel couldn't keep the irritation out of his voice. "I'm not the one that did anything wrong here, Don."

Don took another slow breath. "You're right. One thing I've learned about dealing with church members plagued by guilt is that you have to go slow. Allow them time to tell you something in their own good time."

"Daddy's had forty years to do that."

"He might have told someone."

"I didn't get that impression while he was whaling the tar out of me."

"Something like this takes . . . diplomacy." Don shook his head. "That's not you."

"I did the best I could."

"Yeah," Don said dryly. "I can see how that worked out for you."

"I walked out of there under my own power."

"Daddy was all right when you left?"

"He was. Looked like he was a mite winded, but he had some rounds left in him." Shel's attention was suddenly caught by the sheriff's deputies inside the diner.

As one, the deputies stood and dropped money onto the table. Then they rushed out of the diner.

On impulse, wanting some kind of distraction to break the tension inside the car, Shel pushed his door open and stepped out. He had his NCIS ID in one hand.

"Hey," Shel called. "Gunnery Sergeant Shelton McHenry. NCIS. Where are you guys headed?"

One of the older deputies stopped in his tracks. "Did you say McHenry?"

Don got out on his side so the truck stop's parking lot lights could shine on him. "Andy," he said. "It's Don McHenry. This is my brother, Shel."

"Got some bad news, Don," the deputy said. "Dispatch just called in, said there's trouble at your daddy's ranch."

"What kind of trouble?"

"Dispatch said she heard gunfire. The sheriff told us to keep a lookout over the place. Wayne Hayscott was out that way when dispatch lost communication with him."

"Get in," Shel growled as he dropped into the seat and keyed the ignition.

Don didn't argue. He yanked his seat belt on at the same time Shel did.

By that time Shel had already reversed the SUV and turned the vehicle toward the highway. He glanced at the dashboard clock. It read 21:36 because he'd set it to military time.

Hang on, Daddy, Shel thought fiercely as he blew by an 18-wheeler and barely made the lane change to get out of oncoming traffic. *We're coming.*

By his estimate, they were almost twenty-five minutes from the ranch. The engine screamed in his ears.

⊛ ⊛ ⊛

>> RAFTER M RANCH
>> OUTSIDE FORT DAVIS, TEXAS
>> 2136 HOURS (CENTRAL TIME ZONE)

Tyrel was surprised how calm he was in the darkness. It had been forty years since he'd been hunted.

I guess some things just never go away, he told himself. He still sat a horse the way he always had, still managed posthole diggers with an easy authority, and could still trail a cow across baked earth. The years had added up, but he hadn't changed much and hadn't lost much.

The fight with Shel proved that. Even though his face hurt and his heart was leaden in his chest, part of him still took pride in the fact that he could match Shel. Tyrel hadn't ever let up on himself a single day in his life.

A shadow fell across the bedroom window.

Tyrel's breathing slowed a little more. He didn't move. Instead of staring at the window, he looked away from it. In the darkness, peripheral vision was better than looking at something directly.

Moonlight glimmered on a thick blade that pried at the window.

For a moment, Tyrel allowed himself to think about the men coming for him. Victor Gant attracted a certain kind of man to his flag. Those who stayed with him during the long term were hard men with agendas of their own. They placed their lives above the lives of everyone else.

In Vietnam, Victor's cool composure and emotionless control had drawn several young soldiers to him. He'd promised them that if they listened to him, he'd get them through the war alive and in one piece. Since most of the guys who'd been assigned with him worked reconnaissance, the young soldiers had listened.

Then they'd started counting the body bags and realized that Victor Gant might have been better at keeping himself intact, but that wasn't necessarily how it worked out for others.

And some of them, a lucky few that Victor had gone after, had seen the darkness in him and fought shy of it.

Tyrel hadn't been one of those. He'd been twenty-one years old, scared and alone and far from home in a country he couldn't even begin to understand.

You stay away from there, he told himself. *You got business here to tend to.*

The knife wielder popped the window latch free without difficulty. Security wasn't a big issue in the area.

The man waited a moment. Whispers reached Tyrel's ears and let him know the man wasn't alone.

Tyrel knew he wasn't going to have much time when everything broke loose. He hadn't believed Shel when he said Victor Gant might come after him. Or maybe he hadn't cared. Maybe he'd thought it would be payment of a debt long overdue.

Despite the guilt that had plagued him for forty years and kept him distant from his family, Tyrel was shamed that he wasn't ready to give up his life. He didn't know why that was.

So he lay in wait. Not all of Victor Gant's men would be trained fighters. They might be killers, but there was a world of difference between a man willing to kill and one who had been trained to.

The window lifted soundlessly in its tracks. A man climbed across the sill. A gun was clearly visible in his right hand.

Calmly Tyrel shot the man through the head. The sound of the gunshot was loud in the bedroom. Before the echo had died away, Tyrel crossed the room and took up a position across the dead man's back.

Another man stood only a few feet away. Tyrel shot him through the heart at point-blank range. Satisfied that none of the other men were in the immediate vicinity—though they would undoubtedly be coming soon—Tyrel pushed the dead man back through the window, then threw a leg over and dropped to the ground only a few feet below.

Going out through the window the invaders had tried to come in was a nervy response to the threat. But it was the correct one. Most people who knew they were being chased ran *from* the perceived threat, not toward it.

Tyrel stepped across the other dead man and ran toward the barn.

Hoarse shouts rang out. Footsteps closed on that side of the house.

Ignoring the sounds of pursuit, knowing it was a footrace, Tyrel headed toward the barn.

"Over here!" someone shouted. "He's headed for the barn!"

Tyrel pulled the door open and slid through just ahead of a fusillade of bullets that drummed the heavy wood. Splinters ripped free like confetti.

Pale moonlight filtered into the building, but there wasn't enough to accurately see anything. Tyrel went by feel. He knew every inch of the barn. He'd built it, and he'd been inside it every day since construction had finished.

He took a bridle from the tack hanging on the wall and headed for the mare in the first stall. He'd been riding her for years. When he was in the saddle, he'd often felt they shared the same thoughts. There wasn't a move either could make that the other didn't already know.

Tyrel opened the stall door and called to the mare. She whickered and came to him immediately. He slid the bridle into place, and the bit clacked in between her teeth as he snugged the leather behind her ears. Then he vaulted up across her back. There was a moment of hesitation on the mare's part; then she recognized Tyrel's gentle voice and calmed.

Seated on the horse's back, Tyrel watched as someone pushed the barn door wide. All out of time, Tyrel put his heels to the mare's flanks and guided her toward the barn door. He pulled the .30-30 around, pointed at the center of the shadow revealed in the wide rectangle of soft light, and pulled the trigger. The mare tightened a little beneath him but never broke stride. He'd trained her to deal with him firing from the saddle at wolves that occasionally stalked his cows and calves.

The man in the doorway stumbled but didn't go down. Then the mare hit him and sent him sprawling. Tyrel stayed low over the horse's back as he rode her from the barn. Even without the saddle, he sat her easily, sticking tight.

He had a brief impression of the men scattered around the front of the barn and around the corral. Shots rang out. Some of them cut the air near his head, but none of them touched him or the mare.

Encouraged but knowing how dangerous it was to ride at full speed at night, Tyrel gave the mare her head and let her run. Her hooves drummed the packed earth. She slowed only a moment at the fence, bunching and uncoiling as she sailed over the top post.

She landed roughly on the other side. For a moment Tyrel was certain he and the mare were going to go separate ways, but he clamped his knees tight and hung on. When she recovered and he remained atop her, they had the whole of the wide-open range before them.

Tyrel's heart sang when he realized they'd made it. But he knew he'd never see the ranch again. He'd planned this moment for forty years, but he'd always hoped it would never come. It was ironic that Victor Gant, who'd been the man responsible for all the guilt that Tyrel had felt over those years, would be the one who chased him from the land that had been Tyrel and his family's home.

He put that out of his mind. This life, poor as it had been, was over. Whatever was left, however meager and sorry it might be, lay ahead of him.

44

E SCENE ✪ NCIS ✪ CRIME SCENE

NAVAL CRIMINAL INVESTIGATIVE SERVICE

>> RAFTER M RANCH
>> OUTSIDE FORT DAVIS, TEXAS
>> 2148 HOURS (CENTRAL TIME ZONE)

Victor Gant stood in the darkness and tried to spot the fleeing horseman. He heard the horse's hooves striking the earth, but he couldn't see a thing.

He ran forward and took a position against the corral fence. He rested the barrel of the M4 he carried on the topmost railing and took out the high-intensity halogen flashlight clipped to his belt. With a press of his thumb, he brought the flashlight to life and aimed it in the direction Tyrel McHenry had taken.

It was no use, though. The light illuminated the ground in front of him, but the beam vanished in the dank black of the night.

Victor cursed when he realized Tyrel had escaped. In the next instant a spark of light flared in the darkness. The corral post shivered under the assault rifle, and wood chips flew into the air. Aware that the bullet had missed him by inches, Victor extinguished the flashlight and threw himself to the ground.

The harsh crack of the shot rolled over him.

"Find that muzzle flash!" he roared at his crew. "Find that shooter and light him up!"

Other bikers fell into position against the railing. Some of them raked the darkness with bullets.

Victor lay there for a moment, but there weren't any more shots from Tyrel McHenry. He'd taken his opportunity to make a quick kill and turned his attention to getting out of there.

Grudgingly Victor knew he would have done the same thing. Taking a chance on killing an enemy when that enemy wasn't expecting it was good. Bringing enemy fire to his position, especially when he was in full retreat, was just suicidal.

"Victor," Fat Mike called out of the darkness.

"Here." Victor pushed himself up and stood near the corral. He didn't move away from the fence post. It was also possible that Tyrel would take up one final position and try for a kill once everyone let their guards down.

"Thought he got you," Fat Mike said.

"He almost did."

"He shoots good. Nervy cuss, ain't he?"

"You planning on an adoption, Fat Mike?" Victor demanded angrily.

"Nope. Just observing, is all."

Victor stared at the darkness, then looked around at his crew. He appeared to be two men short.

"I take it Tyrel didn't just escape, did he?" Victor asked. "I guess a couple of men had to go and get themselves shot."

"Dirty Bob and Dead Ear," someone volunteered. "The old man got 'em as they were comin' through the window."

"How are they?"

"Dead. One shot, one kill. That old man must have ice water in his veins to stay holed up like that and come out shootin'."

Victor walked toward the main house and deliberately ignored the fact that the younger biker was referring to Tyrel McHenry as old. Tyrel was a couple of years younger than Victor.

"Anybody else at home?" Victor asked.

"Nope," another man said. "Done been through it. He was here by himself."

And he got away, Victor thought bitterly. His cell phone rang, and he pulled it from his pocket. "Yeah."

"That cop Loco shot was on the radio when he went down." Buster, an ex-communications officer from the Army who'd been discharged for dealing drugs in the first Iraq War, was monitoring the law enforcement frequencies. "Word went out. That twenty is about to be flooded by county Mounties."

"Affirmative," Victor snarled. He folded the phone and put it back in his pocket. Then he raised his voice. "Pack it in. We're outta here. We're about to be eyebrow-deep in cops."

"What about Dirty Bob and Dead Ear?" one of the bikers asked.

"We got a klick-run ahead of us," Victor said. "You want to superman it and hump them out of here, feel free." He turned toward the front of the ranch where they'd left the motorcycles and began trotting.

Behind him, Fat Mike cursed disconsolately. As big as he was, Fat Mike was already carrying the equivalent of a dead man's weight strapped to him.

Victor focused on the run. He'd get another chance at Shel McHenry. Victor felt that in his bones. The big Marine wasn't the type to clear out of a situation.

A grin pasted itself on Victor's face. He'd promised Tran after tonight's attempt that he'd get out of the United States for a while. If the Marine came after him, he was going to have to do it on dangerous terrain.

No one knew Vietnam like Victor Gant did.

⊛ ⊛ ⊛

>> 2201 HOURS (CENTRAL TIME ZONE)

Shel slotted himself into the breakneck convoy that raced down the farm-to-market road toward the Rafter M. He'd positioned himself the third vehicle back. Not close enough to the front of the pack to appear anxious to take over the operation, but not so far back that he missed out on a good look at the scene when they arrived.

"They need to turn off the flashing lights." Don sat in the passenger seat and clung to the seat belt. "Those bikers are going to see us coming for miles."

Shel silently agreed. But he knew trying to tell the deputies that would only start an argument. They were driven by the adrenaline of knowing one of their number had gone down in the line of fire. For most of them, this was probably the first time that had happened. They weren't thinking right now; they were reacting.

"That's pretty smart for a preacher." Shel tried to sound as though he wasn't worried about their daddy.

"It's common sense." Don shook his head. "I grew up watching the same Western movies you did." He pointed. "Look. There's the ranch house."

Shel peered through the night and spotted the house in the distance. He was relieved to see it sitting there quietly in the darkness. He'd been expecting to find it lit up with muzzle flashes or engulfed in flames.

The lead deputy cruiser veered without warning and suddenly raced for the ditch on the right side of the road. Over Shel's shoulder, Max barked and ran to the driver's side window in back. Shel's hand was already on his pistol when he heard the shots.

A moment later, the second deputy cruiser came under fire. Bullets ripped through the windshield and tore across the flashing light bar.

In the next moment, powerful motorcycle engines thundered to life. The bikers rose from the ditch on the right as their machines struggled with the grade because of their weight.

"Get down!" Shel ordered when he noticed Don was sitting frozen in the passenger seat, watching the outbreak of violence around them.

Shel transferred his pistol to his left hand and cupped his right behind Don's head to pull him down. He knew that Max had already gone to cover.

Bullets slammed against the SUV and ripped through the windshield. Safety glass trickled into Shel's lap as he held the wheel straight with his right knee and took aim at the first biker he saw. The pistol jumped in his fist as soon as he had a lock on the target.

The biker jerked, and the motorcycle went out of control. It fell over sideways and skidded across the road under the SUV.

Shel let go of Don and grabbed for the wheel. It didn't do any real good. The motorcycle had lodged under the SUV and made the vehicle unmanageable. Still, he almost had it under control when the deputy cruiser behind him slammed into him. The air bags blossomed with staccato blasts and trapped Shel and Don.

The other bikers sped past and were gone in a heartbeat.

Shel tore the air bag free with his hand and cleared his way out of the SUV. He flung open the bullet-riddled door and turned to face the retreating bikers. In the darkness, he couldn't tell how many of them there were. He opened fire immediately and hoped he got lucky.

If he hit any of the Purple Royals, they gave no indication of it.

A quick check of the vehicles revealed that the first two and his own were definitely out of commission. He ran to the next cruiser as he fed a new magazine into his pistol. Max paced him.

The deputy in the car was bleeding from a head wound while he fought the air bag. A quick glance told Shel that the man had received the wound from the wreck, not from a bullet.

"You okay?" Shel asked.

"Yeah." The deputy nodded but looked out of it.

"Call dispatch. Let them know what happened. Tell them they need to shut the highways down."

"Okay." The deputy grabbed the handset.

None of the deputy cruisers were in any position to give pursuit. With the ditches on either side of the narrow road and the tangled mess of the wrecks, they were trapped.

"Shel."

When Shel turned, he saw Don standing beside the SUV.

"What about Daddy?" Don asked.

Without a word, they turned together and raced for the road that led up to the ranch house.

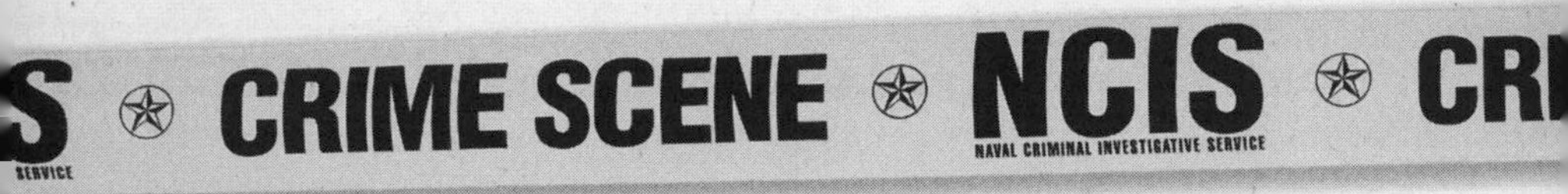
CRIME SCENE
NCIS
NAVAL CRIMINAL INVESTIGATIVE SERVICE

45

SCENE ✪ NCIS ✪ CRIME SCENE
NAVAL CRIMINAL INVESTIGATIVE SERVICE

>> RAFTER M RANCH
>> OUTSIDE FORT DAVIS, TEXAS
>> 2204 HOURS (CENTRAL TIME ZONE)

Please, God, don't let my daddy be dead. As he ran, Don knew he sounded like a child. But that was all right. In God's eyes they were all children. They were supposed to turn to him in times of need and fear. God was a daddy too.

Over the years, Don had known he'd enjoyed a closer relationship with God than he had with his earthly father, especially since he'd been called to lead the church. God had pulled him to that, and Don had never doubted that a day in his life. He suspected that even if he were close to his daddy, he'd still have been closer to God.

Don ran as fast as he could, but he couldn't match Shel's speed. Ultimately Don knew he was going to lose, but the thing that worried him most was that some of the bikers might yet remain at the house, or that Daddy might accidentally shoot them while thinking they were the bikers.

That fear and the adrenaline lent wings to Don's feet. He was less than a hundred yards behind his brother when Shel reached the ranch house.

Shel hunkered down behind the big pecan tree in the front yard. Mama had asked Daddy to put that tree in, and she'd made pies from what they'd gathered every year after it started producing. For a long time after

Mama's death, Daddy had gathered the nuts every year and given them away. Then when Don married Joanie, he'd given the pecans to her. They'd given Daddy pies back. Lately Don's kids had gathered the pecans.

Out of breath, afraid that he was about to throw up from the exertion and nerves, Don bent over and rested his hands on his knees.

Shel faced him, his features calm and set like stone. "I want you to stay here, Don."

"Why?" Don gasped.

"Just stay here." Shel's voice was hard and clipped. It was his big-brother voice. After all these years, it hadn't gone away. But it had been a long time since Don had heard it.

"All right," Don said. He was used to telling Shel whatever he needed to in order to mollify him.

Shel approached the house at a measured run. He signaled to Max, and the Labrador took the lead and stayed to the left.

Don noticed that Shel was going to the rear of the house, obviously circling it. When he knew Shel was too far away to stop him, Don took off like a shot and ran for the front door.

He flattened up against the door like the television cops he enjoyed watching every now and again. Those shows were his one guilty pleasure. He'd sometimes imagined what it might be like going with Shel in his NCIS work.

What it turned out to be was scary. Don's heart beat so hard and so fast he thought it was going to rip right out of his chest.

"Daddy?" Don called. "Daddy? It's Don. Are you in there?"

There was no answer.

God, please watch over us right now. Keep us close. Marshaling his courage, Don tried the door. It was locked, but that made him feel better. If he had to use his key to get in, maybe everything was all right.

Inside the house, Don almost turned on a light out of habit. He caught himself just in time and stopped. Turning the light on would have made him an instant target.

He went through the house quickly, working from the living room to the back of the house, where Daddy's bedroom was.

When he saw the broken window, Don almost cried out in fear. He made himself stay quiet. At the window, he looked down and saw two men lying in obvious death on the ground. Shel was squatted beside them.

"I told you to stay back," Shel said without looking up.

"I couldn't," Don said. "Is that . . . ?" He couldn't say it.

"It's not Daddy," Shel said.

Thank God.

"But Daddy killed them both."

"How do you know that?"

"They've each been shot once," Shel said. "One through the head and the other through the heart. At a distance, that's not such a big deal. But killing a man up close like this . . . and two of 'em, one right after the other?" He shook his head. "That takes some real nerve."

"They would have killed Daddy if he hadn't killed them first," Don objected.

Shel stood and looked around. "I know. I wasn't faulting him, Don. I'm just impressed. Taking a life ain't like it is on television. Especially not if you've already done it before." He paused. "You either learn to accept the need and that dark part of you that can do it, or you eventually get yourself killed. Not every law enforcement person I know could handle something like this. That's all I was saying."

But Don knew his brother well enough to know that Shel was saying more. Evidently Daddy didn't hesitate when it came to killing someone else.

That wasn't any different than Shel, though, was it? Don didn't know the answer. Another question was on his mind.

"Where's Daddy?"

"I don't know." Shel took off walking. "His truck's still out front. There's only one other way he could have gotten away."

Don took a final look at the two dead men, then climbed through the window and followed Shel to the barn.

⊛ ⊛ ⊛

>> 2209 HOURS (CENTRAL TIME ZONE)

Although Don followed him and he didn't want to place his brother in peril, Shel ignored the potential danger. He felt that whatever threat had existed was gone.

Daddy's gone.

That realization haunted Shel, but he felt it was true. He couldn't have said how he knew, but he was aware of an emptiness that had never been at the ranch before. Even when Mama had died, the emptiness had never felt that big.

"He's not here, is he?" Don asked.

Shel didn't answer. He kept his pistol trained on the prone figure lying in front of the barn door. The man didn't move. Moonlight silvered the man's staring eyes.

When Shel reached the man, he kicked the M4 away, then knelt and placed his free hand against the man's carotid artery. Only cooling flesh met Shel's touch.

"Is he dead?" Don asked.

"Yeah."

"They just left him behind like that?"

"In case you're counting, they left the other two behind too. I don't think the Purple Royals are big on friendship once somebody's dead." Shel stood. "Three men. In the dark." He shook his head. "That's something."

"What?" Don looked at him in disbelief.

"I'm just saying, is all," Shel replied. "A lot of men came after Daddy." Pride swelled inside his chest. "If he hadn't gotten away, he might have killed more of them. Then again, since this place is his and he knows every inch of it, he might have killed them all."

"How do you know Daddy got away?"

Shel took his penflash out and played it over the ground. The light showed the heavy horseshoes that scored the ground. The earth was still dark and hadn't dried out yet.

"I'll bet that mare of his is missing." Shel put the penflash away and walked into the barn.

A brief check revealed that the horse was gone, but Tyrel McHenry's saddle still hung on the tack wall.

"He went out light," Shel said. "Rode bareback." He walked back outside. Farther down the road leading up to the house, a few of the deputies were headed toward them.

"Do you think Daddy headed out to get the police?" Don asked.

"No." Sadness filled Shel's heart as he realized what he truly thought. "I think Daddy's lit a shuck for the quickest way out of here. I'm guessing he'll be in El Paso come morning. He'll be in Mexico City shortly after that."

"That's insane," Don whispered, but Shel knew his brother was starting to realize that what he was saying was true. "Daddy wouldn't just run off in the middle of the night."

"Yeah," Shel said, "he would. He had all this worked out, Don. That's why he didn't hang around but decided to take his chances on riding that mare out of here."

"Why?"

"Because Daddy's got military murder charges hanging over him if Victor Gant tells anyone what happened in Qui Nhon. And the military executes soldiers who murder other soldiers. Even if it was forty years ago."

Don was silent for a moment, and Shel dreaded the question he was certain his brother was going to ask next. It was inevitable, though. A similar question had come from the mouths of dozens of family members Shel had gotten to know during his service with NCIS.

"Do you really . . . do you . . . think Daddy murdered somebody?"

Shel blew his breath out and looked at Don. It hurt him to hurt Don by taking away his hope. But Shel believed that if people faced facts sooner, it got easier in the long run.

"Daddy ran, Don."

"Maybe he just went for help."

"It was safer to stay here than to try to get away on that horse. Daddy lit out because he didn't want to be here when the police arrived. If he didn't kill Victor Gant—and there was no way he could be sure of doing that with all those men hunting him—then he knew Gant could get taken into custody. Then the story about the murder would come out. Daddy couldn't afford to stay."

"I can't believe he just ran like that," Don whispered.

"Daddy's been running for forty years. We just never knew it."

CRIME SCENE
NCIS
NAVAL CRIMINAL INVESTIGATIVE SERVICE

46

SCENE ✪ NCIS ✪ CRIME SCENE

NAVAL CRIMINAL INVESTIGATIVE SERVICE

>> RAFTER M RANCH
>> OUTSIDE FORT DAVIS, TEXAS
>> 1038 HOURS (CENTRAL TIME ZONE)

"Must be a slow news day," Estrella commented from the passenger seat. Her displeasure showed in her frown as she regarded the sight.

Will looked at the road ahead and curbed the impatience and frustration that filled him. Ahead, the road was choked by news vehicles and local gawkers. And not everyone had gotten there by car or pickup; a few horses grazed while they were tied to the fence that ran around the Rafter M.

"It's a small town," Will said. "Everybody here knows everybody else."

"Or thinks they do," Nita said from the backseat. "Till something like this happens."

Tall and red-haired, the team's medical examiner peered forward between the two front seats. Normally she was lean, but she was five months pregnant these days. Her hand unconsciously glided across her stomach as Will checked on her in the rearview mirror. She was only just starting to show.

"Small towns are good to live in," Nita went on. "Everybody knows you. Of course, small towns are also bad to live in. Because everyone knows you."

Will silently agreed. "Are you doing all right?"

Nita met his gaze in the rearview mirror and smiled self-consciously. "I'm fine."

"I wouldn't have asked you to come out here if it hadn't been Shel involved."

"With Shel involved," Nita told him, "I'd have been seriously irked if you hadn't asked me."

Will offered her a wan smile. Since she'd come to terms with the issues in her private life and rededicated herself to her husband and daughter, Nita carried a peace about her that Will couldn't help noticing.

"What do you hope to find out here?" Nita asked.

"I don't know," Will answered honestly. "But with the lengths Victor Gant is going to, I want every edge I can get."

A uniformed deputy waved him to a stop. Will rolled the window down.

"I'm afraid I can't let you go any farther, sir," the deputy said with polite efficiency.

"Who's in charge of this investigation?" Will asked.

"That'd be Sheriff Conover, but he's a mighty busy man right now."

Will showed the deputy his NCIS ID. "Get him for me, would you?"

The deputy used the handi-talker on his shoulder and called for the sheriff.

Will got out of the rented car and stretched. He was dead tired. When Shel had called him last night and let him know everything that had transpired, Will had called the team in immediately and requisitioned a jet to get them to Fort Davis. Director Larkin had greased the wheels, and a jet had been standing by when Will arrived at the airport.

Maggie parked the second SUV they'd rented. With all the gear the team packed, they needed multiple vehicles. Remy parked a third SUV behind her, then got out and flashed his ID at the deputy who was trying to wave him off.

A couple minutes later, Sheriff Conover made his way through the crowd and reached Will. He was a tall, thick man with a fierce mustache, a big hat, and mirrored sunglasses.

"Commander Coburn?" the sheriff asked. His gruff voice matched his exterior.

Will nodded and offered his hand.

"Pleasure to meet you, sir," Conover said. "Pity it couldn't be under more pleasant circumstances."

"Where's my agent?" Will asked as he took his hand back.

"Up to the house. Since he's a trained forensics person, I figured it wouldn't hurt none to have him help out some."

"Some lawyer could argue that Gunnery Sergeant McHenry's presence here could compromise the evidence. He has a vested interest."

Conover smiled. "I figure a dumb attorney could work up to that song and dance, see how it flew for a judge at an inquest, but a smart one would realize we got a mess of dead bikers here that ain't local. And this trouble followed Shel's family home from your neck of the woods. Wasn't nothing started here."

Will nodded.

"More'n that," Conover said, "I ain't got enough boys out here to lock Shel out of this." He paused. "I assume you people are gonna take over this investigation?"

"With the family of one of my team in danger like this? You know it."

"They killed one of my deputies last night," Conover said. "He was a good man. A family man. Shel tells me you're good at what you do, so I'm gonna back your play. Anything you need from me, you consider it yours."

"I appreciate that," Will said.

⊛ ⊛ ⊛

>> 1052 HOURS (CENTRAL TIME ZONE)

Don was sitting on the front porch steps and talking on a cell phone when Will arrived. When he saw Will, Don folded the phone, put it away, and got up.

"How are you doing?" Will asked.

"It's tough," Don admitted. "The main thing is that no one knows where Daddy is. Or if he's all right. I've been praying about it since we found him gone."

"The sheriff said he'd put a BOLO out on your father," Will said. A BOLO was a Be On the LookOut order. It was usually accompanied by a description. In this case, the sheriff had posted pictures of Tyrel McHenry. "They'll find him."

Don hesitated. "Shel doesn't think they will."

"He'll probably show up on his own once all the confusion dies down," Will said. "He may have just lain down and gone to sleep somewhere out there." He nodded at the pasture. He knew from talking to Shel and the sheriff that Tyrel McHenry had taken a horse and left the scene. "And Shel didn't indicate there was any reason to think your father was injured when he left."

Don gave Will a curious glance. "Shel didn't tell you, did he?" he asked.

"I don't understand."

Helplessness showed in Don's eyes. Desperation was in there too.

"Victor Gant told Shel that Daddy was a murderer," Don said in a low voice. "Back in Jacksonville. Gant said that Daddy killed a man back in Vietnam all those years ago, and Gant was going to make sure that knowledge became public."

Will listened as Don talked in low tones.

"Personally," Don said when he finished, "I don't see how it could be true. Daddy won't ever win Father of the Year, but he's a good man. What Victor Gant has accused him of, I just don't see that happening."

"Does Shel believe it?" Will asked.

Don paused, then nodded. "He does."

That, Will thought, explained a lot of Shel's strange behavior of late. "Where can I find Shel?"

"He's inside. In Daddy's room. Straight on back."

⊛ ⊛ ⊛

>> 1055 HOURS (CENTRAL TIME ZONE)

Will found Shel in the bedroom. The big Marine had a high-definition digital camera in hand and was capturing images of the broken window with slow deliberation. He glanced up and nodded at Will.

"You got here fast," Shel commented.

"You asked me to come." Will gazed around at the crime scene. It had been expertly marked off. Spent brass lay on the floor with markers beside the casings. He noticed immediately that no bullet holes adorned the walls.

"I hated to ask," Shel said. He captured another image. "I know you've got a full plate with everything back at Camp Lejeune. The last thing you needed was this."

"This," Will said with deliberation, knowing that getting around to the subject of Tyrel McHenry was going to be difficult, "is connected to part of what I've got on my plate. Victor Gant is unfinished business."

Shel nodded.

Will peered over the windowsill and down at the ground. Two dead bikers lay there.

"I told them they couldn't move the bodies till after Nita got here," Shel said. "She came, didn't she?"

"She did," Will said.

"I owe her one."

"She doesn't keep count. None of us do." Will glanced around the room again. "I don't see any bullet holes."

"They never got a shot off," Shel said with a hint of pride. "Daddy sat in that corner there—" he pointed—"and took out the first man as he was coming through the window. The headshot. Then he crossed the room and took out the second. After that, he made his way to the barn and took off on his horse. He left another body."

"Sounds like your father knows how to handle himself," Will said.

Shel nodded. "More than I thought he did."

"The sheriff told me he had a chopper in the air searching."

A look of quiet contemplation filled Shel's face. "Daddy don't want to be found. He knows all that hardscrabble country out there like the back of his hand. He won't be located till he's good and ready to be located."

"I thought maybe that was the case," Will said.

Shel looked at him for a long moment. "You ran into Don out front, didn't you? He told you what Victor Gant said about Daddy."

Will didn't hesitate. In all the years he'd dealt with Shel, there was no other way to handle the gunnery sergeant than in a straight-ahead fashion.

"Yeah," Will said. "Don did."

"I would have told you," Shel said quietly. "But there's no proof that anything Victor Gant said about my daddy is true."

"Do you think it is?"

Angrily Shel took in a deep breath and let it out. "I do, Will. I looked into Daddy's eyes and I saw the guilt there the way I've seen it dozens of times when we've had people in the interview rooms back at headquarters."

Will accepted that. Shel was good at reading people. Will trusted the man's instinct. "All right. The question remains, what are we going to do about it?"

"I don't know."

Seeing the pain in Shel's eyes and in the uncomfortable way he held his shoulders, Will softened his voice. "It's hard to prosecute someone for murder when you don't know who it is that he's supposed to have killed."

"I know. But I think I know who it was." Shel walked over to the closet and lifted a small box from inside a recessed area. "I found this while I was poking around in here. It's stuff Daddy must have brought back from Vietnam." He took a picture out of the box and showed it to Will.

Will took the picture and studied the young man in it. "Do you know who this is?"

"His name's Dennis Hinton. Private first class. Regular army. He was nineteen years old in that picture."

"How do you know that?"

"His name's on the back. That's also how I know this is the man Daddy killed."

Will turned the picture over and read the messy handwriting on the back.

PRIVATE FIRST CLASS
DENNIS "DENNY" HINTON (19)
—MURDERED OCTOBER 15, 1967—
QUI NHON, VIETNAM

Below it was another line of words that had been heavily underlined.

"It's not exactly a confession," Shel said hoarsely, "but it's close enough. If we get testimony from Victor Gant."

Will handed the picture back to Shel without saying anything.

"I'm hosed, Will," Shel said in a tight voice. "If we don't catch Victor Gant, maybe he keeps trying to kill me and gets lucky. Or now that Daddy's gone, maybe he'll try to get Don and his family. I'm not going to allow that, but I can't protect Don's family the way I need to if Victor Gant stays loose. So I'm going to bring him in."

"And when Victor Gant is brought in, he's going to testify against your father."

"You see how it is," Shel whispered.

"I do."

"So I don't know. I don't know if I'm supposed to hope that Daddy is gone and I never see him again. Or if I'm supposed to help turn him over to the military court." Shel paused. "Either way, my family loses."

Will thought about everything that was put before them. Their cases often got complicated. Violence wasn't neat. Not from the perpetrator's point of view and not from the investigator's.

But this . . .

Will didn't even have the words for it.

"All my life," Shel said, "I've always gone after the *W*. I always wanted the win. If I came up short, I was okay with that. I just pushed myself harder the next time." He was silent for a moment. "But there's no win here. No do-over. No matter what I do, I lose something."

"I'm sorry," Will said and wished he had more to give his friend than that. "Look, we've got the team here. Let's see if we can find a room and talk. Figure out what we're going to do. Then we'll break this down just like we do everything else. One step at a time."

"Sure," Shel said. "But I got to tell you, Will, I'll give you everything I've got, but my heart ain't in this."

"I know. But I'll take you with whatever you can give."

CRIME SCENE

47

E SCENE ✪ NCIS ✪ CRIME SCENE

NAVAL CRIMINAL INVESTIGATIVE SERVICE

>> RAFTER M RANCH
>> OUTSIDE FORT DAVIS, TEXAS
>> 1329 HOURS (CENTRAL TIME ZONE)

"Hey, sweetie," Estrella said, speaking her native Spanish. "How are you doing?"

"I'm fine, Mama," her son, Nicky, said, replying in the same language. "Joe just brought us back from the ocean. It was really cool."

A chill ghosted through Estrella when she thought about Nicky out on a boat in the open ocean. Even with Joe Tomlinson, who had practically grown up on water, it was a scary thing. That wasn't a day trip she'd have planned for the two of them. She wasn't a fan of deep water anyway.

During her time in the service she'd served aboard an antiaircraft carrier. The ship had been so big that most of the time there was none of the normal pitch and roll of smaller craft. Still, the first few weeks aboard the ship had left her weak and nauseous despite the medication the ship's medic had signed off for her.

"I was wearing a life vest," Nicky went on. He had a put-upon air. "I didn't like it. It made me feel like a wimp. But Joe made me wear it."

Estrella relaxed a little. She sat at the small desk that Shel had said he had done homework on throughout his childhood.

"Did Joe wear his vest?" Estrella asked.

"Yeah."

"Well, see? If Joe thinks the vest is important enough to wear one himself, then it must be."

"Are you coming to get me today, Mama?"

Estrella stared at the two wide-screen computer monitors that split the work she was doing as they talked. "Not today. I'm sorry."

"So what am I supposed to do?"

"Joe has agreed to let you stay there a little longer. If that's okay with you."

"Sure. I like it here. Joe's a lot of fun."

That declaration hurt Estrella. Nicky was growing up without a father and there was nothing she could do about that. Worst of all, he was getting to the age where he wanted time with a father. Even when Estrella tried to do "dad" things with him, like fishing and camping and throwing a baseball in the park, Nicky was still aware of her being a "girl" when he felt he was supposed to be with a man.

"It'll only be for a couple more days," Estrella said, hoping that the crime scene in Texas wouldn't take any longer than that. "So don't get too comfortable there. And be a good boy, okay?"

"I'm always good," Nicky said.

That, thankfully, was true. Despite the fact that Estrella had had to raise her son in a single-parent household and with a job that could be inordinately stressful, Nicky *was* a good son.

"I love you, baby," she said.

"I'm not a baby."

"You'll always be my baby."

"*Mom . . .*," Nicky protested.

"All right, I love you. If you need anything, call me. And tell Joe thanks for me."

"I will. I love you too, Mom. Bye."

Estrella folded her cell phone and put it away. *You're lucky to have him,* she told herself. *You have no reason to feel sad.*

But she did. She'd never gotten over Julian's death, especially not the fact that he'd committed suicide only months before Nicky was born. That was still the deepest hurt of her life.

She turned her attention to the files she'd downloaded from the U.S. Army databases regarding servicemen in Vietnam and started reading. Once she'd had PFC Dennis Hinton's name and had cross-referenced it with PFC Tyrel McHenry and Sergeant Victor Gant, a lot of the busywork had been eliminated.

What was left was a U.S. Army Criminal Investigation Command report that was interesting.

Estrella knew that Will would want to see the CID report, but she also knew he was busy working the crime scenes. He was also there counseling Shel.

When she'd first heard about the attack on Tyrel McHenry, Estrella's heart had gone out to Shel. She and the big Marine had been close friends since she'd joined the NCIS team shortly after he did. Part of it was the commonality of the Spanish language they shared, but part of it—Estrella suspected—was because they'd both been hurt by family. Julian had left her, and Tyrel had never been there for Shel. Both of them had holes in their hearts and lives that had affected them deeply.

And both of them were too stubborn to talk about their losses. They each believed the loss was theirs to carry alone.

But now Shel's had gone past the point where he could carry it himself.

Estrella only hoped what she was finding out was going to be beneficial rather than hurtful. She was afraid that, just like the phone call to Nicky, it might be a little of both.

⊛ ⊛ ⊛

>> 1721 HOURS

"Private First Class Dennis Leon Hinton was officially declared missing on October 17, 1967," Estrella said.

"Missing? Not AWOL?" Will sat in a chair at the McHenry kitchen table beside Estrella as she walked him through her findings. He was tired but restless, which was always a bad combination for him.

"Yes. Army MPs worked his disappearance as a criminal act from the beginning."

"Why?" Will knew that U.S. soldiers had gone missing in Vietnam during that time period for a lot of reasons. Some of them deserted, and some were killed in DMZ skirmishes or ambushes. There were even times when attacks against U.S. soldiers killed men who weren't identifiable.

That war, more than any other before it, had taught Americans how bad war could be. There, in the middle of enemy territory, trapped in a land where the enemy had no place to retreat and no choice except to fight, they'd learned how ferocious that enemy could be. Vietnamese women carried hand grenades into bars and pulled the pins, killing themselves and all within. Children working as shoeshines covered razors in their rags to ruin soldiers' boots or wound them. There wasn't a place in that country where the American forces hadn't had to defend themselves.

AWOL or desertion would have been easier to accept than kidnapped or murdered. All sorts of crimes had happened over there, on both sides, but they had been eclipsed by the horror of the war.

"Private First Class Marvin Cantrell reported Hinton missing," Estrella said. "According to this report, Cantrell suspected foul play on the part of Victor Gant. Late the evening of the fifteenth, Cantrell had left the bar in Qui Nhon where he'd been with Hinton. Cantrell ended up with food poisoning and was sick for the next two days."

Will followed the information on the badly typed image copy Estrella had retrieved from Department of Defense files. The copy was stamped as property of the Army's CID.

"As soon as Cantrell was well enough, he went to his commanding officer and made the report," Estrella said. "They kicked the report over to the MPs and the matter was turned over to the CID."

"But the CID didn't find anything?"

"No. Those years were the hot ones in Vietnam. River traffic through Qui Nhon was important during those years, and the North Vietnamese were pushing back with everything they had. Their attacks were taking their toll."

"What information do you have about the investigation?"

"Although they don't look it, typewriters being what they were then and correction fluid being all the rage—" Estrella pointed to obvious smears across the pages—"the notes are good. The CID lieutenant was a Philadelphia police officer before he got drafted. He went over there knowing how to conduct an investigation."

"That was lucky."

"It would have been luckier if he found Hinton or figured out what had happened to him." Estrella tapped the keyboard and pages flipped past. "His investigation met with a lot of resistance."

"Because of Victor Gant?"

"Because of a lot of people," Estrella said. "By that time in the Vietnam War, drugs had become prevalent among the troops."

"They were a bunch of scared kids," Will said. "Most conscripted armies are."

"The military forces in Iraq aren't conscripted," Estrella said gently, "and I think a lot of them are scared kids anyway. I was older than a lot of them when I joined the Navy, but I was still scared for a long time while sitting on an aircraft carrier." She paused. "Drugs are a coping mechanism, but they only put things off. They don't help."

Will knew Estrella was speaking from personal experience. He glanced at her.

"I knew someone," Estrella said without looking at him, "who lost himself in drugs. But it wasn't drugs that pushed him over the edge. It was everything that was going on in his life." She shook herself and took a breath. "Sorry. It's a long story and sad."

"If you ever want to tell it to anyone," Will said, "I'm here."

"I know. But today definitely isn't the day for that." Estrella highlighted a section of the report. "The CID investigator, Ramsey, established a timeline for Hinton."

Will stared at the timeline. "Guy was meticulous."

"I know. Ramsey charted everything Hinton did the day he disappeared. The timeline ends here, in one of the local bars in Qui Nhon."

Ramsey's file even included faded color pictures that looked like they'd been taken with a Kodak Instamatic. Scratches marred the pictures' finish and they looked like pale imitations of the originals.

The bar where the timeline ended was a single-story ramshackle building with a corrugated tin roof. Bits of jungle brush peeked out from the rickety wooden steps that led up to an abbreviated veranda.

"Cantrell went to Fat Boy's with Hinton that night," Estrella said.

"Fat Boy's is the bar?"

"Yes. It's also a type of Harley," Estrella said. "The bar's owner was an expatriate American veteran who got released on a medical discharge."

"And instead of going home, he decided to hang around and open a bar?"

Estrella nodded. "That's all covered in Ramsey's notes. The rumor was that Fat Boy's provided drugs to anyone that wanted to buy them. Victor Gant was supposed to be a silent partner."

"Was he?"

"Ramsey couldn't confirm that."

"Why did Hinton go there?"

"The reports don't say."

"Did Hinton go there regularly?"

"I don't know."

Will's frustration grew. It was hard seeing Shel, who was normally one of the most together human beings on the face of the planet, torn up over what he was supposed to do. Will wanted desperately to do something to help.

"Was Gant there that night?"

"Yes. Cantrell's statement confirms that."

"Did Hinton and Gant know each other?"

"There's no indication," Estrella responded.

"What happened?"

"Statements of other witnesses in the bar that night confirm that Hinton left in the company of Victor Gant."

"What about Tyrel McHenry?"

"McHenry isn't mentioned in these reports."

"Does anyone know where Gant went that night?"

"Not that Ramsey ever discovered."

Will pushed up from the chair and looked out through the window. The ranch looked peaceful—except for the sheriff's deputies walking around outside. Will imagined this had been a great place for someone like Shel McHenry to grow up. There was plenty of hunting and fishing, and the ranch work was physically demanding. For a moment he wondered what Shel would have been like as a boy.

Then Will thought about how estranged from his children Don had said Tyrel McHenry was. The man's past, whatever had truly happened, couldn't have been easy.

"There is something we can follow up on," Estrella said.

Will turned to her.

"A few of Victor Gant's cronies are mentioned in Ramsey's reports," Estrella told him. "Since they're all ex-military personnel, I was able to pull them up." She laid a computer printout from a portable printer on top of the table. "Six men besides Gant are named. Two of them were KIA in Vietnam. One went MIA there. Another was killed in a 1997 shootout with the Atlanta Police Department while riding with the Purple Royals. The fifth, Michael Wiley, is still riding with Victor Gant. We tagged him as Fat Mike."

"What about the sixth man?"

Estrella pointed to a name on the page. "PFC Richard McGovern was hit by a Bouncing Betty land mine in 1971 and got mustered out on a medical discharge. He's living in Philadelphia on a military pension."

Will looked at the young soldier's face on the monitor. Back when the picture had been taken, McGovern had been a young man with angular features and hard eyes. He didn't look civilized even in his dress uniform.

"McGovern was there at the bar the night Hinton went missing?" Will asked.

"Yes."

"Where did he spend his military career?"

Estrella checked. "He was assigned to Gant's unit for seven of his eight years served."

"Did you background him?"

"I did." Estrella pulled up another file. "Stateside, McGovern was arrested for selling drugs six times from the age of eighteen to twenty. He entered the military voluntarily to avoid jail time."

"But then he re-upped."

"Yes."

"I don't think McGovern became an overnight patriot," Will said.

"I doubt that."

"Do you have a current address for McGovern?"

"The military sends him a check every month."

"Get me the address."

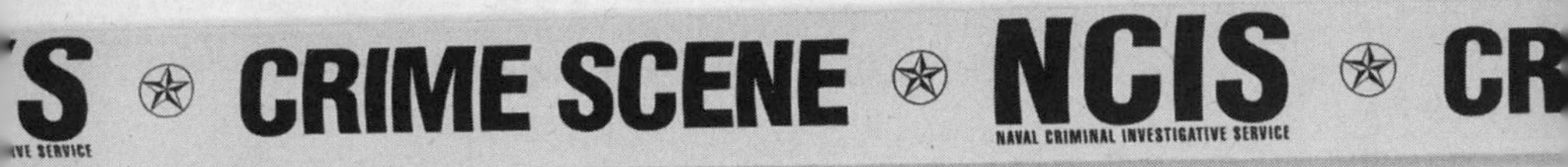
S
CRIME SCENE
NCIS
NAVAL CRIMINAL INVESTIGATIVE SERVICE
CR

48

E SCENE ✪ NCIS ✪ CRIME SCENE
NAVAL CRIMINAL INVESTIGATIVE SERVICE

>> INTERNATIONAL BORDER
>> EL PASO, TEXAS
>> 1942 HOURS (CENTRAL TIME ZONE)

Perspiration trickled down Tyrel McHenry's back as he sat in the back of the cab in the line leading to the border patrol checkpoints. Evening was settling over the area. The eastern skies had turned dark.

Tyrel's eyes burned from fatigue. He hated wearing a ball cap instead of the Stetson he'd worn for so long. But he'd had to wear a hat. His forehead had a demarcation as clear as the Texas-Mexico border from El Paso to Ciudad Juárez. He'd never been outside the house without his hat, and his forehead would have been unevenly tanned. People would have noticed and remembered him, and he couldn't afford that.

He'd also dyed his hair black, something his vanity would never have allowed him to do had he not been forced into hiding. With his weathered tan, he figured he could pass as a Mexican in time. That was the plan anyway. After today he didn't intend to ever step foot on American soil again.

He didn't deserve to. He hadn't deserved that honor in over forty years.

"Senor," the cab driver called.

"Yeah," Tyrel answered.

"Do you have your papers ready, senor?"

"I do."

The cabbie was a round-faced man in his forties. The taxi smelled like cheap soap; a figurine of Jesus stood on the dashboard.

"That's a good thing, senor. These border officials, they are very proud of their paperwork."

Tyrel had gotten rid of his papers. When he'd first returned to the States after leaving Vietnam, he'd planned to relocate to Mexico if worse came to worst, and back then identification wasn't required to pass back and forth between Mexico and Texas.

Relocate, Tyrel snorted to himself. *Why, listen to you, you old fool. This ain't no relocation. You're jackrabbiting to keep your tail together. Like a coward. If you had any pride, you'd have let the Army do what they needed to do forty years ago.*

But he hadn't been able to do that. Back then he'd just been too afraid. Then he'd come home to find Amanda waiting for him and felt like he deserved something good for himself. Then Shelton had been born and Don after that. Once he'd been on that road, he couldn't turn himself in. By the time he'd gotten strong enough to accept what he would have had to do, he would have been abandoning his family. The military and the government didn't help out families of a murdering soldier. Tyrel wasn't sure about a lot of things, but he was pretty sure about that.

After 9/11 and the tight security that went up overnight on people traveling out of and into the United States, Tyrel had known he'd need papers to get over into Juárez if the time ever came. Working with migrant laborers and other men he'd known had given Tyrel the name of a man who could falsify papers. It had cost Tyrel a lot to get a good set.

He didn't know how good the papers were because he'd never used them before. But he was about to find out.

"So, senor," the taxi driver said, "your trip to Juárez, is it for business or pleasure?"

"Business," Tyrel said, hoping the man didn't keep talking to him. He just wanted to get across the border and be gone.

After riding out, he'd freed his horse. Given time, the mare would wander back to the barn. He knew that Don, and Shel for that matter, would care for the livestock. Three miles of hiking had brought Tyrel to Bobby Foyt's place. Foyt and his family were out of town on a last-chance vacation before school started back.

Tyrel had hot-wired the old Chevrolet pickup in the garage, left money for it in Bobby's barbecue grill because Bobby didn't let many days go by without grilling, and driven down to El Paso secure in the knowledge that no one would know the truck was missing for several days at least.

He'd stopped and eaten once outside of El Paso. The television had carried a baseball game and the local news. That was when he found out about the manhunt the sheriff had unleashed to look for him. Tyrel had gone into the bathroom with the hair color and come out with black hair. Then he'd gotten back on the road.

In El Paso, he bought a few things to carry across the border in a suitcase, courtesy of the bargain bins at the Salvation Army. He'd have been able to buy anything he needed in Juárez, or wherever he finally decided to light, but going across the border empty-handed would have drawn attention.

"What kind of business?" the cabbie asked.

"Construction." Tyrel knew enough about that line of work that he could pass for a foreman. He'd learned a lot about woodworking and building when he'd built the ranch house and barn. Then there had been various other projects with neighbors over the years.

"Constuction is a fine business," the cabbie said. "I have done construction work. My father was a cabinetmaker. A very fine cabinetmaker."

Tyrel wished the man would shut up. Waiting in the long line was making him as nervous as a long-tailed cat in a room full of rocking chairs. He didn't need to try to be carrying on a conversation at the same time.

He glanced at the people at the side of the street. The border allowed a lot of walk-through traffic as well. If not for the checkpoint, El Paso and Juárez might as well have been one large city. They were of equal size, but there was a vast difference in the appearance and the economies.

As he watched, a young boy of nine or ten walked beside his mother. The boy was eating a hot dog and holding on to a bright blue balloon. The balloon jerked in the wind and captured the boy's attention.

The young mother balanced a sleeping child in her arms and chatted amiably on a cell phone. She hardly paid any attention to the older boy.

The boy with the balloon stopped suddenly. His balloon floated away and he grabbed his throat. Panic filled his face. His mouth opened to yell—but nothing came out. He grabbed his mother's dress.

Angry, the young mother turned around to admonish her son. Then she saw him holding his throat. His sunburned face reddened more.

Somebody help him, Tyrel thought. *He's choking.*

"Help me!" the young mother screamed. She dropped the cell phone and grabbed her son's arm. Wakened, the baby started screaming too. "My son needs help! Please! Someone help me!"

The bystanders backed away as the boy continued to struggle to breathe.

Tyrel couldn't believe it. Surely someone was going to help.

No one did.

Without thinking, Tyrel threw the cab door open. Images of Don and Shel ran through his mind. He remembered how he'd always been afraid of something happening to them when they were young. It was a parent's worst nightmare.

Like a broken-field runner, Tyrel made his way through the stalled lines of cars till he reached the boy. The woman still yelled for help.

"I can help him," Tyrel told the woman. "Give him to me."

Reluctantly the woman let go of her son. "He's not breathing. He can't breathe."

"Yes, ma'am," Tyler said. "I know." He felt a little panicked himself. When Don and Shel were little, he'd worried about them. Especially Shel because he'd been fearless growing up. Don had had more sense. Tyrel had worried even more when Shel enlisted and went off to fight in the Middle East.

The boy fought Tyrel, pushing at his hands.

"Listen to me, son," Tyrel said calmly. "You're gonna be all right. We're gonna get through this." He forced the boy's jaws apart and peered into his mouth.

There was no visible obstruction.

Tyrel stepped behind the boy and placed his hands together in a double fist just above the boy's navel. He pulled in and up, fast and hard, just like he'd learned to do when the boys were small. In all those years, Tyrel had never had to Heimlich anyone, but once he'd been shown something, he never forgot it.

Nothing happened. The boy still couldn't breathe.

Tyrel knew that a crowd of people had gathered around them. All of them watched. He cursed them all. What he was doing was something anyone could do. The only reason he was there was because no one else would step up.

"C'mon, boy," Tyrel coaxed. "You're scaring your mama. I'm right here, and I ain't gonna give up on you." He pulled again.

This time the piece of hot dog stuck in the boy's throat exploded from his mouth. He sucked in a ragged breath, then cried out in pain and fear. He fought against Tyrel's hold.

"Hold up there, partner," Tyrel said. "Let's make sure we got it all."

The boy trembled as he turned back toward Tyrel. When he tilted the boy's head back, he looked in his mouth and down his throat.

The child was breathing normally now.

"It's okay," Tyrel told him. "It's okay." He released the boy, who immediately ran to his mother.

She was crying and shaking, but she held her son tightly. The boy held on to her and cried too.

"Thank you," she told Tyrel. "Thank you so much."

Tyrel touched his hat and nodded. "Yes, ma'am. Glad I was here to help."

The crowd around them suddenly erupted with applause.

Embarrassed, Tyrel ignored them and turned to walk back to the waiting cab. He intended to finish his escape now that the line was moving again. He was only a few minutes away from freedom.

However, when he stepped from the curb, it felt like the top of his head had come unscrewed and someone had dumped spiders inside. A tickling sensation ate at the edges of his thoughts; then black spots appeared in his vision.

He tried to keep walking even though he felt woozy. He didn't take more than four or five steps before it felt like someone drove a railroad spike straight through the center of his heart. His legs went out from under him and he fell between two cars. On his back, he stared up at the sky and saw the sun dimming in the west.

Tyrel tried to get up, but the viselike pain in his chest grew even tighter. His vision closed to small tunnels. People came over to him and looked down. Tyrel tried to take a breath and couldn't. Blackness consumed him.

CRIME SCENE
NCIS
NAVAL CRIMINAL INVESTIGATIVE SERVICE

49

SCENE ⊛ NCIS ⊛ CRIME SCENE
NAVAL CRIMINAL INVESTIGATIVE SERVICE

>> RAFTER M RANCH
>> OUTSIDE FORT DAVIS, TEXAS
>> 0125 HOURS (CENTRAL TIME ZONE)

Someone was knocking on the door.

Worn and exhausted though he was, Shel woke immediately. Out of habit, he reached for the SOCOM .45 hidden under the cushion of the couch where he slept. Don had tried to get him to come home with him, but Shel hadn't been ready to do that. He'd needed time alone to think and decompress.

In the end, after much talking—which had only further exhausted him—and because Don didn't have the strength to continue, his brother had left. Shel had also invited Will and the other NCIS agents to stay at the house, but they'd declined, and he'd been glad. He'd dropped his duffel on the bed in the room he'd once shared with Don, then headed out to the couch to sleep.

Max was already up and awaiting orders.

The knocking repeated.

The house was dark. After everyone had left at eight o'clock or so, finally relinquishing the site, satisfied there was nothing more that could be learned about what had happened, Shel had raided the refrigerator. He'd found leftover pinto beans and some cold corn bread. He'd microwaved both and ate at the table. He had never felt lonelier or less certain.

"Shel?" It was Will's voice.

"Yeah?" Shel stood by the door and peered through the window.

Will appeared to be alone. His rental SUV was parked out front next to the one Shel was driving.

"Can I come in?"

Shel tucked the pistol in his waistband at his back and unlocked the door. He could tell by Will's face that something bad had happened.

"What's going on?" Shel asked.

"The El Paso police called," Will said.

Shel took his cell phone from his pocket and glanced at it. The battery was dead. During all the confusion, he'd forgotten to charge it. The home phone lines had been cut when Victor Gant and his crew had tried to kill Tyrel. Shel looked at Will but couldn't ask what was most on his mind.

"Your father's been located," Will said. "There was an incident at the border. It appears he stopped to help a boy who was choking, then suffered a heart attack."

A heart attack? The words poured ice water through Shel's veins. *People die from heart attacks.*

"Is Daddy going to be all right?" Shel asked.

Will's face softened. "They don't know. The doctors say it's too soon to tell. They've got him stabilized."

Shel nodded and took in a deep breath. He felt dizzy and hurt all at the same time. "Does Don know?"

"Estrella went to tell him. I figured this was news he didn't need to hear over the phone, and since we're staying at a hotel outside of town, we were about equal distance. The sheriff's loaning us a helicopter so we can get to El Paso sooner."

"All right," Shel said. "I'll get my kit and meet you in the car."

Will turned and headed back to the SUV.

Real fear settled in over Shel as he walked to the back bedroom.

He took a moment to get everything organized, but he didn't know what he was supposed to do. His daddy was in a hospital, maybe fighting for his life. The Marines hadn't had a checklist or training for that.

Shel felt helpless. In a situation like this, Don would pray. Shel envied his brother that feeling of being useful. But Shel knew he didn't believe or trust enough to do that. He'd be a hypocrite if he tried to pray, and he didn't wish for that.

Unable to do anything else, Shel grabbed the handles of his duffel and hoisted it to his shoulder. As he headed for the door, he looked around the house and wondered if it would ever feel like home again.

⊛ ⊛ ⊛

>> LOVE FIELD
>> DALLAS, TEXAS
>> 0239 HOURS (CENTRAL TIME ZONE)

Shaved and sporting a new haircut, wearing a suit for the first time since his last court arraignment, Victor Gant sat in the waiting area for his flight. Beside him, made over in a similar fashion, Fat Mike sat reading a copy of *Playboy* he'd bought in one of the magazine shops.

Neither one of them was *GQ* material.

A few bleary-eyed travelers gave Fat Mike hard stares over his choice of public reading material, but the biker ignored them.

Victor controlled the anger and frustration that slopped around inside him, but only just. If it hadn't been for alcohol, he wouldn't have been able to contain himself. He drank just enough to keep the edge off.

"You're gonna have to let it go," Fat Mike said quietly from beside him. "Maybe you didn't kill Tyrel McHenry, but you seriously jacked his life."

The local news had been full of the attack on McHenry's ranch. Victor had seen footage all day while he'd made the necessary arrangements to catch this morning's flight. If all went well and no one saw through the false papers he was carrying or identified him—which, based on the mug shots they were displaying on the television, Victor doubted—he'd be back in Vietnam in a few days.

He'd be safe.

That irritated him too, because it had been a long time since Victor had truly felt threatened. But there was something about that big Marine, something so *intractable*, that Victor had lost some of the confidence he'd always had even at the worst of times. Shel McHenry was one of those bona fide human assault weapons that just wouldn't stay down.

Victor knew he'd have felt better if Shel were dead. But being in Vietnam didn't mean he couldn't work on that. He still had friends in the States, still had people who owed him favors and money.

It was just a matter of time.

"Did you hear me?" Fat Mike asked.

"Yeah," Victor said irritably. He felt naked sitting there without a gun.

"Says here in this magazine that stress will kill you if you keep it internalized."

Victor glanced at Fat Mike. "You saying I'm stressed?"

"No," Fat Mike replied coolly, suddenly realizing he might be on dangerous ground. "I'm telling you it's a good thing you're not."

Victor turned back to the windows overlooking the airfield. "I'm not stressed."

"You don't look stressed. Want a magazine? I got *Penthouse* too."

"That old man should have been dead last night," Victor said. He spoke in Vietnamese so none of the other passengers around them could understand their conversation.

"He got lucky. That's all."

"Lucky enough to kill three guys."

"You and me, we seen guys go down in the jungle that shoulda lived, bro. And we seen cherries that should have gone down the first time Charlie opened fire live to fight another day. Don't mean nothing. Just means we gotta let it go for now. We've put stuff on the back burner before. Ain't no thing, brother."

"The Marine should have been dead too. Out of the two of them, somebody should have been dead. Instead, we got a lot of dead guys behind us and a whole lotta heat coming down on top of us."

"Maybe this just happened so you can get them both later."

Victor didn't believe that, but he knew he wasn't going to stop trying.

"We get back to Vietnam, you'll wrap your skull around this thing," Fat Mike said. "You'll figure out a way to get them. Nobody escapes you in the long run. But I'm telling you, bro, once you're back in the jungle—where only the quick and the dead show up—you may decide it wasn't all that important anyway. After a few days there, it might not even matter."

That wasn't going to be the case, though. Victor was sure of that. Whatever it took, he was going to balance the scales between himself and Shel McHenry.

⊛ ⊛ ⊛

>> INTENSIVE CARE UNIT
>> LAS PALMAS MEDICAL CENTER
>> EL PASO, TEXAS
>> 0648 HOURS (CENTRAL TIME ZONE)

"Are you his son?"

Shel disengaged himself from the confusion that filled his mind and focused his attention on the nurse who had just entered the ICU room.

She was Hispanic and looked like she was in her early thirties. Her scrubs fit her athletic build well. She wore her black hair pulled up.

"Yes, ma'am," Shel said. His voice was thick from disuse. He'd sat at his daddy's side for hours, worrying about him and wondering what he was supposed to do now. The constant chirping of the heart monitor and humming of other assorted machines provided an undercurrent of noise.

"Don't call me 'ma'am,'" the nurse said. "You'll make me old before my time. My name is Isabella." She turned from the chart and stuck her hand out.

Shel got to his feet and took her hand.

She smiled, obviously pleased. "So, you're a gentleman."

"No. I'm a Marine."

"Is that better or worse?" Isabella's face showed that she might have really been interested in the answer and not just making small talk.

"I guess it depends on who you talk to."

"Well, either way, your father is going to be all right."

"That's what they said." Shel resumed his seat out of the way while Isabella manually took his daddy's vitals. Shel watched her with interest.

"I trust the machines," Isabella said. "They're good. But I don't ever want to get out of practice doing things the old-fashioned way. In case I'm ever in a situation where I have to."

"Redundant systems," Shel commented.

She smiled at him. "I guess you could call it that. I just think of those kids working fast food when the computer crashes. They act like they don't know how to add or subtract or how to make change. Computers are supposed to make things easier, not impossible. *We're* supposed to be the redundant system. I suppose the military is really big on redundancy."

Shel nodded.

"I'm going to be with your father—and, I suppose, you—during this next shift," Isabella said. "The other nurses told me you were here most of the night."

"Some of it, anyway."

"And I'll also tell you that if Dr. Abelard wasn't a fan of the military, you wouldn't be sitting in that chair. He likes his ICU kept clear of civilians. I suppose you can empathize with that."

Shel felt magnanimous enough not to point out that the hospital didn't have enough security people and orderlies in the building to make him leave if he decided to stay. He remained quiet.

"But Dr. Abelard can be a generous man if nobody makes any trouble," Isabella said. "So here you are. They said there were two of you."

"My brother, Don," Shel said. "He was here for a while. But he had to go take care of his family. They're going to stay in town for the next day or so. Until we get Daddy through this."

"Like I said, your father is going to be fine. There's no need for anyone to get stressed. In a few days, barring any complications, we're going to send him home."

But there already were complications, Shel couldn't help thinking. The murder and Victor Gant were out there lurking like land mines along their path.

"We know that," he said. "This isn't about being here waiting for something bad to happen. We're here for Daddy. When he gets better, we want him to know we were here for him."

Isabella smiled. "I can understand that. I just didn't want you to worry needlessly."

"I'm not." He was worried but not over anything the hospital could help with. Shel was more concerned about what the Army was going to do to his daddy once Victor Gant's charges got out into the open.

"They said he Heimliched a boy before he had his heart attack." Isabella held her chart on one cocked hip. "From what I was told, he probably saved that boy's life."

Shel nodded. He'd read the police officer's reports too.

"He had a busy day," Shel said, thinking his daddy had also killed three men who were going to take his life and escaped to the border.

"He'll have others."

Shel nodded again, but he wondered where his daddy was going to spend those days.

"Were you guys in a car wreck?"

Shel gave her blank look.

Isabella touched her face with the end of her ink pen, causing Shel to realize she was referring to the bruises on his face. His daddy had them too.

"I know your father didn't get the bruises on his face from the cardiac event," the nurse said.

"No. It was a separate thing. We were working on the farm. Stacking hay. Things . . . things didn't go as well as they could have." Shel felt bad about the near lie, but he didn't want to have to explain the fight. Dr. Abelard knew, and Will had had to vouch for Shel to be allowed to remain in the room.

"I see." Isabella looked into his eyes, and he couldn't tell if she believed him or not.

Shel crossed his arms and looked back at his daddy.

"He'll probably sleep for a while longer, but if he doesn't or he seems like he's having problems, buzz the desk."

"I will."

"If you need anything, just let me know."

Shel stood again out of respect as the woman left the room, and she smiled at him over her shoulder. Then he resumed his vigil.

For a moment, he let his vision linger on the silent television set in the corner. CNN showed the top news stories. He'd muted the audio.

When he gazed back at his daddy's still form almost lost in the huge hospital bed, he saw that Tyrel McHenry's eyes were open and staring straight at him.

CRIME SCENE

50

SCENE ✪ NCIS ✪ CRIME SCENE
NAVAL CRIMINAL INVESTIGATIVE SERVICE

>> INTENSIVE CARE UNIT
>> LAS PALMAS MEDICAL CENTER
>> EL PASO, TEXAS
>> 0704 HOURS (CENTRAL TIME ZONE)

For a moment, staring into his daddy's partially opened eyes above the oxygen mask he wore, Shel didn't know what to say.

Tyrel didn't look happy to see him there. Then again, remembering how the bruises and scabs on his daddy's face had gotten there, Shel figured his daddy had every right not to be feeling kindly toward him.

"Where am I?" his daddy croaked.

"El Paso," Shel said. "Las Palmas."

Tyrel frowned at that. "Why am I in the hospital?"

"You had a heart attack, Daddy." Shel's voice nearly broke when he said that.

"Don't remember no heart attack. Seems like that's something a person oughta remember. As long as he woke back up." Tyrel looked at the machines. "Well . . . am I gonna live?"

Shel wasn't really surprised by the matter-of-fact tone in his daddy's voice, but it still sounded strange at that moment and in that place.

"Yes, sir."

"That might not be the best thing."

"It ain't like you to give up."

"Didn't say I was giving up, now did I?" Tyrel's voice was sharp and cold. "Just said it mighta been better, is all. Or do you want to try to tell me that me and you in this place right now is what you wanted?"

His daddy's anger turned Shel more angry himself, and that squeezed some of the sympathy out of him. Tyrel didn't look at him, and Shel was grateful for that. He didn't know what would show on his face.

"Reckon not," Shel said.

"How'd you find me?" Tyrel asked.

"The police found you. They tried to book you under the identification you were carrying, but they couldn't."

"They could tell that identification was fake?" Tyrel grinned wryly. "I paid good money for that. I probably wouldn't have made it through the border checkpoint either."

"Running was stupid."

"You calling me stupid, Shelton?"

Even though his daddy was lying in the hospital bed, a chill of deathly fear raced through Shel. Even when they'd fought in the barn, he'd never said anything disrespectful.

"No, sir."

"You'd best not be."

Gathering some of his defiance back, Shel asked, "What would you call it?"

Tyrel shook his head slowly. The mask bobbed across his face. "All I had left. Wasn't anything else I coulda done at that point. Running was it."

"Didn't help anything."

"Everything that coulda been helped was forty years ago."

Shel drew in a quiet breath and folded his arms.

"How's that boy?" his daddy asked.

Puzzled, Shel looked at his daddy.

"The boy that was choking," Tyrel said irritably.

Shel couldn't believe his daddy. The man was lying in bed after a heart attack, had killed three men in his escape, and was possibly facing a military execution, and yet he wanted to know about a boy he'd probably never see again in his life.

"He's good, Daddy," Shel said. "Him and his mama were there when the ambulance got there and took you away. The police interviewed them because you'd been seen talking to them before you went down."

"At least there's that. Boy that young, he ought to do him some more living."

Impatience stung Shel. "What did you think you were doing by leaving?"

"For a smart man who's been in the Marines and taken some of them college classes they offer, you sure act like thinking's a new thing for you."

Heat flamed Shel's face.

"I figured leavin' would be self-explanatory."

"You were going to leave? Without telling me or Don good-bye?"

"I've told Don good-bye lots of times," Tyrel said. "Me and you, we said good-bye in the barn the other night."

That hurt Shel a lot more than he expected it to.

The sound of the hospital equipment filled the room for a moment. Outside, Shel heard the low buzz of conversations.

"Did you kill Dennis Hinton?" Shel asked.

Tyrel turned toward Shel and gazed straight into his eyes. For a moment Shel hoped that his daddy would say no and that everything had been some incredible mistake.

Then, as calmly as if he were ordering breakfast, Tyrel said, "Yes, sir. I reckon I did."

* * *

>> ATWATER APARTMENT BUILDING
>> PHILADELPHIA, PENNSYLVANIA
>> 0819 HOURS

Maggie Foley stood outside Apartment 616 and rang the doorbell.

Beside her, Remy said, "I didn't hear anything."

Maggie hadn't either. She rapped her knuckles against the door and waited. Despite the nap she'd caught on the airplane during the jump from Fort Davis to Philadelphia, she felt bone-tired. The last two days had been incredibly hectic.

Rather than break in on Richard McGovern before eight o'clock in the morning, they'd killed an hour at a diner down the street. At present, they still didn't have the leverage they needed to put pressure on McGovern. All he was guilty of lately was having once been a friend of Victor Gant.

There were two peepholes in the door. One was at normal eye level, but the second one halved the distance to the floor.

"Try knocking louder," Remy suggested. He wore street clothes with a jacket to cover the pistol on his hip.

"I don't want to knock much louder," Maggie said. "People in the other apartments could still be trying to sleep."

Growing up in her father's house, she'd never had to live on top of other people the way the residents in the apartment building had. She couldn't imagine what that was like. Down the hall, she heard the sounds of a television and a baby crying. The odor of frying eggs and coffee filled the hallway.

Remy leaned forward and knocked more loudly.

Maggie felt slightly irritated at him, but she knew he was just doing what he did because he cared about Shel. All of them did.

"I got a 12-gauge shotgun aimed at the center of this door that says you're gonna step off now," a man's voice said. "Otherwise five-o's gonna be scraping pieces of you off that other hallway wall."

"We're with the police," Maggie said.

"'With the police' ain't the same as *being* the police," the man said.

"Is this Richard McGovern?"

"Don't know nobody by that name."

"That's fine. But when I walk away from this door, I'm going to call the Army payroll offices and stop that monthly check that's been coming to this address."

"That's my girl," Remy whispered. "I like that."

"You can't do that," the man said.

"If Richard McGovern doesn't live at this address, I can," Maggie said.

"He lives here," the man grumbled.

"Then I want to talk to him."

"He ain't here."

"Then I'm going to suspend that check until I can verify he lives here."

The man cursed. "Guess you got me up on the wrong side of the bed this morning. Lemme see some ID."

Maggie opened her identification and held it in front of the lower peephole.

"Says NCIS. Richard McGovern was in the Army. You can't go cutting off his check."

"Open up, McGovern," Remy said. "We've come a long way and we're going to talk to you."

"I ain't said I was McGovern."

"Unless you're a midget or a second grader with a deep voice, you're McGovern." Remy tapped the bottom peephole. "Now open the door. Otherwise we're going to get a caseworker out here to review your life with a microscope to make a new decision about your benefits."

"Man, that ain't right. I done give up my legs in the service to my country, and you come here and get all up in my grill—for reasons I do not know."

"Let us in," Maggie said. "We're here to talk about Victor Gant."

McGovern was quiet for a moment. "Now that there's a bad man. Got a lot of bad juju all knotted up in that man's name."

Remy pounded on the door. "Open the door, McGovern."

Down the hall a child cried louder.

Maggie felt bad about that.

"Dude," McGovern said, "chill. People live here."

The locks slid back. Maggie counted five of them. She stood in the doorway and waited.

Richard McGovern, now sixty-three years old, was scrawny, and his ebony skin looked gray. Dressed in a sweater and sweatpants that hung on his too-thin legs, he sat in a wheelchair and looked up at them through John Lennon glasses that made his eyes look too big. His hair touched his shoulders, and a scraggly beard adorned his cheeks. An unfiltered cigarette hung from his leathery lips.

A cutdown double-barrel shotgun lay across his lap. He started to lift it.

Maggie had her Beretta out from under her jacket and pointed at the man in a heartbeat.

At the same time, Remy leaned in and grabbed the shotgun. McGovern refused to let go.

"You're going to release the weapon," Remy said, "or I'm going to break your fingers when I take it away from you. Your call."

Cursing, McGovern let go of the shotgun. "I want that back. It ain't safe living here. I got a right to defend myself. I gave my legs to this country."

"Let's go inside," Maggie said as she put the Beretta away.

"Lady, this is my house. You can't just barge into my house. I got rights."

Maggie took a deep breath, then looked at Remy. The apartment reeked of marijuana. "Do you detect the presence of a controlled substance?"

A smile almost flickered to life on Remy's lips before he caught himself. "I do."

"Hey, it ain't me," McGovern protested. "It's those college kids living in the apartment below me. They smoke reefer, smoke rises, and I'm trapped up here with it."

"Getting by on a contact high?" Remy asked. He kept moving forward and forced McGovern to keep backing.

"I'm not happy about it," McGovern said. "I've been talking to the super about it."

"Anybody else in the apartment with you?" Remy glanced into the small kitchen to one side.

Maggie flanked Remy, staying behind far enough to give herself a clear field of fire if she needed it. According to the files Estrella had gotten about the man, he lived alone.

"No, man," McGovern said. "It's just me."

In the living room, McGovern spun the wheelchair around and rolled into an empty space in front of the television. The blinds were pulled and the room was dark. Some kind of cheap horror movie was playing on the television set. A knife-wielding character chased a young couple through a forest. They were both screaming, but the set had been muted.

Maggie stood in the living room and kept watch over McGovern while Remy quickly went through the rest of the apartment.

"Hey," McGovern squawked. "Hey! You can't just go barging through my house!" He started to roll forward.

Maggie stuck her left foot out and braced it against the wheelchair wheel. McGovern came to a stop rather than push himself around in a circle.

"Let's just stay here," Maggie suggested.

A few minutes later, Remy reappeared carrying a Baggie filled with grass and some pills. "Does this belong to you?" he asked McGovern.

McGovern frowned and looked increasingly nervous. "I haven't ever seen that before. You planted that on me."

"Funny thing about Baggies," Remy said, holding the bag up for a better look. "They retain fingerprints pretty easily. The dust from the marijuana is going to make any prints on today's blunt, or anywhere else in the Baggie, easy to find."

A worried look tightened McGovern's face.

"Want to know what a judge is going to say when he finds out your fingerprints are on the *inside* of the bag?" Remy raised a speculative eyebrow. "Unless you have a really good excuse."

"Look," McGovern said, "I got an okay thing going here. I know that. I don't want anything to screw it up."

"We're not here to try to screw it up," Maggie said. "We're here to get some answers about Victor Gant."

McGovern took a hit off the cigarette dangling from the corner of his mouth. He took it out and looked at it a moment, then dug out his lighter and expertly relit it.

"Victor isn't a man whose trust you betray," McGovern said quietly.

"Do you think you're going to have to betray that trust?" Maggie asked.

"When you're talking about Victor Gant, you're not going to have anything good to say. And no cops—not even NCIS agents—would ever come snooping around to give Victor some kind of good citizenship award."

Maggie knew that was true. She sat in a sagging easy chair across from McGovern. "Do you remember Dennis Hinton?" she asked.

CRIME SCENE

51

SCENE ✪ NCIS ✪ CRIME SCENE

NAVAL CRIMINAL INVESTIGATIVE SERVICE

>> INTENSIVE CARE UNIT
>> LAS PALMAS MEDICAL CENTER
>> EL PASO, TEXAS
>> 0721 HOURS (CENTRAL TIME ZONE)

In the wake of his daddy's confirmation that he'd killed Dennis Hinton, Shel took a moment to gather his thoughts. Then he asked the question that he most feared to get an answer to.

"Why?"

Tyrel lay back and stared at the ceiling. He licked his lips. "You really want to get into this, Shelton?"

"I don't have a choice, Daddy." Shel knew his voice sounded cold and distant. It was the only way he could speak at the moment.

"Might be easier if you had someone else asking these questions."

"Yes, sir. It might. But I don't think, after all these years, that you should be looking for the easy way out of this."

Tyrel snorted. "There ain't no way out of this. If there was, don't you think I'd have found it by now?"

Shel didn't answer, but he had to wonder if he was going to be strong enough to deal with everything he was about to learn.

"And it ain't me I'm worried about making it easier on," Tyrel concluded.

"Not like you to be worried about me."

Tyrel nodded. "I guess I got that coming."

Shel didn't say anything, though he was sorely tempted.

"This might be something your brother is more suited for. I bet a lot of people have come to him and told on themselves. He's probably used to it."

"I bet Don ain't heard as many confessions to murders as I have," Shel said, intentionally being harsh about the situation.

A wan smile pulled at Tyrel's face. "Well, sir, I'd have to say you got me there. I bet he ain't." He looked around. "They got any water somewhere? I'm getting dry."

Shel poured water from the carafe beside the bed into a plastic cup and added a flexible straw. Tyrel tried to hold the cup, but he was shaking so badly that he couldn't do it. In the end Shel had to hold it for him.

Tyrel drank for a moment, then nodded. "That's good. Thank you."

Unable to speak, Shel put the cup to one side. He sat in the straight-backed chair and listened. He wished that Max were there with him instead of off with Don. This wasn't something he wanted to be alone to deal with.

"I knew Dennis Hinton pretty good," Tyrel said. "We was friends. That was back during the days of the PBRs out of Qui Nhon. You familiar with that?"

"Yes, sir."

"They called it the Brown Water Navy. And them boys that worked them boats was some of the bravest men I ever knew. Charlie wanted Qui Nhon and those supply routes along Highway 19 shut down. They worked hard to get it done. A lotta men got killed over there."

"How'd you know Dennis Hinton?" Shel asked.

"Just from around Qui Nhon. He was outgoing and obnoxious. Didn't have a shy bone in his body. They said he was a killer out in the jungle, a good shot and cold enough to get it done. But he didn't glory in it like some did. He was just taking care of his country."

Shel felt a little more saddened. It would have been better if Hinton had been like Victor Gant, a bad man in a bad place. But if Hinton was a good soldier, his loss was even harder to take. And his murder less understandable.

"Hinton wasn't in your unit?" Shel asked.

"No sir. Just a guy I knew from the bars and the football games." Tyrel looked at Shel. "We played a lot of football over there. A lot of us played in high school before we joined up."

Shel was surprised. He didn't know his daddy had played high school sports. No one had ever talked about it.

"I played quarterback," Tyrel said. "In high school. I had an arm. Still had it over there. Denny—that's what everybody called him that knew him—had played wide receiver. They didn't like us playing together. He could get loose, and I could find him."

"You were friends?"

Tyrel paused, then nodded. "Yeah."

"Then why did you kill him?"

Tyrel took a breath and let it out. He licked his lips. "Lemme tell it the way I need to. You got any questions after that, you ask 'em. Okay?"

"Yes, sir."

"Over in Qui Nhon, we didn't think too much about the future," Tyrel said. "It didn't pay much to do it, because every day you'd see guys evac'd out of the jungle. Sometimes they were wounded, but most of the time they were dead. Kinda reminded us all we might be on short time."

Shel knew what his daddy was talking about. Things hadn't been as severe in the places he'd served, but the losses that had occurred made everyone sit up and take notice.

"So we did what young soldiers do when they're away from home and facing death on a daily basis," Tyrel said. "We went numb to it. We told ourselves that it wouldn't happen to us. We kept our heads low during firefights and worked to keep our butts together. You know what that's like."

"Yes, sir."

"Just took things one breath at a time when we were in the field. But back in Qui Nhon, it was different. Soldiers drank, and they spent time with the working girls. I didn't have nothing to do with the women. Your mom and I were exchanging letters, and I guess I knew I had something waiting on me when I got back home even though we hadn't talked about it."

As he listened to his daddy, Shel couldn't help realizing that the Tyrel McHenry he was hearing about was a different man, a twenty-one-year-old who'd never been far from Fort Davis. He hadn't been worldly, and he hadn't seen the horrors of war. Shel remembered what his own loss of innocence had been like, and that wasn't as bad as Vietnam.

"That night I killed Denny, I was with Victor Gant and his team," Tyrel said.

"I can't see you and him together."

Tyrel laughed hollowly. "That's 'cause you only know Victor Gant as a bad man. But back then in Vietnam, Victor Gant was everything we wanted to be. Soldiers told stories about him. The brass deferred to him during military action. He knew Charlie like nobody knew Charlie. They said if you got signed onto Victor Gant's penetration team and went hunting targets out in the brush, he could keep you from getting killed. The way they talked, you'd have thought bullets bounced off of him."

Shel listened to his daddy speak and knew that he wasn't in that hospital room anymore. Tyrel was back in Vietnam.

"We all wanted to be with him," Tyrel said. "Because we all wanted to go back home. They said he was the man that could get you there."

⊛ ⊛ ⊛

>> ATWATER APARTMENT BUILDING
>> PHILADELPHIA, PENNSYLVANIA
>> 0833 HOURS

"Victor Gant was the most evil man I ever knew over there. There was nothin' he wouldn't do. Nobody he wouldn't kill." Richard McGovern took a drag on his cigarette, then blew smoke at the stained ceiling.

Maggie watched McGovern and locked into the man's body language. The wheelchair threw some things off, but there were always tells she could read as a profiler—the eyes, the shoulders, and what he did with his hands.

Remy lounged at the window behind McGovern, just out of the man's sight. Maggie knew Remy had chosen the position on purpose. No matter what he did, McGovern would know Remy was there just out of sight, and he'd have to wonder what he was doing. McGovern also had to wonder how Remy took everything he said.

"For somebody that didn't like him much, seems you sure stayed around him a long time," Remy said.

McGovern tried to look back over his shoulder but couldn't. That frustrated him—Maggie read that in his eyes.

"There was nobody like Victor Gant in the jungle," McGovern said. "The man could keep you alive, that's for sure. We'd be in firefights, nobody knowing who was who, and Victor Gant could keep things straight. Like he had radar in his head or something. Never seen anything like it before. Never since, either." He gave up trying to look over his shoulder and concentrated on Maggie. "I wasn't hooked up with Victor Gant 'cause I liked the dude. I was just looking out for my own self."

"Nobody can blame you for that," Maggie agreed.

"That's what I'm talking about." McGovern nodded and took another hit off the cigarette.

"Do you think you owe Victor Gant anything?"

"You mean, would I lie to protect him?"

"Yes," Maggie replied.

"No." McGovern shook his head. "I haven't seen him in thirty years. Not since I come back with no legs. That day I went down in the jungle, Victor didn't even come after me. If it hadn't been for the PJs, I wouldn't have come back at all."

PJs were pararescue jumpers, Maggie knew, specially trained military forces who went in behind enemy lines or in battle zones to rescue wounded.

"I owe anybody anything, it was them," McGovern said.

"Do you still keep in touch with the men who rescued you?"

McGovern hesitated. "No. I was so hurt, I don't even know who they were. Never found out."

Which means you don't really feel like you owe anybody anything, Maggie thought. It was an interesting insight, but she didn't let anything show on her face.

"How did you know Dennis Hinton?" she asked.

"Man was just around, you know? I played football against him. Pickup games we had during downtime in Qui Nhon. Man had magic. There was another guy we played football with. A skinny country kid with a bad accent and a bad temper. He could throw that pigskin now, I'm telling you. But Country—that's what we called him—he's the one that killed Dennis Hinton."

"'Country'?"

McGovern nodded. "Don't remember his name. We just called him Country on account of the way he talked."

Maggie reached into her file and pulled out a six-pack of pictures she'd prepared. She'd put Tyrel McHenry's service picture in with five other similar headshots.

"Is he one of these men?" she asked as she handed the six-pack over.

McGovern took the card, then twisted in his wheelchair so the light from the window behind him could hit it. He studied the faces for a minute. "You know, it's been a long time. Over forty years. You're not even old enough to remember back that far."

Maggie sat quietly and waited. McGovern was just putting on a show and she knew it.

"But I still remember," McGovern said. "It was this man right here. Top row. Third man from the left. That's Country." He tapped his finger on the image to confirm it. "That's the man that killed Dennis Hinton."

Maggie knew without checking that McGovern had just identified Tyrel McHenry.

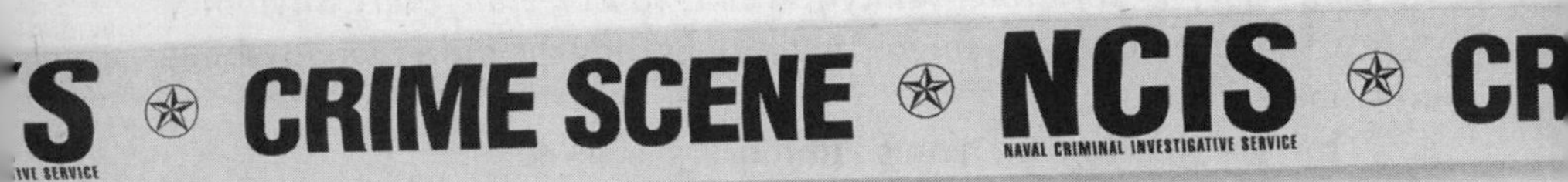
CRIME SCENE

NCIS
NAVAL CRIMINAL INVESTIGATIVE SERVICE

52

SCENE ✪ NCIS ✪ CRIME SCENE
NAVAL CRIMINAL INVESTIGATIVE SERVICE

>> INTENSIVE CARE UNIT
>> LAS PALMAS MEDICAL CENTER
>> EL PASO, TEXAS
>> 0748 HOURS (CENTRAL TIME ZONE)

"I'd met Victor Gant several times before," Tyrel said. He focused on the ceiling and tried not to give in to all the pain and self-loathing that filled him. The medication circulating in his system helped keep him calm and quiet when all he wanted to do was get up and start running.

The biggest hurt was knowing Shel sat there, watching him and passing judgment on him. Tyrel had never wanted to face that.

"Tell me about the night Hinton died," Shel said.

Tyrel listened to the calm professionalism in Shel's voice. He'd never seen this side of his son. Over the years, he'd seen Shel hurt and mad, confused and restless, but he'd never known what it would be like to face his son as a potential enemy. Even the night they'd fought in the barn hadn't felt like this. In the barn, they'd both been mad and scared and not really in control.

Shel was in control now.

Tyrel steeled himself to be just as strong, but it was hard. He was working from a weak position and they both knew it.

"It started at the cantina," Tyrel said. "I went there to drink. It had gotten to be a habit. Not falling-down drunk. I hardly ever got falling-down drunk. I grew up around too many people where that was a way of life, and the pastor back at our church preached against the wickedness of whiskey."

"You went to the cantina because Victor Gant was there?"

For a moment, Tyrel thought about just saying yes and being done with that part of the conversation. Except he knew that would be a lie. Here, in this moment, he needed to tell the truth.

"No, I went there to get drunk enough not to be afraid anymore." Tyrel made himself not look at Shel. He'd never admitted to being afraid in front of either of his sons before. "I was tired of being afraid. I got up in the morning afraid. I went to bed afraid. I had nightmares from hell itself." He paused and let out a breath. "And every waking moment between, I was afraid."

The silence in the room was punctuated only by the undercurrent of voices outside the room and by the monitoring equipment.

"I've never been more afraid in my life. I got to tell you that. I couldn't take drugs the way some others could. Couldn't deny that death might happen to me the way some managed. So every now and again, I drank till I was numb enough to go to bed and get a decent night's sleep." Tyrel paused. "That's what I'd planned that night."

"But that's not what happened?" Shel's voice was gentle.

"No, sir," Tyrel answered. "That's not what happened. What happened was Victor Gant come up in the cantina and started carrying on the way he always did. There wasn't another man I ever met that was like him. I swear to God on that.

"He come in from being out in the jungle for three weeks. Him and all his crew. Victor Gant bagged him two targets that were on the list the CIA had given the penetration teams. They'd killed other Charlie too. We knew 'cause they had the stink of death on them. And that stink was coming from the fingers and ears they'd chopped off men they'd killed to prove it."

"They weren't supposed to do that."

Tyrel laughed bitterly. "That what they tell you in the Marines? Not to take trophies?"

"Yes, sir."

"Well, they told them not to in the Army too. But those men did. They did it to show that they were different, that death couldn't come for them so casual-like, the way it did for everybody else." Tyrel paused, surprised at how easy it was to remember some parts of that night and how other parts had eluded him for forty years. "I was pretty tanked up by then. So I went over to Victor Gant and offered to buy him a drink.

"He took me up on it. And I was drunk enough to tell him I wanted to be like him. Fearless and more dangerous than Charlie ever thought about being. He just laughed at me and told me I wasn't killer enough yet. He said it was gonna take me a while longer 'cause he could see that I hadn't yet got a taste for it." Tyrel stared at the ceiling. "Do you believe that, Shel? that some men just get them a taste for killing? a craving so strong they can't turn away from it?"

"Yes, sir. I've seen it."

"Like them serial killers you hear about?"

"And others."

"What about servicemen? You hear about them getting a taste for it too?"

"Yes, sir."

Tyrel hesitated, not knowing where he was going next. "You've killed a lot of men."

"Yes, sir."

"They teach you not to talk about it and not to dwell on it."

"Yes, sir."

"Do you?"

Shel hesitated. Tyrel heard his son's boot scrape across the floor.

"From time to time," Shel said, "you can't help but think about it."

"Do you ever wish that it didn't touch you? that the killings you were part of weren't part of you?"

"Yes, sir."

"It's worse," Tyrel said, "when you kill a man close-up. When you can taste his breath and feel the warmth of his blood on your face."

Shel didn't say anything.

That didn't matter to Tyrel. He wasn't in the hospital room anymore. He was back in that cantina.

❂❂❂

>> CANTINA

>> QUI NHON, VIETNAM

>> 2031 HOURS

>> OCTOBER 15, 1967

"I want to be like you," Tyrel repeated, looking into Victor Gant's cold, dead eyes. Tyrel knew he was drunk enough that he should keep his mouth shut. But he couldn't, because if he did, the fear would get to him again. "Just like you."

The cantina was hopping. Everybody had drawn pay and was spending part of it on hooch. And all of them had their eyes on Victor Gant and his team of hard cases.

"Careful what you wish for, Country," Victor Gant said.

Getting called by that nickname still bothered Tyrel, but there wasn't much he could do about it. He couldn't remember when it had started or who had given it to him—one of the sergeants, he thought—but it had stuck like road tar.

"I'm serious," Tyrel said. He knew he was standing too close to Victor, but he couldn't help himself. With the rock-and-roll music blasting in the background, it was hard to hear anybody in the cantina.

"Outta the man's face," Fat Mike said. Grizzled and thickly muscled, he stepped between Tyrel and Victor, then put a hand on Tyrel's chest and shoved just hard enough to back him off a couple steps.

Tyrel was embarrassed, but he knew he'd been in the wrong. Still, back home he'd have come back swinging on Fat Mike for touching him. Several of the soldiers and a few of the Kit Carson scouts were watching to see what developed. Tyrel had a reputation for fighting over slights and name-calling that most men simply ignored.

Gathering himself, Tyrel pulled himself up straight. "I apologize. Didn't mean to offend. Let me buy you a drink."

Victor stared hard at him with those dead eyes. "I don't drink unless my men drink with me."

Tyrel looked at all of them. "All right then." He unbuttoned his shirt pocket and took out a twenty-dollar bill. He pushed aside a fleeting concern that he was going to be broke by the end of the night. "I'll buy for all of y'all."

A slow smile spread across Victor's face. "Much obliged, Country," he said in that drawl that told Tyrel he wasn't far from small towns and backwoods himself. "You can even drink that beer with us."

A few minutes later, they were all settled at one of the back tables. Tyrel thought that every man in the cantina was envious of him.

Although Victor didn't talk much, Fat Mike and other members of his group kept the stories flying. Tyrel hadn't been around much, but he knew he couldn't believe everything that was being told. Still, if even half of it was true . . .

During a lull in the conversation, Dennis Hinton walked into the cantina.

Tyrel was a little surprised. Denny wasn't one to go and hang out in the bars, and he sure stayed away from the women. Some said it was because of his raising, that his daddy was a preacher out of Alabama. There were others who said Denny preferred reefer to alcohol. Tyrel wasn't sure who had the right of it, but he did know that Denny hadn't ever come into the cantina with him.

"Denny," Tyrel said, pushing up from the table. "Denny. Over here."

Fat Mike snagged the front of Tyrel's shirt and yanked him back down into his chair.

"That ain't cool, man," Fat Mike said. "If you're gonna sit at this table, you're gonna sit here by our rules. And one of them rules is that you don't act like an idiot."

"But that's my friend," Tyrel protested.

"Maybe you want to go be with your friend," Fat Mike suggested.

Tyrel was debating on that. He'd bought the first round and two more besides. He really was going to be broke by the end of the night. He honestly didn't know how much longer he'd be able to afford to sit in that chair.

"No," Victor said in that quiet voice of his, "let it alone, Fat Mike. Let him invite his friend over if he wants."

"But that—" At a glance from Victor, Fat Mike shut his mouth and sat there silently.

Victor shifted his attention to Tyrel. "Invite your friend over, Country. I'll buy the next round."

Tyrel stood again. "Hey, Denny. Come on over. Victor said he's buyin'."

Denny hesitated a moment, then walked over. One of the other men hooked a chair over with his foot. Denny sat, but he didn't look comfortable.

Proud of himself and his new friends, Tyrel just grinned and ordered another beer when Victor offered.

⊛⊛⊛

>> ATWATER APARTMENT BUILDING
>> PHILADELPHIA, PENNSYLVANIA
>> 0911 HOURS

"Why did Victor Gant want Dennis Hinton to sit with them?" Maggie asked.

Richard McGovern shook his head. "Lady, I didn't know everything Victor was doin' back then. How'm I supposed to know now?"

The man was lying. Maggie knew that with certainty. She couldn't tell exactly what he was lying about, but she knew the deception was there all the same.

"We all thought it was a joke," McGovern said. "Most of us knew Hinton didn't drink. He had him a good dose of religion. That and a good attitude. The way he acted, you'd have thought he could walk on water."

"Why do you say that?"

McGovern lit up another cigarette from the butt of his previous one. "To understand that, you'd have had to be there. You'd have had to be in that jungle, fighting Charlie. Everybody I knew that was over there was afraid." He paused. "Except this kid Hinton."

"He wasn't afraid?"

"Nope. Not a day he was over there. Probably not the night Country shot him either."

"Why?"

"The way I figured it, Hinton thought he had a direct connection to God himself. You could tell it too, the way he came over there and sat down in the middle of us. Like nothin' and nobody could touch him." McGovern shrugged. "Or maybe he just felt safe because Country was sitting there with us. Anyway, he sat down, looked us all in the eye, and ordered a soda pop. Like he was Paul Newman in *Cool Hand Luke* or something."

Maggie waited. The hardest part of conducting an interview was knowing when to be quiet and let silence make the person being interviewed talk.

"After we had a round or two," McGovern said, "Victor suggested we go hunting. And that's when things started to get real interesting."

53

SCENE ✪ NCIS ✪ CRIME SCENE

NAVAL CRIMINAL INVESTIGATIVE SERVICE

\>> INTENSIVE CARE UNIT
\>> LAS PALMAS MEDICAL CENTER
\>> EL PASO, TEXAS
\>> 0815 HOURS (CENTRAL TIME ZONE)

"Hunting?" Shel asked.

His daddy nodded but didn't look at him.

"For what?" Shel tried to imagine, couldn't, and gave up.

"Victor didn't say," Tyrel answered. "Just told us there wasn't nothing like being out in the jungle at night."

"You'd run night maneuvers before."

"Yep. But we'd never run night maneuvers with Victor Gant. Everybody talked about him like he was a ghost out in the jungle. I wanted to see him in action. See if he really knew that much more than I did. My daddy taught me how to hunt at night. We used to go coon huntin' down in the hollers all the time when I was a kid. When I got older, Daddy taught me how to take deer during the daytime and how to track a coyote at night. I was a whisper in the darkness."

Shel listened to his daddy talk. In all the years that he'd known the man, Tyrel had never talked so much about what he'd done. Others had told Shel stories, but Tyrel wasn't one to abide bragging. If he'd been talking to his daddy for any other reason, Shel would have been happy to sit and listen.

"So we all went and got our rifles," Tyrel said. "Then we slipped through security and went out into the jungle."

"Hinton went with you?"

"Yeah. That's where I . . ." Tyrel stopped speaking for a moment. "He didn't come back that night. He died out there."

"Why did he go?"

"I don't know." Tyrel's voice was dry and paper-thin.

"Did you ask him?"

"No. I was twenty-one years old. I was scared to be going, but I was excited too. I was going with Victor Gant. A genuine penetration team legend. There was nothing that coulda kept me from going that night." Tyrel paused. "Except knowin' how it was all gonna turn out."

⊛⊛⊛

>> HIGHWAY 19

>> QUI NHON, VIETNAM

>> 2207 HOURS

>> OCTOBER 15, 1967

An hour after leaving the cantina, Tyrel was still drunker than Cooter Brown. He figured an hour of walking would have put him near to rights, but he was still having trouble seeing straight. And walking straight for that matter.

They were three miles out from Qui Nhon when Victor Gant called a break.

"How are you boys feeling?" Victor asked.

Everybody answered that they were feeling fine except for Denny. He'd been kind of hanging back from the crowd even though he'd agreed to come. Watching Denny now, mad at himself because he couldn't sober up enough to take care of himself and wasn't quite drunk enough to forget about being afraid, Tyrel didn't know why Denny had come.

"That's good," Victor said, "because now we're going to do exercises."

"Exercises?" Denny asked.

"Yeah," Victor said. "A few night maneuvers." He looked at Tyrel. "Country there said he wanted to learn to be a better soldier. Tonight I'm giving lessons."

"Country needs to be in bed," Denny said. "He's three sheets to the wind as it is."

Fat Mike jabbed Denny in the chest with a big forefinger. "You think him bein' drunk is any different than bein' out there in the jungle for four or five days? Dude, you don't get no sleep out there. You're too busy tryin' to grow eyeballs in the back of your head to sleep. You think sleep deprivation is any different than being drunk?"

Denny didn't say anything.

"Glad we got that cleared up," Victor declared. "We're going to divide up into teams for this. Country, you're with me."

Tyrel's chest swelled with pride at having been chosen. He took a fresh grip on his M14 and walked unsteadily over to join Victor.

"Hinton, you're with Fat Mike."

Denny wasn't happy about that.

"Hey," Tyrel said, "I'll see you in a little bit, okay?" He winked at Denny to show him he was having fun.

⊛⊛⊛

>> ATWATER APARTMENT BUILDING
>> PHILADELPHIA, PENNSYLVANIA
>> 0924 HOURS

"Wait," Maggie said, trying to understand everything that had happened on the night of October 15, 1967. "Victor Gant took men who'd been drinking out into the bush to run maneuvers?"

McGovern smiled slyly. "No. You see, that's what he told Country and Hinton. He figured that's the way they'd tell it when they got back to camp."

"Then what was really going on?"

"Victor was using the maneuvers as a cover," Remy said.

McGovern grinned hugely and touched a finger to his nose. "My man here knows the score."

"Then why was Victor out there?" Maggie asked.

"Back in those days, Victor had him a black market and drug scam going with a Kit Carson named Tran."

"Tran who?" Maggie asked.

"I don't know. Victor didn't let anybody except Fat Mike up in his business. And I don't know if he told Fat Mike the truth about everything."

"So why was Victor out there?" Remy asked.

"Man had to pick up a delivery," McGovern said. "He was supposed to get it on the way into Qui Nhon, but the dude who was supposed to deliver it wasn't there."

"Why wasn't he?"

McGovern sighed. "That's another question I can't answer. All I know is that Victor was using those two cherries to cover up what he had going on. If anybody asked, they'd just say they were out running maneuvers. Only that ended up all wrong."

"What went wrong?"

"I went with Country and Victor. The three of us hit the jungle. I was pretty high. In addition to the drinking we'd been doing, I'd been smoking reefer like a mad dog."

"So Country wasn't the only one wandering around messed up out in the dark?" Remy asked.

"Nope. Most of Victor's crew stayed messed up back in those days. How else do you think we made it through all those operations?" McGovern took a drag off his cigarette. "Where the wheels come off was when Country went to take a nature call and saw Tran's boy slippin' around in the jungle."

⊛⊛⊛

>> HIGHWAY 19
>> QUI NHON, VIETNAM
>> 2241 HOURS
>> OCTOBER 15, 1967

While he stood there in the bushes taking care of business, Tyrel tried to get his thoughts together. The fog that had filled his mind back at the cantina was not only proving unshakable but seemed to be growing steadily worse.

That was when he saw the Vietnamese man gliding through the forest.

Tyrel froze in the brush the way his daddy had trained him to. Animals could only see in black and white, and people were so used to looking without actually seeing that only movement really drew attention. Tyrel had tried to get that point across to other soldiers out in the jungle, but not many of them listened to him.

The Vietnamese man was a soldier. Tyrel knew that from the easy way he moved through the trees and brush. If the moon hadn't dusted him silver for just a split second while he'd been moving, Tyrel knew he'd never have seen him.

Unfortunately Tyrel had also lost sight of Victor and the other guy, the African-American one. McGowan. Something like that.

Easing into motion, Tyrel picked up his rifle and stayed within the bush. He moved slowly and cautiously. The adrenaline pumping through his body sobered him up a little, he thought, but his vision was still double and blurry.

At that moment, Victor seemed to materialize out of nowhere beside him.

"Where are you going?" Victor whispered, so close he was breathing in Tyrel's ear.

"Charlie," Tyrel said, his heart thumping in his chest. "Got Charlie in the jungle with us."

Victor looked around. "You sure?"

Tyrel nodded slowly. "Saw him. Saw him myself." He licked his lips. "Might be more'n one of 'em."

"Just slow down," Victor said calmly. "Just slow down, and we'll figure this out right enough. Follow me." He slid into the brush.

Slow and easy, regretting every beer he'd had, Tyrel followed. He was amazed at how fluidly Victor moved through the jungle. There was so much darkness around them that Tyrel almost couldn't see the hand in front of his face. He didn't know how they were going to find Charlie in the brush without getting themselves killed.

Where's McGowan?

⊛⊛⊛

>> ATWATER APARTMENT BUILDING
>> PHILADELPHIA, PENNSYLVANIA
>> 0933 HOURS

"I saw Victor and Country creepin' through the brush," McGovern told Maggie. "Didn't know what they might be doing other than maybe playing war games. But I knew Country was tense. You could see that in every line in that white boy's body." He shook his head.

"Where were you while this was going on?" Remy asked. He didn't care for McGovern. He'd known too many men like him back in New Orleans. His grandma had tried to keep him away from such men, but that hadn't always been a battle she'd won.

Remy glanced at Maggie to check and see how she was taking everything in. She watched McGovern and didn't seem in any way concerned.

"I was takin' care of Victor's business," McGovern replied. "He had a shipment of black tar heroin comin' from Tran. Victor shipped packages like that out of Qui Nhon all the time. We all made money on it."

Revulsion filled Remy.

"Business like that was easy," McGovern said. "All you had to do was be willing to share a bit."

"And Victor was?"

"Victor always was. Man liked him some money, but that wasn't what he was all about. He liked havin' people look up to him. To get that kinda attention, you gotta be willing to give in order to get. Know what I'm sayin'?"

Remy did. "Yeah. I know."

"What went wrong?" Maggie asked.

McGovern took a drag on his cigarette and breathed out a cloud of smoke that rolled across the small living room. "Hinton. He musta got lost in the darkness." He shrugged. "Probably wasn't his fault. Fat Mike didn't like him, and he probably ducked out on Hinton to let him fend for himself at the wrong time."

"What do you mean?"

"I mean, that's when Country shot Hinton. While he was jumpin' at ghosts he thought he was seeing in the jungle."

54

SCENE ✪ NCIS ✪ CRIME SCENE
NAVAL CRIMINAL INVESTIGATIVE SERVICE

>> HIGHWAY 19
>> QUI NHON, VIETNAM
>> 2244 HOURS
>> OCTOBER 15, 1967

"Keep my six," Victor ordered. "I'll watch what's up ahead. You just cover my six."

Tyrel turned sideways as he followed Victor. That way he could watch along their backtrail and protect their flank.

"You stay close, Country," Victor said. "You just stay close and be cool. I'll get us out of this."

Afraid his voice would crack if he spoke, Tyrel instead chose to say nothing. He kept the M14 snugged into his shoulder, ready to raise it up at a moment's notice.

"Where'd you see this guy?" Victor asked.

"To the left," Tyrel said. And his voice did crack. He felt embarrassed.

"It's gonna be okay, Country. I'll get you out of this."

Tyrel knew they shouldn't have been there. He should have

stayed back at the base, crawled into his rack, and slept it off. Instead he had to be stupid and prideful.

A light flared in the darkness.

"Look out!" Victor warned.

Tyrel twisted to track the light at once. He had just a momentary glimpse of the Vietnamese man sighting down a rifle not more than sixty or seventy yards away.

"Rifle!" Tyrel called as he brought his M14 up and started firing. He got four shots off before Victor Gant dropped a hand on the rifle and told him to stop shooting.

"Just hold up," Victor whispered. "Let's see what we're into here."

Breath ragged and hot against the back of his throat, Tyrel stared into the darkness where the Vietnamese soldier had stood. Nothing was there.

Then a figure ran across the darkness to where the Vietnamese soldier had been. It took Tyrel a minute to recognize the man as McGowan.

⊛⊛⊛

>> ATWATER APARTMENT BUILDING
>> PHILADELPHIA, PENNSYLVANIA
>> 0937 HOURS

"I was the one what found Hinton," McGovern said. "He was lyin' up in them bushes where Country said he saw the Vietnamese soldier. Hinton had been shot twice. Once in the face and once in the neck. It was an awful mess, but I seen worse while I was over there." He slapped his useless legs and cursed. "I had worse done to me while I was over there."

"What about the Vietnamese?" Remy asked. He didn't let McGovern's physical disability touch him. Men of his ilk were skilled at using infirmity to get sympathy. Remy knew that from watching all the panhandlers back in New Orleans when he'd grown up.

McGovern raised his shoulders, then dropped them. "Don't know. The only Vietnamese guy I saw that night was Tran's man."

"Do you think that was who Country saw?"

"Man, I don't know what Country thinks he saw that night. All I know is that when I got over to where he was shootin', that poor boy had checked out. When Country got over there, saw what he'd done, he absolutely freaked."

❀❀❀

>> HIGHWAY 19
>> QUI NHON, VIETNAM
>> 2251 HOURS
>> OCTOBER 15, 1967

When he stared down at Denny's ruined face, Tyrel got sick. He turned away from the dead man and heaved into the nearby bushes. The sour taste of vomit filled his mouth and he stank of it.

Victor's hand rested on his shoulder. "Go easy there, Country. You didn't know."

"I killed Denny," Tyrel gasped. He turned and stared at his dead friend. "I *killed* him."

"You ask me," Victor said, "I'd say he killed himself. He should know better than to flash a light out here."

The small flashlight lay only a short distance from Denny's lifeless hand. The beam shone into the grass till Victor knelt down and retrieved the light. He switched it off and slid it into a pocket on his BDUs.

"We've got to get him back to Qui Nhon," Tyrel said. "They've got doctors and nurses there."

"Doctors and nurses ain't goin' to help this guy," Fat Mike said. He'd only just gotten there. "Country put a bullet through his brain-pan." He turned to Tyrel. "That's good shootin' in the dark, man. You got two outta four."

Tyrel couldn't even remember aiming. Everything was on auto-pilot out in the jungle.

"We got to think about this," Victor said. He glanced at Tyrel. "If we take Hinton's body back, try to tell them what we were doing out here, this thing's gonna end your career in a heartbeat. They might put you in military prison for this because you were drunk at the time."

A fear like none he'd ever known assailed Tyrel at that moment. He'd already given up any ideas of going back home a hero. Vietnam didn't make heroes these days. But he couldn't imagine going back as a prisoner guilty of killing a fellow soldier. Even if it was by mistake.

"I know I don't want anything to do with an investigation like that." Victor paused. "And neither do you, Country."

"We can't just leave him here," Tyrel whispered.

"We take him back, there's gonna be an investigation," Victor assured him. "Uncle Sam will rain a storm down on your head. This is the military, Country. They don't give free passes for mistakes."

Tyrel knew that was true. He'd heard the same kind of speech all throughout his military career.

"You got a woman back home?" Victor asked.

Unable to answer, Tyrel just stared at Denny and willed the man to get up and tell him it was all a joke. Except he knew it wasn't a joke. There was too much blood.

"Are you listening to me?" Victor demanded.

"Yeah."

Victor took Tyrel's face between his hands. "Look at me, Country."

Tyrel tried to, but tears were streaming down his face and blurring his vision. He blinked to clear them, but there were more.

"Pull it together and look at me," Victor ordered.

Hurting, more scared than he'd ever been in his life, Tyrel did. Victor's eyes were hard and black. He looked like he'd never been scared a day in his life.

"Do you have a girl back home, Country?" Victor asked.

"Yeah."

"Do you want to see her again?"

Tyrel nodded.

"Then you're gonna have to do exactly what I say," Victor told him. "If you do, we're gonna be shut of this and we won't ever speak of it again. Do you hear me?"

"Yeah."

Victor stared deeply into his eyes. "What I should do is take you back to the post and turn you in myself. I'm a sergeant. It's my duty."

Tyrel knew that.

"But this war," Victor said, "it ain't nothin' like anybody said it would be. We're over here fightin', and it seems we're the only ones that knows we ain't gonna win. We're just gonna keep dying till finally somebody gets tired of sending body bags for soldiers to be sent home in. You listening to me?"

"Yeah."

"So I'm gonna help you," Victor said. "I'm gonna make an investment in you. I'm gonna help you out because I think you deserve it. I don't think you should take the fall for this."

Tyrel didn't even have the strength to ask how Victor was going to do that.

"What we're gonna do," Victor said, "is take Hinton's body deeper into the jungle. Then we're gonna bury it."

"You can't just leave him out here."

"We can't take him with us. We gotta leave him."

"But the animals—"

"We'll bury him deep," Victor promised. "We'll make sure the animals don't get to him."

The idea of leaving Denny lying in a forgotten grave made Tyrel sick again. He doubled over and threw up, but there was hardly anything left. Victor was barely able to get out of the way.

"Stay with me, Country," Victor said. "We're gonna make this right, me and you. We're gonna be all right."

✪✪✪

>> INTENSIVE CARE UNIT
>> LAS PALMAS MEDICAL CENTER
>> EL PASO, TEXAS
>> 0901 HOURS (CENTRAL TIME ZONE)

"So that's what we did," Tyrel said. "We picked Denny up and we carried him farther into the jungle. Found a spot, and then we buried him."

Shel listened to his daddy's cold, emotionless voice and tried to imagine what that must have been like. Twenty-one years old at the time, his daddy had to have been scared to death.

And he'd been living with the guilt for over forty years, Shel realized. How could he have carried that around so long without becoming an alcoholic or an abusive husband or father?

"Somebody back at the post had to have asked questions," Shel said.

"They did," Tyrel replied. "But we stuck to our story. Denny went out with us, must have gotten lost in the jungle or captured by the enemy. We knew Charlie came close to Qui Nhon on a lot of occasions. And Denny wouldn't have been the first soldier to go MIA from there. All of us covered for each other. In the end, the brass wanted Victor out in the field doing what he did best. Killing Charlie."

Shel rested his arms on his knees and tried to think. It was like his brain had turned to mud.

"Did Mama know anything about this?"

Tyrel shook his head. "I thought about tellin' her. I thought about tellin' her a lot. But I couldn't. Your mama was a strong lady, but she didn't deserve to have to try to get around something like that. It was bad enough I came back scarred from that war in ways that never showed. She didn't need that piled onto her prayer list. And there was nothin' she could have done anyway."

For a long time, Shel just sat and thought. But he knew there was no way to avoid talking about what both of them knew was on their minds.

"This is murder, Daddy, and covering it up only makes it worse."

"I know it. I knew it then."

"There are no statutes of limitations on murder."

Tyrel nodded. "The Army will prosecute me. Probably hang me. Especially since I tried to cover everything up."

Shel didn't know about that. He didn't want to think about that.

"What are you gonna do?" Tyrel asked.

"I don't know. This . . . this isn't what I expected."

Tyrel rolled his head to see Shel. "Don't you tell me you don't know, boy." His voice was edged steel now. "I raised you right, Shelton. You know the right thing to do, and you'd blamed well better do it."

His daddy's vehemence took Shel aback.

"I already spent forty years suffering over this," Tyrel went on. "I'll not spend one more day in torment. Do you hear me?"

"Yes, sir."

"I tried holding on to this secret." Tyrel looked up at the ceiling and his voice faded again. "I kept it from everybody, and it kept everybody from me. From the day I got back, I stayed packed and ready to pay for my crimes. I couldn't love your mama like I should have—and God knows she deserved better'n what she got. And I couldn't let you and Don get so attached to me that you couldn't make it when the Army finally come for me. I was a sorry daddy to you boys, and I know that. But I didn't have a choice. I had to let you be strong on your own."

That's why you kept pushing us away, Shel realized. The thought of what his daddy had done—and why—almost made him sick. Even understanding it the way he did, he didn't know how his daddy could have been so rigid and cold as to keep his sons distant all of their lives.

"So don't you let any sentimental foolishness on your part cloud your judgment," Tyrel said. "You turn me in. The way you're supposed to. You do it or I will. Either way, this ends. Do you hear me?"

Shel tried to answer, but then his daddy slumped back onto the bed, and all the alarms went off. By the time Shel got to his feet, a team of nurses and a doctor were inside the room with a crash cart.

"Get out of here," Isabella told him.

Shel hesitated, watching helplessly as the cardiac unit worked to bring his daddy back from the dead.

"Now!" Isabella ordered. Her voice was a harsh whip crack.

Shel left.

CRIME SCENE
NCIS
NAVAL CRIMINAL INVESTIGATIVE SERVICE

55

SCENE ✪ NCIS ✪ CRIME SCENE

NAVAL CRIMINAL INVESTIGATIVE SERVICE

>> CHAPEL
>> LAS PALMAS MEDICAL CENTER
>> EL PASO, TEXAS
>> 1013 HOURS (CENTRAL TIME ZONE)

Shel sat in the back of the chapel with his head in his hands and his elbows resting on his knees. Fatigue battered him and leeched all the energy from him that he normally would have gotten back by simply being still.

All around him, people prayed. Some voiced litanies. Some railed at God. Others made their peace quietly. Max lay quiet and supportive at his feet.

For the past hour, Shel had tried to figure out what path he should take. The problem was, he didn't figure God was behind it all or that God was out to get him. Shel had come to the chapel because he'd wanted to be alone as much as he could. Church held good memories for him from his childhood. He didn't know when he'd lost that feeling. And it wasn't there for him right now either.

This thing—his daddy's situation—was just what it was. That's all. There was nothing to be done about it and nothing else he needed to be doing. He'd just file his report about hearing his daddy's confession, back it up with the recording he'd made, and let justice take its course.

And what are you gonna do then, Shel? he asked himself. *Watch the military kill your daddy? Or watch him wither away inside of some prison?*

Neither of those options sounded good.

Someone slid into the pew next to him.

Shel glanced over and saw Don sitting there.

"I just came from the cardiac ICU," Don said. "They told me Daddy's going to be all right."

Shel nodded. Isabella had already come down and told him that less than ten minutes ago. He'd left word for Don on his cell phone. Don had been getting his wife and kids checked into a local hotel.

"They said you were with Daddy when he had his episode," Don said.

"Yeah."

Don hesitated, and when he spoke again, his voice was harsh. "They said he was yelling at you."

Shel nodded.

Anger showed in Don's eyes. "You want to tell me about that? Because if we almost lost Daddy just because you got into a fight with him and almost killed him that way, I really need to know what's in your head and your heart, Shel. And whether or not I want you to be around Daddy right now."

"You're not going to like what I have to say, Don."

"It can't make me feel any worse than I already do. But I don't want to lose my daddy and a brother all at the same time, so you'd better start talking."

"Okay." Shel took a deep breath and looked up. "But let's get out of here. Go somewhere we can talk."

⊛ ⊛ ⊛

>> CAFETERIA
>> LAS PALMAS MEDICAL CENTER
>> EL PASO, TEXAS
>> 1057 HOURS (CENTRAL TIME ZONE)

It took Shel nearly an hour to tell all of it and finish up with the questions Don had. Around them, families sat at tables and carried on quiet conversations. They all had their own troubles, and Shel saw the weight of them stamped on the people. Just knowing there were that many problems nearby made him feel claustrophobic.

"What's wrong?" Don asked.

"Nothing."

Don frowned at him. "I've known you my whole life, Shel. You'd say nothing was wrong if they cut both your arms off and set you on fire."

Shel forced a grin. "Don't you think that example is a little extreme?"

"For anybody but you, yes. Talk to me."

It took Shel a long moment to try to figure out the words he needed. He'd never been good at talking about himself.

"I joined the Marine Corps to get away from Daddy," Shel said softly. "I couldn't do anything about him. Couldn't do anything about Mama dying like she did."

"That wasn't your fault," Don said.

"I know that. But I felt like there should have been something I could do. I just knew I felt bad staying at the ranch. Everything there reminded me of how helpless I was to fix things the way I wanted to."

Don just remained silent. He'd always been good at listening.

"I joined the Marines because I liked the way they looked," Shel said. "All those commercials made it sound like Marines were these incredible, unstoppable warriors who could take on anything and win." He shook his head and grinned ruefully. "I was eighteen. What did I know?"

"You knew you wanted to help people. That's not a bad thing."

Looking at his brother, Shel suddenly realized they weren't so very different these days. Maybe they really hadn't been when they'd grown up together. Seeing that gave him a whole new perspective.

"You joined the church to help people," Shel said.

Don smiled. "Actually, I joined the church to date the preacher's daughter. That was the only way I could see Joanie back then. But God called out to me, and I answered. I think you were probably called too."

"Not me. It was a Marine poster that did me in."

"And the chance to get away from Daddy."

"Yeah." Shel sipped his tea. "The thing I learned was that no matter how hard I tried, I couldn't save everybody."

"That's not your burden, Shel. God works among people, and he gives them the means to save themselves."

"That's where you and I are going to have to disagree. I've seen a lot of people that couldn't save themselves."

"Like Daddy?" Don asked quietly.

For the first time, Shel realized what was bothering him most. After hearing the whole story, he knew his daddy needed help. Needed it in a bad way and had needed it for a long time.

"I can't help Daddy," Shel said, but it was more for himself than for Don.

"Do you have to tell the military about this?"

"Do you want me to cover it up?"

Don sighed. "No. I suppose enough of that has been done already."

"I think so too."

"And even if we didn't tell them, Daddy would."

"Too many people are going to wonder why Victor Gant went after Daddy," Shel said. "Maybe they'll figure it's me. But Victor Gant could make that phone call at any time."

"It would be hard for the military to prosecute Daddy without a body, wouldn't it?"

"Not if Daddy tells them he killed Hinton. Military courts are different than civilian courts. A soldier's word, unless it's proven a lie, is all the evidence you need if it's an admission of guilt."

"How could they trust Daddy now? He lied back then."

"Not to a military court," Shel pointed out. "And why would he lie now?"

"I'm just saying there could be some confusion."

Shel was quiet for a moment. "Let me ask you something, Don. Suppose we could somehow get Daddy to stand down on this—which, seeing as how we've never been able to convince him of much our whole lives, I don't see happening—and he isn't prosecuted. Where does that leave Daddy with God? Those books have still got to be balanced too."

"God can forgive him," Don said. "All Daddy has to do is ask God's forgiveness."

"Maybe God's the forgiving type—"

"Don't you think for a minute that he isn't."

"—but Daddy ain't. He hasn't given up on his guilt for forty years, and he won't for forty more." Shel rubbed his stubbled jaw. "I've seen men like Daddy. Guilt rides them hard. Tears them apart from the inside. I don't know how he's lasted as long as he has."

"Because of Mama and us," Don said. "He knew we needed him."

"Maybe. But Daddy ain't gonna turn to God. He don't figure he deserves it."

"He might not at first. But if you give him enough time, especially now that the truth is out, he might be able to forgive himself."

"Don," Shel said patiently, "this is Daddy we're talking about. He ain't never cut nobody no slack. When he draws a line in the sand, right there is where it stays."

Don laced his hands together behind his head and leaned back in his chair. "I know. You're right." He was quiet for a time. "What are you going to do?"

"That's what I'm telling you. There's nothing I can do. It's all out of my hands."

"Can you accept that?"

"It's not a matter of accepting it. That's just the way this is."

Don eyed him. "Let me ask you a question."

Shel nodded.

"Why were you in the chapel?"

"Don't go reading more into that than is there," Shel warned. Don had always wanted to bring him in closer to the church—not necessarily *his* church, but any church Shel could attend.

"I'm not reading anything into it. I'm just asking."

"The chapel was a quiet place to think."

"Outside could have been a quiet place to think too."

Shel knew that was true, and he didn't know why he hadn't gone outside.

"You needed comfort, Shel. If how I feel is any indication, I know this is bad for you. This . . . military stuff, that's more your world than mine. And I think you probably know more about what was in Daddy's mind the night he shot that man."

Shel's voice got thick. "Daddy was twenty-one. He wasn't much more than a boy. He was away from home, surrounded by men who wanted to kill him, in the company of strangers who took death for granted, and was seduced by every vice you can imagine over there. Everything that he'd known or thought of himself had been left behind. On top of that, he was more scared than he'd ever been before in his life."

Don just looked at him.

"Yeah," Shel said, "I know what was going through Daddy's mind that night. It's gone through my mind too. Young soldiers make mistakes."

"Do you think a military court will hold Daddy accountable for what happened over there that night?"

Shel let out a tense breath. "I don't know. This would be a close call, and there are a lot of people still sensitive over what happened in Vietnam. But the bottom line is that even if the military chose not to find any wrongdoing on Daddy's part, Daddy's still going to fault himself. Now that this is out, things could be even worse for Daddy. Have you thought about that?"

"What do you mean?"

"I mean that if the military court doesn't see fit to punish Daddy, Daddy may decide to punish himself."

Don paled as he realized what Shel was talking about. "You're talking about hurting himself?"

Shel remained quiet.

"Daddy wouldn't do that," Don said.

"Daddy lost Mama," Shel said. "He doesn't have a good relationship with either one of us. Other than that ranch, what does he have that's going to keep him alive?"

"I don't want to believe that."

"Believe what you gotta believe. But I've seen men that were cleared by military investigations who ended up taking their own lives because they allowed a fellow soldier to get killed or accidentally killed one themselves. The choices you're asked to make out in the field are life-and-death. They're not easy, and guilt comes awful quick and hard."

"There is one thing you can do for Daddy," Don said.

Shel looked away because he knew what was coming, and he really didn't want to hear it.

"You can pray for him," Don said. "You can ask God to touch Daddy's heart and make him strong enough to live through this. No matter what happens."

"That's not how I deal with things," Shel said. "You're the believer. Not me."

"Doesn't take much to be a believer, Shel. Just a little faith. About the size of a mustard seed."

Shel wished he could believe that, but he'd never been able to find even that little amount of faith. Facing what he was facing now, with everything beyond his control, faith wasn't what he wanted to reach for—because he feared that would be even less effective than trying to find an answer himself.

56

SCENE ✪ NCIS ✪ CRIME SCENE

NAVAL CRIMINAL INVESTIGATIVE SERVICE

>> LA QUINTA INN
>> EL PASO, TEXAS
>> 1337 HOURS (CENTRAL TIME ZONE)

Will wore the Bluetooth headset for his cell phone to keep his hands free as he went through the paperwork involving the Army's investigation into PFC Dennis Hinton's disappearance. Something niggled at the back of his mind, not quite within his grasp, but never going away. Over the years with the NCIS he'd learned to pay attention to those details.

"So McGovern confirms the story that Tyrel McHenry shot Hinton?" Will asked.

"That he shot Hinton accidentally, yes," Maggie answered.

"But he was drunk at the time."

"That's correct."

"Did you get the impression McGovern was telling you the truth?" Giving up for the moment on whatever it was he couldn't quite think of, Will got out of his chair and looked out the window.

The sun was bright and hard over the desolate countryside that began just beyond the motel parking lot. Mirages created by the heat shimmered over the twisted trees and scrub brush that dotted the landscape.

"I believed him," Maggie said. "Remy and I leaned on him pretty hard. We left him with the impression that we could take his medical check away if he was involved in any of this more than he said he was or if he was lying about it now."

"Hinton's body is still out there?"

"That's what McGovern said. Remy and I gave him maps, and he tried to locate the area where Hinton's body was left, but—"

"It's been forty years and we can't trust what he thinks he remembers." Will felt frustrated.

"I don't think he was exactly sober that night, either. Tyrel wasn't the only one who had been drinking. All of them appeared to have been intoxicated."

That caught Will's attention and he knew he was tracking down part of what was bothering him. "Not everyone," he said softly. "You and Shel both agreed that Hinton wasn't drinking that night." He turned back to the papers on the desk.

They'd taken a suite at the motel, then set up a skeletal operations base. Estrella manned the computer system in one corner of the room and maintained a connection with the databases back at Camp Lejeune.

"Right," Maggie said. "I'd forgotten about that."

"I almost had too." Will turned from the desk and paced the room. During the past hours, he'd thought about Shel and about the ties that bound father and son so fiercely.

Even Will's divorce and his son's feelings of betrayal hadn't destroyed the bond between them. It could have, though. He was keenly aware of that. Only by the grace of God had his family remained intact as much as it had with all the changes they'd been through.

"We know Victor Gant ran a tight crew," Will said. "He still runs one now. The biker gang might be large, but there are only a handful that control the power within the group."

"Or that know what's going on everywhere," Maggie agreed. She'd looked over the same information he had and arrived at some additional insightful conclusions, but none that were any more on target than what Will had seen.

"Then why go into the jungle that night to get an illegal shipment of drugs with two men who weren't part of your unit?" Will asked.

"As cover," Maggie said.

"Cover from whom?"

"The CID had been keeping a watch on Victor Gant's activities. That's in the reports we've seen."

"Two men isn't a lot of cover," Will pointed out.

"But maybe all you need."

"Tyrel McHenry was still new to Qui Nhon. Dennis Hinton had been there for most of a year. He knew who the players were."

"Meaning he knew who Victor Gant was?"

"Or he had a pretty good idea."

Airport noises sounded in the background at Maggie's end of the connection. She and Remy were already booked on a flight back to El Paso and would be in late that night.

"I don't know where you're going with this," Maggie admitted.

"Tyrel McHenry approached Victor Gant in the bar that night," Will said, churning it through his mind as he put the pieces together. "Why didn't Gant just blow McHenry off?"

"Why should he?"

"Because Victor Gant ran a tight group. He didn't let anyone into his group that he didn't trust. That's covered in the CID reports as well. Since Victor Gant was part of the CIA-sponsored assassination teams, he had a blank check to do whatever he wanted when it came to personnel."

"As long as he kept turning in the results they wanted."

"He did," Will reminded. "Seventy-three confirmed kills' worth."

"Tyrel McHenry wanted to get to know Gant, but Gant had no reason to get to know him."

"I think he did," Will said. He shuffled through the papers.

"Hey, Will," Maggie said, "we're boarding our flight. I'll talk to you again in a little while."

"Sure," Will said. "Get some rest on the plane. I'll talk to you soon." He clicked the phone off and called out to Estrella.

"What?" Estrella asked.

"Maggie's e-mailed a map—"

"I've already got it. I can print it out if you'd like."

"I would. I want to see how big of an area we're dealing with there. In the meantime, do you have the name and number of the CID guy who investigated Hinton's disappearance?"

"Right here." Estrella brought up a screen on her computer.

Will walked over to her desk, then entered the number on his phone. He waited while the phone rang. An answering service picked up. He left his name and number and a brief message detailing what the call was about. Then he studied the maps Maggie had sent.

⊛ ⊛ ⊛

>> 1807 HOURS (CENTRAL TIME ZONE)

A youthful seventy-six-year-old, U.S. Army Colonel Mack Ramsey, retired, sounded robust and energetic. Furthermore, he wasn't bashful about his golf game. He'd retired to Silver Springs, Maryland, and lived there with his wife.

Will talked golf with the man for a moment, having had just enough experience to ask a few questions, and knew that they were both feeling each other out. That was something officers and police investigators did before getting to what was really on the table.

"I know you're a busy man," Ramsey said. "I hear NCIS keeps almost as busy as the Army's CID."

Will smiled at that, knowing the dig was intentional and meant to break the ice.

"Tell me you didn't have someone dig up my phone number just to talk about my golf game."

"I didn't," Will replied. "One of your old investigations has tangled itself up in something I'm currently working on."

"Now you've got my interest. You know, you can retire from the crime business and check in your badge and pistol at the door, but you never check your curiosity. Nope, that goes with you for the rest of your days."

"There was an MIA in Qui Nhon in 1967 while you were stationed there."

"Back in those days, there were a lot of MIAs."

Ramsey suddenly sounded tired, and Will felt guilty about that.

"That's one war that won't ever quite go away," Ramsey commented. "Who was the MIA?"

"Private First Class Dennis—"

"Hinton," Ramsey said. "I remember him."

The fact that Ramsey remembered Hinton so quickly cinched what Will had been thinking. After pulling a long tour like Ramsey had in Vietnam, after dealing with so many investigations, most people wouldn't have remembered isolated cases.

"I'm impressed," Will said. "You've got quite a memory."

"About some things," Ramsey said noncommittally.

"Any particular reason this one stands out?"

"Instead of beating around the bush here, son, why don't you just come out and say what you think you've got to say?"

"I want to lay some groundwork first so you see where I'm coming from. I'm going to lay my cards on the table."

"Doesn't mean I'm going to put mine there, son." Ramsey's tone was guarded.

"One of my agents is Shelton McHenry."

"I knew a young soldier named McHenry."

"Yes, sir. Tyrel McHenry. That's my agent's father."

"Small world," Ramsey commented.

"It is at times," Will agreed. "A couple months ago, my agent had to shoot and kill a young man named Bobby Lee Gant."

"Now there's another name I know."

"His father was Victor Gant."

"Seems like I recall the incident with your man from the news. It was ruled a good shooting."

"Not by Victor Gant, Colonel. Gant has tried to kill my agent in retaliation on more than one occasion."

"You're lucky he didn't get it done. Gant was a killing machine back in Vietnam."

"That's what I've heard. Shel's not an easy man to kill."

"He must not be."

Will shifted in his chair. "During the course of our investigation into Victor Gant, we were told about PFC Hinton. We've since learned that Hinton went missing while in the company of Victor Gant and his fire team."

"That's right. They told me that Hinton got lost in the jungle. It happened to some men. They got blind drunk or stoned, or both, and walked into the jungle never to return."

"But you never thought that was what really happened to Hinton."

At the other end of the phone, Ramsey took a deep breath. "Not for a New York minute."

"Because PFC Hinton didn't drink," Will said, "and he would have been less inclined, according to his service jacket, to drink while on duty."

"Hinton was a good soldier," Ramsey said. "His kind was hard to come by in some places."

"Was that why the CID was using him as an undercover operative?" Will asked.

Ramsey was quiet for a time. Then he asked, "What do you have, Commander Coburn?"

"I've got testimony that Hinton was shot, killed, and buried in a grave off Highway 19 that night," Will said.

The silence stretched over the phone connection.

"I looked for that boy for a long time," Ramsey finally said. "It was like he disappeared."

"He did."

"Did Gant kill him?"

"No. He was shot by Tyrel McHenry."

"How do you know this?"

"Because McHenry told my agent that this morning," Will said.

"Why would McHenry shoot Hinton? I never put McHenry with Gant and his goons. He was the reason I believed it was possible Hinton had wandered off. I wouldn't have believed Gant or his men. McHenry, though, seemed solid. Just green. All those kids were."

"It was an accident." Will described the situation as Shel had given it to him.

"That still doesn't make sense. Gant could have brought Hinton back in and reported the accident."

"Maybe he was so used to covering his tracks by that point that lying was second nature."

"Why did McHenry lie?"

"He was twenty-one years old," Will reminded. "Nothing in his life had prepared him for what had happened out there."

"No. You're right about that. What do you need from me?"

"I need to know about Hinton. I still can't figure out why Gant would ask Hinton along or why Hinton would accept. The only thing I came up with was that Hinton was working undercover for the CID and that Gant suspected it."

"Working undercover for the Criminal Investigation Command was dangerous," Ramsey said. "Men who informed on soldiers ended up dead. Either at camp or—easier yet—out in the jungle. The only law over there at that time was survival of the fittest."

Will waited. Even if Ramsey didn't confirm his suspicions, he felt certain he was right.

"Hinton was working undercover for me," Ramsey said. "I needed someone who could get in on the inside of those men. Hinton went with them that night because of me. He knew I wanted to bring Gant down, and he didn't like Gant either." His voice softened. "I got that boy killed that night."

"No," Will said. "Bad luck did." And he couldn't help feeling that bad luck had struck all the way around. It had also cost Tyrel McHenry forty years of his life.

SCENE NCIS CRIME SCENE
NAVAL CRIMINAL INVESTIGATIVE SERVICE

>> LA QUINTA INN
>> EL PASO, TEXAS
>> 1852 HOURS (CENTRAL TIME ZONE)

"Director Larkin," Will said when the phone was answered.

"Will? How are things there?" Larkin's voice was quiet and controlled.

"Confusing and painful, sir," Will replied.

"With everything you've told me, I can see how that would be the case."

Will paced at the window and watched the sun going down in the west. He tried to frame in his mind how best to ask what he knew he had to ask. He and Larkin had a good working relationship, but he knew what he was about to request might be hard for the director to handle.

"I need you to arrange something for me," Will said.

"If I can." Larkin didn't hesitate, but he also didn't readily agree.

"I want to take my team to Vietnam."

"Why?"

"To recover the body of an American GI who's been missing since 1967."

"Dennis Hinton?"

"Yes, sir."

"Do you know where his body is?"

"I think we can get close enough to find it."

"Hinton's recovery would be more in the Army's interest."

"If Shel's father weren't on the line for a murder charge, I'd agree with you, sir. But that's exactly where Tyrel McHenry is."

"I know this has to be hurting Shel, Will, and I know you take the things that happen to your team personally—"

"Every time," Will interrupted.

"—and I respect that, but the Army isn't going to like being cut out of this."

"The Army can't rescue PFC Hinton," Will said gently.

"Neither can you. PFC Hinton has been dead for four decades. To me it sounds like you're more concerned with keeping Shel's father's head off the block than with conducting a criminal investigation."

Will paused a moment. "I want to know exactly what happened that night, sir. Once we figure out what happened, we'll know who was guilty of what."

"Do you think there's going to be any crime scene evidence left after forty years?"

"I think the possibility exists. As long as it does, I'd rather my people and the NCIS crime labs processed it. I'd just rather trust us."

"I agree."

"We've also got something to save here."

"Will, don't get your hopes up on this one too much. And whatever you do, I wouldn't get Shel's hopes up."

"I don't think getting Shel's hopes up at this point is even possible. But we might be able to tie Victor Gant to a crime that will guarantee that he'll serve his time in a military prison and never see the light of day again."

"You don't think you can do that without going to Vietnam?"

"I'd rather exhaust every avenue."

Larkin was silent for a time. "That's a tall order, Will. Even though Vietnam has opened its borders to outside countries, there's a limit to what they'll allow over there. Getting your people in-country might not be possible."

"It's not possible," Will stated, "if nobody asks. Give me a name at the State Department and I'll be happy to make the request myself. I just thought it would carry more weight from the director of the NCIS. And, officially, NCIS is made up more of civilians than service personnel."

"Not your group."

"No, sir. But not everyone has to know that."

Larkin was silent for a time.

Will stared out the window at a circling hawk and thought about Shel and Tyrel McHenry. That one night had charted their course together even before Shel had been born.

"I don't know if I can make it happen," Larkin said finally.

"Maybe if you posited it as a goodwill gesture," Will suggested. "Everybody wins when we bring a soldier home." That was true even when the soldier was dead. At least the family could have closure. In the end, that was what something like this was all about.

"Let me make a few calls," Larkin said. "But I can't make any promises."

"No, sir. I understand that. Thank you." Will broke the connection and let out a deep breath.

"How did that go?" Estrella asked.

"Better than I expected," Will admitted. "He didn't say no."

>> CHAPEL
>> LAS PALMAS MEDICAL CENTER
>> EL PASO, TEXAS
>> 0718 HOURS (CENTRAL TIME ZONE)

Shel came awake when Max moved at his feet. He lifted his head from the wall behind him and looked around. The nurse from the cardiac unit was at the doorway. Shel started to get up, expecting the worst.

After the second attack in the ICU, Tyrel's doctor had been more aggressive in his treatment. He had started to talk about the necessity of a pacemaker, but Tyrel had turned that down every time it was brought up.

He had also refused to see Shel.

Finally Tyrel had been sedated and put completely under and would be kept that way until the doctor felt he was strong enough.

By all rights, Shel knew he should have left the hospital. He wasn't doing anyone any good there. The relationship he had with his daddy was modeled on this kind of behavior. Every time he'd tried to reach out to Tyrel McHenry, his daddy had rebuffed him. That was to be expected. The biggest surprise was that he wasn't walking away from his daddy this time. That was how he normally reacted.

Some of his concern must have shown, though, because Isabella and a couple of the other nurses had kept him up-to-date with reports about his daddy's condition. Don had gone to the hotel where Joanie and the kids were. Don was also in contact with several of his church family. All of them were concerned about him and his daddy, and they extended their prayers.

Isabella came over to Shel and talked in a quiet voice. "I didn't mean to wake you up."

"You didn't," Shel assured her.

She grimaced. "That's why you didn't wake up until I was staring at you, right?"

"Maybe a little," Shel acknowledged.

"You should get a hotel room. Someplace where you can get a good night's rest." Concern showed in her dark eyes.

"I'm fine. Thanks."

Isabella leaned back against the wall and relaxed. She smothered a yawn with her hand, then grinned ruefully. "Sorry."

"Maybe I'm not the only one missing out on sleep."

"No, you're not. I'm finishing up my master's right now. Night classes. It takes a lot out of me. But the kids help."

"You're married?"

Isabella shook her head. "Widowed. My husband was a fireman. There was a bad fire downtown almost four years ago." She didn't meet Shel's eyes as she spoke, lost in memory. "The building collapsed. Brian didn't make it back out."

"I'm sorry."

"Yeah. Me too." Isabella nodded at the cross at the front of the chapel. "There's not a day I'm on duty that I don't stop in here and say a prayer for him. Some days, I feel like he's here with me."

"Maybe he is."

"I suppose, as much time as you spend in here, that you like churches too?"

Shel shook his head. "That's Don's purview."

She looked at him.

"I like it here because it's quiet and no one bothers you."

Her eyes were deep and intense. "Do you really think that's why you're in here?"

"Yes."

A sad smile pulled at her lips. "Then you've got a lot to learn, Marine. Anyway, I didn't come here to witness to you, though I never hold back in that regard either. I just wanted to see how you were holding up."

"I'm fine. Thank you."

Isabella stood. "I usually take a break for lunch around eleven thirty. If you want some company."

"I'd like that," Shel said.

Isabella smiled. "I'll stop by and get you." She started to go, then turned back to face him. "Try praying, Marine. If you've tried everything else, what have you got to lose? Just make sure that when you do, it's from the heart."

Shel nodded, but he didn't promise anything. He wouldn't have promised Don either.

After Isabella left, Shel folded his arms and tried to get back to sleep. But sleep wouldn't come. He kept staring at the cross and thinking about how Don had put so much faith in God. Evidently Isabella did too.

How could someone do that?

It was beyond Shel to imagine putting faith in anything outside himself. He'd acquired skills and trained his body to take care of him wherever he went. He was a warrior and had stridden across battlefields, through dozens of firefights. He'd been shot at point-blank range almost two months ago. He hadn't called on God then. He'd just healed and gotten himself ready again. That's what he always did. And he kept his wants small, down to things that he could manage.

He'd learned not to ask for big things after he'd discovered that no matter what he did, he couldn't have a relationship with his daddy. The closest he'd ever allowed himself to come to anyone was with Will and the others on the NCIS team. Even that had been scary. He'd known then that he shouldn't reach for anything outside himself.

Losing Frank Billings had hurt. But thinking about Frank now, Shel realized that the thing he most remembered about Frank was his faith in God. Frank's faith had always been there, totally unshakable.

These days, Will had that faith too. It was still new, but Shel had noticed it. And it had come over Will at what Shel would have figured was the worst time ever: after Frank's murder in South Korea and after his wife had dropped divorce papers on him.

How had Will turned to God in the middle of that?

"People who don't have faith turn to God when they don't have anywhere else to go," Don had told Shel on more than one occasion. "It's a shame they wait till then, but that's usually when they get the wake-up call that they need help in their lives or they're not going to make it through. That's the whole thing about free will, Shel. God is there, but he leaves the choice in your hands."

Shel wondered if that was true, though. Did God move in ways to coerce people into believing in him? He figured if he'd asked that question of Don, his brother would have gotten irate with him.

Maybe he'd even committed a sin by thinking that way.

Then again, by believing that God was coercing you into accepting him, wasn't that faith too? Believing that God cared enough to blackmail you into faith was also an admission that you believed. Shel wasn't certain about that.

One thing was certain, though: he didn't have anywhere else to go. No one could help him.

No, he corrected himself, *no one can help Daddy.* His eyes burned as he thought about that. He stared at the cross. *What about it, God? Do I have to knuckle under for myself? Or can you blackmail me into believing in you by threatening Daddy?*

Anger swept through Shel at that moment. But at the same time, he let out a breath and calmed himself. He thought for a long time, but he couldn't come up with another plan of action.

He was at a standstill and up against a stone wall. And all that time, his daddy was fighting for his life.

All right, God, I don't know if you planned this or are just around as you've always been. We can sort all that out later. Shel bowed his head and let go of his anger. He didn't have room in his heart for that and hope at the same time. *Right now, God, I'm asking for your help. Not for me, but for Daddy. I don't know if you take prayers for others, but I know a lot of people pray for other people who have trouble in their lives.*

Daddy's got a lot of trouble in his life. It's been there for a long time. But I expect you already knew that if you're everything Don believes you are. Daddy needs help that Don can't give and I can't give. I'm asking you to give him that help. If he can't help himself, then please help me help him.

Shel sat there quietly for a time and thought about all the Sunday school classes he'd gone to when his mama had been alive. He thought about her too, and for a moment while he sat in the chapel, he could have sworn he felt her around him.

Then the feeling was gone, but a peace like none he'd ever before experienced descended on him. Before he knew it, he was totally at rest and fell asleep effortlessly.

⊛ ⊛ ⊛

>> CAFETERIA
>> LAS PALMAS MEDICAL CENTER
>> EL PASO, TEXAS
>> 1139 HOURS (CENTRAL TIME ZONE)

"Your father surprised the doctor just a short time ago," Isabella said as she placed her tray on one of the back tables.

Shel sat on the other side of the table from her. Max made himself at home to one side. All around them, visitors and hospital staff lunched and talked. It was busy and noisy.

"How?" Shel asked. He dropped part of a turkey sandwich and Max caught it before it hit the floor.

"He's agreed to talk to the doctor about the pacemaker."

Worry gnawed at Shel. "Did something happen?"

"You mean with his heart?"

Shel nodded.

"No. He just changed his mind."

"Daddy don't often do that once he settles on a game plan."

"Just be glad that he did."

"I am."

They ate and swapped small talk for a little while, but Shel couldn't help thinking about his prayer in the chapel and how he'd felt his mama there. Isabella was pleasant and easy company, and she didn't mind keeping up both ends of the conversation when she had to.

As they were putting their trays away and getting ready to leave, Shel's cell phone rang. He took it out of his pocket and flipped it open.

"Did I catch you at a bad time?" Will asked.

"Now is good," Shel replied.

"Estrella found one of Victor Gant's old crew that was wounded before he got out of Vietnam. Maggie and Remy went to see him. He was there the night your father shot PFC Hinton."

Shel's stomach knotted up at little at that. The murder wasn't going to go away.

"He's also identified an area where he thinks the body was buried," Will went on.

Excitement blazed within Shel as he guessed where Will was going.

"I asked Director Larkin to pull some strings with the State Department and the Vietnamese government for us," Will said. "He came through. I just got word a few minutes ago. You were my first call. We'll get to double-down on this one. We can see if we can answer some questions about the shooting that night, and we can bring an MIA soldier back to his family."

Shel couldn't believe it. His spirits soared when he thought about the ramifications.

"When are we leaving?" Shel asked.

"As soon as we can get mobile."

"I'm on my way." Shel closed his phone and put it away.

"Good news?" Isabella asked.

"I don't know," Shel answered honestly. "But it's something to do. Maybe it can help Daddy. I don't know. I'm going to try."

Isabella smiled at him. It was a good smile, one that Shel knew he would remember.

Shel hesitated. "I don't like leaving Daddy right now. Not with him in the shape he's in."

"Your father is a tough man," Isabella said. "He's going to be all right."

"I shouldn't be gone more than a few days."

"If this is something you need to do," Isabella said, "then do it. Your father has one of the best heart surgeons I know looking after him. And I'm looking after him too."

Shel took an NCIS business card from his ID. "I'm going to give you my personal number. You'll be able to reach me anytime." He wrote the number on the back of the card. "If anything changes, I'd appreciate it if you'd call me."

"I will," Isabella said. "Promise."

"Thank you." Shel touched the Marine Corps baseball cap he wore. Then he turned and got under way. Max fell into step beside him, and the dog seemed to understand that they weren't just going for the usual walk.

58

SCENE ✪ NCIS ✪ CRIME SCENE
NAVAL CRIMINAL INVESTIGATIVE SERVICE

>> PHÙ CÁT AIRPORT
>> QUI NHON, BINH DINH PROVINCE
>> SOCIALIST REPUBLIC OF VIETNAM
>> 1341 HOURS (LOCAL TIME ZONE)

"You watch all those movies like *Full Metal Jacket*, you don't expect Vietnam to look like this," Remy said.

Shel gazed out at the long runway in front of him and silently agreed. The city, looking very modern with the tall buildings that hadn't been there during the war, flanked the airport to the southeast and ran deeply into the jungle. The metropolis fought the creeping vegetation back, and a few paved roads snaked up into the mountains surrounding the port city.

"Doesn't look like the pictures Daddy took of the area," Shel admitted. "He was here in 1967. The United States Air Force's RED HORSE Civil Engineering Corps started building the airport for the Air Force use the year before."

"Your father was in the Army, not the Air Force, right?"

"The Army worked the jungles, kept the supply routes clear, and flushed snipers and kill squads from the riverbanks to keep the PBRs safe."

Sunlight glinted off Remy's sunglasses as he surveyed the jungle that began immediately on the other side of the city. It was thick and tall and verdant.

"You ever fought in the jungle?" Remy asked.

"Nope. My first taste of action was eating sand in the Middle East. Did some work down in Africa. A few hot spots in Europe."

"Me?" Remy said. "I wouldn't want to have to run through all that brush and try to fight an enemy that had grown up in that type of environment."

"I know," Shel agreed.

"And most of the American soldiers in that war were nineteen years old. Away from home for the first time and dropped right into the middle of a fire zone." Remy shook his head. "Unbelievable. At least you and me, we've been around the block."

"A time or two," Shel agreed. He stared at the city beyond the long runway and tried to feel his daddy's footsteps in the land. It was strange, but he felt closer to his daddy than he ever had. This was his daddy's battleground, and it was about to become his.

❂ ❂ ❂

>> 1348 HOURS (LOCAL TIME ZONE)

"I hope you realize you're in a unique position here, Commander Coburn."

Will sat in the back of the air-conditioned limousine and stared at the heavyset man across from him. As a military man, Will didn't like dealing with politicos as a general rule. Dealing with their secretaries and lackeys was even worse.

Ashton Finlay was a Yale graduate who hadn't had enough pull to get a cushy State Department job. Instead he'd landed the Socialist Republic of Vietnam and wasn't happy about it. Not many people had to deal with him, and most were likely not impressed. He was in his early thirties and wore good suits. His haircut was neat and he had a fresh manicure.

"How so?" Will asked.

Finlay blinked at him. "Getting the weapon permits for your team wasn't easy."

Will understood immediately that he was supposed to be impressed with Finlay's abilities. "I suppose it wasn't. You did well, Mr. Finlay."

A small, uncertain smile pulled at Finlay's face.

"Of course," Will said, "given the fact that this country is filled with soldiers armed with assault weapons and that my team wouldn't really have anywhere to run even if we did try to initiate World War III, plus the fact that the people in charge of this country don't care that much about the citizens here, maybe that wasn't as hard as one might think."

The smile went away. "What I'm saying is that I stuck my neck out for you people."

"Thank you."

"I wasn't even told what you were doing here."

So that's what this is about, Will thought. "There's not much I can do about that."

"I thought maybe we could talk." Finlay leaned a little closer. "Just man-to-man."

Will leaned closer as well. In a softer voice, he said, "We are talking."

"I thought you could tell me what you're really doing here. I mean, not just the recovery of a dead soldier cover."

"I could," Will agreed, deadpan despite the disgust that moved through him, "but then I'd have to shoot you."

Finlay pulled back. He shot his cuffs and looked away.

Will nodded at the military jeep rolling toward them. "Is that the captain I'm supposed to liaise with?"

After a quick glance through the window, Finlay said, "Possibly."

"Maybe we could go find out," Will suggested.

❂ ❂ ❂

>> 1356 HOURS (LOCAL TIME ZONE)

The Vietnam People's Army captain was in his forties, a quiet and dapper man with an easy but professional manner. His uniform was neatly pressed and clean. His men moved immediately to flank him without a word and without offering direct challenge.

"Commander Coburn," the captain said.

"I am." Will stepped forward and offered his hand.

"I am Captain Cuong Phan of the Vietnam People's Army. I hope you had a pleasant flight."

"That much flying," Will said, "is never pleasant." He took his hand back. "You were informed why we're here?"

"To recover and transport the body of a missing American soldier you believe is somewhere in the area?" Phan nodded. "I have been so informed. But it's been forty years, Commander. Do you really think such a thing is possible?"

"I have hope, Captain. Little expectation, but hope."

Phan looked past Will. "These are all your people?"

Remy, Shel, Maggie, Nita, and Estrella stood behind Will in a ragged line. Max sat alertly at Shel's boots beside their duffels.

"Yes," Will answered.

"So few of you?"

"I hope this is all that it takes. But I've got a few others en route."

"Who?"

"Two specialty dog teams," Will said. "They're civilians trained to find historical remains. Old teeth. Bones. Clothing. Things that you'll find at old, unmarked graves."

"I've never seen dogs like this."

"Well, you will if you'd care to come by and have a look while we're working." The dogs and handlers were due to arrive later that afternoon.

Phan looked at Will. "I have also found out, unofficially, that you've got another interest here."

"We do," Will said and wondered where the captain was getting his information. Will had intended to share it anyway.

Phan smiled. "Since we have started depending on the tourist trade for part of our economy, we have found it beneficial to find out who some of the people are who enter our country. Your Sergeant McHenry is very much in the news at present."

"Your people appear to be very thorough."

"The world is getting smaller these days, Commander. It pays to know whom you let enter your borders. Your country has learned that the hard way."

"We believe Victor Gant is somewhere in-country," Will said. "If we cross paths with him, we intend to take him into custody."

"You would need to seek permission from the government to take him back with you."

Will smiled. "I happen to know that Victor Gant is wanted in this country as well, Captain. If we do have the good fortune to detain him, we'll turn him over to your government initially. At that point, my government would be happy to enter negotiations with yours as to the final deposition of the prisoner."

Phan nodded and appeared a little relieved. "As long as we understand each other."

"I think we do."

"Do you believe the six of you are going to be able to accomplish your goals?"

"I hope so."

"Victor Gant, as you say, is known to us. He's a very dangerous man. A killer several times over. Not just in the war, but during recent visits to our country. We intend to bring him to justice if we ever find him.

Unfortunately Gant remains elusive because he's in league with one of the drug lords in the area." Phan paused and looked at Will. "You people are taking quite a chance walking out into that jungle."

"If there was another way," Will said, "I'd do it."

"Perhaps there is. I was thinking that I could send a few of my men—"

"No more than two," Will interrupted.

Phan smiled. "You know what is on my mind."

"You want to use us as a stalking horse," Will said, "to draw Gant out of the brush."

"Yes. And if we are favored by fate, his partner as well. I have heard Gant has cause to hate your Sergeant McHenry very much."

"Yes."

"You are counting on that."

Will nodded.

"That is very risky business," Phan said.

"I can't think of another way to do it. Given the circumstances, I can't make any promises about the health and well-being of your soldiers."

"I would not ask you for that promise. Working together in this instance will be a privilege."

"I feel the same way," Will said.

"Still, what we do even with each other's assistance will be a very dangerous thing."

"Your men will be in radio contact with you?"

"Always."

"Then it will be less dangerous than if we were to do this thing by ourselves."

Phan gazed at Will with new understanding. "You knew something like this would be done?"

"I wouldn't let anybody wander around in my backyard unescorted," Will replied. "Whether I let them know or not. I appreciate you letting me know."

"You could have asked for assistance."

"I could have," Will admitted, "but I think it was probably easier for you to suggest to your superior that you be allowed to keep an eye on us. Maybe plant guides within our ranks. That way you're in control, on the surface, rather than providing a service."

"I did ask them for permission to spy on you," Phan said with a small smile. "They readily agreed since it seemed we'd be fooling you. Those men take such . . . clandestine action for granted and think they are very clever. They are years from the battlefields. But I thought that you would suspect something was amiss."

"That's why you made the offer directly."

Phan grinned. "So we understand each other."

"Entirely," Will agreed.

⊛ ⊛ ⊛

>> NINE KLICKS OUTSIDE QUI NHON, BINH DINH PROVINCE
>> SOCIALIST REPUBLIC OF VIETNAM
>> 1407 HOURS (LOCAL TIME ZONE)

Soaked in sweat from the heat and humidity that filled the jungle around him, Shel marched resolutely. It felt good to be doing something other than staying in hospitals or being one step behind Victor Gant.

Of course, Shel knew he was about forty years behind at present, but at least he felt he was gaining on something. In fact, he felt more hopeful about things than he had in a long time. He attributed a lot of that to the fact that he had at last slept on the long flight to Vietnam. But he often thought about his prayer in El Paso. In fact, he thought about it enough that he was praying every morning and every evening. Something about that felt right as well.

The team had spent three days in the field so far. Estrella had gridded the area that McGovern, the paraplegic who had been with Victor Gant's fire team, had indicated.

Even though he'd wondered if McGovern had lied to them, Shel couldn't help but remain somewhat hopeful. Hinton's body had to be out in the brush somewhere, but Shel also knew they could be miles from it. Or they might never find it.

Please, God, he thought. *Don't let that be the case.* He knew his daddy needed some kind of closure. So did he.

Shel carried an M4 assault rifle in one hand and a GPS compass in his left. Vines and brush pulled at his combat boots and BDUs, not really slowing him down. A few feet away, Estrella walked her own line of the grid.

He noticed that she looked worse for the wear, and Shel realized he'd been pushing the pace. He felt guilty about that. Remy was about the only member of the team who could keep up with Shel over time.

The historical remains handler working Shel's grid was a civilian, a young woman with red hair and a large, female German shepherd. So far her dog and Max had gotten along fine.

Although Max was cross-trained for search and rescue, his primary training was to find live victims. Locating old graves was specialty work, and the dogs dedicated to that couldn't be trained to search for live or wounded people. The dog handler had mostly kept to herself, and neither she nor her animal had shirked a bit as they'd worked the grids Estrella had laid out.

"Water break," Shel called out when he reached the top of the latest incline. He squatted in the shade of a towering tree but kept a clear field of view on both sides of the incline.

"Thank goodness," Estrella said. She leaned against a tree and drank water from the built-in bladder in her LCE pack. The load-carrying equipment came with a two-liter bladder for storing water that also served to cool the soldier's body.

"Easy," Shel called as she continued drinking. "You don't want to make yourself sick out here."

Estrella eased off of the water and wiped her mouth with the back of her arm. But she didn't cap the plastic straw that was built into the bladder.

She looked at Shel and shook her head. "I don't know how you do it."

Shel grinned. "The few and the proud," he told her.

"Please," Estrella said, rolling her eyes in mock disbelief. She looked back the way they'd come. "We've actually done a lot of work."

"I know," Shel replied. "We're making good time." He tried to remain positive though his impatience was getting higher every day.

But the truth was they were walking the gridlines faster than they'd believed possible. The men Captain Phan had put with them had actually helped speed up the process by restructuring the gridline search party method to push people into motion faster.

Max ranged the countryside, constantly on point, and remained close even though he wandered away till he was out of sight on several occasions. Shel never worried. One whistle and the dog would be at his side.

Although he'd watched, Shel had never seen Captain Phan's men in the outer perimeter. The idea of being a stalking horse hadn't set too well with Shel. If someone who was constantly keeping an eye on a developing situation came in close enough to alter the outcome of a potential encounter, that person could also be too close to leave events unmarked by their presence.

A stalking horse worked best against predators driven by instinct, not thoughts. He didn't want the Vietnamese army to scare Victor Gant away. Then Shel realized that the presence of the army might enhance Victor Gant's desire to attack his enemies. It would be a real coup. If he could pull it off.

Shel became aware that Estrella was talking to him. He focused on her. "Sorry."

"I was wondering how your father is doing," she repeated.

"Fine," Shel replied. "I talked to Don this morning. Daddy's almost strong enough to deal with the pacemaker."

"That's good."

It wasn't, though. Not really. As his daddy had told Don, the only reason Tyrel McHenry had agreed to the pacemaker was because he figured he owed somebody prison time, or a death, for killing PFC Dennis Hinton.

In all probability, his daddy was giving up. Shel had never seen his daddy give up on anything.

Except living his life for his wife and kids. That sober thought rocked him.

"All right," Estrella said, interrupting his dark thoughts. "If you're ready, I am."

Shel nodded and rose to his feet. He took a fresh reading with his GPS, signaled the dog handler, then started walking again. They were staying close to the road for the first sweep. If they didn't find anything, they would go deeper into the jungle.

What they were looking for was a man-size depression in the ground. After forty years, all the flesh would have sloughed away from Hinton's corpse. When he'd been buried, his body had been one size. But after time and nature had stripped his flesh, his body would have been another size, and the dirt on top of his mortal remains would have sunk. Most old graves were found through visual searches.

If the approximate location was known.

And they had the dogs. It was something to hope for.

Shel glanced toward the horizon and saw the black clouds that had been forming to the east were now more vigorous. They were also on a direct approach. The storm would be upon them soon.

59

SCENE ✪ NCIS ✪ CRIME SCENE
NAVAL CRIMINAL INVESTIGATIVE SERVICE

>> NINE KLICKS OUTSIDE QUI NHON, BINH DINH PROVINCE
>> SOCIALIST REPUBLIC OF VIETNAM
>> 1658 HOURS (LOCAL TIME ZONE)

"What do you think they're looking for?"

At first, Victor Gant ignored Fat Mike's question. They sat under a thick copse of brush on a hillside over a half klick from where the Marine who had killed Bobby Lee was searching. Victor held the high-power field glasses carefully so that the sun wouldn't ever reflect from the lenses. There was less and less chance of that happening as the cloud cover from the approaching storm became more complete.

Finally Victor lowered the field glasses and stared at the figures in the distance. Without the lenses, he could barely make out the people searching the land.

"This far out in the brush, there's only one thing they're looking for," Victor said.

"That kid's body?" Fat Mike asked.

"Did we bury anybody else out here?"

Fat Mike looked like he was thinking about that. There had been a number of bodies back in those days. And that wasn't even counting Charlie and the Kit Carsons they'd left lying where they'd dropped them.

"Did we?" Fat Mike asked finally.

"No."

Fat Mike snorted. "They're not going to find that grave." He cursed. "As long as it's been, I don't think I could find it now."

"They brought those dogs for a reason."

"Maybe they're trying to track us."

"No." Victor put the field glasses in the protective case on his hip.

"Do they have grave dogs?"

"I don't know."

"Doesn't matter," Fat Mike said. "There's probably so many people buried out there, they'll never find Hinton." He glanced at the darkening sky. "Not only that, but the storm that's coming is gonna be a toad strangler. The ground we're standing on is gonna turn to muck."

Victor watched in silence.

"You know," Fat Mike said, "I was thinking that if we had a Barrett rifle, something with some serious range, you could settle that Marine's hash and be done with this before they could ever find you. We could fade the heat and be gone before they could catch us. None of them know this jungle like we do."

"No," Tran said. The slightly built Vietnamese crime lord sat farther back and up the hill. His hair was cut short and was mostly gray these days, which amused Victor. "If you attack, even from this distance, the local soldiers will hunt us down. And I don't believe we could escape them before they closed in."

Victor silently agreed with the assessment. He'd noticed the quiet way Tran had been watchful about the NCIS team's search. As always, Tran didn't miss much. Most people didn't get that because Tran was tight-lipped and didn't speak until he had something he was willing to talk about. Outside of himself, Tran was the most vicious and dangerous man Victor knew.

He looked over at Tran. "I don't want to drag this thing out. We know where their base camp is. They're staying out here."

Tran looked at him. Both wisdom and wariness showed on his friend and business partner's features.

"I want to take care of this tonight," Victor told him. "I don't know how long they're going to be here or what they're going to find, but I don't want to wait, and I sure don't want them dragging anything out of the ground that's better off staying buried."

"All right," Tran said. "We do this tonight." His eyes locked on Victor's. "Then you are done with this thing, Victor. Your son would have wanted you to live, and you have wasted enough time with this. You and I, we have a business to run that requires our attention. We have lost some ground in the United States."

Anger roiled up inside Victor, but he didn't say anything. Tran was probably the only man on the face of the planet who could speak to him so bluntly. They'd shared danger for so long that Victor respected the man. More than that, Victor knew without a doubt that Tran would kill him if he started endangering his drug operation.

Thunder rumbled across the sky.

"We may get an early start," Victor said, "if this storm rolls in within the next hour."

❂ ❂ ❂

>> 1823 HOURS (LOCAL TIME ZONE)

Rain spattered against the broad leaves of the trees. Will thought it sounded like he was surrounded by footsteps. His nerves jangled because he wasn't used to being in enclosed places like the jungle. The only enclosed environment he'd dealt with had been aboard ship. But there he could always go up on deck and feel the world open up around him.

Rainwater collected on the ground. It was the rainy season, and the earth was already saturated. Pools formed first; then they began tiny rivulets that gathered more volume and became miniature streams.

The historical remains dog ahead of them suddenly took on renewed energy. The animal hardly ever lifted its head from the ground as it became a flesh-and-blood vacuum cleaner for scents.

Rain wouldn't hamper the dog. The water actually reactivated the smells trapped within the earth, making them sharper and stronger and more easily detected.

Mud clumped to Will's boots and made his feet feel like they weighed a hundred pounds apiece. Walking became a physical toll, and that was without the constant threat of slipping.

"Sir," the handler called.

Will tore his gaze away from searching the trees to keep watch and glanced at the young man working the dog.

The dog had stopped moving forward and was zigzagging through the trees. The sensitive nose never lifted from the ground.

"I think Rusty's found something, sir." The handler was a young man with a forthright manner and a shy smile. His name was Neal and he'd been working with the historical remains dog program for eight years. He wasn't chatty, preferring to get his job done, but he seemed to express himself enough for people to get to know and trust him.

Will stood in the rain. Although his rain poncho had a hood, he didn't pull it up because it would have restricted his hearing and his vision.

"I'd like to give him some time," Neal said. "Let him sort through everything. Kind of a confidence vote. He's been working hard today."

"All right," Will told the handler.

The dog kept wandering around through the nearby jungle, but the outside journeys grew smaller and smaller. Finally, a few minutes later, the dog chose a patch of muddy earth between two towering trees and lay down.

"He's found something," Neal said excitedly. "That's his signal."

Will walked forward and studied the ground. When he squatted and looked across the lay of the land, he saw where an irregular oval had filled up with water where the dog lay.

The oval was definitely man-size.

"Let's close it in," Will said to Maggie. She stood twenty feet away. "See if we've got anything. If we don't, we make camp. We're losing the sun anyway."

⊛ ⊛ ⊛

>> 1856 HOURS (LOCAL TIME ZONE)

Although the night hadn't yet arrived, they were working by lantern light in the thick copse of trees. Shel used one of the trenching tools they'd brought. Will used the other.

Nita stood at the prospective graveside. Although Will had wanted her to stay at the base because of her pregnancy, she hadn't agreed. She'd told him that she'd been praying about the situation and felt she needed to be on hand. Besides, as the team's medical examiner, her testimony about the recovery of the body—or bodies—was important.

Shel was glad she had stayed with the rest of the team. There was safety in numbers, and they could better protect her with them than if she was off somewhere else.

As he worked, Shel's muscles warmed. Even with the storm, the air remained muggy. When the fabric of his shirt kept slowing his efforts, he'd taken the shirt and Kevlar vest off. He'd seen Will glance at him and expected that Will might tell him to put them back on, but he didn't.

"It won't be too deep." Neal squatted beside his dog. "Rusty got a good hit, so you can expect to find something within three or four feet at the most."

Shel kept turning dirt that was just short of qualifying as oozing mud. Every shovelful felt heavier, but he only worked harder.

He thought of the forty years that his daddy had lived with the guilt of accidentally killing a man—a fellow soldier—and burying his body so the family wouldn't know. Of that same forty years when Tyrel McHenry had been mentally prepared to go to military prison for the rest of his life or to be executed. Of all the years that Shel had grown up not understanding why his daddy hadn't taken any real interest in him.

Pain shivered through Shel's heart. All those years of misunderstandings and arguments and hurt feelings hadn't been because of him. Or his daddy. If the situation had been reversed, if Shel had accidentally killed a fellow soldier during a firefight—and such things happened—he honestly didn't know how he would deal with it. Or if he'd be able to live with himself.

And that was now, when he had nearly twenty years of experience behind him.

How could anyone expect a fresh-faced kid away from his home country to handle something like that? More than that, Tyrel had been drunk and been led by Victor Gant. Nothing good could have come of that.

Nothing good did come of it, Shel reminded himself.

Then his shovel pressed against something hard.

Shel got down on his knees and searched for the object with his fingers. The falling rain pooled in the bottom of the excavation. Several times before, he and Will had been forced to saw through tree roots that had grown through the area. This felt different, not as big, not as solid.

His fingers uncovered something round. Hope swelled in his heart.

"Nita," Shel called, trying to keep his voice calm. "I need more light here."

Nita moved immediately and brought the light to bear.

As Shel brushed away the mud and grit, the object became very clear. It was a human skull.

CRIME SCENE

60

SCENE ✪ NCIS ✪ CRIME SCENE

NAVAL CRIMINAL INVESTIGATIVE SERVICE

>> ELEVEN KLICKS OUTSIDE QUI NHON, BINH DINH PROVINCE
>> SOCIALIST REPUBLIC OF VIETNAM
>> 1903 HOURS (LOCAL TIME ZONE)

"Everybody out of the grave," Nita ordered.

Shel stared at the prize he'd found. It was definitely a human skull, and there was definitely a bullet hole beneath the right eye socket.

It remained to be seen who was buried there, though. With the fleshless state the skull was in, Shel knew it had to have been in the grave for years.

Reluctantly he clambered from the three-foot grave. "Rainwater's filling it up quick," he said.

"We can cover the grave." Nita handed him the lantern as she crawled down into the grave with his help. "If need be, we can pump it out tomorrow to finish the reclamation."

Out of habit, not liking standing in dangerous territory without a weapon in hand, Shel took up his M4. He canted the assault rifle against his hip and watched Nita set to work. He leaned in and adjusted the angle of the lantern.

"I need a bucket," Nita said.

Will passed one down.

Slowly and carefully, Nita scooped handfuls of mud from around the skull and threw them into the bucket.

"Dump everything we extract from this point on into the trash bins we brought," she directed. "We're going to have to go through all of it for evidence."

Shel knew that all of the team was aware of that, but Nita was thorough. He waited impatiently as Nita filled the bucket a half-dozen times and Will emptied it. The rain washed the skull cleaner with each passing moment. Nita continued unearthing the body.

All the flesh was gone, carried away by nature's disposal system of beetles and other insects, as well as broken down by the chemical processes within the body.

Estrella stood nearby and ran video of the recovery. Maggie stood near her with an M4 canted on her hip. The two men Phan had sent gazed implacably into the grave. If the sight of the skeleton or the rain bothered them, it didn't show.

A moment later, Nita uncovered the stainless steel dog tags that had been on the body. She used a penflash to read them.

"PFC Dennis Hinton," she said, looking up at Shel. "I'll have to make a comparison of the skeleton to his medical and dental records to confirm that."

"There's no reason to believe anyone else was buried there," Will said softly.

Relief and sadness passed through Shel at the same time. If they hadn't found the body, there was a chance the military might have dismissed charges against his daddy. But now that the body had been found—

"We've got visitors," Remy stated quietly over the radio headsets they all wore.

The announcement jacked Shel's adrenaline. He leaned down easily and picked up the Kevlar combat vest. He shrugged into it without looking away from the grave, as if he were just putting it on.

"Skyview," Will said calmly, "do you copy?"

"Skyview copies," Director Larkin replied over the frequency. "Stand by for computer link."

Before leaving the United States, Will had set up a combat-ready computer support team at the NCIS headquarters in Camp Lejeune. Linked to a geosynchronous satellite over the area, the team was able to scan down and provide information on the site. The satellite's scanners were powerful enough to pick out individual movement by heat signature.

"Standing by," Will said. Then, raising his voice slightly, he said, "Lights out and regroup."

As one, every member of the team switched their lanterns off and shifted.

The trap had been set. Now it was time to see who the true predators and prey were going to be.

⊛ ⊛ ⊛

>> 1909 HOURS (LOCAL TIME ZONE)

Victor Gant knew immediately that something had gone wrong when all the lights at the gravesite extinguished. Somehow, the NCIS group had become aware that they were being stalked.

Prior to the darkness settling over the scene, all the people present had been clearly defined in the bright white electric glow of the lanterns. They'd stood out against the darkness of the trees, shining in the silver rain.

Now they were gone.

Victor glanced to the side. The light had poisoned his eyesight. Black suns dawned in his gaze. His direct vision was dead in the darkness, but he still maintained some of his peripheral vision. Looking directly at something in the darkness was next to impossible anyway.

"They made us," Fat Mike whispered from Victor's left.

"You just now gettin' that particular newsflash, Fat Mike?" Victor growled irritably.

Fat Mike cursed. Then he calmed himself. "We outnumber them, and we know the jungle. They don't stand a chance."

Victor wondered about that, though. The NCIS agents had moved too easily, and they'd known exactly what they were going to do. For the lights to be out, someone had to have seen them creeping through the brush.

Fat Mike started to get up.

Victor grabbed the man's arm and yanked him back. "Stay down," he hissed. "They've got a sniper in the brush."

"What makes you—?"

"Someone saw us. How else would they know we were here?"

Fat Mike cursed again. "Doesn't mean he's a sniper."

"Go ahead and get up," Victor told him. "You let me know how that works out for you."

"I believe I'll just sit here a spell," Fat Mike said.

Victor grinned.

"Why are you grinning?" Fat Mike asked.

"It's always more fun when the people you're hunting know you're coming."

A strong voice rang out. "Victor Gant. This is NCIS Commander Will Coburn. Throw down your weapons and give yourself up."

Victor peered through the darkness. His night vision was starting to return. "That's funny," he yelled back. "I was about to offer you the same deal." He tried to pin the location of the voice.

"This is the only offer you're going to get," Coburn said.

"Well, I got to give it to you," Victor said. "You sound awfully convinced for a man who's about to die."

One of Victor's men suddenly stood up about twenty yards away. Victor started to yell at the man to get down; then he noticed how the man was holding his neck. The man turned suddenly, showing black fluid running between his fingers. Then the sound of a rifle shot rolled over Victor's position.

Another man next to the first man suddenly jerked and lay sprawled. Another rifle report sounded.

"Sniper," Fat Mike breathed. He kicked his feet and jammed his back up against the nearest tree.

"You think?" Victor demanded harshly. In the space of a drawn breath and he was down two men. Whoever the sniper was, the man was good.

Moving slowly, careful to keep the tree between himself and the unmarked grave, Victor hefted the M14 he carried as his lead weapon. He'd never liked the M16 and had never carried one throughout his career in Vietnam.

"Cover me," Victor told Fat Mike.

Immediately, Fat Mike popped out with his M60 machine gun and fired downhill into the grave area. The sudden roar cannonaded between the hills.

Victor sprinted to the two dead men and face-planted on the ground. A bullet zipped by over his head.

"Take cover," Victor yelled.

Fat Mike pulled back in behind the trees, but now the other men opened fire. Assault weapons on full-auto lit up the night.

Victor grabbed the M79 grenade launcher one of the dead men had been carrying, checked to make sure it was loaded and ready, then rolled onto his belly and looked down the stubby barrel at the bowl depression.

Sporadic return fire lit up the darkness around the grave area.

Calmly Victor ignored that. The guy he was looking for—the sniper—would be shooting with measured deliberation, not just shucking rounds and hoping to hit something.

The wet earth beneath Victor seemed to suck him down, like it was calling to him. His elbows threatened to slide out from under him as he scanned the ranks of his enemies. Then he found the sniper. He was certain of it. The man fired calmly and steadily.

Smiling to himself, cursing the unknown man's parentage, Victor took up trigger slack on the M79, then pulled it through. A 40 mm grenade thumped from the abbreviated launch tube. Years of practice had taught Victor that the grenade would travel in a parabola, at first breaking free of gravity, then getting pulled back into it.

Victor was too experienced to stick around and see the results of his handiwork. The grenade traveled relatively slowly. Just as he rolled back to cover, a bullet chopped a small tree in half right beside his head.

Downhill, the grenade hit and exploded. The bright flash of light tore through the wooded landscape and ripped away the night for a heartbeat.

Once more under cover, Victor broke the M79 open and loaded another grenade. This time he rolled back to the other side, once more framing himself on his elbows as he took aim.

The grenade round left flames draped through the trees and brush. Evidently the launcher had been loaded with an incendiary high-explosive grenade. The flames helped reveal the area.

Victor scanned the countryside quickly, knowing full well that he might be equally exposed in the flames. He swept the trees, not seeing anything. Then his subconscious pulled his attention back to his left.

There in the shadows, Victor saw the big Marine. Shel McHenry had leaned into the tree with enough skill that he looked like—at first glance—just another layer of bark.

Victor took aim, then sensed with an animal's instinct that Shel McHenry had also spotted him. Victor pulled the trigger more quickly than he wanted to, and he wasn't certain of the shot. It didn't matter.

In the next instant, the grenade exploded in midair as Victor rolled for cover. The concussive force shivered through the trees and raked the grass. For a moment Victor forgot about being wet and muddy and was just thankful to still be alive.

Evidently Shel McHenry's bullet had, fortuitously, struck the grenade and set it off prematurely. That also meant the Marine had had Victor in his sights long enough to put a bullet in him. They'd both gotten lucky on that score.

Victor pulled the M14 to his shoulder and clambered to his feet. He abandoned the M79 as he awaited Shel McHenry's next onslaught.

But it didn't come.

Cautiously Victor peered out around the trees with one eye. Only a true sharpshooter could have picked him off in the night.

Flames burned in the trees around the grave. Ropes of fire dropped to the ground and fought against the drumming rain brought in by the season. There were no other lights, but every now and again lightning would strobe the sky.

Victor thought he detected movement.

Then he was certain because he saw someone easing through the brush and headed away from him. Whoever it was wasn't going to have much luck, though. Victor had brought enough men to circle the area and cover every inch of landscape.

A bullet ripped across the tree trunk less than an inch from Victor's eye. Splinters stabbed his face. He pulled his head back and raised the radio he carried to his lips.

"Close in," he directed. "They're pulling back, heading toward the west. Don't let them get away. And I'll give a reward to the man that brings me the head of that Marine before we get out of here tonight."

Then he stayed low and moved through the darkness of the night. He and the shadows were old friends, and it was time to introduce Shel McHenry to how dangerous the darkness could be.

61

E SCENE ✪ NCIS ✪ CRIME SCENE

NAVAL CRIMINAL INVESTIGATIVE SERVICE

>> ELEVEN KLICKS OUTSIDE QUI NHON, BINH DINH PROVINCE
>> SOCIALIST REPUBLIC OF VIETNAM
>> 1917 HOURS (LOCAL TIME ZONE)

Shel abandoned his spot and cursed the luck that had put the grenade in his way. Just for a moment there, he'd had Victor Gant perfectly framed in his rifle's sights. If the grenade hadn't intercepted the bullet's path, he was certain he would have shot the man.

The explosion of the grenade had temporarily robbed Shel of his night vision. He blinked against the exploding black spots that Swiss cheesed his sight.

Bullets hammered the trees and brush. The drone of the rain made it hard to hear them slapping branches and leaves, but experience made it easier for him to pick out the deadly noises.

Despite the steady rain, flames stubbornly clung to the trees and the ground near Remy's position. The grenade had come awfully close to scoring a direct hit. Remy was injured, but Shel didn't know how bad it was. The SEAL was still mobile and still death on wheels because he'd accounted for two more men downed. Larkin and the support techs using satellite imagery had confirmed that.

"Shel," Will called over the earpiece.

"Here," Shel responded.

"Pull back."

"On my way." Shel started forward. Max fell into position beside him.

Will was leading the others to high ground in a desperate attempt to get out of the dangerous trap that had whirled up in the low area as Gant and his men closed in on them. According to Larkin's observation, the path of least resistance lay in the direction Will and the others were headed.

"Skyview," Shel said.

"Here," the calm voice replied.

"Did you mark the position that grenade launcher came from?"

"Affirmative."

"Did you find the guy who used it?"

"Yes."

Shel grinned a little at that as bullets dug divots out of the muddy ground around him. "Good. Mark that one as Victor Gant."

"Confirm visual?"

"Roger visual," Shel replied. He ducked beneath a sudden spray of bullets that knocked leaves from the tree branches overhead. A branch fell directly in front of him. "I laid both eyes on him."

"Skyview has located and designated the target."

"Good. Keep him tagged. Then see if you can't figure a way to get me back there to him." Shel didn't intend to quit the battlefield if at all possible without at least taking a run at securing Victor Gant.

⊛ ⊛ ⊛

>> 1920 HOURS (LOCAL TIME ZONE)

Maggie Foley moved through the darkness with Berettas in both fists. Despite her lack of military service, she was a trained combat marksman with a pistol. She had spent hours on the ranges, working with Shel and other military trainers who specialized in handgun maneuvers.

She stayed low as she took the point. Will and Estrella covered Nita as they came up the hill.

"Maggie," the calm voice of Skyview said over her earpiece, "two targets are to your left."

Without breaking stride, Maggie used her peripheral vision to search for the two gunners the satellite team had spotted in the brush. She trusted the tech support staff to keep all the players separated so she would neither receive nor give "friendly" fire that wasn't.

One of the men shifted a little to bring his assault rifle up. Maggie aimed at him off the point, not truly sighting at all, and hit him with at least two of the three bullets she fired. The second man got off two rounds of his own. One of them slammed into Maggie's vest and knocked the wind out of her, but the other went wide.

Staggered, Maggie regrouped and fired again, aiming for the man's center mass. He went down as well. She trotted over to the two men and checked them, noting that neither of them would be getting up again.

She felt bad about that. Killing for her was always hard, but it was often necessary in her chosen field. She turned back to face the route she'd been given to follow.

"Clear," Maggie said. The pressure gripping her chest from the blunt force trauma finally eased and she was able to draw a full breath.

"Skyview acknowledges the clear," the coordinator said. "You are clean and green at the moment."

Maggie kept going, wondering where Captain Phan and his men were.

⊛ ⊛ ⊛

>> 1923 HOURS (LOCAL TIME ZONE)

Remy lay in the grass behind a small outcrop of rock and ignored the pain in his right side. He didn't think he'd taken a bullet, but he had been hit by some shrapnel, and he knew he was leaking blood. The flow wasn't enough to be dangerous or debilitating. He'd been there before.

"Skyview, find me targets," Remy said calmly as he lined himself up behind the M24 sniper rifle he was using as his lead weapon.

"Targets coming," the support guy said. "Confirm three. East of your position. One hundred twenty yards out and closing in staggered jumps."

Remy kept both eyes open as he swung the rifle toward that section of the target area. He didn't focus on anything in particular. Instead he tried to look through his targets, allowing his peripheral vision to track the movements his normal eyesight couldn't see in the darkness.

The men were fleeting shadows. In the night, he couldn't tell if they were American or Vietnamese. He supposed it didn't matter. Either way, they worked for Victor Gant.

He passed up the lead runner as they came in a flying wedge—a point and two wings. If the two men in front saw the lead man go down, they'd go to cover. So he aimed at the man farthest back first, knowing that he could at least have the second shot in the air before the two men heard the sharp crack of the sniper weapon.

He squeezed the trigger, rode out the recoil, and locked on the second man back. By the time he squeezed the trigger, the sound was just reaching the two men. The lead man went down, but the other man behind him spun and sprawled before he could go to ground or find shelter.

The lead gunner took cover behind a tree, but he didn't like where he was and tried to get up and run. Remy squeezed the trigger again. The man crumpled and remained still.

Remy fed more rounds into the sniper rifle and growled, "Skyview, find me targets."

⊛ ⊛ ⊛

>> 1925 HOURS (LOCAL TIME ZONE)

"Will," Larkin said.

"Yes." Will walked slack behind Estrella and Nita. He kept his eyes open and moving. He carried the M4 in his hands like he'd been carrying it all his life. Hours on the practice fields at NCIS had helped him feel like the assault rifle was a part of him.

"I'm patching you through to Captain Phan," Larkin said.

He's going to be surprised, Will thought.

"The two of you need to work out logistical support before you run into each other in the dark," Larkin went on.

"Agreed," Will replied. Escaping hostile fire only to be brought down by support troops wasn't a pleasant possibility.

"I'm bringing him on now," Larkin said. "Captain Phan, this is Director Michael Larkin of the NCIS."

"I hear you," Phan replied.

"We've got communications set up and running in the area. We wanted to coordinate my team's exfiltration from the battleground with you."

"Of course."

Will admired the Vietnamese military man. Phan could change and adapt with the best of them. His ability to do so while on the fly was impressive.

"Will," Larkin called, "are you still there?"

"I am," Will said, then addressed Phan. "Captain, good to have you with us."

"I see our plan worked," Phan said. He sounded a little out of breath, and Will could imagine the man hurrying into the area on foot.

"It did. We also found our missing soldier."

"Then you've been doubly fortunate tonight."

Will drew a flare from his vest and held it in his hand. "I want to get my people out of here. We're coming toward you and I don't want to get accidentally shot."

"I understand."

"I'm carrying a flare," Will said. "I'm going to set it off in a moment. When I do, mark this position. We're coming straight at you."

"Skyview confirms there are no hostile encounters between the NCIS team and the local soldiers," the support guy said.

"Roger," Will said. "When you're ready, Captain."

"Now," Phan said.

Fisting the flare, Will banged the end against the nearest tree. The flare exploded into ruby light that spun shadows over Will. He threw the flare to the right. Bullets chased it across the ground as Victor Gant's gunners cut loose.

Will hunkered down behind rocks with Estrella and Nita, who looked pale.

"Are you all right?" he asked.

"I'm fine," Nita said tightly. She had her arms wrapped around herself. She hadn't often been in the field and hardly ever under these conditions. "I'll be fine. There's just a lot—a lot of noise."

"You'll be out of this in another few minutes," Will said.

"Commander Coburn," Captain Phan called.

"Yes."

"We see you."

"We're actually to the right of the flare. Your right. Behind a stand of rocks."

"Yes. We have you. We'll be there shortly."

"Captain Phan," Larkin said.

"Yes."

"Did you call in air support?"

"No."

"Then we've got trouble. Two helicopters just lifted from the brush only a few klicks from you. They're speeding in your direction and will be there within minutes."

That, Will knew, wasn't good news.

⊛ ⊛ ⊛

>> 1929 HOURS (LOCAL TIME ZONE)

Savage glee hammered through Victor Gant as the two pilots of the helicopter gunships he'd had lying in wait contacted him.

"Bring 'em on," Victor crowed. He gazed up at the sky and saw the helicopters shifting back and forth as they sped toward the rendezvous point.

Both helicopters were outfitted with 20 mm rocket pods and .50-cal machine guns manned by expert door gunners. It was more firepower than the NCIS agents and their Vietnamese army unit could deal with. Their trap had just been sprung and turned into a trap of its own.

Victor smiled and watched the helos zip by overhead as he tried to spot the NCIS agents in the darkness. The helo pilots would have an easier job at it because they were FLIR-equipped. The forward-looking infrared devices would pick up body heat in the darkness.

"Hey, Fat Mike," Victor growled as he watched the choppers sail across the sky just above the treetops, "seems like old times, doesn't it?"

"Yeah," Fat Mike replied.

The dirge of the helicopters' rotors beating the air grew louder.

62

SCENE ✪ NCIS ✪ CRIME SCENE
NAVAL CRIMINAL INVESTIGATIVE SERVICE

>> ELEVEN KLICKS OUTSIDE QUI NHON, BINH DINH PROVINCE
>> SOCIALIST REPUBLIC OF VIETNAM
>> 1931 HOURS (LOCAL TIME ZONE)

Shel pulled back into the shelter of a stand of tall trees just as the lead helicopter opened fire on his position. He hooked Max by the scruff of the neck and pulled him tight, wrapping both arms around the Labrador's neck to shelter him.

The .50-cal rounds chopped through the tree branches and smaller trees like scythes. Leaves, branches, and trees fell to the ground like the rain that continued to relentlessly pound the jungle. Purple tracer rounds made the bullet streams visible, and they danced only a few feet away.

"Shel!" Remy called over the headset.

"I'm good," Shel replied as he watched the helicopter swing around his position. "But this guy must have night vision. He's circling my position like he can see me."

"There's a FLIR mounted on the undercarriage," Remy said calmly. "He's got your number."

Desperation filled Shel as he burrowed more deeply into the trees. The bullets struck rocks and threw sparks that flared only briefly before dying. He caught momentary glimpses of the door gunner hanging outside the helicopter's cargo doors. The chopper looked like a predatory insect in the darkness.

"Know what the weakest point on any helicopter is?" Remy asked almost conversationally.

"The tail rotor," Shel answered. He shifted, dragging Max with him, putting trees between himself and the helicopter gunner.

"Hold tight," Remy warned.

Even as he moved, Shel saw sparks suddenly dance along the helicopter's tail section. The chopper was moving slowly, so the target wasn't as difficult as it could have been. In the next moment, the tail rotor suddenly swung out of control. The pilot tried to recover, but the chopper started turning circles in the sky. Then it descended and smashed into the trees.

There was no explosion. It just went down seventy yards from Shel's position. By the time he was in motion, the second helicopter had marked Remy's position and was moving in for the kill.

"Hang on," Shel said. "Help's on the way." He ran through the jungle, dodging trees and brush. He cradled the assault rifle in both hands as Max loped at his side.

The second helicopter was too far away, on the other side of Remy rather than being between them as the first one had been, so Shel moved toward the downed chopper.

Both door gunners had survived the impact and were struggling to free themselves from the safety rigging. When the first one saw Shel, he reached for his sidearm.

Shel shot the man on the run, stitching a three-round burst from the gunner's hip to his shoulder. The man slumped in the rigging.

The pilot stumbled from the cockpit and brought up his pistol. Before he could use it, Max clamped his huge jaws over the man's forearm and smashed into him, knocking them both to the ground.

The other door gunner turned and fired at almost point-blank range. In his hurry, he missed. Shel spaced a double tap over the man's heart, then tracked a round up between his eyes in case the man was wearing Kevlar.

Shel took hold of the .50-cal machine gun, twisting it experimentally on its gimbal. It still had full movement.

Tracking the .50-cal drone of the other helicopter, Shel turned the machine gun in that direction, found the aircraft, and then lit up the night with tracers. He was wide and low of the helicopter for just a moment; then he tracked the tracers onto the chopper's dark body.

The .50-cal rounds punched through the helicopter's body and marched toward the cockpit. The pilot juked and tried to take evasive action. Shel stayed locked on, knowing the fuel tank was there somewhere.

Finally the tracers ruptured the fuel tank and ignited the gas. In the next second the helicopter became a roiling ball of orange flames and dark gray smoke against the black sky and silver rain. Flaming pieces of the aircraft showered down over the landscape.

"Not bad shooting, Marine," a gruff voice said. "Looks like I'll be walking out of here."

Shel spun as he recognized the voice as Victor Gant's.

"But that's okay, because I'm gonna walk out of here knowing I squared things with my son's killer." Victor Gant stood next to a tree. Only the M79 grenade launcher and one eye were visible.

Shel knew he wouldn't have a chance if he ran, so he jumped back through the helicopter's cargo area toward the open door on the other side. He was in midair when the 40 mm grenade slammed into the helicopter's interior and the explosion engulfed him.

⊛ ⊛ ⊛

>> 1934 HOURS (LOCAL TIME ZONE)

Victor Gant watched the incendiary grenade fill the helicopter's interior with twisting flames. The illumination spun and whirled as it chopped into the darkness. He didn't see the Marine's body anywhere.

Cursing, wishing he'd been able to kill the big man less quickly and regretting that it was already over, Victor tossed the M79 to the side and pulled the M14 into his hands. He stayed low and duckwalked to the back of the helicopter. Staying next to the downed aircraft while it burned wasn't his first choice, but Victor wanted to make certain of his kill.

"Fat Mike," Victor called.

"Yeah."

"You got my six?"

"Like always."

Fat Mike stayed in the brush and kept a weather eye peeled while he held on to his M60 machine gun. If anyone made a move against Victor, Fat Mike would cut the assailant in two with the weapon.

"That dog was with him," Fat Mike said.

"When you see it, euthanize it," Victor said. "We're scorched-earth here."

"Reading you five by five."

Victor felt the pressure of the clock against him. Maybe they'd chased the NCIS team off, but the Vietnamese People's Army soldiers were moving in. His window for escape was closing.

"Victor," Tran called over the radio.

"I'm already gone," Victor replied, but he kept circling the helicopter.

He wasn't going to leave until he saw the Marine's dead body for himself. "You with me, Fat Mike?"

"I'm on your six. You're clean and green."

Victor smiled. It was like old times. Hunting Charlie through the brush had always been a thrill. When he ducked under the helicopter's tail section, he felt the heat pushing at him. It was almost hot enough to sear.

Then Victor saw the Marine. Shel McHenry lay almost twenty feet from the stricken helicopter. He was facedown on the ground, his assault rifle another dozen feet away.

Cautiously, Victor closed on the man's body. "You still alive, jarhead?" he called softly.

The big man didn't move.

"You wouldn't be lying there playing possum, would you?" Victor stepped closer. The M14 led the way. "Maybe I should just put a round through the back of your head to make certain."

Shel McHenry lay motionless on the ground.

Closer now, Victor saw the embers still smoldering against the man's shoulders and back. A fine dusting of them trailed through the short blond hair. Bits and pieces of him were on fire, but he wasn't moving. Victor knew the man was either dead or unconscious.

"I think I'm going to take an ear or maybe a finger," Victor crooned. "Some piece of you to remember you by. What do you think about that?"

A dark shadow rose from the ground and launched itself like an arrow across the broken ground. Victor saw just enough of it to know what it was, and he knew where it was headed.

"Fat Mike!" he yelled. "Watch that dog!" He tried to spin and draw a bead on it. But from the corner of his eye, he saw Shel McHenry rise from the dead.

⊛ ⊛ ⊛

>> 1936 HOURS (LOCAL TIME ZONE)

Later, Shel was never rightly able to say what had woken him from unconsciousness as Victor crept up on him. The last thing he could ever clearly remember was the explosion. The concussive force had blown him clear of the helicopter and hurled him several feet through the air. He didn't remember hitting the ground, but he had the bruises and abrasions to prove it.

But what had woken him remained a mystery. On some days, he thought that it had been a feeling, an outgrowth of the combat senses he'd developed while in action. Other days, however, he was certain it was his daddy's voice, fierce and hard, telling him to get up before he got himself killed. When he told Don about it, Don had another take on just exactly what had happened.

All Shel knew was that he woke and saw Victor Gant drawing a bead on Max as the Labrador streaked for the brush. That had been enough to galvanize him into action. He pushed himself up from the ground, caught Victor's eye rolling toward him, then saw the rifle coming around to meet him.

Shel blocked the rifle with his left hand, felt it chug as it spat bullets into the ground, and curled his right hand into a fist. He put his shoulder into the effort and—even though he was on his knees—got his weight behind it and hit Victor Gant as hard as he'd ever hit any man.

Victor was knocked sideways. Shel yanked on the M14 and pulled it from the other man's grasp. Before he could reverse it and use it himself, Victor came back at him with a Ka-Bar combat knife clenched in his fist. Blood trickled down Victor's face and made him look like a madman.

"Thought you were dead, boy," Victor roared. "I gotta admit, I like the idea of killing you myself even better." He slashed at Shel with the knife.

Shel threw himself backward, rolled, and got to his feet in one smooth move despite the wooziness rocking his skull. He felt slightly disoriented as he moved, but everything was there.

Victor quick-stepped toward him, trying to step on his lead foot, but Shel managed to get his foot away and duck back again. This time he smashed the palm of his right hand up against Victor's elbow and trapped the man's arm for a moment. While he had him blocked, Shel drove an overhand blow into Victor's face that split the man's cheek.

Max's growl in the brush let Shel know he was dealing with a threat himself. A man's frightened squalls echoed around them.

"Come on then, boy," Victor taunted. "Let's see what you're made of."

Shel felt for his pistols, thinking to put a quick end to the knife fight. His holsters were empty. Evidently the explosion or the landing had knocked them free. Reluctantly he gave ground.

Victor stepped forward quickly again and slashed twice. The blade whispered across the front of Shel's Kevlar vest.

"Why are you running?" Victor sneered. "You come all this way to get a piece of me. Well, here I stand. Let's see how bad you want me."

Black anger filled Shel and he almost rushed the man. Remembering how he'd fought his daddy gave him pause, though. His daddy had fought back even harder than he'd expected. Shel knew that Victor Gant would be no less of an opponent.

He also realized that Victor had circled him and was driving him back toward the burning helicopter. He felt the heat blazing against his back and heard the fire crackling in his ears.

"How bad do you want me, boy?" Victor taunted. "Looks to me like you just come all this way to die."

Unbidden, the image of the small chapel in the hospital filled Shel's mind. He'd been at peace there. Even with everything that had gone on with his daddy, he'd been at peace.

All his life, he'd felt he'd chosen a different path to walk than Don. His brother had gone the way he believed God had pulled him. But in the end, had Shel done any less? Even with his world filled with violence and bloodshed, wasn't Shel drawn to the same goal of helping others who were lost and unprotected?

In that moment, with more clarity than he'd ever expected, Shel knew that he wasn't so different from his brother. Don was a shepherd. So was Shel. They just tended different flocks in different circumstances.

And their daddy, though he'd been thrown off-stride, had done the same thing. God had pulled him back to that small town where he'd come from, and he'd given him Mama to love, and he'd given him two strong boys to guide and love as best as he dared.

In all that time, Shel knew that his daddy had never once truly turned away from that calling. Maybe he hadn't had the soft words or the understanding that some daddies did, but his war hadn't ended in Vietnam. For forty years, that guilt had been the biggest war Tyrel McHenry had ever fought.

He'd never once stepped away from the burden God had given him to do.

A calm peacefulness like he'd never felt suddenly filled Shel with clarity. He knew what he was supposed to do, and he knew that there wasn't another path he would ever take.

He stopped backing up before Victor Gant. When he dodged the knife this time, he set himself and delivered a full-on body block that lifted Victor Gant from his feet and hurled him backward. Victor landed and set himself immediately, but it didn't do him any good. Shel came at him without fear, without anger, with only the knowledge that he was doing what was right and what he'd been born to do.

He punched Victor in the mouth and drove him back. "I'm here, Victor." He hit him again, driving him back once more. "Do you feel me now?"

Victor threw a punch.

Shel slipped the punch easily, shoving it away from him. "And I'm taking you back with me, Victor. Not a piece of you. *All* of you. You're going to stand trial for every evil thing you've ever done."

Victor swiped at Shel with the knife, but Shel caught the man's wrist and twisted. The knife dropped from his fingers. Stepping forward, Shel delivered a forearm shiver that knocked Victor backward and almost toppled him.

"Do you feel me now?" Shel asked.

Desperate, Victor tried to kick Shel in the crotch. Shel caught the man's leg, lifted, and twisted. Victor spun and crashed to the ground. When he tried to get up, Shel hit him in the jaw. Then he rolled him over and jacked an arm up behind his back.

Shel knelt on his prisoner, placing a knee in the middle of his back, and pulled a pair of disposable cuffs from his combat vest. He fit the cuffs onto hand, then the other, pinning both behind Victor's back.

"You have the right to remain silent," Shel said, gripping Victor by his long greasy hair and yanking his head up. "Anything you say—"

"I don't think he's going to say much," Will said.

Shel glanced over his shoulder and saw the commander standing there.

"He looks pretty unconscious to me," Will said.

Breathing hard, black spots whirling in his vision and his body hurting from various bruises, scrapes, and burns, Shel looked at Victor Gant.

The man was dead to the world.

"We'll read him his rights later," Will suggested. "When he comes to."

"Good idea," Shel agreed. He let his prisoner's head drop.

"There's something else I need to tell you. While you and Remy have been out here shooting down helicopters and arresting unconscious criminals, Nita found something very interesting about our friend Hinton. Something you're definitely going to want to see."

Before Shel could ask what Will was talking about, a frightened voice called from behind a tree, "Hey! Somebody want to get this dog off of me?"

When he stood and walked to the brush, Shel saw that Max had Victor Gant's henchman by the throat and lying on his back. Shel picked up the M60 lying nearby and pointed it at the big man. He signed Max off.

Fat Mike Wiley stared up at Shel with frightened eyes. "I thought he was going to kill me."

"He could have," Shel replied. "You make any wrong moves, I'm going to let him."

"Not me," the big man said. He rolled onto his face and put his hands on top of his head. "You won't have any trouble out of me."

Shel quickly put cuffs on the man and got him to his feet. Will kept him covered.

When he looked back over the battlefield, Shel saw that Captain Phan's soldiers held the high ground. Maybe some of Victor Gant's people had escaped, but they weren't going to be doing much.

Shel looked at Will and grinned. "We won."

"Yeah," Will said, smiling a little. "I guess we did. You sound surprised."

"Me?" Shel pulled a shocked look. "I never had a doubt in my mind."

EPILOGUE

>> RECOVERY ROOM
>> LAS PALMAS MEDICAL CENTER
>> EL PASO, TEXAS
>> 1017 HOURS (CENTRAL TIME ZONE)

Shel stood at the window of his daddy's room and stared out at the clear blue Texas sky that he'd grown up under. A red-tailed hawk circled the sky and made him think of the ranch and the Indian paintbrush in bloom, looking like the scrub grass was on fire. He'd seen it this morning when he'd stopped by to check on the livestock.

Then, in the reflection, he saw his daddy turn over in bed and wake up. His daddy's eyes stared at his back. He looked older and more fragile in the hospital gown, but there still remained that fierceness that Shel had always remembered about the man.

If he hadn't been through what he'd been through, would he still have that? Shel wondered. It was a worthless question, though. It was part of his daddy's nature. That was like asking if there'd be dust in west Texas.

"You got all the time in the world to be staring through the window like that?" his daddy asked.

Shel smiled. "Yes, sir. I reckon I do. Otherwise I'd be sitting back watching you sleep." He turned to face his daddy.

Max stuck his head up in the corner, looked at both of them, then curled up again.

"How'd you get Max in here?" his daddy asked.

"I made friends with one of the nurses."

"I'm glad my ailing has worked out for you."

"Yes, sir."

"But you got no call to be coming around, Shelton. We're done here. We were done before you up and left a few days ago. Got nothing more to say to you."

"No, sir. I reckon you don't. So I'm gonna tell you a few things."

"I don't want to hear them." Tyrel reached for the remote control on the table between them. He turned the television on.

Shel reached down and pulled the plug from the wall. The television went off.

"Don't think that just because I'm in this bed and outfitted with a pacemaker that I'm feeling too poorly to get up and give you some of what I give you in that barn," his daddy threatened.

"No, sir. I wouldn't think that. But if you get up out of that bed, I'm gonna call that pretty little nurse friend of mine, and she'll have a couple of orderlies strap you to that bed till I finish saying what I've come to say."

"You're just wasting your breath. What I done, I done. Spent over forty years dreading what's coming, and that's over forty years too long in my book."

Shel leaned back against the wall. "You ever talk to God, Daddy?"

Tyrel waved a big hand at him and ignored him.

"I mean, *really* talk to God?" Shel persisted.

"Your brother talks to him enough for all of us."

"I can see how you'd think that. But it's not true."

"Say what you got to say, then be on your way. Surely they got a baseball game on somewhere."

"You know," Shel said, "I've spent all of my life trying to understand you."

Tyrel was silent for a moment; then he said, "There ain't as much to understand as you might think there is."

"No, sir. I have to admit that most of it's pretty simple. Most of it's what I figured it was. Those parts that I liked and understood, I measured them out and kept them for my own. You see, Daddy, if it hadn't been for you, I wouldn't be the man I am today."

Tyrel looked at him and tears glimmered in his eyes. His face quivered a bit but he smoothed it out.

"Got no time for this," his daddy objected in a strained voice. "Nor no reason to listen to it."

"What I am," Shel went on, "what I made myself become, was something I thought was better than you would ever be. But that's not true. I know that now. Don, he got the best parts of you right off. I only thought I had them."

Tyrel tried to speak and couldn't.

"You see," Shel said, "I saw you as this loner cowboy. John Wayne. Audie Murphy. This fierce, hard, proud man that wouldn't take nothing from nobody. I wanted to be just like that."

"You're a better man," his daddy whispered. "You always was."

"No, sir, but I'm working on it. Don understood what you were better than anybody. He took what he saw and he became one of the best husbands and one of the best daddies in the world. He became a leader in the church and works at saving more people than you or I ever will."

Tyrel couldn't speak.

"Don got that from you," Shel said. "I understand that now. He saw you raise us when other men didn't stay with their families. He saw how you were with Mama. He became just like that—never failing, never swerving, never a moment lost when he needed to be a daddy or a husband."

"That wasn't me," Tyrel said.

"It was." Shel's emotions were thick in his words, and his voice almost broke. "It was, but we just didn't see it, you and me." He paused. "I just got back from Vietnam, Daddy. I walked some of those battlefields where you fought, and I found a part of you I never saw before. I tried to imagine what it was like to be eighteen years old, handed a weapon, and sent out in the jungle to kill men I didn't even understand before they could kill me."

"Hard times," Tyrel said. "Those were *hard* times."

"Yes, sir. They were. I could see how a kid could make the mistake of shooting a friend in the dark. Especially when he was drunk and with men who were known for violence."

Tears ran down Tyrel's weathered face. "I killed him, Shelton. I killed that poor boy that night, then helped bury him so his parents never knew what happened to him."

"I know you think you did, Daddy," Shel said, "but that's not what happened." He pulled a packet from the chair beside the bed and handed over eight-by-ten photographs. "This here's what remains of PFC Dennis Hinton. We found him and identified him."

"I don't want to see them." Tyrel held up a shaking hand.

"Fine. Then I'll tell you what Nita found when she examined that body." Shel put the photographs away. "She found slash marks along the underside of his jaw that were made with a sawtooth blade. The kind of combat knife Victor Gant carried back in those days. A lot of guys carried those survival knives."

Tyrel stared at Shel.

"Yeah," Shel said, "that's what we were wondering too. Why would anyone cut the throat of a dead man?"

"Denny's face and chest were covered with blood," Tyrel whispered.

"You shot him, Daddy," Shel said. "But he was already dead at the time. You were drunk and doing something stupid, and I guess if you want to feel guilty about something, you can feel guilty about that. But you didn't kill anyone that night."

Tyrel just stared at his son.

"After we found out PFC Hinton's throat had been slashed, we talked with Fat Mike Wiley, Victor Gant's second-in-command." He smiled a little. "While we were over in Vietnam, we went ahead and arrested both of them."

Tyrel finally found his voice. "Guess you were busy."

"Yes, sir. Wiley wanted to cut a deal. He's gonna testify against Victor Gant and a man named Tran, give up their whole heroin operation, in exchange for life imprisonment. It wasn't a bad deal, because either the Vietnamese or the American military was going to execute him for murder one."

Tyrel lay still and quiet.

"He told us that Victor Gant knew PFC Hinton was working undercover as an informer for the Army CID. They were trying to nail Gant for his black market dealings."

"Denny was working with the CID?"

Shel nodded. "Gant found out. You were Hinton's friend. That night in the bar, Gant used you to get to Hinton. He took both of you out into the jungle. Then he killed Hinton and set you up to make you think that you did it. When you shot Hinton, he was already dead. You didn't kill him, Daddy. You been paying for a crime you didn't commit."

Tyrel closed his eyes. "My God," he whispered. "All those years." He looked back at Shel, and his face knotted as he tried to remain calm and collected. "All those years, I lived just knowing the Army was going to come get me at any time. I've been scared for forty years. I was afraid of letting your mama or you or Don get too close to me. I thought they'd come get me; then what would you do?"

"I know," Shel said. "It took me a while to figure it all out. But I did. You did the best that you could."

Tyrel shook his head. "No. I was never the daddy to you boys that my daddy was to me. You didn't get to know him, Shel. He died before you were born. But he was a good man. Not like me. He knew how to be a daddy. I—I just—"

A fresh lump formed in the back of Shel's throat, and he barely choked it down. "Daddy, you did what you could. And you did every part of it you knew how. In your own way, you were trying to protect us."

Tyrel's face writhed as he struggled to speak. "I remember how it was when my daddy died, Shel. I was seventeen. He died in a car wreck when a drunk in a truck hit his tractor. He was just . . . *gone*. I couldn't stand for you boys to have to go through that. I didn't want either you or Don to feel the way I felt. It was awful and hurt something fierce. I didn't think I was ever going to get over it. Maybe I never did. I didn't want that for you two."

"Daddy, someday we're all gonna have to let each other go. At least for a little while. It's just how things are. But there's something past this life. I've always known that. Don didn't have to tell me that." Shel stared at his daddy. "But we can take the time we have here and use it the best way we know how. That's all we can do."

Tyrel shook his head. "Look at me. I'm old. I'm used up. My heart don't even work the way it used to. There ain't much left."

"There's enough," Shel said. "There's enough if you want there to be. In this case, I feel certain God's gonna make sure of that."

Quietly, hesitantly, Tyrel sat up in bed. Then he pushed himself off it and walked over to Shel. "You're telling me," he whispered hoarsely, "that I'm free. I don't have to look over my shoulder, and I don't have to feel guilty no more."

"No, sir. Not one more second."

"I want you to know that I love you, Shel. I always have. I just couldn't—"

"I know, Daddy. I know."

Carefully Tyrel McHenry reached for his son; then he pulled him into a fierce embrace that almost squeezed the breath from Shel's lungs.

For the first time in his life since he was eight years old, Shelton McHenry put his arms around his daddy and held him tight. His daddy smelled of soap and shaving cream, of old saddles and hay, and he was built rawhide tough from hard ways and mean ways and from working from sunup to sundown.

In that moment, Shel felt certain he knew what God's love was like. It was wild and powerful, complete and enduring, just like his daddy's love had always been though he hadn't known it.

"I love you too, Daddy," Shel whispered. "I love you too."

NAVAL CRIMINAL INVESTIGATIVE SERVICE
MEL ODOM >> BEST-SELLING AUTHOR
PAID IN BLOOD
NCIS
CRIME SCENE
MEL ODOM >> BEST-SELLING AUTHOR
BLOOD EVIDENCE
NCIS
CRIME SCENE
MEL ODOM >> BEST-SELLING AUTHOR
BLOOD LINES
NCIS
CRIME SCENE
TYNDALE FICTION
Available now in stores and online
www.tyndalefiction.com
CP0042